By Téa Obreht

The Tiger's Wife
Inland
The Morningside
Sunrise

SUNRISE

SUNRISE

TÉA OBREHT

a novel

RANDOM HOUSE
NEW YORK

Random House
An imprint and division of Penguin Random House LLC
1745 Broadway, New York, NY 10019
randomhousebooks.com
penguinrandomhouse.com

Hardcover ISBN 978-1-9848-5553-4
Ebook ISBN 978-1-9848-5554-1

Printed in the United States of America

1st Printing

First Edition

BOOK TEAM: Production editor: Cara DuBois • Managing editor: Rebecca Berlant • Production manager: Sandra Sjursen • Copy editor: Bonnie Thompson • Proofreaders: Ethan Campbell, Liz Carbonell, Jennifer Sale

Book design by Diane Hobbing

The authorized representative in the EU for product safety and compliance is Penguin Random House Ireland, Morrison Chambers, 32 Nassau Street, Dublin D02 YH68, Ireland. https://eu-contact.penguin.ie

For Parini, who's been reading about Anton Vargas,
in one guise or another, since at least 2015

Contents

AN INCIDENT OVER HORSEBONE LAKE

August 2024

Now you see her. From above, she's a dark speck against darker water. Head, shoulders, occasional hands. Below, her legs are churning flashes in the green. She's fighting the chaos of the moment, the sense that she's been teleported into this cold horror. For now, she's still screaming. Grabbing at empty space as her clothes continue to swell with water. Her brain is convinced that her feet will eventually find ground. They won't—she's almost half a mile from land, and the lake, where she's fallen, is over four hundred feet deep. In a minute or two, she'll realize the broad strokes of all this and slow her thrashing.

Overhead, the smoke trail the Cessna left behind is already fading. A black drape blurring faintly gray as the wind pulls it apart. It takes Nina a few seconds to tie one thing to the other: her body down here in the water, the smoke's plunging arc up there in the sky.

No plane. There's no plane anymore.

No fireball, either, though. No explosion. That's important.

The dulling cold is in her. She feels as if it's been part of her for a long time, although she can't have been underwater for more than a few seconds.

Something—thick, cold, and living—bumps her leg, and she sets off for shore. Slow progress. She has to think about every move: the reach, the pull. She never really learned how to swim. Lied on her nannying application about having formal training in all four strokes. Her arms ache and disobey. Sometimes they fail, and she dips under. Water up her nose, and in her mouth. The roar of it in her ears. There's no stillness anywhere.

Her shoes are like irons, pulling at her from below. She reaches down and starts to unlace one: there's her distant, slow-motion hand, plucking at the bright green gleam of the sneaker. But then the thought of losing something to the insistent darkness of the lake fills her with panic. It would be like cutting off a piece of herself. She gives up on the laces and swims on, the flooded shoe loose now and threatening to come off with every kick.

A tendril of memory finally comes through.

Ben. Where's Ben?

She glances around. Behind her, there's nothing but flat blue calm, all the way to the far shore. Two miles, maybe more, of this freezing lake, bigger than it had looked through the low clouds when Ben had aimed the plunging Cessna toward it. In the distance, she can make out some bluffs, barren and black, covered in leafless trees, dead, maybe, or burned in one of the many fires Jones told her are forever ravaging these mountains.

The shore she is swimming toward doesn't seem much livelier. A gray beach littered with driftwood that looks like the shed antlers of something huge and prehistoric.

By the time her knees hit ground, she can't even imagine trying to stand. She crawls the rest of the way, drops down into the muck, and lies there. The close-up world appears in extraordinary high definition: coarse flecks of gold and brick-red among the sand grains, a pip of something incredibly green that was once, perhaps, part of a bottle.

Everything around her has already fallen into silence. No plane engine. No water in her ears. No birds. Just her own breath scraping in and out, and the immense indifference of the world going back to what it had been before the sputtering Cessna cleaved into it.

Don't just lie there.

She pushes herself up onto her elbows. Before her, the beach slopes steeply away from the lake and into a dense wall of pine trees. The ones nearest to her are tiny, but the soaring ranks behind them are tall enough to disappear into the fog. There's no sky, no sign of anything beyond them. The fog has fastened everything to the ground.

To her left lies a massive pile of boulders past which the landscape is anybody's guess. To her right, the beach goes on for a good while before curving sharply around the end of what looks like a peninsula, into more trees and out of sight.

Nina turns over slowly until she's sitting up. Her legs look odd, misshapen. White with cold. The stark veins around her knees make it seem like she's infected with some alien pathogen.

"It's all right," she tells her shoes, in the same voice she's been instructed to use with the Devander girls, Bo and Belice. "Hey. We're all right."

Now comes the inevitable vomiting. She throws up lake water and the remnants of this morning's burrito, procured in haste at the Snak Shak by the airstrip outside the so-called town of Hollis, South Dakota. Nina had felt too nervous to eat, but then Ben pointed out that the flight to Moraine would take almost two hours, and that she would start complaining if she got hungry. She had forced herself to finish the whole burrito while Ben's old Park Service bunkmate, Jones, went back over the Cessna's controls one more time.

"Oh, I know," Ben had said, gliding his hand wistfully along the flank of the plane. "I remember."

All the way to Hollis, Ben had talked about this clunker as if it were some magnificent old horse he had been forced to abandon and was hoping to find still alive when he finally made his way back to what he considered his real life. He called it "the Fire

Drake." He had flown it all over the Mountain West. In the year since Ben had last seen it, Jones had given it a new set of tires and a fresh paint job.

Ben must have jumped right after pushing her out of the plane. This probably happened somewhere past that curve of the beach, where the lake, she presumes, continues indefinitely. That's where the fading smoke trail leads. And since no new smoke has appeared, she knows the plane didn't crash and explode. Ben would've jumped and then swum to shore, as she did, just past those trees. He'll be following the shoreline straight back here. She shouldn't go searching for him. She shouldn't move. She should stay exactly where she is until he finds her.

Her phone, miraculously, is still in her backpack. Save for the smashed top corner of the screen, it looks intact. There's no signal, of course. This notification about her seven o'clock dinner reservation at the Black Horse bobbing at the top of her screen must have come in sometime while they were airborne. So, too, a couple of texts from her mother. *Whatever you want Nina.* And then: *Send me text when you get on the road.* And then finally, just twenty-three minutes ago: *Juhu? All okej?*

She thumbs *All okej* into the keys and hits Send. While the progress bar stutters across the top of her screen, she tries to figure out what to type once this first useless communication manages to get out. Her next effort really has to count. She could try: *We had a snafu.* But then her mother would write: *What is snafu?* Resulting in a meaningless back-and-forth, a gigantic waste of time and signal. She has to convey the facts clearly and simply without sending her mother into a tailspin. Something like: *We left the van with Ben's friend Jones and flew in Jones's plane to Moraine. But we hit a bird and had to do an emergency landing.* This is true, in essence. After the bird, and the initial moments of panic following the strike, an emergency water landing had been attempted—and hopefully had succeeded back there behind the trees after Ben had pushed her out of the plane.

Receiving this shock of information, her mother would try to call her and, when that failed, would still type: *Where are you??? What is going on??* To preempt this, Nina should just go ahead and add: *Not sure where we are. But I'm okej. I'm waiting for Ben. Pliz don't panic.* That last part is vital. Don't panic. And it applies equally to everyone involved. Yes, something terrible has happened. The exact kind of something her mother would have warned her about had she known that they were planning to take off in some tiny single-engine, even one Ben had previously flown. But the most important fact is: nobody is hurt. Nina is all right. She's managed to hold on to both her backpack *and* her shoes. Her cellphone not only works, but is charged, for once, to a miraculous 84 percent, thanks to Ben's prescience back at the motel last night. No, she doesn't feel up to standing just yet, but beyond the searing pain in her chest, she clearly hasn't broken anything, and this, too, is a small miracle. Any second now, Ben will come around the curve at the far end of the beach. By then, she'll have gathered enough strength to start hobbling toward him. Rangers are probably on their way here, too—along with whoever else saw the Cessna go down.

A watched message never sends. She places the phone screen-side down on the damp shingle beside her. With her head on her knees, she waits.

The goose pimples on her legs are painful and huge, as if something under her skin is trying to climb out. At least there's sun. Dim, burning somewhere beyond the fog, but still pleasant. She pulls off her sneakers, tips the remaining water out of them. Yanks off her socks. She struggles out of her sweatshirt—the one Violet unironically bought for her at some souvenir stall in Montmartre during the Devanders' anniversary trip to Paris last year—and lays it flat over the stones. It reads L'HISTOIRE DE L'ART and is garishly printed with a grid of emoji representations of different artists—Rembrandt, Picasso, Warhol—each of them rendered in a mimicry of his individual style. Pollock is just a big, incoherent swirl.

Munch is a shrieking oval. Nina's specialization, if you can call it that, is still-life painting of the Dutch Golden Age. There's no emoji for that.

Ben will ask whether she's inventoried their supplies. She puts the backpack between her knees and digs through it. A promising start: right at the top are the two Bulki bars she set aside for Ben this morning. Below them, things get bleaker, though: Her wallet. Her lip balm. A wad of fast-food receipts from their road trip. The spare set of keys to her mother's apartment in Astoria, dangling from a metal icon of the Holy Mother with the infant Jesus, who looks like a surly little diplomat. A lighter that won't start. A glob of clumped God knows what, the weird, gross detritus of nannying: napkins, cheese-bunny dust, a brick of stuck-together crayons that have been dirtying the bottom of her bag since Christmas. But it's not all bad news. There's a working penlight and a mini water bottle, too, almost completely full. Hand sanitizer. Most of a bag of trail mix and two more Bulki bars, flattened to fuck but otherwise intact.

She steals a glance at her phone. The send-message bar is still stalled in the exact same place. Its effort to push through has devoured a heart-stopping 8 percent of her battery life. She puts the phone into low power mode.

What about the Black Horse Grill? Obviously, Nina and Ben will not be dining with them tonight. There will be no fireside banquette, no prosecco, no silken piece of raspberry torte. A no-show. And after she left a message on their machine this morning, asking whether it would be possible to add a third person to their party. "It turns out our visit will be overlapping with a friend's" was how she'd phrased it. "I know this is a long shot, but if you're able to seat a third at such short notice, we'd love to have him join us." Perhaps the folks at the Black Horse would take it as implied that if they couldn't accommodate her request, she would prefer to cancel the reservation. Perhaps, anticipating this, they would even save her the trouble and just cancel it themselves. Maybe they would even waive the $100 cancellation fee. Either way, she would know by 7:16 P.M., when they either would or would not charge her credit card for the no-show. She'll get the charges reversed, of course, when she and Ben get into town tomorrow or the next day. Surely, even in a place like Moraine, Wyoming, this excuse will be a first: "We missed dinner because our plane crashed." The Black Horse is not the kind of place to underreact to a situation like this. They'll probably do something extravagantly classy, like comp Nina and Ben a meal for the hell they've been through. Make the kind of gesture that will amplify the restaurant's already stellar reputation.

She checks her phone. Apparently, it's given up trying to send that text informing her mother that *All okej.* The bubble has turned green.

Nina glances back over her shoulder. The huddled pines look as though they're all tilting ever so slightly toward the same point of focus together, like black-clad mourners over some turn-of-the-century casket. Is she really going to keep sitting here with her back to them? She burrows sideways down into the driftwood, but no matter how she turns, her back is to something that unnerves her.

The sun goes on melting drowsily behind the fog. Her phone clock reads 5:44. It's late August. There will be light in the sky until eight, eight-thirty. There's still so much time for Ben to find her before it gets dark. She squints down the beach, trying to imagine the jolt she'll feel when she finally sees him emerging from the trees at that distant bend. Will there be tears? Probably. She'll jump into his arms, the misunderstandings of last night and this morning forgotten. Trials bring people together. It could be exactly what they need. A massive scare to remind them of what they mean to each other.

She's a little surprised that no rangers have turned up yet. But that's all right. She mustn't forget that Jones is out there, too. Jones knows that they're supposed to be flying to Moraine. He's probably about halfway through his seven-hour drive over the mountains, which should put him in town just before sunset. He's out there right now, on the road, easing the van along, rummaging through their console for her homemade granola, maybe taking a rest-stop nap on their bunk. Whatever he's doing, Ben's dog, Enid, is beside him with her big, lovely, worried face, wearing the bison-print bandanna Nina had tied around her neck that morning. Wondering, probably, in her doggy inner voice, where the hell her people have gone.

When Jones gets to Moraine, he'll go to their motel. Once he finds out that Nina and Ben haven't checked in yet, he'll head to the airstrip. He'll put together that they never landed, and he'll sound the alarm. Of course, Jones is a ski bum whom she's never seen in any state but slightly high—but on the single, vitally important front of outdoor practicalities, he seems to know what he's doing. The hills around Nina will be swarming with Search and Rescue by morning.

She feels confident enough in this to eat one of the Bulki bars. She'd been planning to wait until Ben found her, so that she could share their full inventory with him, but she knows that if he asks her how she's doing and she answers that she's hungry, he'll say, "Then why the hell didn't you eat?" This is some old-world thing, this impulse to leave everything intact until everyone is accounted for. Ben has no patience for it.

The Bulki bar is dense and dizzyingly sweet. Bits of it cling to the food traps between her teeth long after the bar has burned its way down her throat. This is about as far from how she had imagined the evening as anything could be. She's supposed to be looking out over the downtown bustle of summertime Moraine from one of the rooftop tables at the Black Horse and feeling a sense of realignment.

Her mother would say that Nina had doomed the evening herself by putting so much stock in it. She had basically memorized the menu, and had come to the conclusion that even if she and Ben each ordered one of the most expensive starters, and followed these up with the most expensive entrées, plus the bubbly and the shared dessert, she could still afford to pay for the whole thing herself, including the lavish 22 percent tip she would feel obligated to give. The Devanders—Dr. Michael and his wife, Violet (whom Nina's mother, for some reason known only to herself, refers to as the Second Mrs. de Winter)—had given her a little summer bonus, and Nina didn't mind dipping into it for this special meal. Of course, Jones had thrown a wrench into all that by asking where he should meet them for dinner this evening. But he and his tattered jacket and his endless affirmation of the fact that they were all apparently "sending it" had been no more part of how Nina had envisioned the night than a single-engine plane crash in the mountains was.

Maybe this will be one of those weird little cosmic coincidences in which her mother is always trying to locate the divine. An opportunity for providence to show its face and give her a big wink. Maybe Jones will be delayed on his way into town and be forced to head straight to the Black Horse for their seven P.M. reservation. Maybe he'll sit there awhile, merely thinking he'd been the first to arrive, before getting suspicious and then heading out to look for them, thereby sparing her the no-show fee. The absolute least he could do in his big, stupid, useless way.

A cool wind touches her back. She looks over her shoulder again. There's nothing there.

The sudden warbling of her phone shocks her. She flips it over. Not one signal bar, but there's the 307 area code, anyway. The Black Horse, right on cue, bursting through like some great benevolent seraph by sheer force of will.

"Hello?" she cries.

"Hello, Miss Turzick?"

She will not be correcting this mispronunciation. "Yes, hello, I'm so sorry we're late, we've been in a plane crash somewhere over the mountains, please send help."

Send help. You sound insane. Why did you spend the last five hours sitting here, looking stupidly around, instead of planning out what to say if someone managed to reach you?

"Hello?" the Black Horse says.

Then Nina hears the terminal *boop-boop* of the line going dead.

It is so important, in this moment, not to cry. If she starts now, she won't stop for a while, and there's dehydration to consider. She's a theoretical expert in preventing tears in others. What would she say to Bo at a moment like this? "I know you're frustrated. It's okay to *want* to cry. But let's consider the big picture. There's reason to be hopeful. Right? They called you and the phone rang. That means another phone call will eventually get through. You are not beyond reach. You just have to hold it together. You cannot go to pieces. You don't want to be a mess when Ben finds you."

How the clouds begin hurrying as the evening sweeps in. The sun burrows into distant fog across the lake, blackening the bluffs between itself and Nina, putting the little teetering trees on the outcrops into silhouette. Behind this rush of reds and pinks follows a purple coolness. The bellies of the clouds above her stay bright for a long time, then go suddenly gray. From gray, they vanish thinly into the evening dark. She grows cold in a way that makes it hard to think. She draws her bare feet in under herself. Huffs warm breath over her hands. Digs her back into the embankment behind her. The light keeps changing but never seems to fully leave.

Nine o'clock. The hostess of the Black Horse must be flipping the shingle from OPEN to CLOSED by now. Table settings have been cleared. A few stragglers in whose company Nina thought she would be spending the evening are finishing their nightcaps. Dessert wines and Manhattans. Stained tablecloths are being rolled up and tossed into laundry carts. Kitchen noises dying down. A last exhausted sigh of steam from the dishwasher. And Jones—what about him? Where is he right now? Has he realized what's going on yet? Is he roaming the dark driveways around the airstrip in Moraine, asking about the Fire Drake? Or has he himself been delayed—has he texted them on their new group thread: *hey guys, running behind here, just go to dinner without me, I'm gonna hit the hay*? Does that mean it could be morning before he realizes they're missing?

That's right. Get yourself in a tailspin, Neen. That way you can hyperventilate and be your usual useless self.

Before long, a huge, pockmarked moon is clearing the shaggy tops of the pines, flooding the beach with its light. She's never seen a moon this size—not even on her involuntary march along the Nebraska highway the other night. It's a real presence. Unnerving in its immensity. It makes her feel as though something has joined her on the beach, some weird, wild, unnameable thing, and she should keep very still for fear of startling it.

How long has it been since she's spent a night alone? Years, probably. When she was still living at home, she slept on the foldout and let her mother take the bedroom. Since she's been juggling grad school with full-time nannying, she sleeps at Ben's place once a week, on her night off. Or, rather, she lies beside Ben until he falls asleep, and then she eases out of bed and gets dressed and wanders around the living room, trying not to disturb his roommates and occasionally lifting the curtain to watch the action on Avenue B die down. The other six nights, she stays at the Devanders' place on Central Park West, where she has a room of her own but mostly ends up sharing the king bed in the nursery with the Devander girls: Bo, four, and, more recently, Belice, two. She lies between them, beset from all sides by kicks and sighs and little farts, and passes the time answering check-ins and memes from Ben. Around midnight, when his texts wind down, there's just the ceiling and the earworm music in her mind, until dawn lights up the bottoms of the blinds and she finally drifts off.

Over her shoulder, the black trees scrape faintly against one another. They're so densely packed together, she's certain nothing could fit through them to surprise her. Maybe a squirrel or a chipmunk. Anything bigger would make a lot of noise. She'd hear it before it saw her.

Of course, it'll be right on top of you then. Are you ready for that?

She picks up a length of driftwood and rests it across her knees.

Ah, yes. Nothing says "Don't fuck with me" like a hollow bit of dead tree.

An abrupt, agitating terror bores into her. On its heels comes disbelief. Fury with herself for having taken so long to think of it. What if she's wrong? What if Ben hadn't managed to jump out of the plane at all? What if he's still aboard, and instead of trying to find him, she's been sitting here, all afternoon, all evening, all night, while this leering moon beats down on his broken body somewhere in the lake?

She staggers to her feet and calls out Ben's name. The startling flatness of her voice moves out across the water. She can hear it out there in the dark, drifting, growing, leaving her behind. After some minutes, she works up enough courage to try again.

The way the silence returns makes her never want to produce another sound. She feels studied by this punitive, forbidding wilderness. Its agents are the trees and the stones, the relentless moon and its reflection. She doesn't know their language, so she can't figure out the extent of her own transgression in breaching its peace.

The beach seems much bigger than it did by daylight. Huge, really: gray-blue and warped by shadows. Nina wrangles her feet into her damp shoes and starts toward the distant bend. The weeds that tackle her crack and rustle, sink burrs into the sodden tongues of her sneakers.

All this time, she assumed that there must be more beach and more lake beyond this bend, but that's not the case at all. Both end here, at a palisade where the river that feeds this lake leaves the black woods, coursing from a narrow cleft in the rocks. She can't see it very well, but its roar is impressive, and it sends up a fine mist that chills Nina's face. On the far side of the waterfall lies another cove, with another beach, moonlit and silent.

She turns her phone flashlight to its brightest setting and flits the beam back and forth over the water, until finally it catches an answering glint on the other beach. Something. Maybe Ben's phone. Maybe Ben's eyeshine. Do people even have eyeshine? She shouts, "Hey!" There's no answer. No matter how aggressively she waves the light back and forth, she can't get the thing to shine back at her again.

Maybe you imagined it. You're hungry. You're agitated. Don't do anything till you can think clearly. Wait for morning.

But she knows what she saw. And every second counts. If Ben is over there, hurt, and something happens to him while she's waiting for morning, how will she live with herself? She's already wasted precious time sitting around all day. Thinking only of her own needs, as usual, her pulse, her fear, her hunger. What about Ben?

Do not wade out near that waterfall. You have no idea how deep it is. Can you really be this stupid?

Turns out, yes. Yes, she can. Three steps in, and she's lost her footing. The incoming river takes her down and pulls her right under. Washing-machines her, spits her out. For the second time this terrible day, she is trying to tear her life back from this same freezing water. For the second time, she is crawling out to shore.

Her mother had once told her the story of a woman from the old country who had fallen thirty-three thousand feet in the fuselage of an airliner, crashed into the Dinaric Alps, and lived. The woman had been a flight attendant. She had been standing in the lavatory when the plane disintegrated in midair, and it had been the lavatory that fell to earth, intact, with her standing upright in it like a Barbie in a box.

"How?" Nina asked. "How?"

Her mother shrugged. "It wasn't her time."

The woman had been found by—who else in her mother's stories?—a shepherd. There she sat, the miraculous flight attendant, Death's unlikeliest reject, screaming and blood-soaked in the mangled fuselage of what had once been her domain of utmost hospitality, with her back, ribs, arms, and legs shattered, and the heels of both shoes broken off. What a sight for the poor shepherd, who kept getting younger and younger every time Nina's mother told the story, until he was just a boy with a lamb draped over both shoulders, like some sort of biblical Zsa Zsa Gabor.

Day 2

Nina drifts for some time in the enveloping roar of white noise. She knows this setting on the Devander girls' sleep machine. It's called "Tender Rain." Its hum chases her through vague, freezing sleep. Her jaw feels like concrete. Something is digging into her back. There's an odd tension in her stomach—any minute now, she will get up, pee, stretch, pad out to the kitchen for a glass of water. But she can't move. Her toes are numb. The tip of her nose is so cold it hurts. Plus there's the gray sense at the edges of her understanding that something is not as it should be. Something awful is waiting for her. She wants to keep it out for as long as possible.

When she finally sits up, it takes her a beat to remember that there is no white-noise machine, no Tender Rain. There's just the lake, the beach, the distant cove, and the endless rush of the waterfall. Her knees are swollen. Her feet are like boards way down somewhere on the ends of her unfeeling legs. When she tries to move, pins and needles go fizzing through her. She's never been so hungry.

The fog has descended, and is resting against the surface of the lake. In the pale light of the coming morning, Nina is able to parse the insanity of what she tried to do last night. The river to her left is squeezed by a fault line in the cliffs, and the pressure of its emergence is incredible. Like a water jet. Thick foam where the spray bites into the lake, and then a roaming tide of bubbles curling up out of the deep. Beyond this, much farther away than it seemed last night, lies that other beach.

Its shoreline is white with debris. Something long and red has washed up against the rocks. From this distance, it looks like part of the Cessna.

"Ben? Hey, *Ben!*"

There's no answer. Nothing stirs at the sound of her voice.

Are you really surprised? He wouldn't hear you over all this noise if you were yelling through a bullhorn.

She'll have to find some way over to the other beach. Just because she can't see Ben, just because he isn't answering, doesn't mean he's not there. Trapped under the wreckage, maybe. Too injured to call out.

Swimming is no longer an option, though. It's too far. She might not survive a third plunge. There's only one thing to do. She'll have to climb the palisade, find some more manageable fording place in the woods above the fall, and then come down again through the trees on the far side.

The way up is steeper than it seems, though. The angle of the slope forces her to half-crawl, half-climb. Her face is full of freezing spray. She jams the tips of her sneakers into whatever cleft she can find, but her shoes are not meant for this shit. Not meant for cliff faces coated in some sort of brown slime. Not meant for the loose soil, with its matting of pine needles, that she finds above when she finally manages to drag her mist-soaked ass over the top of the palisade. She is immediately covered in pine needles. Up here, at least, the low branches give her something to hold on to, but they also prick her hands, bow wildly under her weight as she continues to pull herself higher. Finally, the slope eases and the ground levels off. The descending water to her right is wide and fast, rushing past snarls of deadfall that have dammed the river. Pine trees stand densely all around her, their Dr. Seuss tops lashing against one another with every gust of wind. A little farther on, the ground starts rising steeply again, and Nina leaves the river behind. She's still pulling herself along by the thin whips of the trees' lower branches. Sap gumming her hands. Dead needles pouring into her socks. A blister is starting on her right heel. She stops to search her backpack for Band-Aids, then remembers that these are in the first aid kit in the van. She keeps going. Her advance flushes weird little mountain birds out of their hiding places. It's hard not to think of bears. Ben has seen his share while doing trail work in Montana these past two summers. Nina has never seen one, but this feels like exactly the kind of place and time for it to happen. Alone, unarmed. Pressing up through the forest with the forest pressing down on her. Sunlight dancing wildly. Flat, alien-looking mushrooms barnacled to the deadfall. Ahead, the fog seems to have lifted. She can see the open sky shining through the trees: flat blue, dimensionless, and empty.

The woods let out onto a rolling, treeless plain. She lets herself rest for a minute. Pulls her sock down to check the blister. Slings the backpack off her shoulders and peers inside at the trail mix and the Bulki bars.

The trail mix is basically untouched because she had forgotten, when she grabbed it off the convenience store shelf before their last hike, that Ben hates cherries almost as much as he hates macadamia nuts. He had refused to touch it. She picks through the pieces one by one, making sure to start with the cherries and macadamia nuts and leave the oats and seeds she'll be able to convince him to eat later on. Everything is damp and tastes vaguely of lake water.

More bad news awaits on her cracked screen: her battery has been draining. Her power sits now at a pitiful 32 percent. She should turn the phone off. But what if, by some miracle, she stumbles into a patch of signal while she's searching for a way onto that other beach? The phone needs to be on for that to happen.

She walks on. The top of the first rise finally brings her within sight of what's been behind the fog this whole time: the mountains.

They're right there. Or perhaps twenty miles away, who knows. They go on and on in either direction. With the snow shrouding them, they look as if they're exploding in slow motion. *Boom, boom, boom,* all the way east. *Boom, boom, boom,* all the way west. Below each dazzling peak, the pines have drawn up their meandering darkness as high as the terrain will allow. Over this tableau, the clouds are hurrying past, and she feels the immensity of their movement in the pit of her stomach—there they go, away from here. And here she is, Nina Terzić, clutching her trail mix in this immense, indecipherable expanse.

Don't cry. The mountains don't matter. They don't mean a thing. There are plenty of mountain towns in what looks like the middle of nowhere. They overnight sushi to towns in mountains just like these. Remember Aspen? There's probably an Aspen around here somewhere.

The important thing is not to drop to your knees and start wailing, and then stress-eat all the Bulki bars.

Remember what you're trying to do: You're trying to find a place to ford the river and get down to that other beach. You're trying to rescue Ben.

She wipes her eyes, adjusts her socks, and moves on.

She keeps the beach behind her and follows what she has decided must be a kind of trail: soft dirt and tamped-down grass weaving between the little dollops of gray sage that fur the hill in every direction. Giant yellow grasshoppers hurl themselves in snapping droves across her path. At the top of the next rise, she stops to catch her breath and take a sip of water.

Have you managed to lose the river? No, it's still down there, in the gulch to her right.

She would have guessed that the way over and down would be clear by now. But the slope just keeps climbing, keeps changing. Her forehead is definitely getting sunburned. At least she's warm now. At least her clothes are dry. She takes off her sweatshirt and ties it around her waist.

The trail narrows through tall purple bushes. They're packed so close she has to shoulder through them. Her attention is so much on her footing that she doesn't realize, at first, that she has emerged from cover onto the crest of a hill directly over somebody's roof. But then there it is, at her feet, just past the edge of the road. A sheer slope, and a ridgepole with some shabby-looking shingles overlaid on either side of it. She stares stupidly down at it all, her brain stacking the disparate elements into one concrete thought.

A house, Neen. This is a house.

She's down the slope, through the thickets surrounding the house, and at the window in no time. The shutters are open. She leans in and shouts: "Hello?"

The room before her appears to be in the middle of some kind of renovation. It's empty of furnishings. Huge sheets of brown paper are taped down to the floor. White dust covers everything.

Coming around the side of the house, Nina finds the rest of town sitting in the shallow little valley below. A dozen or so rooftops scattered along a dirt track, and down there among them, the river she's been trailing all morning, reduced to a slow, glittering thing manageable enough for a footbridge. She can see its little tributaries snaking through the sagebrush all around town.

This is why there's been no sign of Ben. The people who live here probably saw the crash and rescued him. But they couldn't know that Nina had fallen out of the plane, too. She'd had the misfortune of washing up on a beach that isn't visible from up here. They had no way of knowing she was down there.

Why didn't Ben tell them to look for you?

Maybe he was unconscious when they found him. Who knows what injuries he sustained in the crash. They'd probably had to rush him to the hospital. This doesn't look like the kind of place with an emergency room.

Thank God she hadn't drowned trying to swim across in the dark. Thank God that wasn't her death.

She scrambles down away from the house and into the road. To call it a road is misguided. Generous, even. It's just a dirt track, really, barely wide enough for a car. Deserted, on what she now realizes is a Sunday. If anyone has noticed a ragged twenty-four-year-old bursting out of the bushes, they do not emerge to greet her. No one has come out by the time she reaches the first squat little house at the end of the road. And it itself is not a house at all. Just a weathered old barn with staved-in windows, empty, junkyard in the back with a buckled wagon lying upended like some heat-struck beetle. Something about the vibe of the town feels oriented away from her, and it's because, she realizes, there's a steeple at the far end that must belong to the church where everyone has gone this Sunday morning. Won't they be surprised to see her coming through the doors like this on bloodied legs, pine sap in her hair, the L'HISTOIRE DE L'ART sweatshirt around her waist, her whole self stinking of a night alone, of stress and terror.

She doesn't get to rattle anyone with this dramatic entrance, however, because the church is also empty. Also seemingly under construction. There are tarps all over the floor, and the pews have been removed, presumably so that the workers can access the hole in the roof above her, through which sunlight streams. As she stands there, looking up at the hole, a massive brown rat runs along the far wall, turns a corner, and disappears.

How, exactly, does she come to suspect that the town is abandoned? Maybe it's the dust all over everything. Maybe the totality of the stillness. Nothing here seems to have moved in years. Gravity is the only force acting upon the place: everything is caved in or lopsided, the groundward drift of wood and metal. Whatever hasn't capsized has rusted over until it has begun to lose its shape. A mining cart. A claw-foot tub. Some sort of farm machine that looks like a rolled-up millipede wearing a saddle. And the wind, hurrying in little drifts in and out of the open doorways, finding nothing to move but more dust.

Sitting astride a barrel in one of the empty yards, still half-convinced that signs of life are simply eluding her, Nina waits. It's impossible to believe that nobody, *nobody,* will be coming out of one of the houses along the street. She glances at her phone again. Down to 29 percent. Not significantly less than 32, but every digit counts now, and that initial 2 is terrifying. Just behind it follows the red-tinted drop into the teens, and then single digits, and then oblivion. She lives simultaneously in that zone and in dread of it most days. It's a point of incredible annoyance to Ben, who bought her a battery pack for Christmas, teasing that she would deserve a more meaningful gift when she finally stopped being so careless.

She's wasting time waiting for someone to show her that she's wrong about this place. She should keep looking for the way down to that other beach. Once she finds Ben, she can bring him up here for the night. Give the inhabitants a chance to return from wherever they've gone, before she starts breaking into their pantries to scour for food.

The slope that leads to the other beach is much steeper than the roundabout way she came up. The trees are black and broken, as if there's been a fire, and whole swaths of the hillside are completely barren, making her descent slow. She has to edge along crabwise, aware that a misstep is inevitable. When it finally happens, it's almost a relief: her sneaker slips, and then she's on her ass, an unstoppable mass of arms and legs. Nothing in her path but stumps and shrubs, one bone-rattling collision after another. Her final one, near the bottom, is with a fallen log. She manages to hit it backward somehow, then lies there gasping, waiting for the pain to finish bouncing around her teeth and bones. There's a gash on her shoulder. Leaves are in her mouth. But nothing is broken. And here it is: the other beach.

What she mistook for the whole plane is, in fact, only a piece of its fuselage. Siding from the left flank to the tail, stamped with the code X891. There's nothing under it. No Ben, and no footprints to indicate that he might have been here last night and wandered off to look for her. The piece of fuselage isn't even big enough to serve as something he might have used as a flotation device. It's just a chunk of his stupid, beloved plane, uselessly lying there in a mire of other detritus of the crash. Part of a brown leather seat cushion. Indeterminate scraps of metal. Things she didn't even know belonged to a plane's anatomy: foam stuffing, paper, melted plastic.

All the while, she's calling, "Ben! Ben!"

Her exhaustion, held back thus far by sheer force of will or maybe the last scraps of hope, finally overtakes her. It closes over her mind, and then over her limbs, too. She lies down in the shingle amid the wreckage, too tired suddenly even to sob.

Ben isn't here. He isn't coming out of the woods. He hasn't been rescued by villagers.

He's dead. Probably still strapped into his seat, in the remains of the Cessna, somewhere in the crushing darkness at the bottom of the lake. You'll never see him again. He'll never show you his beloved Montana. He'll never write another story. He'll never look at you that way again.

What is she going to tell Ben's mother? She can see herself so clearly, buzzing into the lobby of Teresa's building on West End Avenue. The naked halogens. The intrusive fug of provisionally mopped floors. Ben's mother at the door of 908, fretful and unsmiling. Tiny, swimming in the oversized sweaters she always wears. She's been crying. She has heard already that her son is missing, presumed dead. But, of course, she has questions. She wants to know about the crash. Couldn't Nina have prevented this? Had she even tried to talk Ben out of flying? What about Ben's last words?

Nina will have to be diplomatic about forming a grieving mother's impression of her son's final moments. She can't tell the truth. But she can't lie, either—not completely.

No matter how she frames it, Teresa will respond very badly to the news that her son had no intention of coming home after their trip. That he had all but decided that he—no, that *they,* he and Nina both—should drive on to Montana and, once they reached it, stay there. Maybe there's a gentle way to break it to her. "He was so happy to be back out West. He had so many plans for us—he said he wanted us to move out there one day."

And then, when Teresa inevitably says, "What? *Leave?*" to follow this up with: "You know Ben—he didn't mean a lot of the things he said."

"But why?" Teresa will want to know—of Ben's plans and of his fate. "Why, why, why?"

And Nina will have to tell her: "It was his time." This, of all things.

And you, Neen? What are *you* going to do?

To let her mind grasp the full extent of her predicament seems lethally stupid. In some direction unknown to her and completely undetermined by her prayers lies a road, and that road, after some distance, leads someplace where people live. Between that theoretical place and the horrific cloister of the present moment lie the mountains and the woods, teeming with bears and poisonous berries and freezing dunks in water. The more of these factors she allows into the muffled hollows of her mind, the more their number crowds out her ability to think. She must keep them out. If she fails to do that, she might as well just stay here on this beach and die.

You have to keep doing things. Little things, constantly.

You have to find shelter. You have to build a fire.

For what? With what?

There must be something of use in the wreckage. Get up.

She wanders the debris field. Most of what she finds is difficult to identify. Just vaguely shattered synthetics that were once part of the plane. But here and there, she spots one Bulki bar, and then another, bobbing on the surface of the lake or trapped in some feeble eddy.

She takes inventory again. There's her backpack, her penlight, her phone with its rapidly dwindling battery life. Her lighter—still dead, still useless, but maybe not forever. Bulki bars, ten of them now, boasting an extravagant 270 calories each.

Don't forget the trail mix.

How to ration, she wonders, for the coming days? How long should she expect to be out here? Can she have one Bulki bar a day? Can she have two? Five days seems a reasonable amount of time for someone to find her. But what if she's wrong? What if it ends up being longer?

That's impossible. How many places on this continent don't get a single passerby in five days? Somebody is coming. Somebody with skills and a sense of adventure and a dog. Some *man,* probably. Some man who heads to these mountains once a year for solace and clarity, and whose whole life has been leading up to this miraculous meeting between them, just as Nina's apparently has. It's like one of those grade school time-and-distance equations, which she could never quite crack. If Kento leaves home when he is eighteen years old, works for a couple of years as a barista in some Colorado ski town, falls in love with a mountain-climbing babe and then follows her out to Wyoming, where he stays even after they break up because he's grown to love the mountains, and Nina leaves New York by van at the age of twenty-four, only to find that she lacks the fortitude to stop her boyfriend from getting behind the yoke of a plane he hasn't flown in a year, then how long does Kento have to hike before he stumbles across Nina and, improbably, saves her life?

She should move back up to the town and wait for this cosmically ordained rescuer. He is more likely to find her in an abandoned settlement than down here, sitting in the debris field of the fallen Fire Drake.

But it's already too late. What Nina mistook for ordinary clouds in the distance are rapidly congealing into a storm. The wind has shifted, underlaid with something cool and flickering. The clouds are low, flat, and gray, and they draw over the lake as one solid mass, sudden and absolute. In them is a roll of thunder forty seconds long. It shakes the ground. Distant lightning touches the surface of the lake. Here, there, sometimes in two places at once. Cold, fat raindrops strike Nina from between the branches. Within minutes, her breath becomes visible.

She checks her pulse. It's irresponsibly fast.

Get a hold of yourself. It's just a storm. Yes, you're outside and it's cold. But you don't die like this. You didn't die when that building fell on your pregnant mother. You didn't die in a plane crash. You don't die in a thunderstorm. You are a bear. You go underground for the winter. You are a whale. You go to the bottom of the ocean. Your heart slows down, down, down, until it's very still. You don't die like this.

In truth, she doesn't know how she dies. She has never been privy to this information, even though her mother has had it since Nina was six years old. The source was their downstairs neighbor, Mrs. Tima, her mother's best friend and a noted witch who had accidentally revealed it during a coffee reading, then sworn Nina's mother to secrecy so that Nina could live a full and untainted life.

However, the fact that this information exists, the fact that Nina knows her mother possesses it, has meant that her mother's cautions have to be closely regarded. Any one of them might be coded to protect her from the specific death that awaits her.

For instance, when she was growing up, her mother had always told her, "You only get a certain number of heartbeats when you're born. Some people's hearts beat very slowly. Those people live a long time. Other people's hearts beat very fast. Those people die young."

Nina had assimilated this as a secret warning that her death would be something of the cardiac variety. This was obvious. Her mother was not the kind of person who could keep secrets. She was the kind of person who would insinuate, imply, suggest, circle around the unsaid so pointedly that her real meaning could not be mistaken. And of course it was her duty to warn Nina. Of course she didn't want Nina to accept her fate and take Death's hand when he came and walk off with him peacefully into the dark.

Convinced that she was in charge of her own longevity, and that she should exert whatever control she could over her heart rate in order to prolong it, Nina had developed deep-breathing techniques long before she knew what they actually were. That they sometimes made her pass out seemed a small price to pay for the greater benefit of living into old age. She assumed everyone was privately doing the same thing. And some people, like her dormmate Miles, actually *were.* Miles had been the self-professed "only gay kid" in his hometown of Spain, Texas. He sang a cappella, and was very good at it, but would get so anxious before his performances that he had to take a beta-blocker. Nina had never heard of a chemical approach to the heart rate problem before, but it was compelling enough to try, and Miles was as generous with his pills as he was with his pot and his advice on the perils of professors who made the classroom their dating pool. The first time Nina took a beta-blocker, she let the stillness work its way through her, unable to understand why every single person on earth wasn't on them. She convinced herself it had something to do with the American health insurance system. Most things seemed to.

"I feel like a bear could walk in here right now," she told Miles, "and I wouldn't bat an eye."

But Miles went home a week before finals that spring, taking the beta-blockers with him. And Nina, sitting in her dorm room on Eighth Street, was forced to run the gauntlet of her art history exams without his help. By that point she was already gravitating toward the Dutch masters, mesmerized by the quality of their illusions, and had somehow boxed herself into a study of the opulent horror of *vanitas.* But it was one thing to deal with all those depictions of Death in class twice a week over the course of a semester and quite another to face slide after slide of his leering mug by herself all night long. There he was again. In window niches. On tables. Peeking out from beneath violins. Gnawing on books. There was his wrenched-out mandible, looking like a Lego crab on a bed of fabrics and shells from plundered lands. Nina knew he was no different from the rotting flowers and half-consumed hams that surrounded him: present only to remind whoever had commissioned the painting that their vices were obvious and their existence fleeting. But come on—what kind of people needed such stark reminders? The kind of people, apparently, who would sling a deer carcass, with the abdominal cavity hanging open, over their kitchen table. The kind of people who would sit down to a feast of now-extinct grouse after knocking over every goblet of wine, that's who. None of this was the point, she knew. The people off-scene weren't the point—and yet their ill-fated, absent selves were all she could think about. Imagine their surprise when they walked in on the spectacle of these paintings and saw themselves for what they really were: wrong, greedy, and doomed. Her chest felt tight. She couldn't quite get her pulse to where it needed to be. When she wasn't writing out adjectives that would distinguish her observations about lemon peels from her classmates', she was googling "cardiac distress symptoms," expending far too many heartbeats on the worry of it all. She couldn't shake that one creeping thought: maybe exam stress *is* how you die.

Finally, after two nights of this, she relented and went to the student health center. The GP, Dr. Hall, had incredibly kind eyes, and this made Nina believe that she was beautiful right away. She sat down beside Nina and went over her vitals, then had Nina hop up onto the table so she could listen to her heart.

"Would you say you're feeling more anxious than usual?"

Nina had prepared for this. "I do get pretty anxious around exam time, but I'm doing my best to keep calm and not use up too many of my heartbeats."

Dr. Hall tilted her head. "I don't think I've ever heard it put that way before."

"I just mean—I'm being careful."

"Is that an expression where you're from? To 'not use up too many heartbeats'?"

"Kind of."

"What does it mean?"

"Well, it means, you know, since you only get so many heartbeats, I'm trying to be mindful and not waste mine on panic over something as banal as exams. Because, you know—what if I'm one of those people who's been designated fewer heartbeats than average?"

"Designated? By whom?"

"Well, just." *Death,* she wanted to say, *whatever you want to call him. The thief, the great bewilderer. The unmaker of plans.* "Genetics."

"Oh, honey." Dr. Hall sat back. "That's not how heartbeats work."

"But—"

"Nuh-uh. Nope. Not at all." Dr. Hall returned to the adjoining chair. "I think you have acid reflux caused by stress. When you feel that pressure in your chest, I want you to take a Tums. If it doesn't improve, take another Tums." She smiled at the face Nina was apparently making.

So perhaps, medically speaking, Nina had misinterpreted her mother's heartbeat warning. Or perhaps her mother's whole theory on the subject was nonsense. All the same, Nina had spent most of her childhood in the grip of its implications, and it was too late to shake the habit now. Even if the effects were minimal, surely it was pretty good practice to focus on your heart rate and keep it as low as possible. What harm could that do? Look at the animals that could slow their hearts to almost nothing: snakes, frogs, deep-diving seals, whales, bears, and other hibernating vertebrates. They were some of the most resilient creatures on the planet. And here she is now: making herself into just such a creature.

Day 3

The wretched little town looks even more desolate in the morning fog than it did the previous afternoon. Nina stands among the trees at its southern end, listening for signs of life. Anything at all would be welcome. The slap of a screen door. A dog barking in the distance.

But there's nothing. Only a magpie soundlessly spearing worms out of the ground along the dirt track that cuts through the center of town.

It's very faint, that old track. The buildings are neatly lined up along it. Once it crosses the rickety little bridge over the river and leaves out the buck fence on the north side of town, however, it peters out completely in the sagebrush. She follows it as far as she can, scanning for tracks. But even the footprints Nina left yesterday have been obliterated by last night's rain.

She scrambles up a low, sagebrush-choked hill to get a better view of the whole layout, but ends up wishing she hadn't. What she finds on the other side is despair-inducing. A tiny, overgrown graveyard teeming with rusted crosses. A huge, long-legged building bristling with chimneys clinging to a barren slope. Probably a mine. The mere thought of it is loathsome, this hole in the ground, with the building crouching over it like some primordial mosquito. Overlooking all this unpleasantness are the snow-dusted mountains. Their sides are deep purple, ribboned here and there with vast bolts of gold and orange that must be trees.

How long has this place been abandoned? There's no way to know. To her, all the farm implements look like they're from the fucking Dark Ages. And who is she to guess time by the appearance of things anyway? She once lost a game of Chronology for her whole team on the conviction that the discovery of penicillin predated the invention of the flushing toilet.

If people were still living here thirty or forty years ago, they must have had electricity. Maybe that means there's a power outlet somewhere. She'll have to start going into buildings. It's hard for her to come to terms with just how desperately she's been hoping to avoid this. Each one, to her, looks like the grave of somebody's entire family.

She starts with the building that terrifies her the least: what appears to be a bar right in the middle of town. It's still sporting a faint coat of mint green paint over its clapboard false front, though a log cabin posterior sticks incriminatingly out the back. To her surprise, the door is locked. She's obliged to enter through a front window, which she can barely force open enough to squeeze herself through.

Inside, the air is dry and close. Flies roam the window ledges. Their dead husks litter the floor. There's a deer head mounted on the wall, his face twisted slightly to the right in an attitude of surprise. Something is wrong with his antlers: their points are melting down over his ears, like Dalí's clocks. There's an unsettling discord between the alertness of his expression and the slow drip of his antlers. As if they continued to grow long after the moment of his death.

The tables and chairs have been pulled back from the center of the room, and other members of the deer family are arranged in a bizarre tableau on the floor before her. There must be fifteen or twenty mounts of various sizes and levels of attempted preservation laid out there in a grid. Some are just skull tops with little pointy horns. Some, like the Dalí deer, are the whole deal: antlers, skin, eyes, a black nose painted to look like it's still wet. Somebody, sometime, had been doing a gallery wall and had given up. Or been interrupted. This hadn't happened recently. The heads have been here for a long time. Dust lies thickly layered on the floor between them, in the crevices of their faces, on their lashes and their open eyes. The whole thing could be something out of Claesz or Snijders. Still life with game. The only thing missing is food.

She makes her way carefully through the grid. Behind the bar, she finds an old-timey cash register with half its keys missing. There's a little filing cabinet under the counter. Most of its drawers are empty, but going through them one by one, she stumbles onto yellowed handbills advertising bake sales, cattle auctions, brands.

You are looking, she reminds herself, for signs of *recent* life. A power outlet. A level. A table saw. A crumpled soda can. Something that belongs in this century.

Across the street, in what looks like a defunct hotel, she finds a broken check-in counter and a huge tarped-up table. A listing staircase meanders up to the second floor. The kind of authentic period feature that would be roped off for patrons' safety if the place were a museum.

What is she missing? There should be clues here that are obvious, but she just doesn't see them.

Last year, the Devanders had treated her to a pair of tickets to the hit immersive play downtown. The tickets were a very late Christmas or a very early birthday gift, though Nina would have preferred a bonus, especially after missing so many classes that spring to stay home when Bo had her adenoids out. Ben was already in Montana for the season, his posts nothing but campfires and wildflowers and hyper-saturated sunsets. Nina was, once again, technically single. She thought about inviting a girlfriend to the play but got tangled up imagining the effort it would take to reconnect with Melanie or Gina, and then explain that she and Ben were on a break, and then listen to all the reasons she had been stupid to take him back the last time. Then Nina thought: Just go by yourself. People do things by themselves. You used to, back in high school, when Ben wanted more but you just wanted to stay friends. Remember that? You should do something alone, just to show yourself you can. So she sold the second ticket outside the theater to a middle-aged man who gave her $150 in cash. He hadn't even bothered to dress up for the occasion, a fact that mortified Nina more than she could possibly have anticipated when she found herself seated across from him at a romantic little café table during the magic show just before their admission slot. She felt so implicated by his lack of formality that she kept whispering, "We don't really know each other" to the people sitting behind her. When their time slot was called, she ditched the underdressed stranger and wandered from room to room, rummaging through the desk drawers, leafing through books, studying the posters in search of clues that would help her understand the play's storyline. Every inch of the place had completely stupefied her. She gave up trying to draw meaning from the beeps of the radio transmission in the little hidden bathroom beneath the stairs and instead started following actors whenever one of them dashed past her. All this led to, however, was the sense that more and more information was continually eluding her. At one point, a door appeared in the wall in front of Nina, and a young woman pulled her into a secret room. The young woman was very pale, and had long black hair that was probably a wig. Nina got the feeling that maybe they were about to kiss, but instead the young woman stamped something onto Nina's forehead and pushed her out of the hidden room and slammed the door, which immediately vanished. Nina went away, wondering whether she had hallucinated the encounter. Not long afterward, during the ballroom finale in the great hall, Nina looked down over the second-floor balustrade and saw the underdressed buyer of her spare ticket. He was waltzing with an actress who wore nothing but a fishnet dress made entirely of crystals. He looked like he had understood everything. He was having a wonderful time.

When Nina got home, Violet had wanted to know all about the show. Had it been beautiful? Had it been strange? What was the symbol stamped in the middle of her forehead? They hovered at the bathroom mirror, squinting at the weird neon blotch between Nina's eyebrows.

"What do you think it means?" Violet asked.

"I don't know."

Violet scanned the image with her phone camera, and the two of them spent an hour trying to decipher the various Celtic tattoos it vaguely resembled, without success.

That's how it feels to be standing at the top of the crumbling staircase of the nameless hotel across the street from the Mint Green Bar. Lonely and illegible. Nina can only hope that her journey up the loud, rickety stairs has not roused something on this upper floor. The impulse to signal her intrusion with yet another *Hello?* doesn't quite override her terror of receiving a response. What would she actually *do* if something said hello back? It wouldn't be a living thing. She knows that.

She moves softly from room to room. Stays on the balls of her feet. Any second now, the tortured floor will give way, and she'll come through the ceiling. Or she'll pass through one of the doorways into the presence of some corpse sitting propped up in an old-timey four-poster. Wearing a wig. Wearing a bonnet. Wearing a cowboy hat. She's sure of it. She's seen the films.

Get ahold of yourself. Having a heart attack after seeing a cowboy skeleton is *not* how you die.

In the end, there are no corpses at the nameless hotel. No beds. No power outlets.

There are none at the grocery store, either. None at the schoolhouse.

She drifts down the street from building to building, trying doors, naming aloud the things that are recognizable to her. Mirror. Pipe. Clock. Sometimes she surprises herself by identifying an object that she didn't even know she knew. Bellows. Type settings. She keeps expecting a layer of misperception to peel back and finally make her surroundings more legible. Like, oh my God—that's a line of utility poles! You should follow it.

A pile of dead bouquets, tucked halfway into an alley between two buildings at the far end of town, is the closest she's able to come to this sort of discovery. The pile is almost up to her shoulders, made up of individual bunches whose stems are held together with string. Definitely man-made but, like all the rest, impossible to assess for recency. Flowers die, and dry, and then look the same forever. These are mostly wildflowers. They have crazy seed heads and whip-thin stems. Interspersed among them are a few fierce-looking thistles that have dried down to the shape and sharpness of throwing stars. The way they're laid out reminds her of the tributes that show up overnight on the corner of her mother's block once a year on the birthday of André Waldes, the youngest son of a local Haitian family who'd been shot by police long before her mother brought her to America. Not the kind of thing to rummage through.

The building the flowers are piled up against used to be a stable. From some distant trove of childhood stories, Nina recognizes its wide-set doors. Inside are rows of empty stalls. An old-timey pitchfork stands propped up in one corner, hooked like the claw of some massive extinct sloth.

The mere idea of horses makes this place feel safer than anywhere else in town. They have bound a softness into the air. If they were fine sleeping here once, maybe Nina can be, too.

From the rearmost stall, she can sit in the cool darkness with her back to the wall and see almost half the street, safe in the knowledge that any incoming light stops about ten feet from where she would be visible to anybody passing outside. An important arrangement, given her situation. She settles herself into the corner and stares up at the rafters. "Hello," she says to the empty bird's nest there.

The first intentional sleep of her ordeal happens in that stable. She rolls her sweatshirt into a pillow, tucks it under her head, and closes her eyes. The sunlit afternoon is so blinding that the ambient redness remains even after her brain shuts all the way down. For long, glorious minutes, she's gone.

She returns, sometime after sunset, to another evening storm rattling the stable. Her first thought is full of panic: What if we lose power?

What "power"? There's no sign that electricity had ever come to this place. As far as she can tell, these people didn't even have radio.

And what "we"? What a strange feeling to wake up to, the persistent sense that somebody else is there with her. A holdover from dreams she can't remember. Or just her poor, beleaguered brain clinging protectively to the notion that she is not alone.

She's felt it a few times on this trip. Most recently at the little rest stop in Nebraska last week. She and Ben had been driving for two hours without seeing another soul when they pulled over at a historic site to stretch their legs. The site was historic in name only, the cabin that had once stood there having long ago disintegrated. Beyond it stood a cluster of rock formations, pale and crossed through with orange bands. The tallest of the formations tapered from bottom to top, like a pyramid, and had a knobby boulder bizarrely balanced on top of it like some marvel of engineering. The shabby interpretive panel at the edge of the pullout said these were "hoodoos," and attributed their configuration to wind and water. The panel had even more to say about John Jacob Bradley, the builder of the cabin, particularly about his writings and his dealings with the local Native people, one of whom had clearly been his wife. She stood by his side in the panel's most prominent photograph, wearing an expression of intense exhaustion or outrage or some other emotion Nina couldn't quite place but suspected must correlate to the number of kids that were on or around her. Nina counted six, two of them in swaddles. Over the portrait of Bradley's family, someone had scrawled the word MASSACRE in red paint.

Nina searched the captions under the smaller pictures for any elaboration on this point but found only a brief mention of an "altercation with the U.S. Army, after which the site was abandoned."

Ben turned to her. "Do you have a Sharpie?"

"I don't think so," she said. "Sorry."

While he went off to pee in the bushes, Nina led Enid along the little path around the pond to see if they could find another panel. She couldn't decide if the hoodoo cluster resembled figures hunched around a fire, or a single enormous serpent with a pockmarked boulder for a head. What the Bradley kids must have thought of it. The names they would have given it. The stories. She knew how it worked between siblings: the older ones feeding the little ones' anxieties. Even in their day, the formation must have given the impression that it was staring back. She lowered her sunglasses and scanned the ledges from one end of it to the other, just in case some animal was sitting up there, a bobcat or a coyote, perhaps, or some other tawny thing that could blend in perfectly with these surroundings, and might account for this odd feeling of another presence.

On the far side of the pond, she found a few logs laid out in a vague square on the ground, and a single toppled wall, with the window frame still wedged in place. All those kids from the picture, crammed into this tiny cabin. How had the unnamed Mrs. Bradley managed it? Of course, homes were used pretty much just for sleeping back then. All your chores were outside. Your kitchen, too, Nina was almost sure. And people themselves had been smaller in stature. And the kids—well, from what she'd read, fully half of them probably wouldn't have made it past their first year. He had kept busy out here, her old friend Death. Relentlessly called upon to empty the place. Even before the massacre. Had he spared anybody? Surely one of the kids. Surely one.

Over at the panel, Ben had returned, having apparently located a Sharpie. He seemed to be checking around for witnesses. Why? There was nothing behind him but highway and empty prairie. They hadn't seen another car in about two hours.

To Nina's surprise, he leaned over the panel and started writing.

"Hey!" Nina called, without thinking. "What are you doing?"

Ben didn't seem to hear her. That was probably for the best. He was probably just correcting some mistake he'd identified about the geological features. There was no need to go off on him like that, in an accusatory tone.

After two or three minutes, he motioned for her to come and look. She didn't see why she should—he wasn't done writing yet, and he was starting to smile the way he sometimes did when he'd come up with a really satisfying zinger for a post or a short story. Nina stayed put. He would want her to be in on the joke. If she went over there, she risked seeing something that she wouldn't be able to shrug off, and then the afternoon would devolve in the usual direction.

She finally started back toward the parking lot, Enid plodding along behind her. By then, a few clouds had appeared overhead. Nina crossed through the cool shadows they made and opened the sliding door for Enid and got into the van. Ben was still at the panel, taking a picture of his handiwork. When they drove on, she could tell he was waiting for her to ask what he had written. She hadn't looked at it, and had no intention of asking. If he wanted to, he could tell her himself.

She tries her lighter again, with no luck. If she can get it to work, maybe she can make a fire. Ben has typically been in charge of that process, so she knows very little about it. She would need something to encircle the hearth so it doesn't get away from her and burn this whole place to cinders. Cart before the horse, though—what would she do for kindling? A flower bundle from outside the stable door would probably do the trick, if she can bring herself to disturb it. She wouldn't have to take more than one. Just a small fire, something to warm her. The battered stable roof keeps only some of the rain off her, and her bare legs are always slightly damp.

She can't remember exactly where "fire" featured on Ben's list of wilderness survival necessities, but she knows it must have been on there. Food, too. Resisting the urge to eat the Bulki bars has been a battle, but one she feels she has been winning. It's probably why she's lightheaded, yes. But she's only allowing herself to feel lightheaded now so that she doesn't have to feel lightheaded later. She counts her haul again. There are seven Bulki bars remaining. She's eaten one today already. If she eats another, she'll be down to six. And six seems like substantially less than seven.

Her whole life has come down to the mathematics of loss. Seven Bulki bars, down from ten. Just 12 percent of her battery remaining, down from 84. She hasn't had this much interaction with numbers since high school. But numbers are good. Numbers keep her mind from dwelling on the way her hunger feels—as though it's clawing at her from inside. As though it doesn't want relief but strives to overpower her, overrun her, be bigger than the rest of her. To take up more space in her own body than she does.

Try to go back to sleep. You didn't feel hungry when you were asleep. You weren't thinking about pizza. Or those garlicky marinated mushrooms from Mercato. Or your mother's gibanica.

Her mind has begun involuntarily revisiting the sections of the Black Horse's menu she had managed to commit to memory. The Black Horse is the kind of place that lists the ingredients of every dish without revealing the form in which you might expect to encounter them. *Duck breast, gaufrettes, spinach, maitake.* No verbs, only nouns. The state in which these disparate elements might arrive was anybody's guess. This delightful uncertainty had been one of the many things people couldn't stop buzzing about in the reviews she had studied so obsessively before her and Ben's big meal there. Another point of consensus: the not-to-be-missed espuma.

What the fuck is espuma? She hadn't known when she made the reservation, and she doesn't know now. And at the rate she's going through these few remaining Bulki bars, she'll probably never find out.

It's so like you to think this way, Neen. Fatalistic, woe-is-me shit. People are looking for you. People are coming.

Who? Who is coming? Could anybody she knows even guess, within a thousand square miles, where she actually is?

She thumbs through her old texts to see if she's ever outlined her and Ben's planned itinerary to anyone. Of course she hasn't. In one of her more recent replies to her mother, she did at least mention that they were in South Dakota. But that had been three days ago, in the thick of their misunderstanding about the red marker. Nina had been angry and hurt, and therefore deliberately vague.

Had she told her mother they would be stopping off in Hollis? No. Had she brought up Jones? Not in writing. If she had even mentioned Jones during one of their quick check-ins, usually conducted in the parking lot of whatever diner she and Ben were leaving before heading to their campsite for the night, she probably would have referred to him only as "Ben's friend." What possible headway could her flustered mother, who would often leave the grocery store empty-handed if her cart got overwhelmingly full, make with that?

Maybe she was underestimating her mother. Ajda Terzić could be very stubborn. And the prospect of losing her daughter could light an unprecedented fire in her. Was there some way that she could figure out—through credit card charges, cell tower records, or divination—that Ben and Nina had passed through Hollis? And, from there, perhaps manage to get in touch with Jones?

If so, would Jones rise to the occasion?

Nina doesn't know much about Jones, but in the single photo of him on Ben's grid, he's kneeling on a mountaintop with his arm around some giant dog that looks like it deadlifts sheep for fun. Over Jones's left shoulder—just about visible if you zoom all the way in—is the shriveled face of a dachshund peering out from a little sling that Jones has obviously made for the sole purpose of carrying it up the mountain. The dachshund clearly has no business being on that, or any other, hike. Its left eye is milky with a cataract, and it has the drawn features of something that's been pulled out of a pharaoh's tomb. But its presence is reassuring. If Nina is certain of nothing else, she is certain that Jones is taking good care of Enid.

Is it so outlandish to hope, then, that he might look after Nina's mother, too? That he might fly her out here, help her navigate the search-and-rescue process?

Who knows? In less than a week, they could be sitting side by side in a chopper, somewhere just out of sight of where Nina is now, leaning out of opposite windows. Maybe Jones's hand will be clasped comfortingly over her mother's on the seat between them. What a meeting of worlds. Jones, nervous but optimistic, and probably a little high. Her mother dabbing at her eyes with her free hand, leery of being touched, but leerier still of pulling away, of giving the impression of ingratitude or disdain. The impression that she could be arrogant enough to misunderstand a man's intentions.

Imagine if Jones's intentions toward her mother turned romantic. Wouldn't that be a thing—to somehow limp out of the wilderness in two months' time, only to discover that Jones and her mother, in their grief, have shacked up?

Jesus Christ. She would rather eat her own brain than contemplate such a pairing.

Day 4

Somewhere nearby, an alarm is buzzing.

It's still dark outside, but the stable is incredibly bright. That's because her screen is blazing. Her phone is rattling the floor. Nina leans over it and finds herself squinting into the softly backlit features of Violet Devander's profile picture.

Violet Devander is calling her. Violet Devander is getting through.

Nina fumbles to answer. "Hello! Hello?"

She's still half asleep, still lying on her stomach on the stable floor. Shouting into the unlocked screen. The silence on the other end goes on for so long, she's certain she imagined the buzzing. Then a tiny voice says: "Nini?"

It's Belice. She sounds simultaneously as if she's shouting and very far away—Nina can picture her crouching over Violet's phone and staring down into it.

"Belly-baby, is that you?"

"Looooooo." An interminable pause. "Nini."

"Belly-baby, is Mama there?"

"Uh-huh."

"Belly, go find Mama! Give the phone to Mama!"

There's a rustle as Belice eases to the edge of the bed and hops down. Nina can hear her padding along the hall. Her little bare feet on the pale hardwood. There's a thump as she drops the phone, a deafening crackle as she picks it back up. Her feet have gone quiet. Nina knows exactly what she's doing: she's turning the phone over in her fat little hands, pressing buttons as she goes, looking for animal emojis.

"Belly-baby, go to Mama! Take the phone to Mama, please, baby, right now!"

The little footfalls are off again. End of the hall, and then either left toward the bathrooms or right to the living room and kitchen. Chirping to herself as she goes.

"You're doing so good, Belly!"

"Mama? Mama, phone!"

From somewhere beyond the veil comes the miraculous voice of Violet Devander. "Who is it? Oh, it's Nina calling us!" Thunderous rustling and then Violet again: "It's our Nini! Hi, honey!"

"Violet, thank God!" Why hasn't she thought of a single succinct line that would explain her circumstances to whoever might reach her? She's had almost three whole days to do it.

"Are you guys in Montana yet? How's the trip?"

"Please listen: we were in a plane, and it crashed somewhere."

"Hello?"

"Can you hear me?"

"Hel-loooooo."

"Violet?"

"There you are! So how is it, is it gorgeous?"

"Our plane crashed. Ben is . . . gone. I'm alone, I'm lost, I don't know where."

"Yeesh, this line is terrible, did you say 'lost'? Hold on a second, baby, Mama's trying to hear Nini. Hold on, Nina, it's just chaos here at the moment. Elsie? Can you change Belice?" Back again. "We miss you so much, she's been talking about you nonstop, she keeps saying—"

"Our plane crashed! Our plane crashed! I'm lost, our plane crashed!"

"Ugh, I just can't with this *line.* Let me call you back—"

"No! *No!* Plane crash! Don't hang up, you idiot—*plane crash!*"

She can tell from the silence on the other end that at least some of this has gotten through. "Did you say 'plane crash'?"

"Yes. *Yes!* Plane crash!"

"Wait, were *you* in a plane crash? Are you hurt? Where are you?"

"I don't know, I don't know."

"Oh my God, well . . . well, share your location with me!"

The moment Nina pulls away from the phone to do this, the call fails. She punches the call-back button once, and then again. Darts outside into the frigid air. She tries sharing her location with Violet, and then with her mother. Dials 911. CALL FAILED. CALL FAILED. It's useless. Whatever confluence of unseen technologies brought Belice's little voice to her has dissolved.

Don't just stand here crying, Neen. Go look for a signal. Get out of here and start walking. Anywhere. As fast as you can.

She shoulders her backpack and sets off. Due north, maybe, away from the lake. She follows the dirt track over the bridge, past the buck fence, and into the sagebrush. The valley floor is flat and wide open. There's not much to go by in terms of landmarks, except for the mountains. There's new snow on them this cold dawn. If she can just keep them to her right, she'll be fine.

After what she guesses is about half a mile, she comes into a cramped little grove of emaciated trees. The light of the rising sun, caught in their tiny gold leaves, is disorienting. Their boughs are pocked all over with huge, staring eyes. A small red-shouldered raptor alights on one of the lower branches of a tree just as she is leaving the grove. She stops to take a picture of him. He stares back at her, unbothered, with black eyes that take up most of the real estate in his face. He doesn't look real—the Devander girls will never believe he let her get this close.

Of course, even if she does make it back, whether or not she ever sees the Devander girls again will depend entirely on how much of her little outburst Violet actually heard. She's not sure Violet has ever been called an idiot before. Certainly not to her face. Some women have that good fortune. Maybe, if confronted about it, Nina can pretend she didn't say it at all. Or maybe Violet, in her benevolence, will let it slide on account of the stress Nina had been under, what with being lost in the wilderness. Maybe Nina can emphasize how hard it's been to think out here, powered entirely by terror and Bulki bars.

"I hear you," Violet is likely to say. "But no matter how frustrated you were, it was wrong of you to call me names."

Nina wouldn't judge anyone for mistaking Violet Devander for an idiot. At first glance, anyway, a lot of things about Violet invite the assumption. Her extraordinary beauty. The excited, breathy way she speaks. The apothecary of powders, tinctures, and balms with which she lathers herself, inside and out, every day. The fact that she looks absurd standing next to her husband, who, despite a busted hip and a mild addiction to nasal decongestants, is a neurosurgeon of such formidable standing that he'd managed to hold on to a four-bed, four-bath overlooking Central Park after divorcing his first wife for a woman twenty-five years his junior.

But Violet is not an idiot. Nina knows this. Why did she say it? What if those are the last words she ever utters to Violet?

Don't be an idiot yourself now, Neen. You'll see her again. You'll apologize. This is not how you die.

If Nina has learned one thing from Violet Devander, it's that routines are crucial. "For your sanity," she's always saying. "For your survival. As a *woman.*"

Violet would be appalled at the total absence of routines from Nina's torpid little ghost-village existence. Are you washing your face and armpits in the river every morning? Why not? This should be nonnegotiable. No matter how cold you are from the night before, you should get some of that good cool water on your face. Are you drinking it? Yes? Then why aren't you using it to brush your teeth? A finger brush is better than nothing. Have you figured out your rations yet? You should eat one Bulki bar the moment the sun comes up, and another when the sun goes down. Nineteen grams of protein per—not optimal, but enough to keep you going. If you really can't stand the wait between bars, you should allow yourself one small handful of trail mix, but you should also feel bad about needing it. Every afternoon, weather permitting, you should walk a little bit farther in any given direction than the day before, just to make sure there's not a town over the next hill.

Well, there's not a town over the next hill. Or the one after that.

At the top of the third rise, Nina sits down for a moment in the rustling grass and checks her phone. Still nothing.

Under different circumstances—maybe the actual life from which she's been snatched into this unfathomable new reality—Nina might think: What a perfect day. Warm and stunning. Just below the slope where she's sitting, a little creek comes bursting out of the dark ground. A sudden, glittering emergence. Wild flashes of it wind through the ruddy willows that litter the valley floor. A quarter mile away, the creek leaves these willows and spreads its lazy braids over the sage flats, trapping the reflected blue of the sky in all that yellow grass. Farther along, much farther than Nina intends to walk, the creek starts to pick up more vegetative ornamentation: it is joined by a procession of enormous trees whose overladen orange branches descend almost all the way to the ground. They follow the creek in zigzags until it hits the next set of hills and disappears.

If Montana is anything like this, she understands why Ben loves it.

A dark shape stands up from the bushes below her. For a brief, utterly bewildering moment, Nina mistakes it for an enormous man in a silvery fur coat. But in truth, it's a bear.

Nina's first bear—and from the look on its face, the bear's first human.

She didn't think that it would have such canine features. Like a big, irritated Labrador holding two fistfuls of knitting needles. About ten yards of brush, followed by forty or so of open hillside, is all that separates her from it. She can see the wet muzzle moving with stunning dexterity as it snuffles in her direction. *You know you're in trouble,* Ben has sometimes said, *when you can hear a wild animal breathing.*

Well, you're in trouble now. Maybe *this* is how you die.

Don't panic. You're an elephant seal. The ocean presses in around you. It pushes you down, down, down.

Everything she knows about bears comes from *Winnie-the-Pooh*. Of how much brain, she wonders, is this particular bear? How long will it continue to stand upright? Is there something she should be doing to dissuade it from charging up the hill and ripping off her head? Running isn't it. She knows that. Should she play dead?

During a course focused on self-defense for dog owners, to which Nina had been dragged when Violet first got the family's Cavapoo, the instructor had demonstrated how to wheelbarrow a German shepherd in order to break its hold on a smaller dog. Is that applicable here? The instructor had been a beefcake of probably no less than 220 pounds, and even he seems an unlikely candidate for getting this bear into wheelbarrow position.

The bear, ignorant of the fate she's trying to map for it, continues to stand on its hind legs and glower in her direction.

It takes some effort for Nina to ease herself onto her heels without making any sudden movements, but she does manage it. She should be ready to run. Any second now, the bear might rush her. Yes, she'll be going uphill, but so will the bear, and something tells her that given the disparity in their body size, she will have a brief advantage over this terrain. How that will even out once they start down the other side of the hill is anybody's guess.

The phone in her hand shudders and roars. *Ping ping ping.*

On her screen, a cascade of incoming messages unfurls brightly, like cards pouring out of a magician's hat. Even in the terror of the moment, her brain snatches up details: there's her mother, there's Violet, there's a 20 percent off coupon from her favorite beauty retailer. *Ping ping ping.*

The startled bear drops down onto all fours and goes crashing away through the willows.

Nina is already on her feet, already backing up the hill. She is swiping up to get at the messages, to open the call screen. This is when the keys freeze and the phone finally goes black.

That's it. The last tether.

She's surprised by the disjointedness between her mind and body. The only thing these two separate entities seem able to agree on is that she is screaming. But now her mind pulls away and watches, with a kind of pearl-clutching astonishment, as Nina's body winds its right arm, with the phone in hand, way back. When the arm returns, the phone becomes airborne. Its arc is impressive—she didn't know Nina could throw that hard or that far. There might have been a fate greater than *l'histoire de l'art* for Nina if she'd just put a bit of rage and despair behind her softball pitches in middle school.

The phone hasn't even dropped into the ruddy bushes below the hill yet, and already her mind is ahead of its trajectory:

You idiot. Now you'll have to climb down there and get it.

Not in a million years. She can still see the bear. It has left a path of devastation amid the willows and is standing upright again in the distance at the edge of the trees. The way its forepaws have settled on its chest make it look like it's holding a purse.

It doesn't seem to be thinking about coming back. But then again, it hasn't gone away, either.

It's a long walk back to town for Nina, moving sideways over rough terrain with one eye on where she's going and the other looking out for the bear. It does appear, once, in that grove of bug-eyed yellow trees just a few minutes behind Nina, but afterward, she doesn't see the bear again. Eventually, she manages to convince herself that she's safe to go a few strides at a time without glancing back. At least this way, she can cover some real ground.

She's in sight of the town gate when the next sign of life appears: a turkey vulture hanging in the thermals. Every now and again, the sun catches the brilliant line of silver on the underside of its wings. It's joined by another, farther overhead. They wheel in a kind of echoing symmetry, like toys on a crib mobile, bonded by the funnel of air that holds them both aloft. At some point, a third one swoops in from below.

By the time she reaches the town gate, there are eight above her, plus three or more swinging lazily in and out of the woods that lead down to the lake.

She knows what it means to see them. Something dead has washed up on the shore.

She braces herself against the gate and watches them flying down to the amphitheater of trees. What's strange is the silence. You'd think that such a large gathering of vultures would make noise.

It has to be Ben. What else could be big enough to attract so many?

She should go down there. No matter how tired, no matter how afraid she is, she should go down.

But you don't want to see him like that, do you? All bloated, with the vultures pulling at him. It won't be like a painting. Some bleached skull sitting next to a candle and a bowl of grapes. Death isn't like that. You think you know him because you live with people who do, and you've written a couple of papers about him, but you don't know him at all.

It's the right thing to do. She can't just leave her boyfriend of seven years, her high school sweetheart, on the beach, unburied, no marker, nothing. No witness to whatever end has actually befallen him. No way to tell his mother what happened, and where her boy lies.

It's cute that you think you'll ever be seeing Teresa again. How's that supposed to happen, Neen? No phone. No sense. What exactly have you done to get out of here? How do you think you'll be getting home?

"Well, I'm up here," she whispers. "And you're down there. So I'll have to think of something."

In the stable with only a few hours of daylight left, she prepares for the possible arrival of the bear. Closes the one stable door she can budge. Rolls an empty oil drum in front of the other. The pitchfork will make a decent weapon—it's about six feet long, and even though it's flimsy, she can at least point it at the bear.

If you had any brains, you'd get higher up. Go to the second floor of the hotel, or at least climb onto the roof instead of just sitting here at eye level, waiting for it.

But this feels beyond her powers. The stable is the only place where she's managed to feel safe. She can't give that up, not for a theoretical threat, even if it is a bear. She huddles in her little stall, with the pitchfork across her knees, and eats a Bulki bar. The sunlight coming down through the holes in the roof turns orange, slides drunkenly from one side of the room to the other as the minutes pass. If she didn't have to spend every waking moment convincing herself that she's this kind of animal or that, and willing her heart rate down to nothing, the place would be almost pleasant.

Oh yes. Very pleasant. There's nowhere else you'd rather be.

She can't get this afternoon's walk out of her mind. It had not been impossible to hike whatever distance she covered today and then return. The fact that she'd managed to piss off a bear during her little adventure was unfortunate, yes—but barring this, the landscape was not so forbidding. She could walk for a day or two like that, in decent weather, if she knew she was walking out of here for good. Maybe it's a risk worth taking.

But you have no idea where you are. Where would you even go? It rains almost every night—what are you going to do out there, in the cold, with no shelter? Remember that first night? How many of those do you think you could live through? It's fall. Today is September 3. You're supposed to be leaving Wyoming. You're supposed to be driving up through Yellowstone and into Montana. Instead, you're lying here on the floor of the stable, watching the doorway for any sign of that bear.

If it comes back and kills you, the last thing anybody in your life will have heard from you is that you think she's an idiot.

What a cruel thing to say. To Violet, of all people. Violet, who kept urging her to bring her mother over for dinner, even when attempt after attempt fell through because Nina's mother would suddenly find that she could not convince herself to get on the N train, and Nina would have to rush back to Astoria and find wherever she'd managed to get to and walk her home. Violet, who had gifted her this hideous sweatshirt with a full heart—a loving gesture in its own way, intended to show that Nina had been on her mind even when she was halfway around the world.

Nina had been ready to hate Violet the moment she began working for her, four years ago, recommended by a friend of a friend as a night nurse right after Bo was born. What the hell kind of mother, Nina wondered as she paced the nursery with Bo in her arms at two and four and five-thirty in the morning, outsourced the nighttime care of her firstborn child to a stranger? And not just any stranger but some twenty-year-old with a sparse childcare résumé, struggling through her third year of college. And in the middle of a global pandemic, no less. Some sort of *idiot,* obviously.

This assumption had held fast, even as other details about Nina's hiring began to press back against it. Violet, it turned out, had nearly died in childbirth. Some sort of hemorrhage. Nobody was willing to say much about it when Nina first started working, but it was obvious that Violet needed help eating, dressing, getting to the bathroom. Her blood pressure required constant monitoring. These duties fell to the other nurse—the real one, the actual medical professional, a pretty but unamused fortysomething woman from Manila, whom Nina would occasionally pass in the kitchen as she was arriving for her night shift with Bo.

Violet slept most of the day in the darkened room across the hall from the nursery. She was prone to fits of crying. She refused to hold Bo. She pumped little quantities of milk that Nina dutifully bagged, froze, thawed, and fed to Bo through the long nights. Every once in a while, before they grew close enough for Nina to confess that she, too, suffered from insomnia, Violet would come in and lean over the bassinet and hold Bo's tiny feet in her hands.

"Women like that are dangerous," Nina's mother offered, uninvited. "You're there because the husband thinks she wants to hurt the baby."

This was one of her mother's many theories about Dr. Michael that Nina found implausible. Another was the nature of Dr. Michael's intentions in hiring someone like Nina. Her mother couldn't manage to believe that his only thought was for Violet's welfare. He had never given any indication of having designs on Nina. Even if he had the capacity for such designs—privately, perhaps, or reflexively, the way her mother seemed to think all men had designs on all women—he would be too tired to act on them. Up at three-thirty twice a week for surgery, tousled and bleary-eyed, snorting his Afrin, limping out the door on that desperate hip of his that should have been replaced by now, even though he, and it, were only fifty-five.

When Bo was about two months old, the Devanders added Nina to their payroll. She was to be there most nights and had half shifts four days a week.

Violet was well enough by that point to start receiving visitors. She was the self she had apparently been before giving birth: airy, pleasant, affable. An elegant hostess, floating around the apartment in pale linens through which she somehow managed not to bleed, even though she was still soaking pad after pad, which Nina knew because she was the one shoving the bathroom trash down the chute every night.

In the company of old friends who were themselves new mothers, Violet started talking about what had happened to her. She had been in labor for almost thirty hours. Dr. Michael had been briefly called away to help a colleague in another wing of the hospital. Violet had started to hemorrhage. She blacked out. When she came to, she was outside of her body, a formless consciousness that had snagged on a corner of the ceiling and miraculously stalled there.

"I could see the whole room," Violet would say. "I could see myself on the table, and all this blood on the floor. All the nurses were racing around. I could see Bo—they were taking her away from me. A man was there. He wasn't helping. He wasn't doing anything at all, just sort of standing in the corner. I felt like I knew him, but I couldn't remember where I'd seen him before."

Nina knew who he was. She knew right away. But the women on the receiving end of Violet's confessions—women from the neighborhood mommy groups, women who Nina understood, just from her brief encounters with them as Violet handed Bo off to her for the day, couldn't be trusted with what Violet actually needed—did not. Their knowledge of Death was limited to the effects of aging. They thought all they had to fear from him was crepey skin and perimenopausal midsection weight gain. They fought him at med spas and beauty clinics, wearing their wraps and peels, hiding their stitches from the nannies who gossiped about them in playgrounds and parks.

But to Nina's surprise, Violet, despite all the easy blessings of her life, realized on some innate level that there was more to it than that. Not an idiot after all.

At the suggestion of one of the mommies, Violet started visiting psychics and mediums. Since Nina was living with the Devanders more or less full-time, she was an inevitable party to these sessions. She would accompany Violet to some gorgeous building in the West Village, settle Bo in the travel crib in an adjoining room, and curl up in a chair to eavesdrop. The apartments where these psychics and mediums lived were, without fail, big sterile spaces, with only a few knickknacks of the trade to signal the presence of the other world: crystals, incense, beads. The occasional dream catcher. Where was the mess, Nina wondered. Where were the vinyl tablecloths and the plastic bottles of home-brewed salve? None of these Manhattan psychics seemed to smoke or drink or play cards. Everything about them was so clean—even the way they spoke, smooth, practiced, as if they'd told a thousand women before Violet Devander the exact same thing: "A powerful demon has attached itself to you. But don't worry! I can help you remove him. My Venmo is . . ."

Or: "I'm afraid you've picked up a vengeful spirit. But I've seen this before. I can bind him and move him away from you. I can bundle this service with a maintenance package to make sure he stays away."

Nina wondered how Violet might feel without the pressure of all this language. How she would react to somebody who wasn't slick. Somebody with no social media, with none of the outward finesse of these people. Somebody who would actually tell her the truth.

It took Nina almost a year to work up the courage to invite Violet to Astoria to meet Mrs. Tima, the downstairs neighbor.

"Do you want to talk to somebody *real* about this stuff?" Nina finally asked.

Violet bristled. "What do you mean, 'real'? It's all *real,* Nina."

"I know it's real, I just—" She struggled to explain what she meant. "I wonder sometimes if *they* know it's real. The people telling you that you've attracted a demon only they can stop."

"I'm not stupid." Violet's eyes filled with tears. "I don't believe *everything* they say."

"Come and meet Mrs. Tima," Nina said. "She saved my mother when she was pregnant with me during the bombing."

"Is she a medium?"

Nina hesitated. How to say no, not a medium. More of an enchantress. A back-alley witch, if you will, for the neighborhood, but not the way you think. "She's a healer."

Mrs. Tima cleared some space for them in her schedule the following week. On the morning of their appointment, Violet showed up at the limo carrying a paper bag from Blanc that turned out to contain a bunch of peonies and a scented candle.

"What's this?" Nina asked.

"You said to bring an offering."

The word hung laden between them. Nina had failed to clarify what an offering actually entailed, and was now failing to conceal her disappointment at Violet's misinterpretation of it.

Violet put her hands on her hips. "Flowers and a nice candle. What, it's not enough?"

"I'm sorry," Nina said. "I didn't explain properly. There's a whole thing about presentation. It has to be an *offering.* It has to be, you know, of substance. But don't worry—we'll get something on the way."

When they got to Ditmars Boulevard, they stopped at Baba's for a nut tray and a decorative gift box of world teas, and then at Martha's for buns and pastries. They were forty minutes late by the time they finally knocked on Mrs. Tima's door, but the old woman didn't mind. She hugged Nina, then grabbed Violet's hands and set about kissing her cheeks and stroking her hair. "Beautiful," she said. "Bless you, *lepotice moja.* What a beauty."

She assumed her usual place at the kitchen table, and held on to Violet's hand, keeping her at her side while Nina laid the bakery box and the nut tray and the collection of teas out on the sideboard, and put the flowers in some water. Violet remained trapped in a half crouch at Mrs. Tima's side, smiling awkwardly, and it gave Nina a jolt of pleasure to see her so discombobulated. At least she had the good sense not to try to work herself free, even while the elder was finishing up her cigarette. Once the nub was stubbed out, Mrs. Tima let go, and Violet scurried to the other side of the table and sat down.

They got through all the preliminary questions, the ones about Mrs. Tima's gifts and when they had appeared and so on. There were details here that Nina herself had never heard—particularly about Branka, Mrs. Tima's cat, who was apparently some sort of horny shape-shifter and liked to climb into philanderers' windows and try to suffocate them in their sleep.

Finally they got to Violet and the man in the delivery room.

"She's been told it was a demon," Nina said carefully. "Or the ghost of somebody, maybe her father, who won't leave her alone."

Mrs. Tima laughed in exactly the way Nina hoped she wouldn't. "Tell that child no. Not a demon. Not her father. That's Death, honey. The one and only. The lord of time."

Violet looked both puzzled and amused. "Death isn't real."

"What do you mean, he isn't real?"

"Well, he's not, like, a *person.* He's not . . . somebody. Death is just a thing that happens."

Mrs. Tima pursed her lips. "A thing that happens . . ." She lit another cigarette.

"Anyway, why would he show up and then not, I don't know, take me?"

Mrs. Tima shrugged. "Did he hold his hand out to you?"

"No." Violet gave it another second, just to be sure. "No, he didn't."

"Well, I guess it wasn't your time. Believe me, child, when it's your time, he holds his hand out to you, and you *do* take it. You want to. You're ready. That's how it works."

"Have you seen him?" Violet asked.

"Just once, during the war. Right around the same time Nina's mother did." Mrs. Tima nodded in Nina's direction. "Nina, too."

Violet turned to her with a look of bewilderment.

"That's not true." Nina couldn't shake her head emphatically enough. "I've never seen him."

"What are you talking about? You were there when your mother saw him."

"But I was in utero. I wasn't really there."

"Ehhhhhh." Mrs. Tima tilted her head to indicate that this was a half-truth, when in fact it was a whole one. If Nina had ever laid eyes on Death, she would have taken his hand right away. She wouldn't have hung on for a night under the rubble, like her mother had. She had no fight in her at all.

"So what do you suggest I do?" Violet said. "To get rid of him?"

"Get rid of him? Didn't you hear me say he's not a ghost? He isn't with you, *sine*. He meets you when it's your time. Okay, once in a while he shows up a little early. But then he checks his clocks again. You don't need to worry about him till he comes back. You're not carrying him around. You're free."

For a free woman, Violet looked incredibly pale on her way back to the elevator. They drove home in silence, Nina petting Bo's hair in the car seat, and Violet opening water after water from the limousine door. Then Violet went to her room and Nina didn't see her again until long after the baby's bedtime, when they bumped into each other in the kitchen.

"Do you want me to make you a sandwich?" Nina asked, taking a skillet off the rack.

"No."

"Do you want some tea?"

"No. Thank you."

It was a tone she'd heard Violet use only with people she caught sleeping on the subway grate outside their building. "Is something wrong?"

Violet finally turned to face her. "I think it's really shitty what you did today."

"What did I do?"

"You're trying to make me feel stupid."

"How?"

"By getting your friend to tell me that everybody else has been lying to me. Fourteen different spiritual workers—what, they're all lying, and you two are the only ones who know what's really going on?"

"Isn't that exactly what every other medium tells you?"

"Those people have *credentials.* They know what they're talking about." She wiped her eyes primly with the back of her hand. "I'm not just some moron who'll buy anything anyone is selling. It's not strange or wrong to seek answers when you go through what I went through."

"I know that."

"I nearly *died.* My child nearly lost her mother."

"Believe me, I know. That's why I wanted you to see Mrs. Tima."

"And it was shitty of you to speak together in a foreign language right in front of me."

"I'm sorry. I didn't think we were doing it that much."

"Well, you were."

"She's not completely fluent in English. I translated everything we said to each other."

"Sure you did."

Nina stood there with the skillet still in hand. She had the distinct feeling that she was about to be fired. Or perhaps that she had been fired already, in Violet's mind, and was only just being brought up to speed. She wasn't going to miss the world of the playground and all the other nannies. But she wasn't looking forward to the expression on her mother's face when she came back through the door with her suitcases, or to explaining how she had managed to fuck up such a good thing. "I'm sorry," she said again. "I thought you'd be relieved to know that—that you're not haunted. There's nothing coming after you. You don't have to think about it anymore."

Violet shook her head. "It can't be that simple. It can't."

"Of course it can," said Nina. A flicker of indignation stirred in her. She went straight for Violet's heart. "You can live your life.

You can have another baby. I know you've been afraid to try, but you can."

She had never seen someone's stone-facedness collapse so abruptly. "I really want that," Violet whispered. Now she was crying in earnest. "You know how much I want that."

Nina felt it might be all right to touch her shoulder now. "You're okay."

"I feel funny."

"Funny how?"

"My heart is beating really fast."

"You're okay."

"I'm going to faint."

"It's all right." Nina put the skillet down and took both of Violet's freezing hands in hers. "Just breathe." She puffed in and out slowly until Violet's breaths matched her own. "Pretend you're underwater. So deep there's no light and no sound. Pretend all that weight is crushing down on you."

"What the fuck?" Violet said.

"Trust me. Breathe in. Breathe out. You're a big animal. Maybe an elephant seal. Or maybe a whale. There's a lot of you. A lot of body, and that pressure is pushing down on you from above. It's squeezing you hard. Your heart has to beat very, very slowly to survive it. I mean slowly—really slowly. You have to go down, down, down, down."

Nina rolls onto her stomach, moves the lighter to her right hand and thumbs the wheel. If she can get it to work before the sun disappears, she might still have a fire tonight. Every so often, she manages to get a striving little *fffp* out of it—but no light follows. Her other hand is busy tracing the floorboards. The feel of them is soothing. They're surprisingly smooth. Almost velvety. An artisanal treatment that Violet would love. *Looks nice, but good luck get-*

ting stains out of it, Geraldine, the Devanders' housekeeper, would say. She shifts onto her side.

Here and there, Nina's fingers catch on a sharp bit of something: a rock, a piece of straw, a knot in the board. Her finger hits a groove perpendicular to the one that she is following and changes course. She traces that corner a couple of times, back and forth, then follows the new line directly toward herself until it disappears under the arm she's using as a pillow.

You're lying on something.

She gets to her knees and brushes the straw aside until she can see what's under it: the outline of a trapdoor, maybe two feet by two feet, cut right into the boards. The hinges, which she failed to notice for two whole days, are right there against the stable wall.

Her first instinct is to leave. No good can come of trapdoors and whatever they're intended to conceal.

And yet.

There's no pull ring or keyhole, but there is a knot in the wood that she can use for purchase. She works her finger into it. The door lifts, ever so slightly, then drops back. Dust motes drift around her.

The time has come to ask herself whether she is desperate enough to be opening trapdoors that lead into the darkness under stables. The answer should be yes. Whatever she finds could be of use to her in the ongoing project of keeping herself from starving, freezing, or scaring herself to death.

That last one, though. Opening trapdoors is definitely how you die of the last one.

She heaves the door open and props it against the stable wall, then clicks the penlight on and sends its shuddering beam down into the crawl space. It's deeper than she would have thought. She can see what looks like a suitcase down there. And sacks. Maybe even old clothing. Apparently, she's been lying over some sort of storehouse.

At the sight of it all, a strange warmth starts in her lower back.

She knows a misfire is happening between her body and her brain. But maybe it's not so strange to find yourself warmed by the promise of warmth when you've spent three consecutive nights shivering with cold.

She's never been the kind of person to go for secondhand anything. Even fancy consignment shops smell of rot to her. Imagine the flora and fauna that's been spreading itself all over these rags in the crawl space. Vermin, mold, fungi.

You've been running around bare-legged and without a jacket for days. Picasso and Munch and Warhol can do only so much for you, Neen. People don't die of lice. And almost nobody dies of hantavirus. It won't be what happens to you.

She leans back on her heels and checks over her shoulder, through the open stable door. Above the little tree-studded hill outside town, thunderheads are massing to bring more freezing rain her way.

She sticks the penlight between her teeth and drops down into the crawl space. At the bottom, she has to move around in a half crouch to avoid braining herself on the floorboards.

What she mistook for a suitcase is really a kind of satchel. It's made of thick olive green canvas and has a shoulder strap and a few zippered compartments—features that, even in her present state, jump out to Nina as being not quite of the pitchfork and type-settings era. Finally, finally she has found something that belongs in this century.

She heaves it up over the lip of the crawl space, then goes back down to investigate the remaining rags.

She's surprised that she can tell the difference between one kind of fabric and another: coarse old cotton, soft old velvet. She finds a blanket. She finds a length of cloth and pulls it up toward her, and now, look, with a little effort and courage, a coat is in the crook of her arm. She pushes both items out onto the stable floor.

See? This isn't so bad. Check you out, rooting through musty old clothes in a crawl space. If only your past self could see you now.

The next bolt of cloth has some real heft to it. Nina gives it a little shake to get whatever's caught in it loose, and hears a thump in the darkness. She takes the penlight out from between her teeth and, after a moment's search, manages to locate the dust-whitened but unmistakable sole of a snip-toe boot.

The boot is attached to a length of leg, beyond which she finds a human corpse lying on its side.

Nina has never fled anything the way she flees this. She is simply gone, the way wind is gone, or sound.

Outside, in the astonishing light of the setting sun, she forces herself to breathe. She's a snake, a newt, an elephant seal in the lightless, crushing depths of the Pacific. None of it works. There's no stilling her runaway heart. All the while, she's mopping the tears from her face. Wiping her hands frantically on her bare thighs.

Of course she's been sleeping on a trapdoor with a dead body under it. Of course she has.

Of course its presence is the feeling that has loomed over her in the night, keeping her cold, keeping her uneasy. Biding its time.

You've got to get out of here. You've got to *go*.

She scrambles up the hill and crouches in the bushes and stares down over all the shingles and staved-in cabins. Watching for what? Signs of movement? Will the body walk, now that it has been discovered—will it come staggering out of the stable with its white face and rotting hands, coughing through its mummified vocal cords? She can't shake the impression that it has been toying cruelly with her all this time, lying in wait while the feeling of it at the edges of Nina's perception drew her toward it. Looking for it every damn place: upstairs in the hotel, among the horse stalls, behind the bar. Now that the jig is up, will it dispense with the pretense of normality and hunt her down and eat her flesh?

Stop. This is not how you die.

Night falls. Moonless, for now. Cold, of course, and made colder by a midnight rain that roars down over the ground and the sagebrush, drowning out the comforting shush of crickets and nighttime stirrings. She sits on the hill and watches the stable. Slaps around for the penlight. It's not in her pockets. It's not trapped halfway down her sweatshirt. She resigns herself to the darkness, and after a while welcomes the shocks of distant lightning, which begin illuminating the street.

Day 5

To her surprise, the rain moves on, and the sky fills with stars. Eventually, against all odds, morning comes. Soaked through, she dozes in the warm sunlight on the hill. Wakes to some sort of squirrel flitting around her sneakers, trying to figure out the why of her.

You could leave right now. Just head straight back down to the beach and wait. You won't be any colder or hungrier.

But Ben is down there. Probably in no better shape now, after a night with the vultures, than the corpse under the stable. And this is still a town. Somebody knows about this place. Somebody, for some length of time, has been piling heaps of wildflowers against the stable. Somebody—some joyrider, some lost hiker, hell, some shepherd out of her mother's stories—is bound to come through, or come back, here eventually. She has to *be* here when that happens.

Then you have to find that penlight. You can't spend another night in total darkness. You will go insane.

She retraces her steps back down the hill, scanning the ground for any sign of it. She can't recall her sprint from the stable, but it's reasonable to assume she took the most direct route. On her hands and knees, probably. A magpie crosses her path, alights on the hotel roof, cackles down at her. Loud, ugly thing. She hates its beady eyes, its unwavering stare. As if it delights in her misery. As if it expects something of her.

She comes around the side of the stable and stands there peering through its wide-flung doors. The oil drum is lying on its side. She must have knocked it down as she ran past. She wouldn't have thought she had the strength. The satchel and clothes she tossed out of the crawl space in yesterday's fit of optimism are lying exactly where she left them. They look like they tried to crawl out of the stable after her but died here at the mouth of the trapdoor instead.

You should still use them. That corpse doesn't need them anymore.

This may be the most American thought she's ever had. *Take these clothes from the back of a corpse, Nina. The corpse won't mind.*

What would happen if the head just popped out of the trapdoor right now, like some gruesome jack-in-the-box? She would die of shock. All her heartbeats expended in a single, agonizing torrent.

At least you'd be out of your misery. You wouldn't have to go looking for the penlight.

She knows exactly where it's going to be. That, at least, should come as no surprise.

Her brain makes a desperate attempt to talk her out of her own terror. Maybe she's mistaken. Maybe she's so agitated and hungry that she can't trust herself. Maybe what she saw down there isn't a body at all.

But it is.

When she steps up to the edge of the hole, she can see its dim, horrifying outline in the crawl space below. The woman—for it is a woman—lies on her front, as if interrupted mid-crawl. Her face is mercifully invisible, but a huge net of reddish-brown hair courses over where the shoulders should be. Lying in the midst of all that dead hair is Nina's penlight.

Of course. Where else would it have landed?

She lowers herself down and drops her legs into the hole and sits with her green sneakers floating in the dark.

Don't be too precious about this. Just jump in and grab it. And don't be holding your breath—you don't want to pass out and find yourself face-to-face with your new friend.

The dirt gives way under her feet a little. She doesn't want to look at the body. With her back to it, she squats and starts feeling around. Clacks and rustles—and something living moves away from the body and scurries off into the dark. She glances over her shoulder to make sure it's not coming her way.

Don't think. Just take it.

A hand Nina knows must be her own shoots out and grabs the penlight and, unfortunately, a small fingerful of hair. That fingerful is all it takes to jostle the body. She springs off the ground and grabs the edge of the hole and pulls herself up.

At least she's got enough presence of mind this time to grab her backpack and slam the trapdoor shut.

On her way out, she hooks the satchel and the pile of rags off the floor, one in each hand, and drags them like unwilling children out into the road. The satchel can wait—she leaves it sitting there, between the stable and one of the outbuildings, and hauls the rest straight over to the river. She holds the blanket and coat underwater with the tips of her sneakers. Dust lifts off them, melts, floats away downstream. Eventually she starts rubbing them against the rocky bottom. First the blanket and then the coat. Pulls them out, shoves them back in again. Rinses her hands. Repeats.

She hauls the sopping heap over to the buck fence, wrings each item, shakes it out. The blanket is decent wool—if it manages to resist shrinking to the size of a napkin in this bright sun, it's going to keep her warm.

The coat is thin, but it'll help, too. She checks the label. It's a size 6, and it is the PROPERTY OF LT HAWLEY.

With the blanket and coat drying in the sun, she brings the satchel across the street with her into the Mint Green Bar. She shrugs out of her backpack and allows herself one of the Bulki bars. The light in here is strange, unfamiliar. Little bolts of sunshine course here and there through the ceiling. Between Nina and the cloudy windows lies the craggy debris field of the deer heads laid out on the floor. She can see a little bit of the street through the panes. Nothing new seems to be going on out there.

She sits down with her back against the bar. *Please,* she prays to the satchel between her knees. *Let there be pants. Please let there be socks. Maybe a toothbrush.*

She makes her way through the bag one zipper at a time. In the main compartment, she finds protein bars so ancient she's pretty sure she's seen them in a '90s nostalgia exhibition at the Museum of the City of New York. They feel like a couple of tiles inside their wrappers. Alongside these ossified rectangles is a jar of something called Lutie's Local Award-Winning Pickled Eggs. She holds it up to the light and watches the gray ovals bump around in all that silt-laden brine.

How desperate would you have to be?

You're probably going to find out.

To her utter dismay, the other side of the satchel unzips to reveal nothing but a massive binder crammed with papers. Everything is neatly arranged, hooked into the rings, sectioned off by colorful dividers. The first section is called "Sunrise, Research Materials, etc." At the top of the stack is a black-and-white photocopy of what looks like an old-timey book: *An Incident at Greyrock.* There's a date on the illustrated cover page, but the ink is so faded, she can't decipher it. Behind the next divider are some newspaper clippings, ranging from 1872 to about 1920, also copied onto eight-and-a-half-by-eleven-inch pages, followed by some sort of typed essay or possibly story. Its formatting screams "thesis"—Times New Roman, double-spaced, one-inch margins. The sight of it provokes a wash of intense nostalgia, and Nina thinks, with a weird stab of envy, that its author has probably never received an email from their thesis adviser saying: *It is concerning that even after a six-month extension, your page count has not improved. If something is going on in your life, please share this information with me. I can't help you if you don't tell me you need help.*

There's something heartbreaking about how carefully and precisely all this material had been arranged, only to end up here, under a stable in this godforsaken place.

Nina leafs back to the beginning of the binder. She can't recall the last thing she read that wasn't some variation of *Winnie-the-Pooh*. She has been fastidiously ducking the childhood-development books Violet is always pointedly leaving around the place, on account of their ridiculous titles alone. *Gentlespeak: The Way to a Child's Heart Is Through Your Words.*

The first chunk of pages, the old-timey book, *An Incident at Greyrock,* begins with an interminably drawn-out description of a place called Eula, high in the mountains. Ben would love it. He loves books set in places like this. Places called Jackknife and Dripping Springs. She's tried to read some of his favorites but found herself glazing over whenever any of the characters started fixing fences or branding cattle or staring out over mesas. "What's the difference between a hill and a butt?" she asked him once, earning a look of such indescribable disdain that she'd tried to pretend she was joking.

"Oh my God, Nina," he said. "It's pronounced *butte.*"

It is, Nina thinks, just her luck that the only reading material in this place is the kind of ancient dreck that forces you to get through fifteen pages of general wilderness description before a human being even makes it onto the page. When one finally does appear, he reveals himself to be the narrator, as well as the longtime telegraph operator of the Eula station house. He's sitting in a blizzard by himself, reflecting on blizzards past, at which point three more pages of blizzard descriptions follow. Some of them sound really intense.

Of the old telegraph operator's past blizzards, the most notable apparently concerns the arrival of a noble gunslinger named Anton Vargas and his crew: Fred Kipley and Doctor Maclean. In the illustration on page 20, they are hatted silhouettes who appear in the doorway of a ramshackle hut while streaks of windblown snow swirl around them. The telegraph operator describes them at length, in ascending order of importance: Doctor Maclean, who sounds like a nervous little bad-tempered nerd; Fred Kipley, a steady hand at the helm, with the "serene but distinct features of a half-breed," whatever that means; and Anton Vargas himself, a tall man of mysterious origin with black hair and a carefully tended mustache, dancing eyes, an easy manner. He is the One, obviously, the hero—the dancing eyes give it away. The unlikely trio settles in to ride out the storm. They tell the telegraph operator that they're on their way to a place called Sunrise, a miners' paradise deep in the mountains. The telegraph operator serves them supper, and it's at this point that Nina considers giving up, because of course this is one of those books, like most she adored in childhood, that lavish attention on the descriptions of food. She has to sit here and read about beef stew with carrots and potatoes, and fresh bread, and some sort of cranberry cornbread pudding in a bag—and why, she wonders, tearing shamefully into half of her fifth remaining Bulki bar, is this old telegraph operator, who lives by himself in the middle of nowhere and wasn't planning on guests, making such a massive feast for his solitary snow day?

This is never answered. Sometime after they're done feasting, a telegram comes over the wire, summoning urgent help to a place called Greyrock, which, according to the telegraph operator, is a lonely station house about ten miles north of here. The Greyrock station has been beset by bandits, who are, it is implied, after the whiskey and the women. *Make haste,* the telegram says, and the heroes do. They jump on their horses and charge through about six pages of snow, and past a centerfold drawing of a river crossing.

When they get to the station house at Greyrock, it's absolute chaos. The trees are ringing with the gunfire from what reads like thirty men. The outnumbered heroes engage in a fight for the ages. They burst into the station house, killing all the badmen with one shot apiece. A captured woman named Sadie joins their ranks while they fend off a second wave of attackers from the woods. Anton Vargas directs the action like a ballet choreographer. He quips and jokes, shoots, hits every mark. At one point, he actually says "pshaw." The others take his guidance with reverence. While they're busy shooting, they think about how handsome he is. A lot. Then finally one of the Salt Draw gang sets fire to the station house, and the heroes have to shoot their way out again. In the end, the badmen who haven't been mowed down surrender to Anton Vargas in complete awe of his fearlessness and indomitability, and consent to be taken to Sunrise for hanging. After Vargas shares a passionate kiss with Sadie in the middle of the wreckage, the three heroes—Vargas, Maclean, and Kipley—ride off into the sunset. The sunset goes on and on. A two-pager.

She puts the binder aside and stretches. Goes to the door and looks outside. The street is empty. There's no sign of anything having been disturbed by a wandering corpse. A storm is gathering. She darts outside to get the blanket and coat off the fence, then watches the storm clamber down into the valley, dragging itself along on lightning bolts. The rain sounds different on this roof, like fat sputtering in a skillet. The only thing under the hard sound of it, which gets louder and faster every few minutes as the clouds rush through the valley, is the wind sucking at the roof slats. It makes her think there's an airplane somewhere nearby. A cruel lie told by the weather.

She goes back to her little nest and puts the binder on her knees again. The cloud cover is making it difficult to tell the time, but she's probably due for the other half of her Bulki bar soon. If she distracts herself by reading, maybe she can wait another hour to eat. The newspaper clippings are next, but they're impossible to make out. The type is too small. She tries to squint through a few lines with the aid of the penlight, then gives up and moves on to the next big entry.

It's a novel called "Sunrise," and, like the jacket, it belongs to LT Hawley.

AN INCIDENT AT BURNT CREEK ON THE OCCASION OF A HOMECOMING

1902

"Sunrise"

by LT Hawley

Part I

On a Tuesday in late October, in the twilight of his forty-fifth year, the man they called Anton Vargas came within sight of town. It was not as he had left it, but exactly as he'd pictured it might look almost twenty years to the day since he'd last laid eyes on it. Ugly and unruly and scattered all down the gulch, remade in the time since the first big fire had ravaged its eastern half. Snow on the distant peaks, and the bare mountainsides below appearing drab because of it. Trees all down the slope leading to the lake.

He couldn't bring himself to head in, not yet, so he made camp on the ridge. Clouds gathered, threatened, dispersed. Their underbellies came to be that bewildering gold that Vargas sometimes dreamt of, sometimes thought he recognized elsewhere. By nightfall, it struck him that if things went according to plan, this would be the last time he ever camped anyplace. He got his mind quiet and started listening to the way his horse was breathing, and to the small stirrings in the grass. A coyote was screaming in the trees below. There was an owl somewhere nearby. Far away, down, down, down at the bottom of all hearing, was the hum and clink of Tuesday night in Sunrise.

In the morning, he pulled himself together and rode in. He

wasn't the only Tejano in town, that was certain, but he was definitely the only one wearing blue show boots. A few suits were milling on the boardwalk outside the hardware store. He touched his brim as he passed, and they all tipped back, smiling strangely. There was something antiquated about him, so old-time it was almost novel, the way he rode in, no mules, no companions, totally alone.

He moved his horse over to avoid a passing buckboard.

Along the main street stood some of the remnants of the Sunrise of his time: Sadie's, the Gander. Not one right angle between them. The hardware store's sign was still painted on the alley wall of the only brick building in town, bleached to a kind of velvety blur by ruthless sunshine. The Lavinia, his old saloon, under new ownership yet again, was now painted some garish shade of green.

Sadie's Hotel had taken a bit of battering over the years, but it was still the most spectacular place in town. White with red trim, looking like a grand old paddle steamer had just run aground here, in these badlands. Standing in the entryway moved him almost to tears. Here was the same wallpaper, the same carpet, the same smell of onions and wood chips carried on a hot current of air from the kitchen. The girl at the front desk was a stranger, though. A pretty one.

She lowered her book when she saw him. "Help you, sir?"

He wanted a room for a week, maybe more if his situation should change.

"I got nothing right now but the attic."

"Is town that busy?"

"There's a Stockmen's Association meeting this week."

"Ah," Vargas said. "The attic's just fine."

She squinted at his hat. "You might have to stoop."

"I'm very flattered you think so."

She slid the ledger over to him and he signed himself in, real name and all. He even put where he had actually traveled from: Syracuse.

"Is that far?" she said, turning the ledger around.

He nodded. "Way back East. New York."

"You a lawman?"

"Not lately."

"You look like you'd be a lawman."

"It's the hat," Vargas said. He watched her count his money.

"Up those stairs," she said, "and then down the hall. You'll find another set of stairs going up to the attic. There's two doors up there: yours is the one on the right."

"I know," he said. "I used to live round here."

She brightened. "Really?"

"Helped hang that sign."

"What sign?"

"The one out front. 'Sadie's.' "

"Is that right!" She studied him carefully. "You must've been here in the first days."

"I was—before the railroad came through Hemot," he said. "Where *is* Sadie?"

"In the hereafter. Three years gone this winter."

"I'm damn sorry to hear that," Vargas said, though he had feared, even suspected, it.

Sadie might have been gone, but traces of her were everywhere. In the absurd little salt and pepper collectibles squatting on every shelf. The antelope skulls on the dining room wall. The floral wallpaper on the upper landing.

In the room at the top of the stairs, the bed creaked under his weight. He sat, winded from the climb. His window overlooked the shingles of an adjoining roof, which had not been there in his day. Neither had the fancy cowhide chair. Nor the bathtub.

He took the letter out of his pocket and put it on the nightstand. It was a ceremonial gesture, really. He wanted to do something to signify that it had arrived here, at last. It didn't seem right to just let it go on sitting exactly where he'd carried it for months. But he didn't like the feeling of separating it from himself. He folded it up again and put it back where it belonged.

The newspaper office had moved to a bigger place, two blocks down the street. Vargas went over just before closing time, and took off his hat as he entered. People were still milling around in the anteroom, waiting to file their adverts with Fred Kipley, who looked no different today than he had twenty years ago. His hair was still utterly black. He still wore it short. He still peered down at the type with the same rumpled frown that had sterned him up in youth. The only variant of note was the deputy marshal tin fastened to his lapel. Vargas waited in the back of the room until the last of the customers had gone.

Kipley glanced up at him. Then he stood back and stared.

"Is it you?" he said.

"I'm afraid so."

Vargas had not expected an embrace to be waiting for him at the end of this greeting, but it was.

"Christ," Kipley said, clapping him on the back once more. "You look awful."

"I feel it."

Kipley closed up and brought him over to the Lavinia for a drink. At least this way, Vargas didn't have to work up the courage to go there alone. The man Vargas had sold it to had sold it again, apparently, and the latest owner had outfitted it with all the trappings of a respectable place. Nothing of Vargas's tenure remained, save the mule deer head: old, gnarly, and melting above the door.

Kipley got halfway through his beer before he spoke again: "This is not how I foresaw my day."

"Mine is going more or less exactly as I hoped," said Vargas. "Except for Sadie."

"You've heard."

"Is that her daughter runs it now?"

Kipley took a moment to wipe the foam from his upper lip. "Her niece, Maura."

"There's something of Sadie about her eyes." Vargas took a tentative drink and imagined it going down his throat and ravaging his insides.

They went back to sitting in silence for a while. "Where's Preacher?" Vargas finally said.

"I'm not telling you."

"Why not?"

"Because it's been too long, and he'll kill you, and I won't be responsible."

"That's between him and me."

Kipley shrugged in his loose-shouldered way. "Not if I keep my mouth shut."

"What if I need a doctor?"

"We got a new one," Kipley said. "I'll introduce you."

Vargas thought for a while. "What if you let Preacher know I'm here?"

"So he can shoot me instead of you? No thanks."

"I can get it out of somebody else," Vargas said. "I came to you first because it seemed like the decent thing to do."

"I hope anyone else you might ask would tell you to go to hell, too."

Vargas passed on Kipley's offer for another beer and steeled himself for an order of beef stew instead. But the Lavinia's cook, it turned out, had changed along with its owners, and the stew came out warm and luxurious and studded with hunks of soft carrot and potato. He couldn't get over it.

While he was scraping the last of it off the bottom of the bowl, trying to figure out what approach to try on Kipley next, a scrawny, cave-chested young man with a mass of dark curls came bustling through the door.

"Pardon me," he shouted over the suppertime din. "Has anyone seen Jules?"

"Who in hell is Jules?" someone yelled back.

The young man looked baffled. "My brother, he's—he's one of the Abadie kids."

"Abadies got so many kids, youse probably just mixed them up with each other."

"Jules," the young man said again. There was a murmur of irritation from the other tables, which seemed to fluster him. "Well, we'd be much obliged if you send him home if you do see him. Or let us know if you happen to remember seeing him today."

He let himself out gingerly, and Vargas watched him cross the street to Sadie's.

"That'll be a task for you, I'm sure," he said to Kipley.

"I hope not."

Pain woke him in the middle of the night. Tight and sour in his belly. He turned this way and that in the hard little bed, trying to get comfortable, surprised, despite himself, that Sadie's hadn't offered the reprieve he had hoped it would. Sentimental bastard, he thought, why on earth would it? The pain never left him for long.

Outside, stragglers were making trouble in the road in numbers far smaller than he had expected to hear. A man was shouting, "Harry! Harry! Harry!" in escalating desperation, until Harry, from somewhere nearby, finally answered, "*What?*"

Vargas gave up trying to settle himself, got dressed, and went downstairs. The girl, Maura, was up by the oil lamp, reading her book behind the counter, frowning Sadie's little midnight frown.

"Don't you sleep?" Vargas asked her.

"Someone has to make sure the building stays upright."

"Where would the new doctor's place be?"

"Are you poorly?"

"I need something to help me sleep."

He followed her directions to the infirmary. Halfway there, he realized there *was* no new doctor's place; it was just Preacher's old place, occupied by a new doctor. A light was on inside. He waited, uncertain that he could bring himself to go in just yet. But the pain persisted, so he knocked. The new doctor, just the other side of a kid himself, came to the door in his nightshirt.

"I've a terrible pain," Vargas said.

"Can't it wait till morning?"

He sat on the examining table while the new doctor got himself dressed. It was strange to see the place so changed. Clean and expansive, and missing the hemmed-in feel of Preacher's infirmary. The log walls had been painted, the cot relocated behind a screen. This new doctor did not go bumping into a forest of herbs that hung from the rafters as he drifted back and forth from his desk to the examining table. Vargas wondered if he had inherited any of Preacher's old instruments. If he lived upstairs, as Preacher had.

The new doctor had Vargas lift up his shirt so he could listen to his chest.

"Does this pain come over you often?"

"Now and then."

"How long now?"

"Some months." The hands that began palpating Vargas's stomach were shockingly cold. "I was hoping for something to help me sleep."

"I'd have you head to Cheyenne at your first opportunity," the doctor said. "There's a specialist there."

"I've seen a specialist."

"And?"

"And I need something for the pain, and soon enough I won't need even that."

"I'm sorry." The new doctor removed his glasses. "Well, at least we don't have to dance around it."

"We don't."

"Would you like your level of relief to be oblivion or something slightly south of that?"

"Slightly south."

"Your name?"

"Anton." He watched the doctor scribble it down. "Vargas."

Sadie's niece hadn't flinched when he'd said it, either. Maybe the new doctor was too young to recognize it. Or maybe he just hadn't been in town long enough to know what it meant.

While a bottle of laudanum was being procured for Vargas, the same kid who had disrupted the proceedings at the Lavinia earlier in the evening burst through the door.

"Knock!" the new doctor cried.

"Apologies," the kid said, bowing to the doctor, then bowing to where Vargas sat buttoning his shirt. "We need you out at the house right away. My mother is very bad."

"I'm with a patient."

"Please, sir, she's in a fainting way."

"Give her some water and smelling salts," the doctor said. "I'll be along just as soon as I'm able."

The young man's forehead nearly touched the ground for bowing. He closed the door behind himself, and his face appeared hazily in the window while he waited.

Vargas eased off the examining table and started buckling his belt. "I guess Jules Abadie hasn't made it home yet."

"He will." The new doctor started packing his satchel. "I put my mother through much worse when I was eight or nine."

Vargas thanked him for the medicine. His hand was on the doorknob when the doctor called out to him. "You must be in a bad way to be throwing that name around," he said. "Even if you really *are* Anton Vargas."

He woke to somebody pounding on his door. Terrible sleep had put him in terrible humor, and he wrenched the door open. Kipley was out in the hall.

"Good God," Kipley said. "Did you get any sleep?"

"Some."

"Are you rested enough to join me up at Burnt Creek?"

"What the hell for?"

"I'm heading to the Abadie place," Kipley said. "No one's seen that boy in two days."

"Probably fell down a mine shaft."

"That doesn't happen as often as you'd think." Kipley looked him over. "Can you be dressed in five minutes?"

"I don't see how I'm a necessary part of this excursion."

"I figure I'd let you make yourself useful. Keep you from lurking around town, telling everybody who you are."

"I don't tell people who I am, Fred. They know me on sight."

"Well, get dressed anyway and come down. Let's see if they know you on sight at the Abadie place. We'll have a feed after."

When he got downstairs, Kipley was waiting for him outside, hanging off the footboard of a motorcar. Vargas hadn't expected his first-ever car ride to happen like this, squinting against dust and wind while nursing a laudanum hangover. Kipley gripped the wheel, jolting the car left and right. Vargas figured he should have gone on horseback—but how many new experiences could he expect to be afforded now?

The Abadie homestead was out past Burnt Creek, set back from the road in a stand of willows. There were only two rooms to the whole cabin: the back room, which held exactly one mattress, and the foreroom, which was empty save for the stove and a long table with some chairs around it. This room seemed to be taken up almost entirely by the father, a bearded giant of a man as pale as the moon. Vargas had only ever seen this pink-gray tint in the faces of people in paintings, and those only in the occasional manor house,

English or French, where he'd been invited as a guest of his one-time employer, Montana Jack. Irises so light you'd think the sun would turn them to cinders. The mother was half his height, a sternly handsome mestiza. She stood at the table behind her husband, slapping a wheel of dough, two-handed, with no trace of the fainting way that had brought her eldest son to the doctor's door last night. The Abadie offspring, of whom Vargas counted anywhere between five and seven, were scattered around the place and in a constant state of movement.

While the father ranted in what Vargas guessed might be French, the bewildered eldest son hurried to translate.

"Went off to work two mornings ago," the father was apparently saying. "Never came back."

"Where does he work?" Kipley asked the son.

"Over at John Daisy's house."

Vargas watched Kipley's face for a reaction but found none. "Have you called around to ask after him?"

"Me personally?" the eldest son asked.

"Weren't you the one out searching for your brother last night?"

"Sure was."

"So what did Mister Daisy say?"

"Well, Mister Daisy wasn't there, but his wife, she said Jules left in good time."

Now Kipley looked oddly at him. "I wasn't aware Mister Daisy had a wife. What's her name?"

"I—I don't know her name, sir."

"But she said your brother left in good time?"

"That's right."

"And what would she—or you—consider 'good time'?"

"I guess about four o'clock."

"You guess?"

"Well, that would put him home in time for his chores."

Vargas hoped that Kipley would meet his eye, but this would

require him to look over his shoulder, and Kipley wasn't about to do that, not when he had the kid so squeezed.

"Could your brother have run away?" Kipley asked.

"No." This was the mother. "He's a good boy." She had stopped thumping the dough and was leaning over the table. "He goes to school."

The enormous father finally got a grasp on the exchange and thundered in: "Good boy—how? Four o'clock, five o'clock. One day, two days. No wood chopped, nothing. Where is he?"

"We'll try to find out for you." Kipley put his hat back on.

As they turned to leave, the mother called out after them: "Find my boy!"

Outside, a further Abadie kid or two flitted into the brush beside the car. The sun, directly overhead, glinted off the burning metal. Vargas crouched down and rested his forehead against the door. He was thirsty.

Kipley's boots scraped into view beside him. "What's the matter?"

"I'll be all right."

He heard the eldest son come out of the cabin and make his way toward them.

"Deputy," the son said. "Where are you headed next?"

"Not sure," Kipley said. "Any suggestions?"

"I guess you should talk to Mister Daisy."

"What for? I thought the fictitious wife told you Jules went home in good time." Kipley moved closer to the kid. "Why'd you say you went over there when it's obvious you didn't?"

"I'm sorry, sir. I told my parents I did, and I couldn't own up to the lie in front of them. Mister Daisy—well, I don't like to go over there."

"Why not?"

"It's such a strange house. So grand. It makes me feel small."

"Well, I hope you feel even smaller now," Kipley said. "Your brother missing two whole days, and you with a chance to help, and choosing to lie instead."

Vargas peered over his shoulder in time to see the kid scraping dejectedly back toward the cabin.

"I see age hasn't softened you one bit," he said to Kipley.

"Lying little shit. And his brother gone, legs probably broken down some mine shaft."

"I thought you said that doesn't happen much."

"Come on." Kipley pulled him to his feet. "Let's go see John Daisy."

"You said we'd have a feed."

"We will, by and by. Don't you want to see how grand this house is?"

It wasn't the grandest house Vargas had ever seen, but it was certainly grander than anything he had ever expected to be built in Sunrise. It stood about a mile from town on a bald limestone hill, surrounded on all sides by sagebrush. It was a tall, square building with a balcony all around it, held up by huge wooden columns.

They found Mister John Daisy awake, which, the butler who led them through the corridors mentioned, was quite unusual. At this time of day, Mister Daisy tended to be taking his afternoon rest, preferring as he did to compose his memoirs in the evenings. Vargas stayed close on Kipley's heels as they moved through the dark interior of the house, which was illuminated at haphazard intervals by the occasional transom outfitted in brilliant glass.

John Daisy was a magnanimous little bull of an Anglo. Straightforwardly handsome, even at his age, and even with thinning white hair. His eyes were heavily lidded, fiercely blue. He seemed thrilled to be shaking Kipley's hand. "It's been far too long—and look! Is this a new deputy?"

Vargas felt his hand being involuntarily taken from his side and pumped. He did not introduce himself.

"Mister Daisy," said Kipley, "do you know of a little fella in your employ, goes by Abadie?"

"Young Jules," John Daisy said.

"It seems he hasn't returned home since he was last here two days ago. Understanding that this is an imposition on your time, would you object to my asking your staff what they may remember about when he was last seen?"

John Daisy did not object. In fact, he demanded a thorough investigation. While he led Kipley around the hushed army of his underlings, Vargas slipped into the hall. He let himself wander. Most of the rooms were spare, as though John Daisy were still in the process of moving in. Just behind the grand staircase, Vargas stumbled into the library, where all of John Daisy's decorating efforts appeared to be concentrated: here were game tables, plush sofas, bookshelves that soared to the ceiling as in the old houses of Europe. Shadow boxes and pedestals of every kind mazed around the room. Upon closer inspection, these turned out to contain mostly Indian relics: arrowheads, buffalo bones, scrapers, the tattered edges of leather or clothing.

He found his way to the back portico by the rear kitchen door and stood there, looking out over the hills. Below him, in the far distance, through what remained of the old pine forest, he could see the gloomy blue of Horsebone Lake.

Kipley appeared at his elbow.

"Strange house," Vargas said.

"You don't know the half of it."

Kipley led him downstairs and around the side of the house, across a stretch of bald ground that had been stripped of sagebrush, to the edge of a vast pit.

"Is this a mine?" Vargas asked.

"An old buffalo jump," Kipley said. "Daisy's workers found it a couple years back when they were quarrying stone for the house. You ever seen one?"

Vargas shook his head.

"In the old days, way, way back, this here was the cliff's edge. And the ancients would stampede the buffalo over it and butcher them at the bottom."

Vargas inched to the edge and peered down. The afternoon shadows had slanted so that almost nothing was visible, save a few dead roots. "How deep is it?" he asked.

"I don't know."

"Think your missing Abadie might be down there?"

Kipley looked at him strangely. "No," he said. But he took off his hat and crouched down all the same, frowning into the void. After a moment, tentatively, he called: "Jules?" When no answer came, he shook his head in what seemed, to Vargas, like disgust with himself. "Why do I ever indulge you?"

By the time they left, the sun was getting low. The meal Kipley had promised they would share had never materialized. The day was wasted, and Vargas felt strangely adrift in his own mind. He touched his inside breast pocket and felt the letter there. No Preacher, and no sign of anyone who knew where Vargas might find him. Before him lay only the prospect of a juddering ride back to town with Kipley, who was apparently planning to extend this misery into the following day.

"Tomorrow," he was saying, "we'll muster a search party."

"What do you mean, 'we'?" Vargas said. "What do you need me for?"

Kipley treated him to a big wolfish grin. "I intend to use people's awe of you to catch them off guard."

"I notice you didn't use John Daisy's awe of me back there."

"When it suits me, I will." He started the car and aimed it carefully down the road.

"Don't you got an under-deputy whose job it is to go around with you and do your bidding?" Vargas asked.

"I'm finding you rather a disappointment, Anton." One of the wheels hit a pothole, and the jolt briefly snatched the smile from

Kipley's face. "Haven't seen me in twenty years, and here I am, generously inviting you into my duties, and all you can think is to get away from me."

"I don't have time to be hunting down runaways with you. I got plans."

"What plans?"

"People to see."

"Who?"

Vargas thought about it. "Ned Ritter."

"He died."

"Father Andrej."

"Gathered up his little round church last winter and followed half the town's Russians to the new diggings in Montana." Kipley turned to look at him. "Damn near everybody you knew here has moved on, one way or another. And you should know that whenever I'm asked if you're Anton Vargas, I intend to say that you don't want it known that you've come back. So don't be thinking Preacher will get wind of it from somebody else."

"So he's around here somewhere."

"I didn't say that."

Back at the hotel, Vargas found Maura squinting through a new book, picking something out of a bowl on the desk before her.

"What's this, what's this?" He peered into the bowl. "Are you eating piñons?"

She poured some into a cup for him. He carried them upstairs and sat by the window and cracked them between his teeth, one by one, until the lights in the distant houses went out. He had managed to find a relatively painless position in the chair, and fell asleep this way. He dreamt of taking his cup of pine nuts out onto the balcony. Outside, snow had fallen on the silent world. He could hear the distant quitting bell from the Lavinia mine clanging away. In the dream, he went back to sleep and woke to find a badger standing out on the balcony, helping itself to the piñons, which Vargas had been stupid enough to leave out there. He stood for a while in the doorframe and watched the badger obliterate his precious snacks. The moment it looked up and saw him, the doorframe vanished. Now Vargas could feel the cold of the snow. The badger licked its claws, like a person, one by one, and then started down the ladder, which had suddenly come to adjoin the dream balcony. Vargas followed it down, along the street, and out of town. Everything around him was as it was in real life, save for the snow and the badger walking out ahead of him. They carried on some sort of unspoken conversation, Vargas and the dream badger, came to some sort of understanding—he knew this because the badger stopped glancing over its shoulder to check that he was still following. It led him through the willows along the creek. They passed the Abadie homestead, with its every sorrowful light shining. They passed beneath the old Flood and Hindle arrastra, and then started climbing the switchbacks to what Vargas remembered was the old Robles place. The dugout was empty, the fire tamped down. The badger rummaged through the cupboards while Vargas looked around. The ashes in the hearth were still warm, and from them he pulled an arrowhead the size of his hand. When he raised his head, he realized the badger had dug a hole right in the middle of the floor and was climbing into it. Vargas brought himself to the hole's edge, looked down at the bones piled along the bottom, and woke up.

So searing was his pain when the dream released him that he thought at first he must be hungover. He was still in the chair. The sky outside was beginning to lighten. He stood, threw up, went along the hall to the privy, and flushed the contents of his chamber pot down the hotel's marvelous new toilet.

By the time Maura came to freshen his room, it was early morning. He was up and dressed, and he felt certain he was hiding how terrible he felt.

"Your hand," Maura said in dismay. "What happened to it?"

The knuckles of his left hand, save for his thumb, had swollen to almost twice their usual size. He hadn't noticed because of the pain in his back. "It happens sometimes," he said.

"Should I get the doctor?"

"I've already seen him." He rubbed his eyes. "You don't know where the *old* doctor went, do you?"

"I don't."

"He used to work out of the same place. Maclean—goes by Preacher?"

She shook her head.

"You don't know, or you won't say?"

"I never met the old doctor. I wouldn't know to tell you his whereabouts."

It was hard to guess by her face whether Kipley had told her to keep her mouth shut about Preacher. Surely she would seem more puzzled by the question if she weren't just hurrying through a script. In years past—during his days as a range detective, for instance—he would not have been so easily brushed off. He'd been almost forty pounds heavier in the whole of his health, and taller, it seemed, because of it. People had this way of looking at him—sidelong, with their heads tilted down, as if the prospect of meeting his eye carried some risk they felt but couldn't name. They did not simply go on punching down the pillows and smoothing out the sheets, politely ignoring the lingering stench of his vomit.

"I'm Anton Vargas," he said.

"Yes."

"You've heard the name before."

"Yes, sir, you gave it when you arrived."

What a game little liar she was, Sadie's niece. Practiced and flat, deliberate about avoiding his eye. He felt a sudden, long-dormant urge to grab her by the shoulders. But he resisted it and stayed in the low little chair by his empty chamber pot.

Maura straightened her apron and gathered up the used linens. "Will you join the search again today?"

"I guess so. Fred Kipley's bound to need all the help he can muster."

But the help Fred Kipley had managed to muster was actually considerable. The boardwalk was thick with men in various states of self-aggrandizement. Vargas watched them from the hotel doorway, gnawing his morning biscuit. Fred Kipley came out of the newspaper office and hauled himself onto the hood of his car to present the general layout of the day: they were to extend the search now to five miles south and five miles north of town, riding in pairs.

Vargas's partner in this endeavor ended up being a broad-shouldered, orange-haired youth of about nineteen whose whole face was a triangle drawn down to his chin. His name was Dillon. He had little by way of eyes, and he rode to the right of Vargas without saying a word. Every so often, believing himself in charge, Vargas shouted, "Jules!," which prompted his companion to echo the call.

By sunset, they had gone all up and down Harlequin Butte.

"Figure it's time to head back?" Dillon finally said.

"We ought to make a fire first. Give that boy something to orient himself toward, if he's out there alone in the dark."

They got the fire going and sat down beside it for what Vargas promised wouldn't be long. Its first smoke was heavy, lurching this way and that on the evening wind. Sitting there on the ground, he realized he should have stayed mounted—the pain spreading through his back moved fast, ratcheting him around the middle. He wasn't sure he could get his voice through it to speak, and was thankful now that Dillon did not seem inclined toward conversation.

Below them, the distant torches of the other searchers were bobbing through the trees on the opposite side of the valley. Vargas felt a swell of sadness. The torches were so far apart. So much unsearched darkness lay between them.

"I can't figure how that boy ain't found his way back," Dillon said, as if reading his mind.

"Me neither."

"To tell you the truth, I think we're looking for a corpse. I think we been looking for a corpse all along."

"You're probably not wrong about that." Vargas rubbed his hair under his hat.

Dillon picked at the toe of his boot for a minute. "Is it true what they're saying about you?"

"What are they saying about me?"

"That you're Anton Vargas."

"What does that mean?"

Dillon blinked. "I didn't figure it needed explaining."

"Let's pretend it does." He leaned forward and prodded the fire. "Let's pretend I never heard of Anton Vargas before. What would you tell me?"

"I guess I'd ask you if you'd ever read a dime novel in your life."

"What else?"

"I'd say you should learn your history some. Study up on that Greyrock business."

"How do I compare to the dime novel version?"

"You're shorter. Darker, too."

Vargas let himself laugh at that. Across the fire, Dillon's face broke into a wide grin that sucked his eyes all the way back into his head.

"What are you doing here, Mister Vargas? Last we heard, you was overseas in some Wild West show."

"I'm looking for Preacher." Vargas spoke slowly. "You know who Preacher is, don't you?"

"The old doc. He was around when I was just a kid." Dillon shuddered. "Crazy for them injections. Give you one as soon as look at you."

"Probably saved your life once or twice with those." He had to tread very carefully here to get what he wanted. "You happen to know where he ended up?"

Dillon thought about it. "He was tangled up in some bad business up at Fort Searles, wasn't he?"

Vargas nodded. "I mean after that. You hear anything of him since?"

"No—I think he was real bad off for a while, and when the army started searching for him, I guess he up and moved."

"Where to?"

"No idea." Vargas could feel him blinking stupidly in the dark. "How come you're looking for him?"

"I owe him a debt."

"Sounds like something you'd say in a dime novel."

"Yes, but in the dime novel I'd mean it sinister-like, and here I mean it sincere. I owe him, and it's about time I paid up."

"I could ask around," Dillon said. "See if anyone knows where he's got to."

"I'd be grateful to you. More grateful, still, if you keep my name out of it when you do the asking."

"Okay." Dillon's big, dumb, admiring gaze was making Vargas uncomfortable. He wondered how he'd ever had a taste for young men like this.

"Weather's coming," Vargas said. "You cold?"

"A little."

In past times, he might have used this as an opportunity to suggest they share the saddle blanket to get warm, and see what Dillon thought about that. But as it was, he said, "Go on home, I'll be along."

Vargas watched Dillon walk his horse down the hill. He wasn't ready to return to Sadie's yet. He wasn't ready for sleep or for strange dreams, and it was cold enough out here to count on staying awake. He took the letter from his pocket, read it, and put it away again.

Why did he bother? He knew the whole thing almost by heart. No new phrases were going to materialize on its pages while it waited there in his coat.

He hadn't banked on how tired the day had made him, and once again he failed to recognize that he had slipped into a dream until he saw the badger. It popped up on the far side of the fire with an expression of grave impatience. Last night's cup of piñons was back in its claws.

"Son of a bitch," Vargas said to it.

As before, it led him down the hill, past the Abadie house, and beneath the arrastra. This time, it dropped below the ground early, and he followed it into the earth, through tunnels full of bone and obsidian, until it finally surfaced in a dugout. Coming in this new way, Vargas needed a moment to recognize that the badger had led him to the Robles place again.

When he woke up, snow had fallen. He shook it off his hat and boots, brushed it off the horse's saddle, and rode farther into the hills. Daybreak wasn't too far off, but everything still felt adrift in the resplendent stillness of the midnight world. Over his right shoulder blazed the Abadie house, and through the willows beyond, just as in the dream, was the old arrastra. He had helped to build it, before the stamp mills came. He dismounted and sat under it awhile, looking up at its massive wheel while the snowflakes broke gently against his face.

An invitation was waiting for him when he got back to the hotel.

"The pleasure of your company is requested at the Stockmen's Association banquet tomorrow," Maura said, holding the card out to him across the counter. "At the home of Mister John Daisy."

"My stars." Vargas whistled. "The home of Mister John Daisy."

"Will you need your other suit pressed?"

"I'm real flattered that you think I have another suit."

He sat at a corner table in the dining room while Maura brought a plate over to him, even though he didn't want anything: not the biscuits, not the bacon, and certainly not the egg, hard-boiled, sitting grandly in a porcelain cup festooned with garish rabbits. Town was filling up, and the room was busy. A slightly bucktoothed youth at the next table was staring at him through the steam of his coffee. The instant Vargas met his eye, the young man looked away and frowned meaningfully down at the morning paper.

Vargas brought his half-eaten egg over to the kid's table and sat down.

"Let's get to it, Bucky," he said. "What do you want?"

Briefly, it seemed like poor Bucky might put on a show of ignorance. But he spared Vargas the indignity. "We heard you was in town," he said excitedly. "I had to come see for myself."

"And what do you see?"

He gestured grandly. "Here you are."

"What do you want?"

From his satchel, Bucky pulled a leather folder, which, when opened, revealed a stack of loose papers and clippings and magazines. *An Incident at Greyrock* was right there, on top of it all. Vargas hadn't held a copy in many years.

"Have you ever seen one in such good condition?" his new friend said excitedly.

"Maybe when it was first printed." Vargas leafed through it. There he was, a shadowy figure, bursting through the telegraph station's door with a bunch of faceless accomplices.

"Would you sign it, sir?"

"What are you going to do with it?"

"Do?"

"Are you fixing to sell it or keep it?"

"Oh God, sir—keep it! Keep it, of course." There was something in Bucky's voice that called to mind a child grabbing back its toy.

Vargas cleared his throat. "What else you got?"

"Oh—so much more. Look."

Vargas tried to follow the cascade of the young man's words as papers continued to spill out of his satchel and onto the table. Shooting-exhibition tickets. Handbills for various stage performances. Vargas managed to say, "Congratulations on your archival efforts—this is really something."

Bucky held up an ace of spades. "Can you authenticate this?"

Vargas stared at it. "It looks like an ordinary ace of spades."

"Far from ordinary, sir. This was your winning card when Calico Sam drew on you in Calistoga."

"If you say so."

"But do *you* say so, sir? That's the real question."

"Where'd you get it?"

"One of your fellow players picked it up after you moved the fight outside."

He tried to remember anything at all about Calistoga, playing cards there, or moving a gunfight outside. It would have been his preference to keep the fight exactly where it was. There would have been no point in shooting his assailant in the street rather than at the table, where they were not more than elbow room apart, and he was about to say so when Bucky held up a handbill advertising a boxing match between Wheatfield Will and Youngheart Juan in Langsford Hole, 1878. An upwelling of recognition moved glacially through Vargas. Its resonance grew long after his companion had started up his breathless questions again.

"Were you at this bout, sir? Do you remember?" he was asking proudly, as if he himself, rather than the passing time, was the architect of all of Vargas's memories. "Here's a photograph taken of the crowd in the street the day before—look closely, sir, please, and tell me: *Is this you?*" He was holding out a newspaper clipping of a tintype. His dirty fingernail was pinned to the head of a wide-eyed kid with the wispiest mustache Vargas had ever seen.

"Yes," Vargas said hoarsely. "That's me. That was taken the day I lost my tooth."

It had been written of Anton Vargas that he was born at a stagecoach stop and raised by an uncle. That was partly true: the stagecoach stop where he grew up had indeed belonged to his uncle, but his uncle had belonged to the bottle, so Vargas had more or less raised himself. This resulted in his entering adolescence a quiet, earthbound, raw nerve of a boy, reckless and quick to anger. His uncle's customers were forever threatening to put manners on him, and it was through these lessons that the aforementioned tooth would become a liability. He was schooled—usually by way of haymakers—for his tone of voice, his stubborn eye contact; for the familiar way he spoke to travelers' daughters; for his failure to spit out his chew when addressing his elders and betters; his failure to calculate the correct change for a pound of sugar; his failure to properly stable a horse. To his credit, he never had to learn the same lesson twice. Still, all that learning—never objected to, nor prevented, by his uncle—had taken a toll on the poor tooth: an upper molar on the left side of Vargas's face, which stood in the path of most punches that came his way. Already little more than a painful stump, it took its final instruction from a man named Boss Worth, a white-haired bullwhacker of volatile disposition, who, during the longest night of Vargas's life to date, lost every penny he had at poker, staked his six-gun to cover the debt, wept profusely when he lost that too, and then smashed Vargas in the face for presiding over his humiliation.

At dawn, hungover and contrite, Boss Worth offered Vargas a place among the twenty wagon teams he was leading to the new gold diggings at Sunrise. Vargas didn't believe him—passers-through had offered him a way out before, only to disappear—but Boss Worth was serious. He *wanted* men like Vargas among his teamsters. Which was how, with a tooth he didn't realize was rotted and splitting, Vargas had ended up in Langsford Hole, stalled out with a hundred other freighters by a blizzard that had broken over the pass, obscuring what everybody insisted was a hell of a view of distant peaks.

Perhaps on a nicer day, with no mud pooling in the streets and no ice floes browning in the river, Vargas might have felt differently about the place. But he was shivering with pain. Whenever his tongue bumped the doomed tooth, his swollen gums bled freely.

The only thing on Boss Worth's mind, however, were the handbills papering every door in town. He clapped Vargas's shoulder and sent a red pulse through his jaw. "Holy hell, boy!" Boss Worth said, shoving a handbill in his face. "How do you like that?"

Vargas didn't like it at all. He studied the handbill. It informed him that a gigantic white Ohioan by name of Wheatfield Will O'Leary was preparing to face his latest challenger, the sinewy Youngheart Juan, right here in Langsford Hole. A FIGHT FOR THE AGES! the handbill promised. WHO WILL GET SORTED OUT?

They were wondering this very same thing in the streets, too: in the mercantile, and the livery, and at the saloon where Vargas found himself at lunchtime, frowning into a bowl of beef and barley stew while Boss Worth interrogated the assembly of local drinkers as to the predicted outcome of the fight.

Cooling lard yellowed the surface of the stew. Vargas had been trying in vain to finish it. He could get his mouth just about open enough to push the tip of the spoon past his teeth. The serving girl stopped by his table again. "Something wrong with your meal, sir?"

"No, ma'am," he said.

"You don't look all that well."

He tried a smile. "I'm all right."

He could sense her counting his bites while she cleared the adjoining table, and he tried, for her sake, to make better progress this time, even with his eye watering and everything around him blazing like tin on a hot day.

Later, when it was made clear to him that their stopover would be extended until after the fight, he abandoned Boss Worth at the poker table and drifted into the street. He thought the fresh air might do him good, if he could find any.

A lot of that afternoon's detail would fade from him, but not the spectacle he encountered at the far end of the thoroughfare: in the middle of a sizable crowd, there stood a little teeter-totter, up and down whose wobbling ramp a line of geese paraded in endless orbit. The lead goose, distinguished from the others by a tiny top hat, was in the thrall of a young woman in a very short dress and spiderweb stockings, who guided it through loop after loop with the aid of a wand.

Behind this bizarre little tableau, there stood a ramshackle wagon across which a huge banner that read DOC HIRAM'S INDIAN WONDER TONIC had been draped. A lectern, puzzled out of old crates, had been erected on the wagon, and a man in the starched white apron of a surgeon stood behind it, peering down at the gathering crowd. At his signal, the goose girl gathered up her wand and her seesaw and led her geese away. The man in the apron raised both hands for silence. Vargas took him to be the Doc Hiram of Indian Wonder Tonic fame.

"Esteemed citizens," he said to the crowd, "I see from your faces that many of you are afflicted by ailments that vex you, that strain your nerves, strain your purses, strain your very souls. I am here to impart to you the wisdom given me by the Apaches—those ancient and venerable people whose tribal elders often exceed a hundred years in age, owing to the potent miracles to which I am fortunate to be initiate."

If Vargas was going to leave, he'd better do it now. But he was all the way in the front, and trying to extract himself might draw unnecessary attention. Doc Hiram had launched into a tale of abandonment by comrades in the wake of a terrible bout of catarrh somewhere on the plains of Texas thirty years before, and his surprising rescue by a band of wandering Apaches. Following a six-week convalescence, Doc Hiram received from these most surprising hosts a parting gift of cure-all tonic, made from the powdered root of a sacred tree, using a formula so secret that, even now, it could be shared with none of his acolytes.

Doc Hiram picked up one of the brown bottles that had appeared on the lectern and held it aloft. "Catarrh?" he said. "Why, there isn't a man alive whose respiratory ailments could not be eased by a dose of this potent elixir, nor a cough that could outflank the ancient healing herbs contained herein. Rheumatic gout? Begone, scourge—no more shall you addle the joints of the old and the hardworking. Plague? Walk through a tenement with a swab of this stuff generously applied under your nose and watch the miasma dispel. I am, in fact, freshly arrived from New York, where some of the most putrid subjects I have ever gazed upon were living stacked on top of one another in dank and windowless dwellings—this miraculous concoction cut a swath through all their many woes."

About halfway through this sermon, Doc Hiram removed the stopper from one bottle and began flicking droplets of the miracle potion over the gaping crowd. A cold little splash hit Vargas. He willed himself not to flinch. But Doc Hiram had noted its trajectory. "My good man, yes! Your poor face! No longer will you suffer from your piteous malformations. One dose of this, and your features will right themselves again."

His features, Vargas thought, weren't the problem—and he intended to say so, if only he could open his jaw enough to shout back. But Doc Hiram's attention had already been commandeered by a loud voice from the rear of the crowd shouting, "Foul! Foul! Foul!"

Its source was a man, not much older than Vargas, from whose vicinity several bystanders were fleeing in embarrassment. He was shouting, "Foul!" over and over again, as loudly as he could, causing equal parts laughter and confusion among the onlookers.

He was a short man, lean and dark-haired, and outfitted in a dusty black suit slightly too loose for his frame. His hat was crumpled in his fist. He had the wildest black eyes Vargas had ever seen.

This, then, was how Anton Vargas met Doctor Thomas Maclean, the man everyone called Preacher: at a medicine show in

Wyoming Territory, drunk with pain and unaware of how close he was to death.

Doc Hiram, meanwhile, was trying to subdue his heckler with flattery: "I recognize by that handsome coat and familiar satchel that I have a colleague in you, sir."

"No," the other said. "Though we may both call ourselves 'doctor,' only one of us carries the real weight of that title." The crowd let him move up toward the wagon. "Tell me more about the mysteries of this elixir. By smell I'd guess it's, what—paregoric? With some bitters? Rosemary? Savory?"

Doc Hiram laughed stiffly. "The formula is, as I said, very ancient. But it is infused with the aromatics of sacred ground, resplendent with all the myriad notes of nature."

"It's alcohol," the angry little doctor said.

"Doc Hiram's Indian Wonder Tonic is, in fact, a beverage favored by many of the most devout temperance societies. As a tonic that originated from the deep-seated ceremonies of the Red Man, it is utterly devoid of spirits."

"What are its effects?"

"Generally curative."

"And how should I expect to feel after imbibing it?"

Doc Hiram, as if he'd been waiting for this very moment, pointed to the crowd: "We have among you one of the very finest advocates of this potent elixir. Mister O'Leary, what manner of feeling overcomes you when you nip a bit of Doc Hiram's wonderbrew?"

He was pointing at a man whose tremendous frame was sausaged into a ridiculous and far too small herringbone suit. Vargas recognized him from the prizefight posters: it was Wheatfield Will.

"Mr. William O'Leary professes daily use of Indian Wonder Tonic!" Doc Hiram was saying. "It is an essential part of the regimen that keeps him so vital and so strong, and will surely advantage him in his bout against the formidable Youngheart Juan

Vasquez. Mister O'Leary—Wheatfield Will!—would you answer the question posed by my doubting colleague over there?"

Wheatfield Will looked around. "What's the question?"

"How does Doc Hiram's Indian Wonder Tonic—also good for children!—make you feel?"

"Oh," Wheatfield Will said. "Strong."

"Anything else?"

"Real strong. Right after I take it, I get to feelin' like I could run to Oregon. Like I could pick up a whole wagon."

"Do it, then," the heckling doctor called from the crowd. "Pick up a whole wagon."

Doc Hiram pressed on: "And does it make your senses tingle, your eyes sharpen? Does your very soul feel elevated to superhuman heights, so that you become more than man, the ultimate version of yourself?"

"Yeah," said Wheatfield Will.

"And will you be using Doc Hiram's Indian Wonder Tonic in readiness of tomorrow's bout?"

"You bet."

A cheer rolled through the crowd. Wheatfield Will shrugged out of his suit coat and got to the business of flexing through his shirt. The heckling doctor stood by, shaking his head.

"Are there any among you," Doc Hiram continued, "who are ready to commit your well-being to the effects of this remarkable medicine?" He located Vargas in the crowd again. "Sir—you look like a man in desperate need of relief." He held one of the brown bottles out. Vargas stared at it. "My good man, just think. For only two dollars—two dollars only! consider the frivolities in which you indulge for a far greater expense!—you could forever rid yourself of that monstrous goiter."

Over the eruption of laughter, Vargas heard the heckling doctor behind him: "Whiskey's twenty-five cents a shot over at the Langsford Tavern, and a much quicker route to the same result."

But Hiram had Vargas—if not on faith, then on the sheer panic of having made him the center of attention. He wasn't the Anton Vargas of the Greyrock Four yet—he was Anton, alone and suffering. The bottle sat in his view, the only thing not blurred at the edges. Doc Hiram was saying, "Young man, I can see that you came to me today made low by pain. My colleague there has shaken your belief—and for that, on this single occasion, I am willing to grant you the boon of lowering my price to *one* dollar. One dollar only, young man—to look your old self again, to get the light back in your eyes. When did you last spend a dollar on so worthy a cause?"

Vargas couldn't remember. The heckling doctor had come up to him through the crowd and grabbed him by the shoulder. He was trying to get a better look at Vargas's face. "That's not a goiter," he whispered. "That poison will do you no good—you need real help."

But the bottle was already in Vargas's hand.

He paid the dollar and took himself off to a secluded corner of the livery to drink his medicine. What he felt, for the most part, was sleepy. Still, considering that the pain had kept him up for several nights, this was an improvement. He curled up on some hay bales and dozed.

When the stablehand found him and threw him out, it was dark. The pain had returned and, with it, a terrible headache. Vargas drifted into the street, wondering whether the lamplight of the windows really *was* such a vile orange, or if this was the sheen of things when you were beyond hope and full of Doc Hiram's Indian Wonder Tonic. Whores whistled down to him from the balcony of Curly's Dancehall. He wandered in and rested against the doorframe, watching the whole saloon whirl to the disharmony of a piano and fiddle that were being played at slightly different tempos.

There, two tables over from where he stood, sat the heckling young doctor from that afternoon. He was tucking in to his dinner.

"You!" Vargas said. The poker players looked up. Vargas went over and dropped into the chair opposite the doctor. He was trying to smile, and felt almost certain that he was succeeding.

"You were wrong" was what Vargas was trying to say. "That tonic's a miracle after all."

The doctor lowered his spoon. "Oh, I can see that."

"Wrong wrong wrong," Vargas told him. "Dead wrong."

"Got you feeling better, has it?"

"Better. Very better."

The doctor nodded. He wiped his mouth with his napkin and rose slowly to his feet. "Mind if I see how you're getting on?"

"No need," Vargas said. He was trying for a nonchalant wave, but he couldn't feel his arm. "Don't amend yourself."

"Stay still, please."

"No, no, don't amend yourself!"

According to Preacher, who loved to tell this story, Vargas kept saying, "Don't amend yourself" over and over again while the doctor signaled bystanders for assistance, and he went on saying it even when they laid him out on the table and pinned his arms and legs. The smell of the abscess, Preacher would later tell him, was indescribable. He'd never seen anything like it: the flesh dark and swollen, the nodule so massive that its capillaries were visible even in the gloom of the tavern. Preacher drained it with a needle the serving girl boiled for him, and the pus went everywhere. At some point in the fray, the poor tooth was pulled.

Vargas had no memory of any of it. He would only remember waking up two days later in what he took a long time to realize was the rattling back of a freight dray.

There was a hole in his gums where the tooth should have been. His thoughts were like going uphill through mud. He went on resting, tilting his face up into the cool air rushing by. The dray was speeding along a pine-timbered ridge. He was trying to work his way through the mazes in his mind when the driver turned and looked back at him. It was the heckling doctor with the startling eyes.

"Well," he said. "You're up." He stopped the horses. "And you look better."

He climbed over the freight and into the back and started pulling at Vargas's eyelids, feeling his forehead, peering into his mouth.

Vargas couldn't get a word in. Finally he managed to say, "Where's Boss Worth?"

"Set out two days ago, I'm afraid," the doctor said. "But he left this for you." He held out a leather pouch that turned out to be full of coins. "It's about five dollars."

That didn't seem right. Vargas had ridden with Boss Worth's outfit for weeks. His head swam. "There should be more."

"I didn't rob you, if that's what you're about to suggest."

"I'm not about to suggest shit," Vargas struggled to say. "I'm asking why I'm here with you, missing money and teeth, instead of on the way to Sunrise with my outfit."

He expected a defensive answer but found nothing on the doctor's pale, unusual face but steadiness. "Look. You were sleeping it off when Mr. Worth came looking for you. He was all set to leave. I told him he'd have to wait till you were fit to travel. I didn't think you'd be out more than another day or so, but he seemed to have urgent need of pressing on."

"I can't figure it."

"Maybe the Youngheart Juan fight didn't go his way."

"Maybe."

"It would certainly explain why there's money missing from your purse."

"I guess it would." Now the doctor was trying to palpate some part of his neck. Vargas pushed him away. "That still doesn't answer what the hell I'm doing here with you."

Preacher gave him a cool, irritating smile. "I have a freight contract that was already delayed thanks to the storm. It was wait out your recovery and lose my contract, or bring you along and make my next stop."

"I wasn't asked!" It hurt to shout.

"You weren't fit to be asked. You aren't fit for much even now." The doctor put a hand on his shoulder. "Please don't take a swing at me. It isn't going to impress squirrels and quill pigs, and they're the only ones out here to witness you getting laid out for your bad manners."

He was right. And Vargas didn't feel up to fighting just now. In a little while, maybe, after some water and a few hours of upright sitting, he might revisit the notion.

His rescuer, meanwhile, had softened. "You headed anyplace in particular?"

"My outfit was going to the Sunrise mines."

"And now? Think you might go there still?"

Vargas shrugged.

"Well, my freight's due in Eula. You know it?" He didn't. "After I make my delivery, if you feel like yourself again, I'll drop you in Sunrise. Does that sound all right?"

"All I got to pay you is what's in this bag."

"Don't worry about that," the doctor said. "It's a long way to Eula—lending a hand, once you feel up to it, will be of more use to me than five dollars."

Vargas climbed into the box seat and sulkily covered his knees with the other half of the doctor's blanket, and they went on. The sun dipped, bloodying the clouds, and the air took on a strange, damp sweetness that reminded Vargas of something he couldn't quite name. The doctor wouldn't let him hold the reins, which was all right. Keeping himself upright was just about all Vargas could manage.

"I don't get it," he finally said. "Why do you drive freight, if you're a doctor?"

"Don't men take whatever jobs they can?"

"Most people can't hardly get one," Vargas said. "Let alone two."

"I must be lucky."

The doctor spoke as though he were some esteemed high roller from Chicago, but up close the frayed edges of his suit far outnumbered the newly mended parts. He was constantly chewing on a piece of licorice stick wedged inside his cheek. Vargas decided that the doc couldn't be more than two or three years his senior. How did life season people so that some were that much more assured of themselves than others?

Vargas opened the coin bag and rummaged sullenly through its contents. At the very bottom, his fingers hit something other than metal. He pulled it out. It was small, yellow, and mangled.

"What's this?" he asked.

The doctor glanced at it. "Your tooth." Then he winked. "Something to remember me by."

Patients called him Doctor Maclean, but to friends he was Preacher. This, he intimated, was what Vargas should call him.

They went on into the twilight until they could barely see the road and grew nervous that the horses would lose their footing. The second the landscape opened up a little, Preacher put the carriage over the grass and into a clearing. It was a small enough campsite, clear of fallen branches, and above them the trees funneled into a round of moonless sky through which the stars advanced. The wind was picking up, and the boughs creaked and sawed against one another.

Preacher went to find wood, and Vargas laid the bedrolls and the blankets out and tried to start a fire. He made a sorry pile with the twigs he found but was too worn out to do much more with it. He sat down and wrapped himself in the blanket and waited.

Now that the sun was down, the temperature had dropped sharply, and the fog that paled the air made it moist and, therefore, worse. He was sitting like this, ascribing the slightly foul odor that plumed around him every so often to the doctor's sick-looking wheel team, tied up by the dray, when a gray horse, wild-eyed, came tearing out of the shadows. Vargas fell backward, and the horse flew by and crashed through the thickets to his left. It vanished as quickly as it had blown in. Vargas lay stunned, listening to its thunderous course through the foliage, and then got up and followed its route to the edge of the clearing, and stood stamping around to shake off the abrupt cold.

Preacher reappeared a short while later with an armful of cuttings. He studied the ruined saplings on either end of the clearing. "What did you do?"

"It wasn't me." Vargas pointed. "Runaway horse."

Preacher frowned. "Wonder who he's run away from."

The cold came in, and the dark. They struggled to light the kindling.

"First night out in the open?" Vargas said.

"No." Preacher smiled. "Yours?"

Before long the rain started, and they tarped the dray and lay side by side among the boxes while the water found its way through and dripped down on them. The scent of the rain-freshened pines cut faintly through the vague, rotten smell from earlier. Vargas's heart was banging so wildly that he had to shove a fist into his armpit just to give himself a little distance from the feeling.

"Do you reckon we're near a bear's den or something, and that's the smell?" he finally asked.

He could just about hear Preacher over the rain. "You smell it, too."

"Maybe we should move on out of here."

But where would they go? It was pouring now. They had no sense of the rivers in the area, and they might end up on the wrong side of a box canyon looking at a wall of water bearing down on them, as had happened to a now-dead associate of Preacher's.

"How come everybody's got a friend they know who died of something that's exactly like the predicament they're in now?" Vargas asked.

It was decided, more by abandonment of scheme than by consensus, that they should stay put. Vargas couldn't call what they did sleep: every twenty minutes, one of them would shift to evade the dripping, and the whole dray would shake and groan. Then they'd lie again in the dark in silence, willing each other to courage or unconsciousness, whichever came first. The horses wouldn't let up their snorting and chuffing. Once in a while, lightning cracked overhead, and the whole stained horizon of the tarp would blaze a brilliant white.

"It feels like we're hiding from the lightning," Preacher said.

Vargas watched the words purl out of his mouth. "As long as it don't bring a tree down on us," he said. That, too, had happened to a friend of a friend.

Preacher smiled. "It reminds me of being a kid. We had terrible storms in New York." Then he laughed. "My father got mad as hell when he found out how bad the lightning frightened me. I was about ten, and he didn't think it fitting. So he'd slink into my room when the thunder got going and hover above where I was shaking under the bedclothes, very close and dead still, for however long it took the storm to subside. And when I finally braved up enough to pull the covers off my face, I'd see him standing there like he'd climbed out of hell, and my heart would just about fly out of my mouth."

"What'd he do that for?"

"Guess he was trying to give me something worse to be scared of. It didn't take more than a couple of times for me to weigh out that nothing bad ever did happen to me on account of the lightning, save the shock I got from seeing my father there."

All this lined right up with what Vargas had been told about fathers. "I'm from Texas," he said.

"You get bad thunderstorms there?"

"Don't know. I got put on a train for Oklahoma when I was six or seven, ended up at my uncle's mercantile till about a month ago."

"How's that tooth?"

"I don't even feel it."

"Good. It would've been some labor to share a tarp with the breath you had on you the other night."

Preacher's telling the story about his crazy father must have worked some strange, stuporous magic on him, because he fell asleep right after and didn't stir. Vargas stared up at the tarp and willed the coming day to brighten it. By the time this happened, he was so exhausted from his heart's fits and starts that he wasn't sure he'd be able to do much except go on lying there. The rain had stopped, and he pushed the tarp away. It was still quite dark, but he could see the serration of distant mountains taking on the first pink of dawn. In a few days, Preacher would tell him this was called alpenglow.

All through the night, the trees hadn't stopped creaking. He traced the length of the pines from ground to sky, one by one, the shocking darkness and height of them.

Preacher suddenly sat upright beside him. "Jesus."

Vargas followed his gaze. Directly above them, where the pines tapered to black, he saw the flash of spurs.

The rope was still creaking by the time they put enough distance between themselves and the tree to see the hanging body in full. The dead man had been there a week, give or take. Even from the ground, Vargas could make out the tattered buckskin jacket, coated in runoff from the ravens that had taken his eyes.

Vargas asked: "Do we cut him down?" He did not want to.

"I don't see how," Preacher said. "I don't see how he went up in the first place. That's about the highest bough I've ever seen."

Preacher went and got his rifle out of the dray. He backed to a spot opposite the tree where the ground sloped up a little and sighted on the rope.

"You're not serious," Vargas said.

The bullet glanced off the rope and then sang off the tree behind it. The twang roared over them. The body jerked on its tether. A nighthawk shot out from some hiding place among the folds of clothing and sent a wash of mess raining down on them. Something thumped in the nearby grass. The man swung on, creaking.

"Christ," Vargas said.

While Preacher lined up his next shot, Vargas went over to investigate the debris.

"Hold on," he shouted over his shoulder. "He's got a neck board." Vargas crouched over it. "The rain's washed it out. I think it says, 'Jo . . . something. Jo Something, hung this day for crimes against nature.' "

That settled it. By the time Preacher put away his rifle, Vargas had already hitched up the wheel team. His jaw was clenched so tight he thought his gums might start bleeding again. He didn't know why he felt this way. Preacher didn't seem too nonchalant about it, either: he was kicking ash over their unlit hearth and securing the freight.

"Can't keep from thinking about all that rain," Vargas said, raking his fingers over his scalp. "All that rain, and him up there, and us under him."

If there had been a fire, they would have burned the tarp, but they just left it there under the tree with Jo Something's shadow swaying over it.

At the first pond they found, they stripped down and plunged in. But they still had to get back into their clothes afterward, and whether it was really there or not, Vargas couldn't get away from the smell.

The mountain hamlet of Eula hadn't yet begun to dig out from the blizzard. Snow had fallen for three days, and now lay shining in the draws. The weight of it had caved the roof of the forge—just as well, the elderly telegrapher told them, because the blacksmith was a hated fellow in these parts, and they were pretty sure the cave-in had driven him off for good. From the look of things, he wasn't the only one who had cleared out. Save for the telegrapher himself and a horse rimming the fence of a distant field, Vargas couldn't see another living soul.

They found two more people at the dry goods store: Mrs. Vickers, an attractive redhead who ran the place and immediately laid into Preacher about the delay of her goods, and Fred Kipley. A stranger to them for that brief moment, he was a lanky, hard-featured brooder nursing a solitary drink at a corner table. It would take Vargas years to notice that some people never questioned his parentage, while others assumed him to be Indian right away. Mrs. Vickers had done the latter. Toward the end of her tirade about soap and crooks and beans, Kipley stood up to refill his glass.

"You've had enough," Mrs. Vickers said to him. "Don't ask for no more until five o'clock."

"All right." Kipley sat back down.

"Your five o'clock one's on me, friend," Preacher told him with a smile.

"Don't talk to my customers," Mrs. Vickers snapped. "You don't gotta talk to nobody but me."

She marched Preacher outside to inspect the freight. Vargas moved a chair closer to the fire and listened through the window to Mrs. Vickers's ongoing furor, amplified by the ramshackle condition of the dray and every item on it. Kipley, meanwhile, took the opportunity of her absence to go behind the bar and help himself to another whiskey. He noticed Vargas watching him. "First time up here?"

"No," Vargas lied.

"That's a thin jacket for a man who's been up here before."

"Well, *you* look about ready to camp on the summit. What's that you're wearing?"

"Buffalo."

It looked like what Vargas imagined a lion might be. The closest he'd ever got to a real buffalo was when some Nebraska trader, overnighting at his uncle's place, died in his sleep. Vargas had been tasked with going through his belongings before trying for the next of kin. He never did find any money or cards or letters, but one of the old man's saddlebags was filled with acrid yellow powder. His uncle had told him this was buffalo bone. They'd traded it to the vinegar factory in Dorrett for ten dollars. He wanted to touch the robe, but Kipley didn't look like the kind of man to let you near his clothes, and definitely looked like the kind of man who would judge you for being dumb enough to ask.

"Anyway," Vargas said. "I've been kept warm enough. By fever. I had a festering tooth and my friend the doc pulled it for me. Without the benefit of dope."

"You don't say."

"I damn near died."

"Are you sure you didn't?"

He wished people would stop leaving him alone with strangers.

Preacher and Mrs. Vickers returned, both in better spirits. She got him a drink, on the house, and one for Vargas, too, and loudly maintained that Kipley was not to have any, to which Kipley just nodded and sank into the depths of his magnificent robe.

The door swung, and the old telegrapher came in, stomping the snow from his boots.

"A curious message just come in about Splitrock."

"What is it?" Mrs. Vickers said.

The telegrapher looked with suspicion from Vargas to Preacher. Mrs. Vickers's shrill announcement that they were all right, for God's sake, didn't seem to put him much at ease. It was Kipley nodding that started him reading in the end:

> *Station storm ravaged. Send resupply at once. All possible urgency, Splitrock.*

Vargas didn't know what any of that meant. The telegrapher seemed equally mystified by it. He read it again.

"That's unfortunate," Mrs. Vickers muttered.

"And strange," the telegrapher said. "We don't got but one connection—and it's not Splitrock. It's Greyrock."

Greyrock was an old Pony Express stop about ten miles north of Eula. There was nothing there but the supply depot, occupied now by a strange Swede who had been running the telegraph out of it for about two years.

"But where's Splitrock?" Preacher asked.

"Way north, in Montana," Kipley said from his corner. "They wouldn't be looking to us for any kind of help. It would take us weeks to get there."

The five of them sat a long while and mulled over the telegram's meaning. It was decided that whoever had sent it must have mixed up the names: the words Greyrock and Splitrock were close enough, after all, even if the places were not. This made sense to Vargas—but the telegrapher shook his head.

"I know the operator up there. He wouldn't make a mistake like that," he insisted. "A misplaced letter here and there, I can figure. Even garbling the name altogether. But to mistake a full name—and to put down the name of a real city that just *happens* to be someplace else? It don't seem right to me."

"Why would he write any name at all?" Preacher wondered aloud. "He knows you know the telegram is coming from Greyrock. Perhaps he really *does* mean Splitrock."

They laid out a map and looked at it together. Vargas followed Kipley's finger as it tracked the distance north way, way up to Splitrock.

"That's damn far," Kipley said.

"What if the stationmaster is injured?" Vargas said, remembering the way he'd felt with the tooth addling his brain. His thoughts had all pressed into a great, indecipherable jumble. It had been a struggle to peel the right words from the wrong ones. Maybe the stationmaster was similarly afflicted. Maybe his roof had caved in, or maybe he was starving or freezing to death.

"He might have had a stroke," said Preacher. "You said he wasn't very young."

The telegrapher was nodding somberly. "I'd buy that over him making this kind of mistake."

"We'll have to go up there and look in on him."

Preacher succeeded in persuading Mrs. Vickers to donate a pound each of sugar, flour, and coffee, some bacon, and a sack of potatoes for their journey. She grumbled about it the whole time, kept picking the items up as if she couldn't believe what she was parting with.

"It's very Christian of you," Preacher said.

"I won't take counsel on what's Christian from some fork-tongued, grave-robbing sawbones," she fired back. "I know how you people get your schooling."

Preacher bowed low. "I've never heard my career summarized so succinctly, ma'am."

They hitched Preacher's wheel team to one of the sleds from the livery. The telegrapher forced Vargas into a warmer coat. Kipley took the reins, and the sled hissed through the fresh powder. Vargas looked out the back and watched the white spray of their wake, the chimney smoke of Vickers Dry Goods absorbed into the pale swath of the fields. The late afternoon was gray and windless, but his face was already stinging. They went down a hill and cut across a frozen river. Preacher seemed delighted with everything: he pointed out the snow-caked husk of a beaver dam among the willows. In the evening, they hit cover, a tight little pine woodland. Mounds of powder broke over them whenever wind shook the sagging boughs.

The Greyrock station was even sorrier than the old telegrapher had led them to believe: nothing but a stockade with a buried fence and an ancient barn half-suspended by what was left of its supports, crooked as the jaw of a corpse. They could see the station house and the yellow squares of light cast by its windows.

Vargas half-stood to get a better look. Preacher, without turning, shoved him back into his seat.

Kipley drew the sled to a stop in a stand of trees. By now it was past twilight. They sat in silence for so long that Vargas could feel his cold-stiffened coat beginning to creak around him. "What are we doing?" he finally asked.

"I'm thinking," said Kipley.

They sat gazing out over the glittering field to the station house. Vargas thought he could see shadows moving in the windows.

"Mr. Kipley," said Preacher. "I'd say it's about time we knew your thoughts."

"I'm thinking about Splitrock," Kipley said. "I'm trying to remember *how* I know the name."

Vargas knew it, too. Vaguely, distantly. Then it came to him.

"Didn't bandits ambush a relief team at Splitrock a couple months back?" he said, more to himself than to anyone else. "I read about it someplace. 'Slaughter at Splitrock.' Something like that."

"That's right." Preacher was grating a gloved palm against his bottom lip. "Those bandits were hanged."

"Maybe there's a posse waiting for us here that took inspiration from them," said Kipley.

"But wouldn't it defeat their purpose to call attention to that association?" Preacher shook his head. "To refer to Splitrock by name?"

Kipley spat into the snow. "That's what I can't figure."

"If there *are* bandits here," said Preacher, "maybe they weren't the ones who sent the message. Maybe the message was sent by someone who wants us to remember what happened at Splitrock."

They hitched the team and followed the edge of the clearing around the side of the station house. There was an old dugout there, with a high, narrow window near the eaves that stood dark. Farther still through the thicket, they came in sight of the old barn, the snow piled along its roof looking like stuffing that had burst from a doll.

They were tracking back through the trees, a little higher in the cover, when Vargas heard something, a tinny silver click, barely a whisper, somewhere to his right. There were three horses hitched up among the trees.

Three horses hidden in the woods, Kipley decided, meant at least three men holding the station house. They would be expecting the help from Eula to arrive within the next several hours. Whoever was in that station house across the field knew that they were coming.

Preacher said, "I haven't been in a gunfight in quite some time."

"Well, you're here," Kipley said, clapping him on the shoulder, "so I guess you did all right in the last one."

They reviewed their arsenal: Vargas's six-gun, two Colts, a Winchester repeater, and a huge, unwieldy Sharps rifle that looked like it hadn't been fired in a century. Preacher wanted more reconnaissance, and set off to get it. Vargas and Kipley watched him cross the field behind the house. Every thirty feet or so, he slumped into the snow and lay still. This was deliberate, Vargas kept telling himself: Preacher was just being cautious, staying low.

"If they get him," he finally asked, "do we return fire?"

"We sure do," Kipley said.

When Preacher returned, he outlined his findings: that high, narrow window in the dugout must lead to a storeroom attached to the main building. There might be a tunnel somewhere in the hill leading up through a trapdoor and into the dugout, but they didn't have time to fuck around and look for it. There was only one thing to do: Two of them would have to come through the front door of the station house. But a third man should climb in the back first, through the dugout window, and wait there to support their fire.

"Why can't we all go the back way?" Vargas said.

Preacher shook his head. "Because only one of us is squeezing through that window."

It was Vargas.

He was halfway across the field to the dugout when it occurred to him that he was short a few useful details. How, for instance, did Kipley and Preacher intend to signal that they were coming into the station house? Would there be a whistle? Was he supposed to come out shooting or just point his gun at the nearest man and pray that this would convince him to drop his own weapon?

Some ten yards from his destination, he dropped and lay still and listened for signs of movement. Then he went for the window.

Inside, it was freezing. Yellow light from the adjacent room sat trapped in a thin line under the door. Vargas floated in darkness until the edges of the empty stock shelves started to sharpen. For a minute, it seemed that the only thing in there with him was the smell of sod and damp. Then a cloud of breath erupted to his left. He could see a cot in the far corner, with its rumpled mound of blankets from which a woman's head loomed up in the dark.

"Who the hell are you?" she whispered.

He didn't know what to say, whether to say anything at all. He took a step toward the cot and his leg met a heavy mass, and he went down. His landing was broken by something cold and stiff, something that had buttons and sleeves and two knees and viscous pulp where its face should have been.

"Oh God," he said, too loudly.

The woman leapt out of bed, pulled him onto the cot, and threw the blankets over him. The dugout door opened, and light poured inside.

"Ain't I told you keep quiet?" said a man's voice from the doorway.

"I'm freezing," the woman said.

"Shut up. I won't tell you again."

Then everything went dark. They listened for the sound of life resuming in the other room: murmurs, a chair being dragged across the floor.

The woman found Vargas amid the blankets. "You got my telegram," she said.

In later years, owing to the many reenactments they would do together, he would come to believe that these were the first words Sadie Wilkins ever said to him. She had dark hair and a stern face older than her years. She wasn't hurt, but she'd been locked in the storeroom since that afternoon. The rigid body Vargas had tripped over on the floor was the old Swedish stationmaster.

"How many men are in the other room?" Vargas said.

"Fourteen," Sadie told him. "Maybe more." She was frowning. "Are *you* the entire rescue party?"

"No, I'm just the one who could fit through the window."

"Where are the others?"

"They're coming."

There was no signal when Kipley and Preacher came. They just kicked in the station house door. Vargas heard it on the other side of the dugout wall. He wasn't ready. By the time he got himself into the next room, he was bursting in on a standoff very much in progress: Kipley was aiming at a bearded man by the stove, and Preacher had his pistols trained at three surprised lads seated at a corner table.

It took Vargas a few seconds to realize that the total number of badmen in the room was significantly fewer than fourteen. He was about to share this revelation when he heard a shot. It knocked him against the back wall. The six-gun in his own hand roared, once, in the general direction from where the bullet that hit him had come.

The kid who'd shot him—the one Kipley and Preacher had failed to notice when they burst in—had been hiding behind the front door. Vargas's return volley hadn't even clipped him. He was just standing there, reloading at his leisure, while they all stared at him.

Then Preacher shouted, "Go ahead, then! Load up! Kill me! Come kill me!" Five foot five of glorious rage. Just standing there in the confusion.

A fresh volley of bullets went twanging around the room. Vargas couldn't tell who was shooting at whom, what was ricochet or not. He himself fired just one more time, blindly, prayerfully into the fray. When he did, a spurt of blood erupted from the kid behind the door. He capsized, howling and trailing red slop.

Vargas had assumed that the act of surrender would be quite ceremonious—but he'd never been in a gunfight before. It turned out that you knew it was over because the guns fell silent, and the survivors looked around at one another, and then those at a disadvantage put their hands up. Kipley started disarming the badmen, pushing them onto their stomachs one by one. Vargas watched these proceedings from the corner where his legs had given out. Preacher was fussing over him. The pain in his shoulder was just beginning. He stared at his sleeve in wonderment. It was a magnificent deep red color.

The kid Vargas had winged with his final shot was still howling on the floor nearby. His neck was wet with blood.

"Have I killed him?" Vargas asked.

Preacher squeezed his shoulder and went over to the kid. He stooped and picked something black and wet off the ground.

"No," he told Vargas. "You took his ear off."

The kid held out a hand for the ear, but Preacher stepped back and pocketed it.

"You'll get yours, you shit," the kid said to Vargas.

Preacher gave him a gentle kick. "He got his already."

"Well then, you'll get *yours.*"

"Shut up, Perkins," one of the men under Kipley's rifle said.

Sadie finally appeared in the storeroom doorway. "Where are the others?"

Kipley took a step back from the window. "What others?"

Preacher turned to the earless kid. "Is the rest of the posse waiting on you?" he asked. "Are they out in the woods?" He took off his glove and snapped a flail of empty fingertips across the kid's mutilated ear. "Where are they, Perkins?"

Perkins wailed. "Yes, they're in the goddamn woods."

Preacher and Kipley put out all the lamps and got down beneath the windows. They tried to convince Sadie to wait in the dugout—eighteen inches of dirt, Kipley said, the most unbreachable room in the whole place—but it was a waste of breath. In the end, Preacher handed her one of the fallen men's rifles.

Two hundred yards to the tree line, Kipley told them, would make the incoming fire wide and haphazard. He was right. The first volley sheared the bushes around the station house and sent the windows raining down on them. "Don't waste your munitions, let them grind theirs down," Kipley said—but it was hard to keep from returning fire when glass was biting into your skin. Every few minutes, Vargas surfaced the muzzle of his gun and fired blindly into the trees.

The barrage lasted an hour. They were white with wood spray. Blood was blackening in the thousand tiny nicks and cuts that had split their skin. A stray ball clipped Preacher's ribs, and tending to it took him out of the fight for almost twenty minutes.

An incredible, unbearable thirst overwhelmed them as the stove roasted the stale air inside the cabin. Vargas's mouth was so dry that the act of turning his head caused his throat to spasm. They couldn't continue without water. A break in the shooting led them to draw straws over who would risk the field for a good scoop of snow; it was Vargas.

The instant his boots hit the station house porch, the balls came twanging off the doorpost, shattering crockery and ribboning an old flag that leaned against the wall. He went headlong into the gunfire until he reached the snow, and drove the bucket into it. Then he came swearing back.

Huddled in their porthole positions, they sucked fistfuls of snow. The coming dawn, Kipley warned, would put the badmen at a much greater disadvantage. They would be looking to end this standoff while they still had the cover of night.

They tried: for half an hour, with the sky already paling, the incoming fire came only from a little stand of bushes just behind the outhouse. No sooner had Vargas relaxed into the notion that this might mean the badmen's numbers were diminished than an acrid smell broke through to them. One of the gang had set fire to the far side of the roof. The heat of it eating through the sod was already incredible.

"Right," Preacher said. "That's that."

They moved to the dugout: he and Preacher, and Kipley with his Sharps rifle roaring, and Sadie and the earless kid. Kipley soaked rags in the snow bucket, and they wrapped their faces up and took sharp, shallow breaths to keep out the smoke.

"Dig," Vargas said, and went to his knees, sliding his hands through the packed dirt of the floor. "Dig."

They could hear the flames bellowing through the station house timbers, the percussion of shattering glass. Smoke came in great, ragged clouds. At Vargas's side, the earless kid sobbed as he dug.

"Don't be scared," Sadie told him.

"Go to hell."

She reached over and twisted the leftover nub of his auricle.

They finally hit the rim of the trapdoor and cleared the margins. Below was the crawl space, a narrow tunnel of darkness. Vargas dropped in first. He held a hand out for Sadie, but she told him to keep moving. He felt his way along the wall, stumbling over rocks and roots. The air grew cooler as he went. At the end, the ground rose and the world opened up around him. The sky was red with fire. He ran for the trees. Overhead, clouds were peeling back from a pink and faraway dawn. The snow tugged at his feet as he climbed. He found a little wedge cut into bluff, where the firs were tight and low, and he waited for the others. Together, they watched the station house burn. The roof came down, a thunderhead of black ash. Embers drifted, speckling the air like orange fireflies.

What was left of the posse now emerged from the trees and ranged around the remnants of the building. Vargas crawled up beside Sadie and sighted down. Seven men were overturning logs and pushing their boot toes through the ash heap. Preacher dropped three, one right after the other. Kipley dispatched an outlier who was running for cover. Sadie, to the surprise of everyone, cut down two of the remaining three.

Afterward, they went down to what remained of the stockade. The heat from the fire had melted the snow all the way back to the fence. Preacher got his medicine bag from the sled and went around checking their sorry little band one by one: Sadie's scrapes and bruises, Kipley's rifle-burned hands. He propped Vargas against the fence and cut away his sleeve. Vargas closed his eyes. There were minutes of wet meat moving around, and a searing tug that swooped through him. Then came the needle, the rasp of the thread.

"Good man," Preacher said.

He left Vargas slumping there and went over to help Kipley inspect the scattered dead.

"Hey," Preacher shouted to Perkins. "Are any of these wanted men?"

Perkins was sitting against a nearby tree stump. He didn't seem to hear. Kipley lobbed a clump of snow at him and tried Preacher's question another way: "Is there a bounty on any of you bastards?"

The kid shrugged.

Preacher went over to him. From the pocket of his destroyed coat, he fished out the kid's ear. Perkins didn't seem to recognize it.

"You hurting bad?" Preacher asked him.

Another shrug.

"You don't seem to hear very well."

"I said all I got to say," Perkins said. "I told you you'd get yours."

"You *did* say that." Preacher surveyed the carnage. "Given the outcome, I don't think you got a bright future in soothsaying." He pushed Perkins's head to the side and leaned close to inspect Vargas's accidental handiwork. "This was some lucky shot," he said.

"Tell you what. While you try to remember whether or not your dead comrades are wanted men, I'll fix your hearing for you. It seems only right."

Preacher rinsed the severed ear until it was just a bloodless rubbery flap in his hand. Then he rolled the kid over, put his knee against the kid's neck, and stitched the flesh back on, so immune to the other's kicks and shrieks that his brow didn't show a bead of sweat when he finally stood up again.

AN INCIDENT AT THE CABIN BAR OUTSIDE THE TOWN OF SALT DRAW

2003

When Coll finally got home, his sister, Freenie, was still awake, piping icing flowers at the kitchen table. Before her sat a huge pastry stone overrun with battalions of faintly pink roses. The closer they were to the edge of the table, the worse they looked. Freenie's belly, coming up on seven months now, was noticeably in the way of their advance.

All around Freenie lay evidence of their mother's ongoing struggle with the cake for Trudie Early's wedding: pans, spatulas, empty cartons of eggs. In the water-filled sink, Coll found a mixing bowl thick with half-dried buttercream. He washed it, and under it found another, and another one under that. At the very bottom was a small pot full of a burned black substance that not even the steel scrubber could dislodge.

The two dogs were asleep under the table. The rest of the house was dark, Coll's parents upstairs in bed already. The Monopoly board was laid out in mid-game on the coffee table in the adjoining darkness of the living room. Coll could tell, even from here, where Freenie had been sitting at the board. She was clearly way out ahead of their parents, but, according to his father, the game always had to continue until its end, even if the other players stood zero chance of clawing their way back from the entrepreneurial devastation Freenie had wrought.

Freenie had small, stern eyes made smaller and sterner by the glare of the track beams overhead. He could feel her gaze following him as he moved around.

"You look like you threw up," she said. "You drunk?"

"No."

It was not a lie. Coll dried his hands and sat down at the far side of the kitchen table and watched her work. He was thirsty, but he didn't want to give her reason to question his sobriety again by getting up for a glass of water. He couldn't tell if his nausea was owed to the two beers he'd consumed, or to the scene he had just left behind, or to some combination of both.

"Were you down at the Bighorn?" Freenie asked.

"The Cabin."

"Ew. With Charlie?"

"He cut out after one drink."

"Maybe you should have, too."

"I'm not drunk."

Pink sugar roses continued to appear hypnotically on the pastry stone. "How was it?"

"Fine."

"Christ, Coll, don't tell me everything all at once. What's the gossip?"

"No gossip."

She squinted at him. She was getting ready to ask him why he was acting so strange. He could tell.

"Bob Fournier was there," he offered.

Freenie made another vague noise of disgust. "Was he trying to put his hand up some poor co-ed's shirt again?"

"No, thank God. But he had a wolf with him."

He hadn't meant to bring it up at all, let alone put it *that* way. As if it were somehow funny. As if a wolf had accompanied Bob Fournier into the bar at ten-thirty on a Thursday night. In a suit and tie, from the way Coll had phrased it, standing up on its hind legs. Elbow on the bar, asking AJ for a whiskey ginger.

"What wolf?" said Freenie.

"What do you mean, 'what wolf'? A wolf."

"He had it in the truck?"

"No," Coll said. "In the bar." His voice was going all strange on him. He finally met her eye. "What?" He knew what.

"Mira Greyfeather let Bob bring a wolf into her father's bar?"

"No." Coll shook his head. "Mira wasn't there." He should have left it at that, but Freenie was bound to hear more about it from somebody, and then she would ask him why he hadn't told her the truth. "And it wasn't the whole wolf."

"What do you mean?"

"Oh for God's sake, don't make— It wasn't *whole,* Freenie. Okay? That's all."

"What does that *mean*?"

"What does it sound like?"

"I don't know, Coll. In what way was the wolf 'not whole'? Spiritually? Mentally? Had it lost some part of itself along the way?"

"Oh yes, Freenie. The wolf was spiritually incomplete."

There had been a head. There had been a tail. Certainly a couple of limbs. But it had been hard to tell one piece of wolf from another in the gloom of the bar. Coll didn't want to think about it anymore, and he certainly didn't want Freenie forcing more details out of him so she could piece the scene together and picture it herself.

"Did people tell Bob to go fuck himself?"

He looked at her. "What do you think?"

"Those pieces of shit."

"Yeah."

"So what did you do?"

"What do you mean?"

"Did you just sit there like a chickenshit?"

"I helped AJ get him out of there."

That seemed to pacify her. She sat back, a little out of breath, trying to smooth out the place where she'd crushed the piping bag in her fist. When she thought this hard, this furiously, she looked like her baby pictures: all cheeks, no fucking around. After a while, she said, "Why would he bring it in?"

Coll shrugged. "To show it off, I guess."

" 'Show it off'?"

"Yeah, just. Show it around to everybody. Let everybody see it. What was left of it, anyway."

She slammed her chair back from the table. Before Coll could get up to intercept her, she was already out the kitchen door. A few seconds later, the truck's high beams blinded him through the window, and he saw them sweep the yard as Freenie hauled through a U-turn and disappeared up the driveway.

After a while, the sound of the engine faded. Coll's eyes were dry and gritty. He took Freenie's seat and picked up the piping bag. Incredible force was required to squeeze even one rose onto the paper. How was Freenie managing this with her fat little pixie hands?

Their mother appeared in the kitchen, dressed in her robe, glasses on. "You're home."

"Just helping finish up here," he said.

"Where's your sister?"

"She went out for a minute."

"It's one in the morning."

"She'll be right back."

There was no point in urging his mother to return to bed. And any attempt to explain what was happening—she's driving to the Cabin in a fit of rage!—and why it would amount to nothing—AJ has definitely closed up by now, so she's going to bang on the windows and find absolutely nothing there—would only result in more frustration and worry.

His mother moved the kettle to the stove and started clinking through the cupboards. "Do you like that shade of pink?" she asked him, meaning the icing.

"It's very nice."

"It's called Pastel Peony. Two parts red, one part white, and the tiniest dot of yellow, just to give it some warmth. Look at you go, Coll. See, this is why you order cake from a local place, and not some heartless, fancy-pants bakery out in Moraine. There's not a single part of this cake that hasn't been touched by our hands."

He smiled. "I'm not sure I'd put it that way to Trudie."

"Why? Oh—Coll. Don't be cynical."

She was halfway through her cup of tea when the truck lights swung back into the driveway. Coll looked at the clock. It was one-twenty. There was no way Freenie had managed to make it to the Cabin before AJ hustled the last of the stragglers out and locked up. Still, he could tell by the way she was careening down the hill that she was livid. He could see his mother, through the steam rising off her tea, grasping for what to say to Freenie. She didn't want to sound too reproachful. But it was also impossible not to mention that she had noticed, and disapproved of, Freenie's decision to take off like this in the middle of the night. "Are you all right?" was her phrasing of choice when Freenie came barging through the door.

"No," his sister said. "I am not."

"What's wrong?"

"What the fuck happened at that bar, Coll?"

"Freenie," their mother said. "The baby."

"It can't hear me, Mom." She jerked her chin at Coll as if she were calling him out into the street. "There's something you're not telling me. There are blood trails all over the place, leading from the door to the parking lot. What happened?"

"I told you," he said. "It was awful."

His sleep was strange and fitful. Brief dreams that stayed with him in feeling only. Waking up repeatedly to the sense that he was feverish.

In the morning, he made himself coffee with the cat underfoot. His mother had moved the pastry stone, with its encampment of stiffening roses, onto the breakfast counter. He tried one. The sugar in it shot cold pain through the exposed root of his molar. He held the side of his face. When his eye finally stopped watering, he went out into the cool fall morning. Up the drive, through the frozen leaves, to get the sodden newspaper. There was new snow on the high peaks. From the empty road at the top of the hill, he looked back at the house, its huge log posts and the naked aspens sitting white around it. Way down by the creek, the willows were turning red. The osprey nest on the pole his father had put up sat empty.

It was worth remembering, especially after last night: not everybody had a home they loved, or parents they could stand to live with. Nor did everyone's father survive a heart attack. Nor did everyone's college give them a chance to defer their classes for a year so they could go home, and save up, and help out.

He had worried that returning to Salt Draw in the middle of his senior year would feel awful. Like falling back down a cliff's edge after you thought you had safely climbed out. Instead, the warmth and familiarity of his parents' house had managed to work against the panic that still overwhelmed him whenever he found himself drowning amid the locals he'd grown up with. It was what had allowed him to weather missing his first opportunity to return to college, and then his second. Now, almost three years since misfortune had reconvened them, the Yards had slotted back into their old ways: joking around, playing board games, taking little fishing trips to the Medicine Bow wilderness. Most days, Coll didn't even feel like his parents were walking the knife's edge of medical bankruptcy. And work hadn't been nearly as difficult to find as Coll had feared. Intermittent, maybe, but always available when he pursued it: a shift at the Moose here, a couple of hours coaching girls' volleyball at the high school there. It didn't come close to the money he'd expected to make in Denver, even as a history major with no graduate degree, but he also didn't need that kind of money out here.

And, most importantly, he had time. Time to go back to school. Time to catch up to friends like Mira, who had been lucky enough to finish college uninterrupted.

For now, he was surprisingly, refreshingly busy. He had learned the ropes of local bureaucracy and was closer than ever to getting a state-level historic landmark designation for the little ghost town of Sunrise—which, without his intervention would frankly continue to sit abandoned way out on his grandfather's land forever. On top of this, he had managed to hold on to his position as the head of the Salt Draw Historical Society, which would have been impossible with classes and activities crowding his schedule. Every year, he was shaping and refining the Greyrock reenactment, not from some dorm room in Denver but while living just fifty miles down the road from the old mines. He could go back to the source any time he wanted. Walk around Sunrise. Sit and meditate by the roadside grave of Anton Vargas. Of all the things he had managed to accomplish in the three years since he had quit school, he was proudest of Old Sunrise Days. He had managed to make it something the whole county could be proud of and look forward to. None of that would have been possible if he had stayed the course he had planned for his life.

The dogs, Sadie and Flip, were dozing on the porch. Was he ever going to be able to look at a dog again without thinking of last night? What a horrible feeling. He wanted to keep it all within himself, starve it of oxygen until it went out. At the same time, he wanted to disperse it a little, get out from under it. He was disappointed that the latter impulse had won out, even slightly, in his admission to Freenie last night. She didn't need to be thinking about what had happened. She knew exactly what kind of men would have Bob Fournier's back at the Cabin at last call on a Thursday.

He went down to the dogs, making kissing noises, and sat between them on the porch stairs. Fickle Sadie, with her gray-spangled snout and dead blue eye, moved away from him immediately.

"Come on," he said. "Don't be like that."

He drove into town the long way. Fourth sunny day in a row, but snow was beginning to persist in the shady places: dirty, insistent, thinned by all the melting and refreezing. An ugly base layer for all the snows yet to come.

The Gold Dust Diner was quiet: just a couple of old folks eating, and Celia at the register, and Fisheye Jim listing over the griddle, obviously trying to recover from whatever he'd been up to the night before. Coll realized as soon as he walked in that it was the wrong place to reconstitute his faith in his fellow man. The new waitress who waved him toward one of the empty booths looked familiar. It took him a minute to place her: Jess Blaine, an English lit student of his father's—one of those gum-cudding, Shakespeare-resistant entities that drove his father to despair. Unlike most of this year's crop of sophomores, she was not the surprise youngest sibling of any of Coll's old high school classmates. But that knowledge, for some insane reason, didn't keep Coll from saying, "Young Jessica! But soft!"

She apparently had no idea who he was. "We don't turn the soft-serve machine on till noon," she said.

"Oh, I just—I just." He raised the menu to evade her glare. "I'll have the short stack, thanks."

She flipped his cup over, poured coffee more or less into it, and swept away.

He got the audition scripts out of his satchel and spread the pages out before him. He had done a lot of thinking about what range of scenes would give him a good sense of everybody's abilities. He wasn't sure he'd hit everything, but his time was limited, as was the patience of his would-be actors, especially the ones who were counting on getting the same parts they had played last year, and the year before that. He had reworked the blocking of the play to fit the new venue, but he had really only added two scenes. One was the tragic discovery of Anton Vargas's corpse at the Remmick dugout. The other was a scene for the women, all on their own, away from the men. He was excited to present this part of the script to Mira. It was the one thing he had been looking forward to, the one good thing about today. She had promised to come. He was ready to start feeling like himself again. Forget the whole sordid business of last night, who'd done what and why. It had nothing to do with him. It was as alien to him as coyote whacking, or poaching elk out of season, or anything else Bob Fournier had ever done or said. Why should he give it any more thought than he did the rest of Bob Fournier's transgressions?

He was easing into his first sips of coffee when he realized that Gabe Early was sitting by himself in the booth just opposite. He hadn't figured Early for the type of man to treat himself to a solo breakfast the day before his daughter's wedding—but then, maybe that was exactly when you needed solitude the most. Coll raised his mug in greeting, and Early, apparently not needing solitude at all, picked up his half-eaten steak and eggs and came over to join him.

"You don't mind, do you?"

"Not at all."

Gabe Early had the jowly, earnest face of a beaver. He had run the hardware store alongside Coll's father back in the '80s, while the last of the Kipley County mines were dying. Then Coll's father had gone into teaching, and Early had stumbled into rodeo management. Now he ran a dude ranch twenty miles out Bancor way. It was a sweet little setup, all hats and spurs and chow bells clanging, that basically had summer tourists paying Early to do his chores for him. "Badly, though," he would say in his own defense. "Very badly." Not so badly, it seemed, that he couldn't afford one of the grandest houses in Salt Draw, in addition to the ranch. This was to be the site of his youngest daughter Trudie's wedding, and the final resting place of the cake Coll's mother was making.

Early nodded at the pages spread out in front of Coll. "I don't want to disturb."

"You're not. I'm sick of looking at this script."

Early's smile was full of sly pride. "My boy's gonna knock your socks off." He was referring to Alex Almador, one of the new pickup men from his rodeo, whom, for reasons Coll could not fathom, Early had persuaded to audition. "He's got a beautiful singing voice."

"It's not a musical, Gabe."

"So? Ain't you the director, writer, and every other damn thing? Write him a song. He'll leave them all in pieces."

Early dragged the condiment caddy into the middle of the table and started rooting around among the creamers. "How's the cake coming along?" he finally asked.

"Lot of parts to it," Coll said. "All over everywhere."

"Is that good or bad?"

"I guess it would be bad if there were lots of parts *after* it's delivered."

"I guess so."

Early was starting to get that same look that had begun wearing away Coll's father. Something resigned about the eyes, something newly grim in the set of the mouth. It made Coll worry that maybe the world was getting away from everybody, even the good souls among these men who had raised him. Even the ones whose sons weren't enlisting.

"You all set for tomorrow?" Coll asked.

Early shrugged. "I guess so. Couldn't really tell you if we wasn't. I just sign the checks and say, 'That's nice.' "

"Are you all right?"

"Boy, I don't know. Can I ask you something?"

"Sure."

"Do you like Brett? Is he an okay guy?"

"I mean, I don't know him *that* well. But sure, he's always seemed fine."

"But how? What about him seems fine?"

Coll sat back. "Well, I guess he's a quiet guy. Seems like he gives things a decent amount of thought. Buys rounds when it's his turn." It suddenly hit him what the actual question was. "And he *loves* Trudie, Gabe. You can bet on that."

Early demolished the sugar packet house he'd been building. "Maybe this is just something a man goes through when his baby gets married."

Maybe, Coll thought. Maybe it was the kind of thing that would be alleviated if a man had seen his baby at her bachelorette party down at the Moose, table dancing and jumping onto random guys' shoulders, from the front, like Xenia Onatopp.

"I feel like there's bad signs going into the weekend, though," Early went on. "Moon looked strange last night. Couldn't get to sleep. Nancy said all her dreams were backward. Plus there's the other thing."

"What other thing?"

Early flagged down Jess, and she refilled his cup. When she was gone, he leaned forward. "Something went down at the Cabin last night."

An eerie little jolt poured through Coll, from his ears all the way through the soles of his feet. It felt like going down a hill at fantastic speed. Ten o'clock in the morning, and already it was out in the world.

"'Something'?" he said. He realized, too late, that he should have said, "I know." But he had lucked somehow into a question that had two sides: On the one hand, it gave the impression that he didn't know *what* the something that had happened was. On the other, it was vague enough that he could, in due course, reveal that he actually *did* know—had known all along, had known when it began, and when it was underway, and afterward too, and had known since then, and knew now.

"I guess there was an incident," Early said. "With an animal."

"Oh!" Coll thumped a hand over his heart. "I thought maybe someone got stabbed."

He sat on the apron of the stage at Salt Draw Elementary, watching the hopefuls arrive. Never mind what had gone down last night. *These* were his people. The artists and the musicians. The caretakers and the historians. Even with the spotlights against him, he could identify them by shape or gait alone. Terry Larkin, who sold wooden carvings at Mountain Man rendezvous all over the West but returned to Salt Draw each year to don the enormous buffalo skin robes of Frederick Kipley. Patti Clarence, the chief librarian. Colleen Harding, who ran the children's collection, and who was here to play Sadie Wilkins for what Coll presumed would be her sixth and final time. Sadie Wilkins had been only twenty years old, after all, when she became part of the Greyrock Four. Colleen looked good for forty—but she was definitely forty. He had let it slide, just like he let other things slide, because all these people came through for him, and for Vargas, and for Old Sunrise Days year after year—though every now and again somebody new showed up, too, and surprised him. Today, he really hoped it was going to be Gabe Early's pickup man, Alex Almador. Alex was already here, all the way in the back, slumped down in his chair. Coll had only ever seen the kid on horseback. He was all of seventeen, big-eyed, lean as a sighthound. For getting stranded riders off a bronc, you could find no better man. He rode fearless, right up in the stirrups, but Coll had never heard him speak. He had a terrible premonition that Alex Almador's voice maybe hadn't even dropped yet. If that turned out to be the case, he had no idea how he was going to handle the situation. The promise he'd made to Mira last year—to try, really try, to find somebody Mexican, or at least Mexican-adjacent, to play Anton Vargas, even if it meant broadening the casting call to include the neighboring county—would stand only if the kid could actually pull it off. You couldn't just *look* the part. You had to have presence. Gravitas. You had to convince the audience that you were capable of both inspiring men and killing them with an equal measure of consideration. You had to remind people that Kipley County had, among its founders, at least one person who was worth a damn.

And this year would be more challenging than ever, because Coll was moving the performance up to Sunrise and making it immersive. The audience would be right there. This close. Walking among the actors. They would be able to see every hesitation, every twitch. Coll himself had played Vargas for the last three seasons, and even he couldn't be sure how his nerves would hold up at such close range.

He counted the heads out there in the gloom. Fourteen so far. He could tell Mira wasn't among them yet, but he shaded his eyes and looked more closely, just in case he had missed her when he first came in.

He got up.

"Okay, everybody," he said. "Let's get started. I'm Colin Yard, I head up the Salt Draw Historical Society." A voice from the back whooped. "Thanks, Tina. Anyway, most of you know me. I see a lot of familiar faces."

He heard a murmur from what he presumed were the familiar faces.

"The reason I wanted to meet up ahead of next week's auditions is that we'll be doing things a little differently this year. I want everyone to be on the same page, so there's no confusion after the roles have been cast."

He had expected dead silence to greet the news of something changing, and it did. He took a step forward and put his toes over the edge of the stage. "As most of you know, the Greyrock reenactment is part of our Old Sunrise Days celebration, which is entering its seventieth year. One of the challenges we've faced is forcing this incredibly complex, multi-part story into the confines of an hour, plus staging it here at the elementary school. Last year I had the chance to attend an immersive theater experience in Denver, and the whole time I was there I was thinking, Why aren't we doing this?" From the way people were shifting around, he could already tell there were going to be questions. "So this year, we'll be moving our reenactment up to the old town of Sunrise."

There was a murmur, and a few gasps. Of delight? Of frustration? He couldn't say. The important thing was to keep plowing ahead until he had gotten through the whole spiel exactly as he had rehearsed it. He was a little more than halfway through. Next up were the hard-sell bullet points: "First, this will enable us to stick more closely to history by using the sites of Sunrise in a unique and exciting way to tell the story of Anton Vargas, the Greyrock Four, and the founding of our community. Second: timeline! We can expand the second half of the play to incorporate a look at what the Greyrock Four did after the raid on the station house. Just imagine: walking into Sadie's Hotel, and there's Sadie, right behind the counter. Walking past the old ruins of the Remmick dugout, and there's the slain body of Anton Vargas, with one in the back and one in the head, and the strange envelope with the arrow lying beside him."

Travis raised his hand. "Isn't the house where Vargas died way out in the Warrens?"

"Well—sure, yes."

"Are we gonna go out there?"

"No, we'll be using a building in the town itself for the site of his death."

"So but—so but, it won't be the Remmick homestead."

"No."

"So, that won't be accurate."

"Any structure up there is more accurate than the elementary school gym, Travis." His laugh was meant to be light, but it came out all pitchy. At least Mira wasn't here to witness it. "Third, the historical society has been working very diligently to get the buildings in Sunrise into shape for historic landmark designation, and we feel that presenting the play up there will be a good way to get the community excited about this new opportunity, which we hope will bring more visitors, and more tourism dollars, into the county."

Tourism dollars were a touchy subject. You didn't want to end up like Moraine. He could feel people thinking it. He hurried along.

"The reason I've asked you all here is to make you aware of this plan and answer any questions about it. Acting in front of a live audience is one thing—most of you are used to it. But immersive theater is a different ball game. It's going to ask a lot of you, and maybe that's more than some of you feel like doing. I want to make sure everybody who intends to audition next week is prepared and aware and comfortable with all these changes." Without the benefit of Mira here to start the applause, he hesitated. "I know it sounds different. But different is good! Different is exciting! I'm excited, and I hope you are, too."

He could hear the back door opening and shutting. "Hello," he said cheerfully, "come on in, sit down, sit down," but when he shaded his eyes, he could see it was just Carl, the janitor.

"So." Travis again. "So but, will we be rehearsing all the way up there?"

"Another great question, Travis. Thank you. No, we'll be rehearsing right here in the school, like always. The week before the play, we'll have two dress rehearsals at the site."

"And the audience? How are they getting up there?"

"Same as they get here, Travis. They'll drive."

"Over all those ruts and potholes?"

"I mean, they live in Kipley County . . ."

"Still. Lotta old folks."

"The senior center will be providing shuttles. And the Big Powder Inn and Suites has generously agreed to donate their airport bus to bring our audience up to town."

"What if somebody needs to go to the airport?"

On his way home, Coll worked up enough courage to stop by the Cabin. To him, it had always been a horrible place. There was only ever one reason to go there: Mira's old man owned it, and she could be reliably tracked down here if she wasn't at any of the other bars in town. He couldn't remember the last time he'd come by during daylight hours. It looked unassuming, even quaint: a model log home Mira's dad had bought from a purveyor who was going out of business and towed onto this dirt lot, where he'd initially intended to open a gas station selling Indian trinkets.

Coll was surprised to find the door open. That particular Cabin fug he hated was overlaid with the poisonous memories of last night. His breakfast pancakes threatened to back up on him. He braced himself against the doorway in an effort to keep them down, and this was how Eric Greyfeather, emerging from the back room with a mop and bucket, found him.

Mira and AJ's father was a tall, lean, unnervingly beautiful man. He had done a brief stint in Hollywood in the mid-'90s, in what he called the "Indian fetish films," some of which Coll would occasionally catch on Lifetime in the wee hours when his insomnia drove him to the living room sofa. The films ran a very predictable course: they were usually set anywhere between 1700 and 1890 and featured unhappy homesteading wives played by unhappy B-list actresses who invariably got stolen from their unhappy homesteads by wandering bands of braves, actors who were half-naked no matter the era and no matter the tribe. Eric Greyfeather had played half a dozen such half-naked persons during the course of his short career. It was always profoundly weird to watch him hooking semi-reluctant white women lustily around the waist while they swooned and tilted their faces up toward the same strong jaw and black eyes that Mira had inherited from him. Unnerving when Coll had been a teenager, and especially unnerving now.

"Hi there, Mr. G," Coll said, violently aware of the fact that he had not come here prepared to encounter anyone but Mira.

"Good morning, Colin."

His tone was flat—but then, had Eric Greyfeather's tone ever been anything but flat? He had always made it a point to be as unfriendly as possible to every guy friend of Mira's, especially the white ones, which Coll found very hurtful. Just because Coll happened to be white didn't mean that he understood Mira any less. There were plenty of things she had shared with him that her father knew nothing about. Things that Eric Greyfeather would be astounded, probably even livid, to learn about his daughter. Like the fact that she had once sold homemade screen prints of some dead woman named Annie Mae Aquash to raise bail money for fellow students in her class who'd been rounded up for spray-painting what the newspapers called "anti-government propaganda" on campus buildings. Or the fact that she went around telling everybody who would listen that she wasn't American at all. Coll didn't quite understand how that worked, but he respected the fact that she seemed, for now, to really believe it.

Now Coll found himself wondering: Was Eric Greyfeather's tone flatter than *usual*? And if so, what did that indicate? Had he heard about the previous night from AJ? Almost certainly. No matter how much AJ might have wanted to conceal the fact that he'd lost control of the bar, he'd have known that things would be much worse for him if his father learned about it from strangers.

Coll went for it: "How's it going today?"

Eric Greyfeather looked at him as if his head were on backward. He gestured to the empty bar. "As you see."

"I just thought maybe the Californians had already come in. You know, for the wedding. The Cabin is on Brett's list of must-dos."

"No, Colin, the Californians have not come in for the wedding." He was definitely mad. Sharper than usual. He plunged the mop into the Pine-Sol-laden water and pumped it up and down a few times. "What can I do for you? Get you a beer? Shot of whiskey?"

"No thanks," he managed. "I'm just looking for Mira—is she around?"

"Nope."

"'Cause she missed the pre-audition meeting, and she said she'd definitely be there."

"Oh."

Eric Greyfeather got back to mopping. Coll held his breath. It seemed to him that the mop was pointedly circling the site of last night's assorted horrors—but then, everything had gotten so messy so fast, and there had been so much movement, so much noise. If Eric Greyfeather was trying to tell him something, just about every surface in the place was ripe for insinuation.

"Well, would you mind telling her I stopped by?"

"I'm sure you'll talk to her at the wedding."

"Of course." He considered pointing out that the wedding was tomorrow. Did Eric Greyfeather think Mira wasn't going to call him to explain her absence from the meeting before then? "How about you, Mr. G?" he asked. "Will *you* be there?"

"No, Colin. I will not."

He mumbled an excuse and felt his way back outside. Was there anything more depressing than a dive bar parking lot in broad daylight? Across the street, Fletcher Sternin's horse paddock was nothing but overturned brown earth. The horses were way out across it, outlined against the distant trees. Coll shaded his eyes with his hand and studied the lot's ground. There were definitely streaks of something brown and recently dried in the dust. Freenie had called them blood trails, but you had to know exactly what had happened to assume that. They could have been anything: grease, or beer, or vomit, or any suspect fluid you might expect to find weaving out the door of a place like this.

One of the trails led to the spot where Coll's truck had been sitting last night. He followed the other around the side of the

Cabin as if he expected to see Bob Fournier still parked back there. But all he found were the rusty dumpsters sitting side by side.

When he got back to the house, he checked the mailbox. There was nothing inside but a postcard of a turbaned badger on a black background looking ruefully over its shoulder. Something about it was vaguely familiar—the blue-and-white headwrap, the earring. Minus the badger, he could *almost* call to mind the original painting it was trying to reference. Something old, and without a badger. The words that kept popping into Coll's brain were "Mona Lisa," but this, he knew, was wrong. Unless it wasn't. He turned the postcard over and read the message.

You'll never be forgiven.

At first, he thought it must be a Reverend Leon note. Reverend Leon lived out in the Warrens, in a tent on land that had been mined by his great-grandfather. Every six months or so, Reverend Leon was shaken by some vision or other that led him to write missives of condemnation to every person in town who hadn't stopped by to hear him preach to a congregation of what Coll assumed were mostly squirrels and magpies.

On closer inspection, however, something about the postcard didn't add up. Reverend Leon usually sent notes in proper envelopes. His most recent one had arrived at the Yards' this past July. On its cover: a wistful little red-cheeked snowman waving at Santa's sleigh and reindeer, which were silhouetted against an enormous moon at the top of the frame. Inside the card, Reverend Leon had scrawled the words *The Lord of all sees yore sins repent repent repent repe* in black Sharpie that had run out before he'd quite managed to work in another whole *repent*.

The handwriting on this postcard was all wrong, too. Something about it exhibited tremendous self-control, in aesthetics if not in sentiment. The writer had used a plain regular pen to write,

You'll never be forgiven.

So neatly, measuredly.

Who needed forgiveness? And who was going to be withholding it so resolutely from them for so long?

As he stood there, looking down at the text, he heard a vehicle clattering up the road behind him. It was the mail truck. Sid Pillwater was waving at him from behind the wheel. Coll stepped back to let him pass.

"I can't believe you'd deliver this," he said when Sid's mirthless jowls appeared in the driver's side window.

"What?"

Coll waved the postcard incriminatingly. Sid took it from his hand. "In what world do you think I could deliver this?" he asked. "It don't got no address."

"Well, how did it get here, then?"

Sid shrugged. "Sounds to me like someone was interfering with federal property."

He dropped the postcard disdainfully into Coll's hand. Then he started putting the Yards' bundle of bills into the mailbox. Coll watched him. "Sid, I'm right here."

"So what?"

"So you know I'm going to take them out the minute you're done. Just give them to me."

"We've been over this, Coll."

"Would you ever take a bribe?"

"Of course not."

"But a really good one, Sid. Like—like free breakfasts at the Gold Dust for a year. Or a guarantee that you'd get to play whoever you wanted in the Greyrock reenactment, no term limits, no questions asked."

"Don't tease."

"Who would it be, though, Sid?"

Sid looked at him solemnly. "You know who."

"Who?"

"My man Fred Kipley, of course."

"Of course."

When he got down to the house, Coll found Freenie sitting on the porch steps with her head in her hands. He touched her shoulder.

"Don't," she said. "I'd literally kill you for a cigarette."

Inside was the predictable chaos of cake-delivery eve. His mother was sitting at the kitchen table crying, even though nothing appeared to be wrong. Four white sponge cakes of varying sizes were all perched on their respective cooling racks. The piping bags were laid out. Various cutting boards and scrapers and armatures of support were glistening on the prep table. In the corner stood the box the cake would be delivered in, looking like the white cardboard coffin of a very short man. Coll's father, in a typically misguided effort to defuse the tension, was for some reason folding a piece of parchment paper into a chef's hat.

It was, Coll realized, the right moment to distract his father with a mystery. He held out the postcard. "I think this came for you."

"What is it?" His father adjusted his bifocals and squinted at the text. "Ooh, sinister! Reverend Leon?"

"I don't think so, actually."

"You're right. Punctuation? What was I thinking?"

Coll turned the postcard over to the picture of the turbaned badger. "What's the reference here?" he asked. "I feel like I've seen it before." He hesitated. "It's not the *Mona Lisa.*"

"No." The smile on his father's face told him he should have stopped before this last guess. "No, it's not the *Mona Lisa.* What is it?"

"I don't know."

"Sure you do. Come on."

"I can't remember."

"This is a take on *Girl with a Pearl Earring.*"

"That's right, that's right." Coll nodded. "She's a girl in that one."

His father stared at him coolly. "That's right, Coll. She's a girl. Johannes Vermeer did not choose the American badger as the subject of this seventeenth-century Dutch portrait."

"Haga waga to you, too, Dad," Freenie said from the doorway.

"Oh, come on. You kids used to know all this stuff." He clucked in something like wistful recognition. "Vermeer. It's at the Met, I think. Or maybe in London? Honey, is someone we know in Europe right now?"

Freenie was peering over his shoulder at the screed on the postcard. "Apparently, someone we've pissed off."

"Maybe it's the baby's parents," Coll tried. "Maybe they've gotten wind of the way you swear around the baby and stay up late watching B-list lesbian horror."

Freenie tilted her head. "Or maybe it's the ghost of that wolf you let Bob Fournier desecrate."

Their mother lifted her head from her hands. "What?"

Coll snatched the postcard back. "Why would you say something like that?"

"Isn't that what happened?"

"*No.* I didn't—"

Freenie crossed her arms and made a face that was supposed to look like Coll at his most useless. " 'I didn't, I didn't.' Did you do anything? Call anybody? Or did you just stand there?"

"I did plenty. I helped AJ. A lot. And it wasn't easy, you know. A bunch of guys were in there, all of them drunk as shit, half of them carrying. And I was the only one besides AJ trying to calm everybody down."

"Oh wow, you and AJ. Just a couple a heroes."

"I'm sure you would've done better, Freenie."

"Stop it," their mother said.

"Well, that wolf wouldn't have ended up in pieces all over town if I'd been there. I can tell you that much."

"Good for you, Freen."

He stuck the postcard under the junk mail pile and turned on the kitchen computer to check how the pamphlets he had ordered were coming along. He found only an email—another one—that had come in two days ago from Louise. He recoiled the moment he saw her name. She was just following up to see if he'd had a chance to read her book or, failing that, if he'd given any thought to her request for a tour. He typed, *Do I seem like I have time to read your book?* in a new draft, then deleted it quickly. He imagined her peering into the kitchen from the email at him, as though the computer were a portal: his exhausted face obstructing her view of the scene behind him, where Freenie was putting on a hairnet with one hand while she stroked their mother's shoulder with the other, and his father was, for reasons clear only to himself, opening up the standing piano and rooting around for sheet music.

Growing up, he'd always felt that his hippie father was a bit of a liability. Slight, earnest, blinking steadily out from behind the same pair of oversized glasses since the late 1970s. Emanating a kind of small-bodied guilelessness that made Coll nervous for him. As if he were just looking to get beat up, or worse. Once, during Coll's short-lived dalliance with high school wrestling, Coach Donovan had caught Coll glaring at him between push-ups and screamed, "Don't be looking at me like that, son—I'm pure Kipley County! I'll eat you alive!"

This warning, basic though it was, had embedded itself in Coll. He had felt so strongly that it was meant not just for him but for his father, too. Dr. Finch Yard, PhD, off in his own head, reciting Shakespeare to the indifferent children of hunters and ranchers. Referring to the Shepard boy as "Matthew," even in public, as if he had known him, when everybody else, including the people who thought he hadn't deserved to die like that, could only bring themselves to call him "that poor kid from Laramie."

And yet, Kipley County had never actually managed to eat Dr. Yard. It had just grown more caustic around him, terrifying Coll, but never his father. Eventually, it gave up and moved on to eating other people, most notably Coach Donovan himself, who tried to kill his wife, Linda, when she left him, and ended up doing twenty-five to life down in Rawlins, while Coll's father went on puttering, hair combed, glasses sliding down his nose as he stood in the strong current of the river, up and downstream of other people's less resilient fathers. More recently, Coll had come around to the idea that maybe it wasn't so bad to be Dr. Finch Yard. Maybe it was actually something to admire—this ability to hold firm, to talk to anybody exactly as they were, to roll through the world unmoved by the pressures and perceptions of other people. It was, perhaps, not entirely dissimilar to going through life as Anton Vargas. Both men were outsiders in their own way. Right in themselves. Unassailable.

His mother was up and in her wedding finery before the rest of them, sitting primly beside the cake as if she were praying with it on the morning of its execution. Despite her nerves, she had managed to get the tiers all plumb, and to do some very elaborate buttercream piping from top to bottom. The sugar flowers shone out from among the vanilla folds.

"It's your best work yet," Coll told her.

He went outside to get the truck ready so that his mother could have a final, private cry before she pulled herself together for the festivities. It was a fine morning, warmer than yesterday. The mountains had stayed clear of new snow for the wedding.

He wiped down the truck bed as well as he could. The new tarp his mother had bought was still sealed in its wrapper on the garage worktop. He was sitting on the tailgate, trying to wrestle it open, when he glanced up to find a brunette coming down the driveway on foot. She was in her late twenties, maybe early thirties, dressed in plain jeans and a plaid shirt almost comically too big for her. She had a bulging army-green musette over her shoulder, and was carrying a large paper bag in her left hand. When she saw him sitting there, a huge smile broke over her face, and she waved.

"Hi there!"

Did he know her? He couldn't place her at all. Behind him, in the house, he could hear the dogs hurling themselves against the back door at the sound of her voice.

He stood up off the tailgate. "Can I help you?"

"I hope so," she said brightly. "I'm sorry to intrude. Someone in town gave me this address—I'm looking for Colin Yard?"

"That's me."

"Oh! Wonderful!"

"I'm so sorry," he said. "Who are you?"

She held out her hand at a rigid right angle. "I'm Louise Hawley. From Denver? I wrote you that I might be passing through this week?"

"Oh!" he said sheepishly. "That's right, that's right."

"I'm sorry to barge in on you like this," she went on. "But I'm not in town for very long, and it's been a couple of days since I sent the last email, and I wasn't sure if you'd seen it, and . . ." She hung her head in a way that was meant to signify her contrition, but she was still half-smiling. "I took a chance that it wouldn't creep you out if I just showed up." She raised the paper bag. "I brought breakfast bars. As tribute. They're not homemade, though—I don't live here."

"You didn't have to do that." He had no choice but to accept the bag. She was going to stay holding it up like this until he took it from her. "I'm so sorry I haven't gotten back to you."

"That's all right. I thought it would be easier if I just caught you for a second."

"I'm afraid you've caught me in the middle of getting ready for a wedding, though."

"Oh! You're getting married!" She looked from the truck to the tarp in his hand, and back again.

"No, no," he said. "A friend is. My mother made the cake. We're about to drive it over there. That's why I'm not wearing my suit."

He was just babbling now because he felt bad to be caught out like this, ignoring some pretty Denver girl's emails, as if he had no manners at all. He'd brought this on himself. Would it have been so difficult to fire off a couple of sentences to her yesterday, instead of sulking about her persistence? Although, really, it should have been *her* feeling bad, walking up on him like this, unannounced on a Saturday morning. She seemed to know that—had known it before she set out. Hence the breakfast bars. "Look," he said. "I hate to run out on you. I know I owe you some answers. But we really do have this wedding. Are you still around tomorrow?"

"I am!" she said brightly. She had the energy of an army recruiter.

"You know the Gold Dust Diner, in town?"

She agreed to meet him there midmorning, which he guessed meant ten or eleven o'clock. He realized, as they were fumbling through their goodbyes, that he should have offered to drive her to wherever she was staying, but she was already walking briskly back up the driveway.

They all got ready and caravaned over to the Earlys', Freenie driving the pickup with Coll wedged in the bed, in his blue suit, bracing the cake box and thankful that the morning was too cold for bugs. Two fastidious car-lengths behind, his parents followed along in the sedan. Coll waved. From the passenger seat, his mother gestured insistently for him to hug the cake box with both arms.

The clouds were high up today, colossal, rolling along like some ancient herd. Now and again, in the distant, golden fields, he caught glimpses of pronghorn bucks wheeling in crazy circles around their little harems.

At last, the truck eased into the driveway, past the sign that read THE EARLY'S in massive Western type.

Coll knew exactly what his father was saying down in the sedan: "What's that apostrophe doing there? What is it *doing*?"

He spotted Mira almost as soon as they pulled onto the gravel lot just below the Early house. She was an astonishment floating from one end of the porch to the other in a dress so yellow his beleaguered brain smelled lemons when he saw it. The strength of his reaction made him thankful that he was here in somewhat of an official capacity—he couldn't just rush over and make an ass of himself right away. He would have to wait until after the unloading of the cake.

He and his father got it out of the truck bed and halfway up the hill to the house before a couple of the other men saw them and hurried over to help.

"Don't, boys, don't," his father cried, but you couldn't dissuade cowboys from making themselves useful. They seized the cake box from all sides and rushed it into the house as if it were some huge white battering ram, Coll's mother trotting along behind and shouting admonitions until she witnessed its safe arrival in the kitchen.

He was wiping his hands on a dish towel when Early sped by him in a huff.

"Can I help?" Coll asked.

"Yes!" Early, still running, beckoned. "Yes, help."

Their destination was the barn, where they set about unfurling yards and yards of twinkle lights that Nancy Early had insisted were absolutely, definitely, one hundred percent all there.

To Coll, it seemed somewhat late to be doing this, a fact he decided to bring up at the risk to his life.

"Don't tell me," Early said. "Take it up with Bob fucking Fournier."

Coll didn't know what surprised him more: the shock of hearing Bob Fournier's name or the shock of hearing Early cuss.

"What happened?"

"He was supposed to rig all these up last night, but he never showed. This morning I call the house to ask him where the hell he is, and I get Estelle—'So sorry, Gabe, Bob can't come. He's *sick.* He's *real bad.*' I asked her, 'Well, has he had a goddamn stroke, Estelle, between last night and today? Because if not, I should be looking out my window and seeing the half mile of lighting I ordered for my daughter's wedding all strung up and ready to go.' She says she's just getting dressed to run him to the hospital in Casper, and she doesn't have time for any of my bullshit. Well, I'll tell you who's gonna have time for my bullshit."

The thought went unfinished, so Coll never did find out who would have time for Early's bullshit. He couldn't pretend to be sorry that Bob wouldn't be here this morning. Still, he wouldn't wish illness on anybody. Not even on Bob. Especially not the kind that warranted a trek to Casper. Not just sick, Estelle had said. "Real bad." What did that mean? He tried not to think about it as he scurried up and down the ladder in the barn, slinging threads of light over the rafters, while various Earlys moved tables and hay bales around in an effort to delineate the dance floor below.

It was a lovely ceremony. Blessings, poems, readings from *Pride and Prejudice.* Elizabeth Cutbach, whom Coll hadn't seen since high school, had driven all the way up from Salt Lake City to sing "My Own Home," from *The Jungle Book,* during the processional.

From his place five rows back, Coll watched Early burst into tears the second she got to the part about Father hunting in the forest.

Mira was fourth of six bridesmaids, doing more for that yellow dress, in Coll's opinion, than the bride was doing for the big cream-puff monstrosity she had inexplicably chosen for her special day. He tried to think of the smoothest way to express this, in terms that would move Mira without seeming to put Trudie down. "I thought the bridesmaids weren't supposed to outshine the bride" was the best he could come up with, but he would have to garnish it with something adequately jokey, maybe a thumbs-up, to keep it from sounding desperate.

And he was struggling with when to deploy it. She was nowhere to be found during the pre-dinner mingling, and then there were the speeches. He managed to end up just behind her after Kelly Murray dropped out of the buffet line.

"Hullo," he said.

"Hullo," she said, without looking up from the chafing dishes. "I'm undecided—steak or ribs?"

"I mean, both," Coll said, unsure of whether he wanted his big pronouncement to coincide with Mira spearing a rack four ribs wide onto the mountain of mashed potatoes and green beans that already overwhelmed her plate. By the time he realized that, actually, given the nature of their friendship, this would have been the perfect moment, the DJ was already revving up "Say My Name" and Mira was streaming with all the other yellow dresses onto the dance floor. He tried to follow her there, but it was chaos as soon as Trudie and Brett came out, pumping their arms, and before he knew it, he found himself amid the Californians, looking around in wonderment at the sloppy ease with which they moved. The last time someone had tried to do the Worm at a wedding, it had been Coll's father, and they'd ended up having to drive to the urgent care in Brecon.

More speeches, sweatier now, breathless and lurid with booze. Then the moment of reckoning: the cutting of the cake. Coll watched his father try to beckon his mother out of the shot as Brett and Trudie huddled together over the glistening white tiers, but she remained there, expectantly, waiting for the cake knife to find its way out of the newlyweds' hands and into hers. The first piece she cut, for them, was massive. The cake equivalent of starting a message in letters that would never, ever fit on the card. As the line started to form behind the couple, Coll's mother got the hang of it, cutting slimmer and slimmer, so that by the time Coll drew up to her elbow, the slices were so thin they wouldn't stand up.

"Two, please," he said.

He brought the other one to Mira. She had taken off her heels and was sitting on a bench at the far end of the barn. He bowed with exaggerated solemnity before her and held out the plate.

"Oh, *cake*!" she said. "Thank you."

"Mother Yard's achievement of the year," Coll said.

She smiled. "Let's give it a whirl."

It was good. Not as good as cake from Moraine would have been, but an improvement on the Yule logs that caused his mother no end of grief every Christmas.

"I like the contrast," Mira was saying, "That tart little hit of—what? Raspberry?"

"I think it's huckleberry."

"Good palate, Coll."

"Well, I'm the one who had to scrub two burned batches of it off the pots, so . . ."

She made room for him on the bench. She was eating slowly, languorously, gazing out over the dance floor, bouncing one bare foot a little in rhythm to the music.

"You look so beautiful," he blurted out. It was not what he had intended to say. He tried to cover for himself, but the thumbs-up he'd been holding back only made the whole thing worse.

"Thanks," she said softly. "The dress does a lot of the work."

"It's not the dress. It's you." He sat there for a minute, stunned by his own audacity. Uplifted by it. Who knew he had it in him? It was all out in the open now, this unspoken thing between them, and there was no going back. "The Roundtrees are playing the Golden Calf in Moraine next week," he found himself saying. "I think we should go together. Make a whole day of it."

"That sounds nice, but I don't think so."

He was so taken aback by the flatness of her refusal that he needed a second. "Why not?" he asked. "Is there somebody else?"

"No, Coll."

"Then why?"

"Because I think I've been a bit mistaken about you, and I don't feel like spending that kind of time with you right now."

" 'Mistaken'? What does that mean?"

She rested the plate on her knees and turned to face him. "The person I thought you were wouldn't have been all right with what happened."

"When?"

"At my father's bar."

"I wasn't all right with it," he said. "It was awful."

"So why did you just stand there and let AJ hang?"

"But I didn't—"

"Coll." She held up a hand. "Come on. Did you really think my brother wouldn't tell me?"

"What did he say happened?"

"I'm not gonna go into it."

"So I don't get to defend myself? What did he say?"

"That you got right in there with the rest of them."

He was so angry that he blurted the stupidest thing he could think of. "A second ago you said I was just standing there letting AJ hang, and now you say I was getting right in with the rest of them. Which is it, Mira?"

She leaned out over the bench to get a better look at him. "Are you serious?"

"Look. There was a lot going on, and all of it happened so fast.

Ask AJ—we were both trying to figure out what the hell to do. Neither of us had been in that situation before, we didn't know most of those guys, and a lot of them were really drunk, plus you know how Bob gets—"

"I understand that. It's disappointing, but I understand it. What I *don't* understand is why you joined in."

"That's a *lie.*" It wasn't.

"I believe my brother."

He wished the silence would actually be silent, not filled with terrible music. "Well, I'm sorry. He's wrong. I did everything I could."

She stood up in a way that was clearly meant, *Sure you did, pal.* He had never felt such a weird, sticky nausea in all his life. The fact that she was squeezing his shoulder made it so much worse. Anyone watching them would be able to tell that she was trying to let him down easy—her, Eric Greyfeather's petty-criminal daughter, who worshipped insurgents and bailed out vandals, and had blown Billy Horse in the back of the bus on the basketball team's return trip from Laramie six years ago and apparently forgotten it.

"I'm not mad at you, Coll—I just can't go with you to Moraine next weekend. I need to think. Okay?"

He shrugged his assent and watched her head away from him, into the cone of light purpling the dance floor. The arms of women pulled her into their midst, and then her arms appeared over their heads in turn, as if the last ten minutes hadn't happened at all.

To make matters worse, Bobby Calvert, the youngest heir of the Calvert Cattle Co., lowered himself onto the bench beside Coll.

"Hey," he said intimately. "The guys and I have a question."

"What?"

"Is your sister, like—pregnant?"

He sat with Bobby's arm around him, watching Freenie disrupt the dance floor. She was not more than fifteen feet away. She had taken off her tuxedo blazer and was pumping her arms up and down to the best of her ability, given the challenge of her current proportions. Whenever she ended up in profile, she looked like she had swallowed a watermelon whole.

"Yeah, man," Coll said. "She's pregnant."

"Do you know who knocked her up?"

He looked into Bobby's big, stupid face. "Nobody, Bobby. She's a fucking surrogate."

"What's that?"

"A rich couple is paying her to carry their baby."

"Oh." Bobby's whole face was straining with thought. "So, like—did she have to fuck the husband? 'Cause we all thought she was . . . you know . . ."

Outside the tent, night had fallen. The stars were out. The Earlys' sloping yard was dotted with firepits, around which partygoers were huddling against the nighttime chill. Coll stood and breathed in deeply. The funny feeling from last night and this morning had been greatly compounded by the whiskey. He was sullen and sad, and amazed by how fast the adrenaline-fueled hope of the past few hours—the past few years, really—had been ground down to nothing, replaced by something awful and thin and ugly.

His chest was so tight that he found he had to cough.

Around one A.M., he steered the truck gently home. His parents had surprised him by staying on for one more reel. Freenie was asleep in the rear cab. At the junction of Grand View and Parmer Roads, he found himself turning left. It wasn't really voluntary—more like the wheel just spun in his hands, and he was on his way to Bob Fournier's place.

From the top of the drive, he could see that there were lights on inside the house. But only one of the Fourniers' trucks was in the driveway. He cut the lights and eased downhill toward the house, pressing the brake now and again, just gently enough so that it didn't screech. The porch lights were on. Coll pulled up as close to the house as he could and tried to see through the windows. Four or five dogs were milling around in there, but there was nobody on the sofa. Nobody in the kitchen.

Freenie had shifted in her seat, and her jaw was now hanging open. Slight snores.

Coll slipped out of the truck and went up to the house. It was a good way to get shot, this. He admitted to himself that on top of his fresh heartbreak, drink had probably been involved in his decision to come here, given that he wasn't even sure what he was looking for. What evidence of affliction was left behind when a person needed to be rushed to the hospital? An overturned chair? A shattered coffee table where the patient went down? A bottle of aspirin spilled all over the counter, maybe? The Fourniers' kitchen was a mess, but nothing jumped out at him as especially incriminating.

"What the fuck, Coll?"

He jumped. "Jesus, Freenie."

She had materialized out of the dark behind him. "Where are we? I need to pee."

"Get back in the truck."

"Is this the Fournier house?"

"Will you please keep your voice down?"

"What are we doing here?"

By the time he heard the porch door open, it was already too late.

"Who the hell is that?"

It was the voice of Bob Fournier's firstborn son, Paul, the useless one. He had tormented Coll throughout middle school, until finally, in ninth grade, he ran afoul of the lethal confluence of Chaucer and Coll's father, and stayed behind for one year, then two, receding into the distance and getting smaller in Coll's imagination, if not in actual size. He opened the screen door and leaned out of it. There was, of course, the silhouette of a rifle in his hands. Coll watched it swing in their general direction.

"It's Freenie Yard," his sister said.

"Who?"

"Freenie and Colin Yard."

"What the hell are you doing out here in the dark?"

"Got turned around coming home from the wedding."

"Some turn-around. Turned *all* the way around."

Freenie shoved past Coll. Her silhouette blocked the incoming light from the door. Coll wanted to shout after her not to advance toward Paul—but she was already doing it.

"Can I come inside?" she said. "I need to pee."

She didn't wait for Paul to answer—she shouldered past him and went into the house. Coll watched her crossing the kitchen, with the bewildered Fournier dogs swarming around her, in the direction of what he presumed was the downstairs bathroom. He was now alone with Paul.

"We heard about your dad," Coll said.

"Mom took him to the hospital this morning."

"Is he okay?"

Paul's sarcophagus shoulders rose and fell in a shrug.

"What happened to him?" Coll pressed.

"He's sick."

"Yeah, but—how?"

"What do you mean, 'how'?"

"Was it a stroke? A stomach ulcer? Something else?"

"The fuck business is that of yours?"

"Just trying to be neighborly. Gabe Early said he was real badly off. We were all bummed he missed the wedding."

Paul failed to surprise Coll by spitting on the ground. "He kinda couldn't breathe. Went all red around the eyes and whatnot. Wasn't really eating."

"That sounds serious."

"I guess we'll see."

Freenie's shape hurried back across the kitchen on the other side of the window. Coll heard the screen door slap shut behind her, and she was at his elbow in the cold night air again. The scrim of drink was beginning to dissipate, and it was starting to occur to Coll what a profound mistake he'd made in coming here, and with Freenie in tow. No sooner had the thought flickered through his brain than she became utterly herself: "Heard your father's sick."

"That's right," said Paul.

"Real shame," she said.

Coll nudged her. "Freenie."

"What? I'm just torn up about it."

Paul managed to catch the discrepancy between the content of her words and the tone of her voice. "You think you're being funny," he said.

"Not at all," said Freenie. "I don't think it's funny when people who dismember animals get what's coming to them almost immediately."

"Freenie."

"I don't think pieces of shit with homicidal impulses don't belong in decent society and should be run out of town."

Paul, finally, had had enough. "Get the *fuck* out of here, you ugly little dyke," he shouted, swinging the rifle in their direction as if it were a broom.

Only in this horror-stricken moment of grabbing her under the arms did Coll appreciate how much extra weight Freenie was carrying around in that belly. He pulled her onto her heels like an appliance dolly and started dragging her back toward the truck. But she wasn't done. "I don't hope that he dies a slow and horrible death!"

He threw her in through the half-door and slammed the truck in reverse up the drive. The gravel snatched at his wheels, yanking him here and there. Through the juddering windshield, he saw Paul put the rifle up, and saw the blue flash of it down by the house. The bullet went nowhere near them—that was part of the demented point Paul was making—but Freenie still yelled, "Dumb fuck!" through the open window.

Then they were on the main road and peeling away.

"What is *wrong* with you?" Coll shouted back at her. "You're supposed to be keeping calm!"

"Must be the hormones," Freenie said, in her normal voice. She lolled back in the seat sulkily, and he felt a sudden upwelling of love for her. Minus the belly and the tiny spray of premature grays around her forehead, she could still be that grubby, angry little teenager he'd pulled out of fistfights with boys twice her size on nights out. They'd been the stewards of their little group, the Yard twins, back in the days when they were all hanging out in basements and cattle pastures, and obliterating their BMX bikes in the badlands on terrible, tentless overnight trips to Horsebone Lake.

He looked back into the rearview mirror to find her face looming just over his shoulder. "Who else should we pay a visit?"

"Hm?"

"Who else was there on Thursday night?"

He had to watch the road. "I told you. There were, like, ten other people."

"Who?"

"Couple of guys I didn't recognize. And, like . . . AJ."

"AJ helped him carve up the wolf?"

"Of course not. Nobody *helped.*"

"But nobody did anything to stop it, either. Including you."

"That's just not true, Freenie."

"What did you do?"

"I told them to fuck off and cut it out. Like, go someplace else. I backed AJ up."

"Look out, everybody, there's not enough room in the cab for you and the balls on this man. He backed AJ up." She fanned herself dramatically.

"What do you want me to do, Freenie?"

"I want you to feel bad about it. You should feel like shit."

"Okay."

They drove on in silence, the whole awful mess of it roiling in his stomach in a washing machine of whiskey and cake and midshelf prosecco and what he was beginning to suspect had been some bad shrimp. He was so incredibly thirsty.

He knew who else had been there, of course. It wasn't just a handful of strangers who had stumbled into the Cabin after coming down the Hemot Pass in the middle of the night on a Thursday. But he was keeping their names to himself for Freenie's own good. Pregnancy hadn't made her any less the kind of person who would fly off the handle at a moment's notice. She wasn't like Mira: quietly judgmental, personally cutting. Even now, if she found out the names of the other participants, she was liable to track them down and ask them about it outright. She could get all kinds of wrong impressions about what had happened.

Better to stay quiet and maybe check up on Bob Fournier. Maybe get ahold of the hospital in Casper and ask them how he was doing. It was serious, right? It had to be, otherwise he would have just gone to Brecon. It must be something cardiovascular. Maybe he should get Estelle on the phone so she could clarify. He'd better do it soonish, before it occurred to Paul to call his mother and report on the Yard twins' midnight visit.

When they got home, he ushered Freenie off to bed and sat at the kitchen table by himself. With the cake gone, the whole room looked bereft. He gathered up the scattered cake boards and brought the crusty spatulas over to the sink to soak. Stood there for a while, staring down at his hands reddening in the water. He could feel this, the heat of the water. *Really* feel it. He could feel the prick of the submerged knife his hand brushed against, too, and the strange tingling along his scalp that overcame him when thoughts of Mira at the wedding crashed through his brain. What a fucking nightmare.

The phone rang behind him. He crossed the kitchen and grabbed it off the hook before it rang again and woke his sister.

"Well, *well,*" he said in the low country drawl he reserved for the rare occasions when his father was drunk. "I presume you kids won't be driving home?"

There was an odd clicking on the other end.

"Hello?"

Someone drew a deep and distant breath. "There's still time."

"What?"

"For you. There's still time."

Then they hung up. Coll went on standing with the receiver in his hand. He had the distinct sense that putting it back on the hook would sever not only his tie to the moment but also to his memory of it, causing it to recede from him like a dream. Already he was unsure about the voice, whether it had belonged to a man or a woman, and what it had actually said.

A few moments later, he heard his parents' voices in the driveway. They wobbled through the door. His mother was clutching the hem of her skirt. Her shoes, tiny little kitten heels she'd bought in Paris thirty years ago, were dangling from her fingers. His father tottered in merrily behind her.

He pointed at Coll. "Oh good," he said. "You're still up."

"Up for your jokes," Coll muttered.

"Finch—tell Coll what Trudie said about the cake. Tell him!" His father opened his mouth but was too slow to start. His mother kept going: "She said it was the most delicious cake she'd ever had, and it looked even more beautiful than the one she'd seen in *Western Bride,* and she was so happy she hadn't ordered a six-hundred-dollar cake from Moraine that had to be driven here in a Porsche."

"That's right," his father said dreamily.

"It was delicious," Coll told them.

"I think the huckleberry jam between the tiers really did the trick."

"Everybody said so."

His mother took his hands and gave them a little squeeze. She looked as if she were about to cry, which meant she'd had at least six glasses of sparkling. She shook her head, wiped her eyes, and turned to survey the kitchen. "Oh, I'm going to miss that cake. It had real presence. You know? Real presence." She put her hands on her hips. "But what a mess."

"I'm just cleaning up now," Coll said.

"No, no."

"Yes. Go to bed."

He waited until his mother had gone upstairs. Then he turned to his father. "Did you just call?" he asked.

His father was getting the orange juice out of the fridge. "Call what?"

"Call here. Call me. Just now."

"No. Why would I?"

"Well, somebody did."

"At three in the morning? What did they want?"

"I don't know—they just sort of hung up."

His father went to the phone and dialed star sixty-nine and stood there for a minute. Then he shrugged. "Busy signal."

Coll took the receiver from his hand and listened to the frantic bleats. His father was watching him oddly. "What's wrong, Coll?"

"Nothing."

"Unnerving, to get a call in the middle of the night. You feel like you're missing something urgent." His father clapped his shoulder and headed for the stairs. Halfway up, he paused. "You know what—somebody *did* call for you. Earlier."

"When?"

"Last night. They asked for you, and when I said you were in the shower, they said they'd try again today."

"Who was it? Why didn't you tell me?" He hadn't intended to sound so angry.

"I just forgot. In all the chaos of getting the cake ready, I just forgot." His father stood at the stairs. "I'm sorry, Coll—but if it's important, I'm sure they'll call back."

"Did you recognize who it was?"

His father thought about it. "A girl, I think."

"A girl—you think."

"Why are you talking to me that way?"

"I'm not." He felt sheepishly sixteen again, standing in the same spot as he had during the interminable high school years, explaining himself to his father in the softly ticking, half-dark house. The phone, incriminating portal to all things his parents must never know, hanging just to his left, exactly where it always had.

His father put his hands in his pockets. "You haven't gotten mixed up in anything, have you?"

"'Mixed up'? In what?"

"I don't know. All this business with the debts and the hospital bills. Your sister's not the only one who makes rash decisions for the sake of the family. *Function is smother'd in surmise.* I just want to make sure you're not in over your head trying to help me and your mother, when we're really going to be fine."

"Are you asking if I've signed up to carry a millionaire couple's lab baby to help save the ranch?"

His father laughed. "Something like that."

"Don't worry—I haven't."

"Well. All right, then." But still his father didn't move. "If there's anything you want to talk about, I'm here."

Then he went upstairs and turned off the light.

The gods did not intend sleep for Coll that night. He lay awake staring at the ceiling of his room, and then he went downstairs to lie on the couch and stare at the ceiling there instead. The density of his thoughts was stifling. Under normal circumstances, he could get some reprieve by focusing on Mira, on their next encounter, the steady march toward their inevitable getting-together. But that outlet had vanished. A terminal new reality had taken its place. She had been mistaken about him. She didn't feel like spending that kind of time with him right now. What did "right now" mean? A week? A month? He had the deadening sense that it might mean "ever again." Just before dawn, the cat came in from outside. Wild thing, survivor of countless battles with the unseen, it sat on the chair opposite him with its leering green eyes and wouldn't come any closer, no matter what he did to encourage it. He wondered if it could tell that he was feeling clammy, that he had a headache, a funny tingling sensation numbing his fingertips. Maybe having a cold made you smell different to animals. Vulnerable and grotesque.

He was still by himself when the sun came up, and when nobody had stirred by nine-thirty, he left them a note and drove into town for breakfast. It was just him at the diner, and he wondered if practically the entire town had gotten hammered at the Early wedding and was sleeping it off. Since there was nobody there to judge, he took the opportunity to order strawberry-rhubarb pie for breakfast and drop a couple of quarters in the jukebox. He was in the middle of subjecting Celia, behind the counter, to the fourth Warren Zevon song in a row when Perch Driskil came in. The sheriff studied the baked goods display for a while, ordered, then put his back against the counter to take in the rest of the place.

Coll hadn't looked away fast enough to avoid his eye.

The sheriff nodded. "Morning."

"Hit your quota after the Early wedding?" Coll called across the room.

"A bonanza. Almost got your parents, but I had Mary Reese pulled over when they came weaving along. Mind if I sit with you?"

He did, in fact, mind, but he didn't say so. The sheriff was the tallest man in town and impossibly wiry, as if he'd been salted and left out through the winter. There was speculation that an erstwhile heroin habit had plagued him during the three brief years he spent in Cincinnati, but no one had ever had the courage to confirm it with him personally. More puzzling still to everybody in town was the way he ate: unstoppably, like a train engine taking in coal. Sitting across from him in uneasy silence, Coll watched him put away a skillet of biscuits and sausage gravy in three long, pensive bites before he raised his head again to check on the progress of the next part of his meal.

"I'm glad I bumped into you," Driskil said. "Saves me the trouble of coming up to the house."

Coll's stomach plunged. "What's going on?"

"Trying to get a better idea of what happened the other night over at Eric Greyfeather's place."

Coll wasn't sure how to play this. Obviously, he couldn't feign complete ignorance. Driskil knew that he had been there; otherwise he wouldn't have been on his way to the house to find him. On the other hand, he didn't know what part of the evening, aside from the general unpleasantness of the whole affair, actually warranted the involvement of police.

"How can I help?" he decided to say.

Driskil blotted his mustache with a napkin. "I guess you can tell me what you remember."

Coll kept his hands on the table. "Well, are we talking about the same night? I mean, are we referring to the same incident?"

The second the words left his mouth, he knew he'd made a mistake. There had been no other incident, and barely any time, besides, for one to occur.

"That depends," Driskil said. "What incident do *you* mean?"

"The one with Bob Fournier."

"Go on."

He took a breath and looked around the diner. "I went in around ten, I guess."

"Alone?"

"With Charlie Boughton. He and Janet just broke up."

"I heard."

Of course he had. Small-town gossip. How long before word of Coll's own Mira-inflicted humiliation reached the sheriff's office? Two days? Three? Was it circulating already?

"We were there for about half an hour, maybe. Had a beer each, and Charlie went home right around the same time Bob came in. He seemed like he was drunk already, which was really all I noticed about him at first."

"You didn't see the wolf?"

"Not right away. I think he had it in his bag."

"Then what happened?"

"Well, Bob was just sort of sitting there, doing shots. Being loud. Being Bob. And at some point I looked over and it seemed like there was a dog sitting between his knees with its head on the table."

"And that was the wolf."

"Well," Coll said. "The head, anyway."

Driskil nodded, unfazed. "Did anybody say anything to him?"

"It took a while because of the way he was holding it. But yeah, people started to notice what was going on. Then AJ said, 'Get the eff out of here with that coyote, Bob.' "

"What did Bob say to that?"

"He said, 'Boy, what kind of Indian are you that don't know a wolf when you see one?' "

"Then what?"

"Bob started buying rounds. Bragging. He told us he'd run it down somewhere up in the Ridges until it collapsed. Then he killed it and dressed it, I guess, and brought it with him."

"Did he give a reason for bringing it in?"

"He said he was taking it home for his kids."

Driskil's next serving of breakfast arrived. He offered Coll some of his pancake, which Coll refused. He didn't feel like eating, but it turned out he felt even less like watching Driskil obliterate yet another giant plate of food. Halfway through, Driskil made a rolling motion with his fork. "Go on."

"Well, I guess Bob wanted people to interact with it."

"What does that mean?"

"He wanted people to notice that he had it. He put the tail around his neck. Like a boa."

Driskil made a face. "A strange man, Bob Fournier."

"You're telling me."

"So, *did* people?"

"Did people what?"

"Interact with it?"

"Some."

"What was AJ doing?"

"He was telling everybody to stop and get the hell out."

"And you? What were you doing, Coll?"

Why did he seem to be the only one getting this question? Was anybody asking it of Bob Fournier? No—Bob was in Casper, resting up, while Coll was answering all around town for what *he* had done. Coll hadn't killed the wolf. He hadn't hacked it to pieces somewhere out in the blue-white solitude of the high peaks. He hadn't brought its head and paws and tail into the Cabin with him on a Thursday night. He hadn't *done* anything, had merely responded to what was being done around him. A first for Coll, being in that situation. Had never seen a wolf in a disembodied, or any other, state before. It was dark in the bar. It had taken Coll a really long time to realize that what he thought was Bob Fournier's dog wasn't a dog at all. That its eyes were open and unblinking. That it hadn't, at any point, withdrawn its absurdly long, purple tongue back into its mouth. That, in fact, the head resting on the table in front of Bob Fournier wasn't attached to anything. Coll wasn't the only one who didn't clock it right away—a half dozen men must have walked up to Bob Fournier and then backed up, raising their voices in laughter and feigned disgust. "What the fuck is wrong with you, Bob?" was the chorus of the evening, even from the drunkest patrons. It was what Coll himself was thinking, and no doubt what AJ was thinking, too. And "What the fuck is wrong with you?" is a tough thing to be thinking about a guy when it's obvious that he's looking to be asked precisely that question by anybody who dares. What Coll *had* done, to his own detriment, was stare a little too hard and a little too long at the spectacle before him—but, again, this was owed to the bad lighting and the general chaos of the place. If either had been slightly better, or if Eric Greyfeather had been behind the bar, or even Mira herself, Bob Fournier would already have been out on his ass, and Coll would not have been staring obviously enough for Bob to notice him and say, "Who the fuck is that over there? Is that, what do you call him, the theater kid, is that Baby Vargas?" He followed this up by sticking one of the wolf's severed paws up over the edge of the table and wiggling it at Coll like a cancan dancer's leg. There was only one thing to do to defuse the situation, and Coll did it: he raised the dregs of his beer in Bob Fournier's direction, hoping that would end the exchange. But no—Bob continued to wave the wolf's paw at him and then said, "Come over here, Baby Vargas, I got a surprise for you." Coll demurred, finished his beer, and, at the first moment Bob looked away, darted into the bathroom and locked the door. He splashed water on his face and tried to plan his escape. He would cross the room calmly, go out the front door, get into the truck, and drive home. Sure, maybe Bob would try to intercept him, or even follow him into the parking lot, but so what? What's the worst that could happen? He'd owe AJ, come back to pay his tab tomorrow, and the two of them would have a laugh about how crazy it had all gotten so fast, like one of those things you sometimes read about happening in a neighboring county or down in Texas, but thank God nobody had been seriously hurt. But by the time he went back out into the barroom, somebody had wrested control of the jukebox from AJ and cranked it up to karaoke, or at least sing-along, volume. Bob was on his feet, in the middle of the floor, singing the new Johnny Cash cover of "Personal Jesus" with the wolf's tail wrapped around his shoulders and the sad, grinning head under one arm like a helmet. All the other men had formed a circle around him and were gamely providing backing vocals, torn, it seemed, between their desire to see how far this latest madness of Bob's would go and their desire to stay just out of its reach. Coll's whole brain emptied. He knew then that he should have just stayed in the bathroom. There was no getting out without crossing the floor, and there was no crossing the floor without passing Bob. He started to go the long way, behind the bar and around the bussing station, but Bob was on the lookout for escapees. He saw Coll, cut across the room, and slid, with staggering precision for a man of his size, across a table to block his path. One of the wolf's paws, severed just below the elbow joint, was making its way through the purple gloom of the Cabin toward Coll's face. Bob wanted him to flinch, to protest, to be a girl about it. All he had to do was not be the thing Bob's eyes were accusing him of being: afraid. He snatched the wolf's paw, which was thin and gritty and light as air, held it up to his mouth like a microphone, and, to Bob's surprise and delight, started bellowing into it with all the ferocity he could muster, given the tremor in his knees. The song went on for a long time. Transitioned almost imperceptibly into the next one. Bob had him around the shoulders, pressing him into his side. Every now and again, the wolf's-tail boa around Bob's neck brushed against Coll's cheek. Coll couldn't tell if the musty smell was coming from the tail, or the bar, or just Bob Fournier himself, who wasn't so terrifying at this distance, who was a giant and soft around the middle. How many of the men in this room knew that? How many of them could claim that they had flipped Bob Fournier's opinion of them upside down with one single gesture, one single moment of bravery and self-reliance? Not many. Maybe not any. Through his sweat, hoarsely revving up for the next song, Coll glanced around the room and saw in their faces the new reality of himself, pressed as he was into the protective, benevolent dough of Bob's armpit, and knew that none of them would ever look at him the same way again. None of them would forget that at the end of the third song, when AJ finally got his wits about him and threw the lights on and pulled the fire alarm, Bob Fournier had slapped Coll's cheek approvingly, and the two of them had staggered, arm in arm, out into the parking lot.

So, yes. Sitting across from Driskil, Coll shrugged. "I helped get Bob out of there."

There was no need to mention that in the cool night air beside Coll's truck, Bob had presented him with the wolf's paw as if it were some ceremonial rod, or that Coll had taken it before climbing into the truck and driving away. Or that he hadn't gone more than two miles before he'd glanced over at it on the passenger seat, swerved onto the shoulder, and puked his guts out. These details would be known only to Coll, and to the wolf's paw itself, which he had left half-buried in a thicket on Ledger Road.

"So how did it all come to an end?" Driskil was asking.

"AJ pulled the fire alarm."

"And that was it?"

"That was it."

Driskil mopped his hands and face with the beleaguered expression of somebody who had just pushed a car up a steep incline.

"It was awful," Coll volunteered. "The whole thing, start to finish."

"Awful is one thing. Illegal is what I'm supposed to determine. Was any of it illegal."

It seemed that Driskil was, perhaps, waiting on Coll's own opinion on the legality of what had happened. Coll couldn't profess it. But there were things he, too, wanted to know. "Who called you? I mean—who told you about it?"

"I was already hearing some about it on Friday. Now maybe Eric Greyfeather wants to press charges."

"Against Bob?"

"Bob, and I guess whoever else participated."

Coll nodded. It would be insane to ask whether the sheriff thought this might include him.

"And then there's the health angle, of course."

"Health angle?"

"Well, yeah. I heard that some people touched it."

"That's right."

"Well, we can't have folks handling predator carcasses with their bare hands around here, Coll. Thank God most people knew better."

His stomach clenched. "Is that what's wrong with Bob?"

"We'll know when he gets back from Casper."

If Coll was going to confess that he had gone down to the Fournier place with Freenie last night, he had better do it now. It seemed like the kind of thing that would be relevant—or, rather, it seemed like the kind of thing that would become relevant once Driskil realized it had been omitted from the telling.

"Paul hadn't heard from his mother when we went down there last night," he said, trying to sound casual.

Driskil looked up. "How *is* Paul?"

"Pleasant as ever, like his dad. Just a real swell guy."

"Friend of yours?"

"God, no."

"So why were you down there last night?"

"We heard Bob got sick. We were worried."

"That's mighty kind of you."

"Can I ask you a question?"

"Sure thing."

"What do you think he could've picked up?"

"Oh, you name it. Rabies. Canine wasting disease. We'll know more when we test the head. Somebody found it stuck up on the stop sign at Sweetwater and Lowell."

After Driskil cleared out, Coll sat there thinking about what he should do next. He had told the truth—maybe not every detail, but the substance of everything had been true.

He was still feeling feverish—there was pain behind his eyes, just above the sockets. Deep pain, persistent, sitting unreachably back there. That was just what he needed, a sinus infection. He should go home and try to get a little more sleep.

But instead, he looked up and saw the Denver woman from yesterday morning—Louise. She had come in while he was talking to Driskil and was sitting at the counter by herself.

He had forgotten about her. He had forgotten that he was supposed to be meeting her here. That *he,* fool that he was, had asked her to come. Why hadn't he just told her the truth? That he had neither the time nor the inclination to deal with her nonsense. Now, instead of going home to rest, he was faced with the inevitability of talking to her for God knows how long. He hadn't even mapped out the broad strokes of what he wanted to say.

He got up and went over to her. "Hey."

"Oh hi!" He'd never met someone so cloyingly, relentlessly cheerful.

"Sorry about that," he said. "Can't really tell the sheriff I have other plans."

"Of course. How was the wedding?"

"So much fun." At least she didn't pry. That was a pleasant surprise. "And you—did you have a good night?"

"Yes. I'm staying over at the Jackalope Motel. It's really lovely."

He'd heard a lot of adjectives used to describe the Jackalope over the years, but "lovely" had never featured among them. "And—did you sleep . . . good?"

He could feel the soul of his father, all the way across town, withering at this turn of phrase. Louise, for all her talk of manuscripts, didn't seem to notice or mind. "It was *lovely.*"

Her eggs arrived—runny and served only with a side of plain, unbuttered toast. Coll took the counter stool beside her while she primly dispatched them.

"I'm sorry to barge in on you the way I did," she said.

"That's all right," he said. "*I'm* sorry I've been so slow to get back to you."

"Well, with reenactment season coming up, I'm sure you're very busy."

"We've never called it that, but I guess that's what it is." He hadn't updated the Old Sunrise Days website in a few months, but he could vaguely remember having set up a countdown clock.

She was looking at him steadily, with anticipation. He didn't know what else to say. "I really like the book," he lied.

"Oh wow." She clapped a hand over the mouthful she had just taken. "You mean it?"

"Of course." He hoped there was some finality of tone in his response that would keep her from asking him to elaborate.

"Well," she said. "That means a lot. Thank you for taking the time."

Celia appeared at his elbow with a fresh cup of coffee. "Are you gonna eat something, hon, or are you just gonna move from table to table, watching other people eat?"

"I had a slice of pie," he protested.

"Do you want another one?" she asked, as if he had any choice in the matter.

"Sure. Thanks." To Louise, he said, "What can I do to help you?"

"I'd really, really like to see Sunrise." She mistook his pause for hesitation, and jumped straight in again: "I know it's on your family's land, and I've read about how difficult it is to get up there because there's no paved road and a bunch of collapsed mines. So if it's simply not possible, I understand. But if there's any way at all—gosh, I'd be grateful. You shouldn't feel any pressure. Really. I know that's not what it seems like because I showed up at your house yesterday, but I do mean it. You can just say, *Louise, there just ain't no way in a month of Sundays.* Sorry, I don't know what that accent was. You don't sound like that. I'm just nervous. But I'm sure that as the head of the historical society, you know so much, and it would be invaluable to see the place and hear what you have to say about it."

His heart swelled up with camaraderie. He knew what it was like to have a rehearsed little speech go belly-up on you faster than you could get it out. "Okay, yeah—no problem," he heard himself say. "We can go up there."

As soon as he uttered this, he realized that he had done so for her reaction. And sure enough, she looked like he'd just handed her the moon. It made him profoundly uncomfortable. While she was offering to buy him breakfast, he sat with the feeling of stupidity that now followed his largesse. A trip all the way up to Sunrise, and with this cold coming on. Laden with fresh heartbreak. Tomorrow spoken for. Plus, he was going to have to spend today skimming this book of hers. There was no getting around that. He couldn't get through the drive, and the whole morning there, and the drive back knowing absolutely nothing about what she had written. Even worse, she wanted feedback. What was he supposed to say?

At first, he couldn't find the damn book. When had it arrived? He had to search through his emails all the way back to their first exchange, which had happened, he realized with mounting horror, more than a year ago. She had mentioned the book and mentioned wanting to be taken up to Sunrise—vaguely, gingerly. "If you should ever happen to be leading a tour up there," she had written, "I would move heaven and earth to come along." It had annoyed him even then, this pressure masked as politeness, and it annoyed him all over again to revisit it now. Two weeks after that exchange, he had given her his address, which must mean that the book had arrived sometime between that email and the next one she sent, "just checking that the book had gotten there safely." Where the hell was the mail from last May? Where would he have put it? He searched all the usual places: the junk drawer, the filing cabinet where his mother hid the bills she couldn't stand to deal with. He went to the garage and rifled through the paper recycling. What did the book even look like, he wondered. Was it just a stack of pages? Or had Louise had it professionally bound?

He found it at last in one of the basement donation boxes. Saved by his father's inability to get rid of anything between covers. It was white paper, cut down to book size and held together by glue.

The kind of job for which a respectable small-town printer might be responsible.

Coll had spent the whole goddamn day searching for it, and now he had to hurry through dinner to start reading. Afterward, he went upstairs and tried to get into it, but he kept closing his eyes against the headache and waking up twenty minutes later in a panic. This was what he got for just trying to be nice. If he'd known what a morass of fallacies and wild speculations the book actually contained—things that, he suspected, belonged more in the pages of the lesbian pulp novels his sister was still sentimentally hiding under her bed, rather than on any shelf of actual literature—he never would have lied about having read it in the first place. But he *had* lied. And he'd told Louise that he had enjoyed it. He had missed his opportunity to tell the truth: that if Louise was going to just make things up, she should simply go ahead and invent a main character and a town, instead of coming after Anton Vargas. Or, for that matter, anybody who had actually been a real person.

Around nine-thirty, he went downstairs. Freenie was subjecting his parents to some lurid Golden Era film about, as best he could tell, a cursed goblin living in the basement of a hotel, roaming the hallways at night and hovering over sleeping women.

"*Phantom* knockoff," Coll said, settling into an armchair and turning on the little reading lamp.

"You're a fucking *Phantom* knockoff," Freenie said. "This is a classic."

When he woke up again, he was on the couch, by himself, alone in the dark. His whole chest was drenched in sweat. Somebody—who but his mother?—had covered him with the warmest blanket in the room and turned off all the lights. He couldn't see a goddamn thing, save for the wildly flashing screen, on which the classic goblin was continuing to creep around, this time in some sort of cemetery.

His headache had progressed to an uneven throbbing right behind his temples. In addition to this, he had only two feelings. The first was the vague dread of having no idea of the time but knowing there was so much of Louise's book left to read.

The second was the certainty that something was in the house with him.

He knew it was there because he felt observed, and this made him too afraid to move. It was not dissimilar to the feeling he had experienced as a child of being the only one awake, the only one aware of the shadows moving across the bedroom wall, and he had had to whisper, "Freenie. *Freenie!*" so that she would roll over in the top bunk and, in telling him to shut the hell up, shatter both the silence and the solitude of his terror. But Freenie wasn't here—she was all the way upstairs, presumably dreaming about the baby's perfect number of fingers and toes.

He was on his own.

Nothing seemed to be moving in the living room. He could hear the kitchen clock going steadily about its business. He couldn't tell whether the thing in the house with him had just arrived or whether it had been there the whole time he was asleep. The right thing to do would be to turn on the lights. But it was so far to the light switch, and the thing, whatever it was, felt close.

Last fall, a bear had broken into Jim Cutbach's cabin. Jim had been home alone, Noreen having gone to the church to help with the clothing drive. Jim had stepped into the kitchen to start heating the macaroni Noreen had left thawing for him on the counter. The bear stood up on its hind legs when it heard him come in, its face caked in frozen macaroni, and laid him out with one swipe. After it had gnawed on Jim's legs for a spell while he played dead, it let itself out through the back door, never to be seen again. What surprised Jim most, in every accounting of the story, was how silent the whole ordeal had been.

"Hey, bear," Coll whispered, just in case.

Where were the dogs? Why weren't they going crazy?

He had to find his courage now. He couldn't go on lying here so uselessly. He eased the stifling blanket off himself and sat up.

There was nothing behind the couch. Nothing under the coffee table, either. He put his feet down on the carpet and paused for a moment to make sure he hadn't been heard. Then he stood up.

There was nothing behind the armchairs. Nothing in the weird darkness that accumulated around the little old woodstove in the corner.

But there *was* something in the kitchen. It was faint, but he could hear it moving around in there. He was right by the woodstove—he should bring a poker with him, just in case. A ridiculous thing to do, but possibly life-saving. He tried to lift it off its hook, but the metal groaned, so he gave up and inched over to the kitchen doorway.

He could hear the dogs now. They were under the table, growling deep in their chests. Blue light was high-beaming into the kitchen from around the curtains. It looked like a car was sitting just outside the window, blasting its brights into the room, though he couldn't hear an engine running. In fact, he couldn't hear anything at all.

But he *could* see the outline of a person sitting at the kitchen table.

"Hey!" he said, and the person turned.

It was Bob Fournier.

"*Jesus.*" Coll lurched to the doorframe to steady himself.

"Coll." Bob grabbed his chest. "You scared the shit out of me."

"I scared the shit out of *you*? What the hell are you doing here?"

"I'm just out of the hospital."

"But you don't live here, Bob, you live at *your* house."

He should have known it was a dream. Parts of it were certainly beginning to feel like one: the bright light, the rumbling of the unseen dogs. The fact that he couldn't feel any part of his own body except for the crushing pressure of his headache—intermittent now, and entirely without pattern, so that it was a surprise every time it returned. A sudden pickax, right behind one eye.

"I didn't say I was *home* from the hospital," said Bob. "I said I was out. Pay attention."

Coll took the chair opposite him. He tried to find the dogs with his feet, whether to reassure them or himself, he wasn't sure, but they were out of reach. He could hear them down there, going on as if he hadn't entered the room at all, as if he weren't here to protect them.

"What's the matter with them?" Bob asked, jerking his head to indicate the darkness under the table.

"You scared them."

"Is it the way I look?" Bob scratched his arms. "Estelle says I look off."

He was right about that. He seemed older, somehow. In the pale blue light, his face was marked by new wrinkles, deep as the gouges in a woodcut. His lips were cracked, and little lines of blood were beginning to emerge on them, as if he hadn't had a drop of water in about a week.

"Maybe you're dehydrated," Coll said.

"I feel fine. Just a little itchy."

"I'm going to get you a drink." He filled a glass with water and brought it back and pushed it across the table to Bob. "Do you want some food? You look like you're wasting away."

"That's what they called it," Bob said.

"Who?"

"At the hospital. Wasting disease."

"What's that?"

Bob gestured at his face. "Whatever this is, I guess."

Coll sat back. "Are you—are you supposed to be out, among people?"

"Sure."

"Are you contagious?"

"They didn't say."

"So you're fine now?"

"I think so. I was feeling real bad for a while. Like, crazy for a while. I don't remember much. They had to tie me down."

Coll was shamefully aware that he was tracking Bob's movements, marking everything he touched. The edge of the table. The sides of the chair. The water glass, though he still hadn't drunk from it. Plus all the scratching, the flakes of his skin coming off in little backlit puffs whenever his nails bit into his forearms. The unkindness of this impulse, Coll would deal with that later. Right now it felt important to contain whatever it was this dream Bob had brought into the house.

"Why did you come here?"

"Estelle brought me."

"Oh." He paused. "Is she . . . waiting outside?"

"I think so."

"Does she want to come in?"

Coll opened the back door. The driveway was empty. Above the dark line of the cottonwoods, the night sky was clear and throbbing with stars. Bob came and stood beside him, and Coll stepped back to give him room.

"Where's your car, Bob?"

"It must be at the top of the drive."

"But that's just the street. Hey! Where are you going?"

He watched Bob head up the driveway in the absolute darkness of the world. Once the trees had him, he was gone, reduced to the scraping of boots on gravel. After a time, even that faded. Coll called out once, "Bob? Estelle?" but received no answer.

When he got back inside the house, the feeling that had filled it was gone.

Coll scrubbed his hands in the kitchen sink. He had to move quietly—he could only imagine his mother's reaction if she came downstairs and saw him spraying down the door handle and the chair Bob had been sitting in with bleach. He wrapped the glass Bob had touched in a kitchen towel and shoved it deep into the trash can. Then he knelt down to try to get the dogs out from under the table. They hadn't moved, and they wouldn't stop growling.

Louise was already there when he pulled into the Gold Dust Diner's parking lot the following morning. She was sitting on the little bench outside, wearing jeans and boots and a thin black coat. She didn't look entirely like she was playacting in a western—but something about the sharpness of her boot toes and the fit of the coat tilted at that idea ever so slightly, and it compounded the vague indignation that her so-called book had left him feeling.

She informed him that she had felt so energized she had walked all the way from the motel, bright and early, passing the little shuttered shops along First Street, so she could enjoy the quiet. "These high plains mornings," she said. "My gosh."

"You want a coffee?" Coll asked.

"They're not open."

Of course. It was Monday. How stupid of him to forget. He peered through the glass dejectedly.

"We'll get something on the way," he said, knowing full well that there was only the Big Chief gas station between here and the turnoff for Hemot.

He expected Louise to be all chatter, but she just sat quietly beside him, looking out the window. They drove north out of Salt Draw, past the last stoplight, past the Mormon temple, past the gardening center where Mrs. Reynolds was just opening up, laying out the last few pots of her fat marigolds.

"How beautiful," Louise said.

It *was* beautiful. This was one of the great things about city people—they always marveled at the things you took for granted. They were also repulsed by some of them, thought they should be different without asking the why of anything.

Was she waiting for him to say something about the book? Probably. He couldn't tell. She didn't seem agitated. In her lap, her hands were still. He didn't know where to begin, or how ugly all this had the potential to get.

"So I read through the book again last night," he lied. "Because it had been so long since my first read, and I wasn't sure if I remembered everything."

"That's so above and beyond," she said. "You didn't have to do that."

"No, no. I mean, here we are." She was looking at him. He didn't want to turn his head to meet her gaze. "Is it the first thing you've ever written?"

Out of the corner of his eye, he saw her whole body sink a little. "Ah," she said. "The reread didn't go well."

"What? That's not true at all!"

"Does it seem like the first thing I've ever written?"

"No, ma'am. Just wondering. I don't know much about creative writing. My father teaches literature, though. At the high school." They passed the sign for the outdoor survival workshop. "I didn't know it would be an offensive question."

"I've written other books, but they went nowhere."

That was good. At least the feeling wouldn't be new to her. "How did you pick Anton Vargas and Sunrise, of all things?"

"Well, funnily enough, it's a story that was in my attic my whole life, and I never even knew it was there."

"Your attic?"

She took off her coat in the way of somebody gearing up for a long story. "A few years ago, my nana asked me to help her clear out my grandfather's stuff. He was much older than her, and he'd worked as a newspaperman, and then in the civil service. The attic was just full of his papers and boxes and books, old stuff, you know, stuff she couldn't even see to read anymore. She wanted me to throw out the things that didn't matter and, you know, find a way to preserve the rest."

"That's a hell of a task."

"It took almost a year. And it turned out that my grandfather, among other things, was one of the volunteers for the Wyoming Posterity Project. You know, he went around the state, interviewing people about their lives. And one of them was—are you ready?—Fred Kipley."

"Are you serious?" She was grinning broadly at him and nodding. "Fred Kipley? *Frederick Kipley,* of Kipley County?"

"Isn't that incredible?"

"I mean—that's so strange, I've never heard of a WPP interview with Frederick Kipley. Why was it in your grandfather's attic?"

"I dug around a little to figure that out, and what must have happened is, the funding was cut right around the time he made it. So I think he just took the reel home and forgot about it."

"Wow."

"And, of course, I didn't know Anton Vargas from Anton Chekhov—but then I looked him up, and, you know, it's so interesting to read about these local heroes—"

"Well, I would say *regional* hero . . ."

"—these, you know, exhibitionists-cum-lawmen. I just became obsessed. And it was such an incredible contrast between what's been written about him and what Kipley says in the recording. And, of course, none of the rest of the materials have the benefit of the recording, so it makes sense that they're a bit skewed. But it did feel a little like bursting in on a piece of history with a hammer, you know?"

That sounded about right. "I would love to hear it sometime."

"*Well.*" She winked knowingly and started unzipping her satchel. He listened to her rummaging around. A moment later, she rested a cassette on the dashboard between them.

"No way," said Coll.

"Is now the right time?" she asked.

[Crackling, throat clearing.]

—Recording commenced by myself, Lars Hawley, here at 603 Little Wolf Road, in Denver, Colorado, on this date of November 19, 1936. Can we begin with your name, please, sir?

—I'm Frederick Kipley. Murrow is my middle name. [Long pause.]

—Deputy U.S. marshal.

—That's right. Retired.

—Please tell me about yourself.

—Well, I was a citizen of Sunrise from pretty much its founding until the Lavinia mine closed. I live in Denver now. My wife is a photographer for the land survey. We have two daughters . . .

—Forgive me, Mr. Kipley, I meant your accomplishments.

—My accomplishments?

—Yes. I believe you started out a newspaperman. At the Santa Rosa Herald*?*

—That's right. Did a stint at the Telegraph*, up in Ershel, for a time. And after that I went to work for the* Sunrise Gazette.

—Which you then inherited from Bartholomew Daggins . . .

—Barty.

— . . . twelve years later. Please go on.

—Well, as I said, we live in Denver now, which has several very fine newspapers. Our daughters are here as well. We got seven grandchildren, and an eighth on the way—

—I'm sorry, sir—I meant, please go on with your accomplishments.

—I see. Well, I was deputy marshal of Sunrise, like you said. I was also fire marshal for a time. I directed the commission for health and peacekeeping.

—And you served as mayor.

—Later on, yes. Briefly.

—When did you become the namesake of the county?

—Just a few years ago.

—That must have been a great honor.

—It was. [Long pause.]

—Forgive me, but you seem a little reticent.

—I guess speaking on myself don't come easy to me. I'd rather speak on my friends.

—Then please do that, sir, and maybe we'll get round to yourself in due course.

—That sounds fine. [Long pause.]

—When you say "friends," do you mean the company referred to as the Greyrock Four?

—Sure.

—What can you tell me about them?

—You know, when you read the Greyrock *dime novels—and forgive me, it's been a while, but—*

—I actually have a copy of An Incident at Greyrock *right here for you.*

—Imagine that.

—Figured you might like to see it.

—Thank you. [Paper rustling.] Ha. I'd forgotten this. [Long pause, papers rustling; a throat clears.] See here? This wording makes it seem like we were running together for a real long time, Preacher and Anton and me. But what always struck me—what moves me still when I think back on them days—is that we were three complete strangers, four once Sadie came along, thrown together into this crucible by chance.

—You hadn't been previously acquainted?

—God, no. Preacher picked Anton up at some carnival, I guess, where he was dying of a rotted tooth. Basically kidnapped him and brought him up to Eula to deliver freight. And I was stuck in Eula already, passing through on my way home to Ershel, and they picked me *up when we got the telegram from Greyrock.*

—And Miss Wilkins?

—I guess Sadie had been on her way to Eula when her stage stalled out in the storm. They stopped at Greyrock to wait it out, and then the Salt Draw gang fell in on them. Now, again, what you haven't read was what happened before *the three of us got there. See, Sadie had been living in Denver with her pa, and she'd had some learning as a typist and a telegraph operator. She knew her dits and dahs. So when the Salt Draw gang came in and blew that poor old Swede stationmaster to bits, and realized the storehouse was empty, they were raging because there was nobody alive to send the telegram and lure us into the trap. But then Sadie thought fast, and she told them, "I can do it, I can send the telegram." And in the moment of transmission, she decided to type "Splitrock" instead of "Greyrock," hoping*

to tip us off that something was amiss. Took a huge risk, counting on nobody to notice that she was doing that, and on us to realize it.

—I guess it paid off.

—It certainly did.

—I'd be worried it wouldn't work. Wouldn't catch it myself in a thousand years, sir, if I'm honest.

—Well, that was Sadie. That was her way.

—Can you tell me about her?

—Sure. [Long pause.] You know they used to say in Sunrise that you could always tell a full moon was coming because Sadie was out doing something she shouldn't be doing with someone she shouldn't be doing it with. That was her way, too. She wasn't over-beautiful, which I guess is evidence of God's thoughtful moderation. But she was a charming woman. Heart like a lion. Very smart. Could make you laugh.

—It sounds like you were well acquainted.

—Not as well acquainted as she was with Anton. I mostly kept an eye on her. Every now and again she'd pick the wrong kind of man to keep her company, and that man would get some notion about how she should behave, and then I'd have to show him the way out of town.

—She took part in the Greyrock shooting exhibitions?

—Oh yes. She was a real ham, Sadie. Shooting. Hollering. The crowds adored her almost as much as they did Anton. And she didn't mind reliving it.

—Did you?

—Well, I lost hearing in my left ear during the Greyrock fight. Couldn't ever feel anything in the last three fingers of my right hand again. There were long periods, even years afterward, when I couldn't get to sleep at all. So yes, I did mind. Preacher did, too.

—You mean Doctor Maclean.

—That's right.

—Why did he mind?

—Preacher had some learning as a priest before he became a doctor, and with it came a very particular way of thinking about things. He understood the purpose of those exhibitions, especially after the town began to prosper.

He understood what we were there to do. We were meant to help cast this spell: that we were bringing order and goodness to a place which had never known either. That we were the appropriate keepers of that land. That our unlikely victory in the Greyrock shootout was evidence of the fated glory of the camp and, therefore, the town and, therefore, the nation. You see? Preacher didn't like that. He didn't care for glory. And he didn't care for nation. And he especially *abhorred our two-faced dealings with the Cheyenne, given what the government just put them through, dragging them down to Oklahoma to starve, and then setting the whole damn army on them, man, woman, and child, when they broke free for home.*

—Did you agree with him?

—On principle. But I'd been raised to believe that rage and vengeance serve no purpose. That any amendment to the way people feel about other people ought be pursued through neighborliness and Christian living. I've seen some things since then, and I feel quite differently now.

—Differently? How?

—I should have been throwing dynamite through windows with Preacher. Whether it did any good or not. But my mother was still living, you see.

—Would she have objected?

— [Laughter.] Lord, yes.

—But wasn't she Indian?

—That's right. Shoshone.

—Would you care to speak on her?

—Well, now. Should I? I don't know. [Creaking of chair.] She was a girl when she was sent off to live with my father, who I guess was old French, from the north. He'd had some friendly dealings with her people and was trapping at that time along the Three Forks up in Montana.

—Is that where you were born?

—I believe so. Two more children came after me, but we had a very harsh winter, and I was the only one left. My father was troubled by drink. He died a few years later in a manner suited to his predilections.

—Oh, goodness. [Nervous laughter.]

—Is something funny?

—No, sir. I thought . . . I was just . . . imagining what manner of death you could possibly mean.

—What were you imagining?

—I don't know, sir. Something related to his trouble with drink, I guess.

—Such as?

—I really couldn't say. Maybe a fall down a ravine.

—What else?

—Nothing, sir. Nothing.

—What if I told you my mother killed him with a piece of his own trap wire?

—What?

—That's right. Damn near sawed his head off, strangling him on the kitchen floor.

—Dear God . . .

—I'm only having fun with you, son.

—Oh!

—His liver failed.

—Is that . . . is that *true?*

—Of course it is. Don't worry about it. Go on there with your questions. What else have you got for me in your little notebook?

—I don't know, sir. I had no plans to ask about your mother. [Prolonged throat clearing and shuffling of papers.] After your father's . . . death, did she return to her people?

—No—by then her band had been summoned to the new agency, but they refused to go. She had a dark feeling about their prospects. So she took the name Mary Kipley, and had us both baptized to Christ, and kept us living in that little house, unnoticed as we could go, until she had enough money to apprentice me to the newspaperman.

—Where'd the money come from, if not your father?

—My mother had a buffalo herd.

—Oh!

—See, on the rare occasion he was sober, my father would take odd jobs. One of them was buffalo hunting for the railroad. I'd seen it done once or twice—and let me tell you, once or twice was enough. You can't imagine the

smell of that meat sitting out in the sun. Sometimes, the orphaned calves, if they were young enough, would grow confused and follow the hunters home. That's how we ended up with a bison calf, a little bull. My mother took to it and raised it up. Kept it in the back pen with the goats and the donkey. After we buried my father, she bought a few yearling bison cows from our neighbor and started her own herd. When the government finally threw up their hands in despair over what had happened to all the herds, they came to her, and folks like Bill Cody, to help revive them.

—She sounds a very steadfast person.

—She was. And a woman of profound faith. She and Preacher used to sit around and ramble about Scripture together into the wee hours. She adored him.

—I'm surprised to hear that. Wasn't Dr. Maclean arrested for an unprovoked attack on Fort Searles?

—It would be more accurate to say that he was pursued.

—But never captured.

—That's right.

—Were you with the party that tracked him?

—No. I was a year or two from lawkeeping yet. But Preacher was very beloved in that country—you couldn't throw a rock without hitting a household willing to hide him, whites and mestizos alike. We let his Wanted posters get papered over. Forgot to tell new arrivals to keep an eye out for him. That kind of thing.

—Do you have any idea what became of him?

—None whatsoever.

—Were there rumors, whispers?

—There are always rumors and whispers.

—But nothing came of them.

—No.

—So he disappeared, Anton Vargas left, and you became a lawman.

—Mostly in name. Just about everyone was deputy something or other in them days. Sunrise was so far from anywhere, it'd take a week or more for the law to reach us. So whenever the actual marshal was in town, he'd

round up those of us who hadn't yet seen the inside of a jail cell and deputize us all together, just so he wouldn't have to be running back and forth all the damn time.

—Was that how Mr. Vargas was deputized?

—I don't know. He led a big life away from Sunrise. All kinds of people deputized him for all kinds of things.

—Tell me about Mr. Vargas.

—You've waited so patiently.

—Sir?

—No, no, really. You haven't hurried me along at all. You haven't tried to turn the conversation toward him. Don't think your restraint went unnoticed.

—I really did want to hear about everyone.

—But now, at last, we've come to Anton. What do you want to know?

— [Nervous laughter.] How did he compare to the dime novels?

—He wasn't as handsome as they made him out to be.

— [Laughter continues.] Was he at least as charming?

—He made himself that way. Wasn't born a gallant, but wanted very much to live up to it.

—Did he succeed?

—How should I know?

—Well, did you *admire him, Mr. Kipley?*

—I had some kinship with him. He grew up not too different than I did. A stranger to where he came from, and to his people's language. I admired his stubbornness. He didn't like to admit when he didn't know something or when something was new to him. So he was always volunteering for things he wasn't suited to.

—What kind of things?

—Well, being a dime-novel hero, for one thing. When I met him, he couldn't ride for shit. Hated crowds. He'd hardly ever fired a gun. But that didn't stop him following Preacher and me straight into a firefight. See, when Anton volunteered for things, it forced him to overcome the not-knowing—so he could eventually make himself suited to just about any-

thing. He had his faults, though. Looked out for himself. Always. Always above all else. It drove Preacher crazy.

—I heard that they were sometimes at odds.

—Sure. Preacher used to say, "Between us, Anton and I could just about make up one person of any use. If he had my convictions or I had his sense of self-regard, we could really get some good done."

—Is it true that Mr. Vargas returned to Sunrise shortly before he was killed?

—That's right.

—What do you recall about his return?

—I recall feeling very old. Now that I am old, of course, I think on how foolish that was. But it had been twenty years since I'd laid eyes on him. In them days, people would go off, and you'd likely never see them again. There'd be letters once in a while. Or news from mutual acquaintances. But with Anton, the news was constant. I'll admit I was responsible for some of it. I had a paper to run, and he was a big name. Riding with this outfit, with that one. Lawman. Range detective. Sometimes you'd hear so much about him, you couldn't help but suspect he must be in three or four places at once. It made you feel that you were living a bit of some other life alongside him.

—Because of your kinship.

—I just mean—anything that involved one of us Greyrock Four always involved the other three. We were just that way. When Anton died—well, let's say, nobody wants to find himself the last man standing among comrades.

—Did you see him, after he died?

—I was the one that found him.

—Much was made of the circumstances of discovery. The bullet in his right shoulder, indicating that he was shot from behind but probably not killed. The preserved arrow he was carrying in his pocket. The second bullet in his head.

—You're going to ask me if I think he killed himself.

—Do you?

—I don't know. Maybe. Anton was very sick when he came home. As I recall, he wasn't given very long to settle his affairs. He was helping me with the case of a boy who had gone missing, one of the Abadie children from Burnt Creek. But his own priority was to find Preacher before the end.

—Really! For what reason?

—To reconcile, I imagine. Or at least to atone for what happened between them.

—[Long pause.] Obviously, I have to ask what happened between them.

—Do you?

—You're having fun with me again, sir.

—Am I? [Long pause.] You're all right, Lars. Don't be so nervous. I am *having fun with you. [Shuffling in chair.] As I understand it, Anton was meant to take part in Preacher's assault on Fort Searles way back when.*

—Goodness! Is that true?

—But at the last minute, he changed his mind.

—Why?

—Couldn't tell you. We never did discuss it.

— [Long pause.] Well, did *he find Dr. Maclean?*

—I don't think so.

—I just wonder . . . given the circumstances . . . perhaps he did, and their reunion went poorly?

—What do you mean?

—Perhaps it was Dr. Maclean who killed him.

—I doubt that. I doubt that very much.

—But weren't they, in essence, enemies?

—There was more to it than that.

—More—how?

—More. You can always tell when there's more between people. Even when they don't admit it.

—I'm not sure I understand what you mean.

—Yes, you do.

— [Long pause and shuffling of papers.]

The tape clicked and whirred. In the passenger seat, Louise was smiling so broadly Coll could see her big bleached premolars even without turning his head. And thank God, too—he didn't *want* to turn his head. Everything from his scalp down to his shoulders felt like it was on fire.

"Isn't that incredible?" she said.

"I'm speechless."

He really was. What a mistake he'd made, agreeing to listen to it with her right away. He should've asked to be allowed to hear it for the first time in private. That way, he could have taken his time with what Fred Kipley—or, rather, the *alleged* Fred Kipley—had to say. Instead, here he was, trying to figure out where to even begin with this barrage of new and absurd information, while some gloating woman, a complete stranger, studied his reaction.

"I feel like I really would have liked Kipley," Louise was saying. "He seems so clear-eyed about everything. He's what, over eighty years old at the time of this interview? And all his stories are still so vivid."

"I guess he's been reliving them over and over," Coll said. "Telling them to himself. Trying to figure out how everything really happened."

"He fills in a lot of the gaps."

"I wonder if there's a way to authenticate it," Coll said. He realized immediately that this was a thought he should have kept to himself.

"Why?"

"That's just the next step."

"Is it? I didn't realize. How does that work?"

"I'm guessing you have the original reel-to-reel?"

"Of course."

"Well," he said, "you make a few copies of the recording. And then you give the original reel-to-reel, as well as the tape you made, to experts who can date it, and who can stack it up against other interviews Kipley may have done to check facts and dates and the consistency of his voice. That kind of thing."

"I thought you said there weren't any other Kipley interviews?"

"Well, none that I know of."

"These experts," she said, turning toward him pointedly. "Any idea where I might find them?"

"You're in luck." He gave her a big, hammed-up wink. "You, at this very moment, are sitting next to the head of the Salt Draw Historical Society. And I speak for all of us when I assure you that we would be *delighted* to review your submission and pass it on to the appropriate bodies."

"You're not one of those historical societies that disappears records that don't corroborate your preexisting assumptions, are you?"

"Only when it comes to mining claims." It hurt to grin so widely for so long. "I'm joking."

They went on for a while in silence. Then Louise said, "I'm sorry, I should have given it to you to listen to at home."

"Not at all! Why?"

"It's a lot to process."

"There's no processing," he said. "I'm a student of history. If I can't appreciate an out-of-left-field recording that screws with what I know, who can?"

She turned to him with a pleasant smile. "What does it screw with?"

Where to start? "I just think it's so interesting," he said at last. "That Kipley says he lost hearing in his left ear."

"Oh," she said.

"That's the kind of fun little detail that can get buried under dense history. It would just never come up in any scenario other than an interview like this."

"I see."

"*Fascinating.*" He drove on for a little while, then glanced over at her. "Don't read too much into the authentication thing—it's just part of the process. An annoying, laborious, but very important part of the process."

"Do you want a protein bar?"

"No. Thanks."

He listened to her rummaging around in her satchel.

He was so agitated that he failed to register the slow-moving sedan on the shoulder with the little flag sticking out the driver's window. The sound of its horn blared after him, and while he was looking in the rearview, Louise shouted, "Watch out!"

The huge black asses of a line of steers had materialized in the lane before him. He hit the brakes, the truck fishtailed a little. Louise slammed both hands on the dashboard. "Sorry about that!" he said. "Roundups all over the place."

"Roundups," Louise said, with amazement.

They eased along beside the herd, passing one cowboy, then another. Ahead of them, a mottled, short-legged dog flew in and out among the cattle's legs. After a while, the road rose up, and they were in red rock country, sweeping through turns as wide and languorous as rivers. At the top of a switchback, Louise exclaimed again, and he was forced to pull over so she could gaze down at Crimson Canyon.

"It won't show up," he told her when she took out her camera. "Not the way it looks in real life."

Why didn't she know that? She should know that, if she was writing about this place. If she was writing about Anton Vargas.

They passed the sign for the Big Chief Rest Stop, and pulled off at the gas station there. Louise insisted on paying so fervently she damn near body-checked him at the pump when he got out of the car.

"All right," Coll said. "You win. Thank you." He didn't want to go on this tour with a curdled feeling between them. "Do you want some jerky or something?"

"Sure." She smiled and slid her sunglasses onto her chin and squinted at the gas pump console.

At least she wasn't coming inside to make faces at all the fake turquoise and hunting knives, and to be appalled by the Big Chief fortune-teller machine that stood in the back of the store. Yes, the whole thing was kind of crass, the chief sitting there in his full war bonnet, with that mechanical jaw forever opening and closing, and yes, his voice had probably been recorded in the 1950s. But as far as Coll was concerned, you had no right to any opinion about it if you hadn't sat in the back seat as a kid and prayed and prayed that your dad would pull over here and let you out of the car just so you could drop a quarter in the coin slot and snatch Big Chief's ticket out of the dispenser and read it aloud to everyone on the drive to Brecon. It occurred to Coll, as he stood there triggering Big Chief's pan flute intro, that he wouldn't have to argue with Mira about this any more. A small mercy.

He looked up. Louise had wandered in. She was standing with her weight on her back leg, studying a display case beside the cashier. As Coll came up to her, she turned to him with an inscrutable smile.

"What award?" she said.

"Excuse me?"

"What award?"

She gestured to the display case. It was a tall hutch made of some kind of dark unvarnished wood, and its every shelf was laden with pickle jars: carrots, gherkins, swampy eggs that could have been fake dinosaur eyeballs in some gruesome Halloween oddities shop. Across the top of the hutch was a sign with a couple of fake roses stapled to it. The sign read LUTIE'S LOCAL AWARD-WINNING PICKLES.

"And," Louise went on, "does the 'local' apply to the award or to the pickles?"

"The pickles," he said.

She looked at him, and he realized she had obviously been kidding. He'd come off as prickly. He tried to iron it all out. "Let's ask," he said, and leaned toward the cashier. He didn't recognize the guy, and remembered too late that the previous owner, Will Harkee, had left for Utah last spring.

"Hey, man," Coll said. "Who's Lutie, and what award did her pickles win?"

The cashier was a blond, wide-eyed dullard of the variety that drove Coll's father insane. Fourteen at the very most; he'd probably lied about his age on his employment form. He blinked in the direction Coll was pointing. "Huh?"

"The pickles, man. What award did they win?"

The kid considered it. "I guess a pickle award."

"No!" Coll stepped back. "Not an interior design award?"

Louise brushed past his shoulder. "Don't mind him," she said to the kid. "We're just being silly." She slid a medium-sized jar of the eggs onto the counter. "How are these?"

"I don't know," said the kid. "I haven't tried them. I don't like pickles, and I don't like eggs."

"Well, then. I wouldn't try them, either."

She paid for the eggs and the gas and went back outside. Coll picked up some sour cream and onion chips and a bag of Debner's jerky. The throbbing behind his eyes made him certain he wasn't going to be partaking of either. What he really wanted was water and for someone to dim all the lights: the fluorescents, the sun, everything. He would never have been so rude to the kid, not in front of somebody like Louise, if he weren't feeling so terrible. He bought a bottle of water and drank it, standing there in the cool of the convenience store.

When he got outside, Louise was leaning against the car. "I love the smell of the air here."

"What, you don't have diesel in Colorado?"

She tilted her head. "You okay?"

"I think I'm getting a cold."

"Oh, I'm sorry. We can go back."

"No, no." God, the sun. It hurt to smile—hurt his eyes, his teeth. "We're nearly there. You'll love it."

"All right. But only if you're sure. And only if you promise to tell me if you start feeling worse. Okay?"

Louise smiled, and Coll was surprised to find that it revived him. She was humming with excitement. She couldn't wait to get out to that wrecked little place he loved so much. Well, he couldn't wait, either. He hadn't been up in almost a month. He was going to walk her around and talk about the town and the mines and the school and what Anton Vargas had *really* been like, no matter what notions she might have brought here, and not let her unfinished pipe dream of a book, or this little cold of his, get in the way of a nice afternoon. He'd save the ace up his sleeve for the return journey: later on, with his headache defeated and a new, lovely, peaceful understanding between himself and Louise, he would cross the highway at the bottom of the Hemot City turn-off and pull nonchalantly up to Anton Vargas's grave. He could all but picture the astonishment on Louise's face when she squinted at the little tombstone obelisk with the bronze revolvers crossed on top of it and realized what she was actually looking at. She would say, *Oh my gosh, I thought he was buried up at Sunrise?* and Coll would say, *Not since 1995.* And he would tell her how his grandfather, never one to bother with bureaucracy, had moved Anton Vargas down to this roadside spot among the ancient cottonwoods on a whim, all by himself, one weekend when Coll and Freenie were in Denver with their parents. And how, really, history had held very little interest for Coll until he found himself responsible for helping his grandfather maintain the gravesite. There was something meditative, something almost spiritual about cleaning the slab, and gathering wildflowers to put on the grave, year after year, on the anniversary of Vargas's death. Something magical about seeing the occasional passing car pull over and read the plaque and stand there in awe. Every so often, Coll would find offerings—shell casings or figurines or coins—and understand, all over again, that people outside of Kipley County, people not unlike Louise herself, actually knew who Anton Vargas was. And that Coll's responsibility to preserve this knowledge was something sacred. And then Louise would understand, and hug him, and go off home and put all her energy to better use.

"Come on," Louise said. "I have some ChapStick in my bag. Your lips look like they're splitting a little."

By the time they got to the first house of the lower mining complex, Coll had heard the story of her life: daughter, granddaughter, volleyball player, former graduate student at Colorado State. Recently single, and happy about it. She was thinking about applying for a writing program next fall, but to do what there, he couldn't say. She had briefly considered becoming a physical therapist, only she found the pressure of constant communication challenging.

"I like being quiet," Louise said.

She could've fooled Coll. The ibuprofen she had given him had taken the edge off his headache—it was now just a dull thing sitting in the middle of his forehead—but Louise's voice was working hard to resurrect it.

There were some advantages to her already being familiar with the place. When they pulled into town, she jumped out of the car and stood there with a smile that made Coll feel like maybe John Hammond should hobble out of the bushes and welcome her. It was exactly the kind of reaction he always hoped people would have up here. She didn't even seem bothered by the disarray—all the farmyard junk from the various eras of Sunrise's booms and busts that he'd been hauling from house to house, yard to yard, while he tried to figure out what curatorship actually meant in a place like this. "They're all going to end up in displays," he told her. "I just haven't organized everything yet. And be careful in the Lavinia—I'm working on a retrospective of deer mounts, so they're all over the floor."

He stood in the street and watched her disappear into the buildings one by one, unsure of the right balance to strike between being helpful and letting her explore. She would be gone for five, ten minutes and then come bounding out, writing furiously in the margins of a fat binder she had taken out of her satchel.

"What are you looking for?" he asked eventually.

"I don't know," she said. "Just the feel of it, I guess."

The feel of it. He knew what she meant.

"Can I go upstairs?" he heard her yell from inside Sadie's.

"I wouldn't," he shouted back. He often did it himself, but only because he knew the stairs very well. He didn't feel like fishing her out from between them. Nor did he have enough money to repair the damage if she fell through. After the reenactment, maybe he would. If the immersive approach took off and lured people from the surrounding counties.

He searched the car for more water. Louise's Nalgene was sitting in the cupholder, and he took a surreptitious sip. A shitty thing to do, he thought, especially if he was coming down with something. She was a nice, enthusiastic person. Overly forward, yes. Extremely chatty. Utterly wrong about Anton Vargas. But he didn't have to give her the flu. He drank until the bottle was almost empty, then dashed the dregs into the dust. He left the Nalgene cap off so that he would remember to tell her to clean it.

Then he went to look for her. She was sitting in the grass by the river.

"Less of it survived than I would've thought," she said wistfully when he sat down beside her.

He wondered how many ghost towns she'd been to before. "You have to remember, this was good wood, good iron," he said. "People took as much as they could carry when they left. Plus all kinds of things work on old buildings. Time. Gravity. Weather."

"Teenagers," Louise added brightly.

"Normally, yes, but they don't bother coming all the way out here. Nobody does."

Louise surprised him. "You're gonna change that, though," she said, squeezing his hand firmly. He could have wept. Perhaps he had judged her too harshly. He felt a sudden, overwhelming urge to apologize, but she saved him by moving on. "What about the Daisy house?"

"Burned down, I'm afraid."

"And the buffalo jump?"

"That's only ever been a rumor. We've never been able to locate it. If the grants start coming through, we're going to get the university out here to dig around and try to find it." She nodded. "It wouldn't look the way you describe it in the book," he decided to say.

"What do you mean?"

"It wouldn't just be a hole in the ground."

"Well," she said. "I mean, it would. Before excavation. Depending on the circumstances."

"I'm just saying." He studied her face. "Is any of this useful?"

"Very. Thank you."

"Sure. I hope you'll be able to work the truth of what you see here into your book more."

If she heard him, she didn't show it. Or perhaps his light critical touch had been effective, the information absorbed and registered. He should give himself more credit. After all, he'd been working with community theater actors for a long time. He knew how to talk to people about their weaknesses.

"Where did he die?" Louise asked.

"Sorry?"

"Vargas. Where did they find his body?"

"*Oh.*" Coll turned and pointed. "About ten miles that way. There's no road anymore, though. It's just a little dugout in the badlands that Herman Remmick built to get away from the lightning." She looked crestfallen. "But I can show you the stable where we're going to have the audience pass his body," he hurried to say. "It looks a lot like the place where he died."

They walked over to the stable together in the sunshine. He wondered briefly why he had said that. The stable was nothing like the place where Vargas had died. Coll had only seen the actual shack once, the summer his grandfather took him out there, but he could remember it clearly, a tiny little place below a ridge on the open plain. Nothing around it except for an old cedar tree. The roof had come down into it.

He climbed over the stable threshold and held his hand out to help Louise inside. "So this place actually did triple duty," he volunteered. "It was built in 1913 as the main livery, obviously. But it was also the marshal's office slash jailhouse whenever he was in town. And it had a root cellar."

"Kind of like an old-timey fridge," she said.

"Exactly." He kicked the dirt around a bit. "In the immersive experience, this will be the last place the audience passes before they head into the festival tent." He moved to the rear of the stable. "We're going to have a big, dark curtain over the back, like this, to make it look more like the dugout. And whoever plays Vargas is going to be propped up on the floor like this . . ." He sat down and scooted back and slumped against the wall. His head was swimming.

"Okay," she said. "Wow."

"Actually, will you do me a favor? Will you go outside and walk past and see what it looks like from out there? This will help a lot. I haven't had a chance to try it out with anybody."

She went out and vanished briefly. She reappeared moments later, walking by slowly, taking big thumping footsteps.

"Am I just walking by, or do you want me to look inside?"

"Let's try both. See which one is better."

"Okay, here I come, just walking by. You're kind of shadowy back there—I don't see you very well." She leaned against the doorway. The light around her was barbaric. He shielded his eyes. "I think you might need a spotlight or something, to illuminate you. Especially if you're performing during the day."

"That's a good note." He needed to stand, but it was so cool in here. A reprieve for his head. "Anyway," he said. "I think it'll be a big hit."

"It'll be amazing. Maybe I'll drive up for it."

"You should."

He forced himself to his feet.

"So what's your take on Vargas's death going to be?" she asked.

"What do you mean?"

"I mean, are you going to position the actor a certain way so that the arrow in Vargas's pocket is visible? Is the gun that fired the head shot going to be in his hand, if he took his own life? Or not, if you think somebody else killed him?"

"We don't really do that," Coll said.

This was when he realized his cellphone was buzzing in his pocket. It took him by surprise. He couldn't remember the last time he'd gotten signal up here. He flipped the screen open to what was apparently a fourth incoming call from Freenie.

"Is the house on fire?" he asked.

"Coll," she said. "Where the fuck have you been?"

"Up in Sunrise for the day." He gestured an apology to Louise and headed out toward the middle of the street.

"Has Mom called you?" Freenie was asking.

"No. Just you. Over and over and over again."

"Well, sit down."

"What's going on?"

"Are you sitting down?"

"Freenie, please. The dramatics."

"Okay, okay." She took a deep breath. "That piece of shit Bob Fournier is dead."

"Dead?"

"That's right."

He wanted to tell her that it was undignified for a pregnant woman to sound so gleeful about somebody's demise, no matter how awful the person had been. "Who told you?"

"Casey. She had a shift on the ward he was in."

"What happened?"

"I don't know. They just found him in his hospital bed yesterday afternoon."

"Yesterday—afternoon?" A crackle spread through the back of his skull. Yesterday afternoon. "Freenie, that's not possible. I saw him last night. I mean, I think it was a dream, but still—in the dream he felt alive, Freenie, there's no way he was dead."

"—ead." Her voice buzzed and snapped. "—agged and tagged and headed to the funeral home."

"What did he die of? Hello? Freenie!"

He checked the phone. It was back to its home screen, and all the bars had vanished from the top corner.

The headache had expanded to engulf his neck, too, and his upper shoulders. He'd heard about things like this—stress headaches that could pulverize your brain—but had never experienced one himself. He wondered if he was having an aneurysm. Maybe he should tell Louise, ask her to drive him to the hospital. She was standing by the Lavinia, looking out into the distance, at the dry sage flats and the blue iron sky, as if she were in a dream, and he was filled with so much confusion and rage and despair.

Had anyone besides him and Bob been stupid enough to touch the wolf that night? Of course not. The others were all hunters. They knew better. They had no need to prove anything by touching it. And, predictably, none of them had seen fit to warn him against it.

"Everything okay?" Louise said when he reached her.

"Just this headache."

"Still?" She squinted at him. "You don't look so good, Coll. Maybe we should head back."

"We will," he said. "We can take another minute. I'm all right."

What was he doing? She was giving him a chance to get out of it, and now here he was, committing further. Maybe he felt that rushing back to Salt Draw would be some kind of admission.

Some acknowledgment of fear that his headache was not, in fact, the flu.

Of course it was the flu. Of course it was. Even if the wolf had played some part in Bob's demise, Coll and Bob were not on equal footing where resistance to infection was concerned. Bob was old. Ancient, really. Bob had eaten red meat and smoked two packs a day all his life. Bob had been fifty-two when he'd had his first heart attack, on the floor of the Obsidian Casino, and had notoriously refused an ambulance in favor of driving himself to the hospital. He'd survived two more heart attacks since and had passed a kidney stone last year that was rumored to have been the size of a dime. He had spent his whole long, misery-inducing existence making himself vulnerable to whatever that wolf may have been carrying. No wonder he'd gotten sick.

Coll shook his head to clear his vision and tried a smile. "What were we talking about?"

"I was asking about how you plan on portraying Vargas's death. And you were saying that you don't really 'do that' here."

"Right."

"But I didn't really understand what it is you don't do."

"We don't make guesses about how he died. We want to make sure that the scenes we portray *really* happened."

Some kind of baffling thought flashed through her. He watched her try to contain it. "Well, he didn't *really* die in the stable, right? But that's what you'll be showing."

"Okay, but the stable itself is real. It was here during Vargas's time."

"It wasn't, though." She tilted her head slightly. "You said it went up in 1913. Vargas died in 1902. He never set eyes on it."

"But people who knew him did."

"So your litmus test for inclusion is: connection to people who knew him."

"There's no litmus test."

"And I just played you a recording of somebody who knew him, detailing facts you didn't previously know. So I'm just curious about why none of the Kipley recording gets to be part of the reality you're portraying here."

"Well, maybe it will, eventually. Once we authenticate it."

Why was he explaining himself to her? She was a stranger. A tourist. He had taken the time to go through her ridiculous book and was now in the midst of doing her yet another favor, bringing her up here, during what little free time he had, despite feeling worse than he'd probably ever felt in his life, and she didn't even have the manners to say "thank you" before subjecting him to an inquest on how he was choosing to structure an event he'd been in charge of for years. Years. Something that stood at the very center of his life. Something that he was working fastidiously to make part of the town's life, too.

And now she had the nerve to go on standing beside him with this expression of utmost dejection, as if he'd wounded her so very deeply.

"I worry that you don't think the recording *is* authentic," she said. "Or maybe you don't *want* it to be."

"That's ridiculous," said Coll. "Why wouldn't I want it to be?"

She shrugged.

"I'm a *historian,*" he went on. "It's not my place to *want* things to be true."

She squinted at him. "Everything you present here is something you *want* to be true."

"That's a very simplistic way of putting it." He forced himself to slow down and take a breath. "By that logic, everything in your book is something *you* want to be true."

"There's nothing in the book that I'd mind being true," she said. "Plus, I worked off the recording. And you're working off dime novels and a script that was written over a hundred years ago."

"And pictures, and interviews, and tons and tons of archival material collected over Vargas's lifetime."

"Most of which was intended to make him look good." She was speaking so slowly. "I have access to that material, too, you know. It's fluff. The only place I've ever caught so much as a whiff of the actual *person* Vargas might have been is the Kipley interview."

"How convenient for you." He smoothed out the gravel in front of him with the tip of his work boot. She was giving him the kind of silence he could tell he would have to break first. "We don't make assumptions about Vargas's death, or about parts of his life we can't access. It's enough for us to know that he died here, close to home, and just accept the fact that we may never learn the whole story."

"But aren't you curious? He was dying. He was on bad terms with Preacher. Don't you *want* to know what happened?"

"Sure. But just because I want to know doesn't mean I'm going to chase every explanation until I've made one up."

Now she was gazing at him almost pityingly. As if all this wrong-headedness of his was about to bring her to tears. "But when new information comes along and you ignore it, it's the old information that becomes made-up."

"New information? What, ten unverifiable minutes of some old man who claims to be Fred Kipley rambling about his mother and saying that—what?—Preacher had a moral compass, but Vargas was just some self-serving coward who sucked cock and fell upward into fame?"

She went deadly quiet. "So that's the problem."

"What is?"

"Him and Preacher."

"No," he said. "No, no. Personally? I don't care about it. At *all*." Except for the absurdity of it, of course, the insane notion that his audience could be brought around to it. Even if it was true, and Louise had somehow correctly interpreted this alleged Kipley's insinuations at the end of the recording she had just dropped into his life, what exactly did she expect Coll to do with the information? Was he supposed to write a brand-new scene into the reenactment, forcing some sort of quiet, hand-holding moment between himself and whoever ended up playing Preacher? How about a big musical number in the moonlight—would that make her happy? Would it be an adequate stand-in for the raunchy parts of her book? If that's what she was thinking, she was welcome to try fundraising for next year's performance herself. See how much cash she could get out of the parishioners of the First Baptist Church of Salt Draw once they'd seen Coll's leading men grabbing each other's asses onstage. The whole project would be put to death in the Letters to the Editor section of the *Gazette* immediately. Try going around town as "Baby Vargas" after a debacle like that.

Louise didn't have the sense to stay quiet for long. "I really don't mean to upset you."

"Don't patronize me." He was struggling to articulate the feeling that was tightening his chest. To separate it from the miserable lancing of his headache. "You're misunderstanding me on purpose. We have this *small thing,* you know. This small thing. This tiny part of history that belongs to us. And I don't want it to be fucked with or misrepresented by someone who, frankly, doesn't understand it or care about it."

"But I do care about it."

"Sure." He tried to take a deep breath. "But not. You know."

"Not like you do."

"I just mean that you care about it in a kind of abstract way. You found it in an attic. Good for you. I've grown up with it. Everybody here has. Anton Vargas, he's *our* guy."

"Of course."

"So—maybe leave him to us. You know? Just leave him alone."

"When you say 'leave him alone,' do you mean stop asking about the reenactment or stop writing about him?"

"I don't know," he said. "Both."

"That doesn't seem fair."

"You can do what you like, obviously," he said. Did he mean that? He wasn't even sure. Everything was quite scrambled.

She folded her arms across her chest and looked off into the distance. He could tell she was searching for a way to change tack, to restore the rapport they'd had when they first arrived here. How long ago that seemed.

"Look," she finally said. "I know you love your town—"

"Stop." He hadn't meant to hold up a hand so close to her face, but the headache was disrupting his depth perception. And his point still stood. "I don't love my town. You don't know anything. Anything. *At all.* You don't—" The little step back she took was so offensive it made him dizzy. He was just trying to make her understand the totality, the outrage, of her ignorance. "Jesus. You don't even know that the fucking canyon *won't show up* in the picture!"

AN INCIDENT IN THE WARRENS ON THE OCCASION OF A REUNION

1902

"Sunrise"

by LT Hawley

Part II

Vargas had meant to rest only for a short while, but when he woke up, it was dark outside.

He stayed on his back, waiting for feeling to return to his extremities. How distant he felt from himself. The only thing close to him was the knowledge of the wasted day. He had tired himself out talking to the bucktoothed kid who had overwhelmed him with all the pamphlets. And for what? The chance to recount a few old stories to a worryingly fascinated stranger?

At least he had woken up with that sense of elation that sometimes accompanied his dreams about the past. The sense that he was eighteen, a little besotted with Sadie, already half in love with Preacher. He lay in bed now, as he had in previous years, feeling their presence in the room with him. Recently, he had come to believe that the subjects of his thoughts must be aware that they were on his mind. How could they not be? The feelings in him were so strong. As though, in unconsciousness, he had disturbed the surface of some pond that existed in them all. This was how he had known that Sadie must be dead. It was how Preacher surely knew he was here. Had known that Vargas was coming.

He took a deep breath. The place smelled as it always had.

Maybe Maura was laundering the sheets exactly as her aunt had done. Same soap and all.

He got up and went downstairs in his socks. The front desk was vacant. So this, then, was when the little night-owl niece retired. For a moment, he took in the blue stillness of the hotel. Then he went into the kitchen. There was an old cuckoo clock hanging among the pictures and newspapers on the wall. He had to come right up to see it: it was a quarter to two in the morning. He had slept for almost eight hours.

It frightened him, this persistent need for rest so close to the end. The specialist had told him he must obey it. "What for?" Vargas had asked. Soon he would do nothing *but* rest. If, indeed, he was going to the place of rest. There were plenty of reasons to think he might not be. A couple of grave markers in Nebraska and Montana whose cattle-thieving occupants he had interred with probably less cause than he had laid claim to in court. Plus some criminally bad stage performances he had given over the years.

And the buggery, of course.

Not to mention the thing he was here to atone for.

Anyway, it was all in the letter.

He wished he could remember what he had said to his little bucktoothed admirer. He could tell, just from the feeling shimmering around inside him, that he had gotten maudlin, and possibly revealed too much. That he had talked about things he should not have. Or, rather, that he had talked about things that made *him* wistful, but that other people didn't really care to know.

This had always been a problem, this gulf between what he knew and loved about his friends and what people actually wanted to know about them. People didn't really care that Sadie sometimes dabbled in magic, collecting chicken feathers and animal bones as keepsakes. Or that Kipley's mother had converted to Christ, and that Kipley felt it would be an unforgivable betrayal of her if he were to ally himself more closely with the part of him that was Indian. People's curiosity about Preacher ended with the origins of his nickname: yes, he had studied to be a priest before he got to be a doctor; but when he left the robes, the pontificating came along with him. People didn't care that Preacher read prodigiously. That he liked a card game. That he was an artful physician. That he balked at what he termed the stand-back-with-your-hands-on-your-hips ministering, both medical and spiritual, that had cost so many lives on the frontier. That he did not believe in the delineations of importance that divided physicians and surgeons, because according to Preacher, you couldn't hope to excel in one field without having attained success in the other. People didn't care that his patients adored him. That he was lithe and quick and funny. Intensely private, so that you only knew what he was thinking if he wanted you to, unless you were close enough to him to guess. Even the things he enjoyed, he preferred to do alone. Other men laughed; Preacher smiled wickedly, unhurriedly, even when he found something hilarious. Other men crowded the piano when they were drunk; Preacher got mawkish and sang Irish coffin-ship dirges by himself in the corner until bystanders suspended their merrymaking and wept. He was suspicious of all things occult, not because he didn't believe in the divine but because he believed so intensely in the abusive nature of anyone who claimed to speak for it. He wasn't afraid of a goddamn thing. You felt it off him, and it made you braver.

"I can see why you don't like to let people hear you talk about him," Sadie had told Vargas once. Probably right here, in this kitchen through which he was now rummaging, an old man in search of the makings of a sandwich. Or maybe upstairs, some unclear night back when they were young and drunk and Sunrise was just booming.

Each of them had managed to get some foothold in the community that probably would not have been available to them had they been anyone but the Greyrock Four. Vargas had managed to persuade the Lavinia's owner to sell it to him for a reasonable price. Preacher, an encouraging but hands-off backer in this enterprise, had started ministering to the sick, both in town and on the neighboring plains, hoping to be of service to any stragglers among the Cheyenne who might still be trying to reach their kin in the north. Kipley had taken a job assisting the old newspaperman, Daggins. Sadie was helping out right here. It was called the Hotel Newell back then and was mired in such misfortune that nobody else would get within a mile of its accounts. First old man Newell had died of fever one spring morning. Then the Travertine mine had caved in on the son, Jim. This had left only the widow Newell, a sordid little woman with all the charm of shoe leather, who wouldn't be succumbing to whatever curse had taken her husband and son. Sadie helped out—mostly, by her own telling, to see what would carry the old bird off in the end. But a strange thing happened: the longer Sadie stayed under the thumb of the widow, the more determined she became to fend off whatever threatened to remand the widow to her judge. It was Sadie who nursed her through measles. Sadie who carried her out of the building when the first fire obliterated the town. Sadie who helped her rebuild the back part of the hotel. So it was Sadie's name that went on the deed to the place, and Sadie's name that ended up on the shingle above it when the old lady finally went to her reward.

"It's a fine place," Vargas had said, sitting across from Sadie in this very kitchen. "I think you'll make something of it."

Vargas and Preacher had hung the shingle for her that morning, with Sadie shouting instructions from the street below. Then Preacher had ridden out to help a laboring woman somewhere near Searles, leaving the rest of the Greyrock Four at the hotel to await the arrival of Daggart Caul, the dime-novel writer who would pen *An Incident at Greyrock,* and the first two plays it spawned, and make them all famous.

The writer was a somewhat notorious merchant of yarns who had been introduced to them by one of the miners. His original name was Henry Miles, but he had changed it to Daggart Caul. He was one of those brash, hollering, cherry-nosed characters who colored their hair and never seemed to fully hear what you had to say, no matter how slowly or deliberately you said it. Vargas had scant experience of such people back then. He had encountered a few of them in his lifetime, usually at passing carnivals. All he saw was the transformation of his spoken words into writing, and the transformation of that writing into words that sounded even better spoken out loud than his original ones had been. He was spellbound by the process, the enthusiasm with which Daggart Caul asked each of the Four to recount what had happened, the theatricality of it all. Sadie seemed to share Vargas's enthusiasm, even though she was having trouble making Caul understand that *she* was the reason for the telegram that had brought the rest of them up to Greyrock in the first place: she had studied briefly in her father's telegraph office in Denver, and when the bandits fell upon the Greyrock station house and needed food and supplies, she had volunteered to send the message, and, in a decision that would change all of their lives, she had changed the name Greyrock to Splitrock, praying that whoever received the telegram would notice. The plan had worked beautifully. She thought this detail, which rested on a thorough knowledge of telegraphy, might be of some importance to Caul's telling, but the writer didn't quite seem able to grasp the specifics.

Kipley, who had figured Daggart Caul out within eight minutes of meeting him, was sitting at the back of the hotel dining room, against the window, and insisting that the phrases he remembered uttering during the prelude to Greyrock, as well as the siege itself, not be changed in any way for either the book or the performance. This led to a lot of the lines being eliminated altogether because Caul couldn't quite make them work with what he was having the others say.

They had been at this for about three hours when Preacher finally came barging in. They heard the front door slam, and then his voice in the hallway roaring, "Did you know that there are *officers* up at Fort Searles?"

"Preacher," Sadie called. "The lodgers. It's late."

"Apologies!"

He came into the kitchen shrugging out of his coat. There was a tiny spot of blood on one of his shirt cuffs. He looked exhausted. "Officers," he said. "Can you believe it?"

"Preacher," Kipley said, nodding toward their guest. "This is Mister Caul."

"How do you do?" Preacher shook Caul's hand without looking at him. "Officers," he said again. "I went out to what I thought was going to be a trading post, and instead, they brought me into the fort. Imagine my surprise to find it manned! And not just manned but bustling. Not just with enlisted men but with officers. And their wives. Who are up there giving birth."

"What's wrong with that?" Vargas asked.

"According to treaty terms, Fort Searles is meant to remain empty," Kipley said. "It's still on Indian land."

"Not just the treaty of '68," Preacher said. "Of '51, too!" He stood there shaking his head in disbelief that, Vargas suddenly realized, was directed not at Vargas's own ignorance but at the obscenity of the whole thing. "Officers."

Kipley smiled wearily. "Our guest was asking me how you got to be called 'Preacher'—thank you for demonstrating so aptly." He nodded toward Caul again. "We've just been working out the script for the book and the play."

"What book?" Preacher said. "What play?"

"Greyrock," Sadie said patiently. "Sit down. Do you want a drink?"

"Oh, of course, of course, the book! The play! I'm so sorry." He rubbed his eyes with the look of a man who'd thought he was moments from going to bed but had now discovered that this plan was quite out of reach. "Have I missed it? I meant to be back sooner."

"Well, Doctor Maclean, we've been rehearsing one of the most important moments of the whole affair: the siege itself!" Caul said grandly. "You're just in time to spare me the embarrassment of reading your part. Would you mind joining in?"

Preacher took the script from his hand and read it over. Vargas could tell that he was barely standing up. They all clustered together and resumed reading the play aloud. Preacher staggered through his lines. When he came to his big moment in the shootout, he faltered. "What's this?" he said. "I—I'm sorry, I can't. This is a ridiculous thing to have me say."

"I beg your pardon," the writer said from the corner. "But your compatriots have attributed these utterances to you."

Preacher stared at the pages again. " 'Go ahead, then, kill me, come and kill me.' I can't imagine ever having said that."

Vargas spoke up: "That *is* what you said. I remember."

"*I* said this?" Preacher stared at him incredulously. "When?"

"When you saved my life." This came out all wrong, and he blushed stupidly. "I guess that's why I'm certain of it."

"I don't remember this at all." Preacher no longer sounded irritable. Just a little bewildered.

"Well, you were in the moment. I'm sure if it had been me saving *your* life, you'd remember what *I* said."

Vargas looked around the room awkwardly and caught Sadie smiling at him.

"I'm sorry," Preacher said. "I don't remember." He tried the lines again, but this attempt went no better than the one before. Stilted, jarring. It would turn out, of course, that he was neither a very good nor a very game actor. But they didn't know this yet. "My apologies," he finally said. "I cannot get up on a stage and say this."

"That's no trouble," Caul said in a voice that did little to conceal how much trouble it actually was.

"It's a shame," said Preacher, "because they're good lines."

"I thought you said they were ridiculous," Kipley said from the corner.

"Well." Preacher fixed him with a glare. "Coming from me, they are."

"Perhaps the doctor has a point. Perhaps these lines would be better suited to one of the other players. Mister Kipley?"

Kipley shook his head. "Don't look at me. I already told you I'm only saying the things I actually said."

"So you did, so you did. Well, we can't have Miss Wilkins making such utterances. We would be run out of town immediately." He chuckled. "I suppose that leaves Mister Vargas. Would you be willing?"

Vargas turned to Preacher. "That all right with you?"

"Of course."

So, ironically, this was how Vargas ended up being offered the lines for which he would become known. Less than five years later, he would be screaming them in arenas in London and Paris, often in fanciful contexts in which they had not been uttered, and in which he himself had never been at all, most notably in the vanguard of a Sioux cavalry charge manned entirely by fellow Mexicans in buckskin and war bonnets. Those words—"Go ahead, then! Kill me! Come and kill me!"—were shouted at him in passing by admirers and hooligans on the streets of St. Louis and New Orleans, whispered to him by women who hoped that he might take an interest, and plastered in speech balloons over his head on handbills and in comic strips long after Daggart Caul had left this world with a bottle in his hand and five dollars to his name. To Vargas's knowledge, he himself had never uttered the words anywhere except on the stage or in the arena. And to his certainty, he never came close to delivering them with the actual fire that had caused him to remember them all those years ago. He thought of Preacher whenever he said them.

There was a noise in the front hall. Vargas turned around. Somebody had let themselves in and was coming very softly toward the kitchen. From where Vargas was standing all the way against the dying stove, it looked like a man. Some guest, sneaking in after a visit to the cathouse. Vargas watched the figure head for the stairwell. The stairs creaked—twelve of them to the second floor. Then the footfalls continued along the hall above Vargas's head. They paused at the bottom of the staircase leading to the attic, and then continued up.

It took him a moment to put it all together. The other room in the attic—the one beside his—was unoccupied. This meant that whoever was going upstairs was heading to *his* room. Vargas's own.

And him downstairs, without his gun. Halfway through a cold ham sandwich.

What a fool he'd been to let that kid with the pamphlets lure him into a conversation about himself in a public setting. Anybody could have overheard their exchange in the dining room. Any good-for-nothing looking to make a name for himself by putting Anton Vargas down while he slept, unarmed, defenseless.

He should slip outside and go over to Kipley's. But then he wouldn't know who had come after him, or what they wanted.

He got a knife out of one of the kitchen drawers and hurried up the stairs. It was his great fortune to still be so light on his feet. The attic landing was empty. The door to Vargas's room was slightly ajar. He lined himself up behind it so that he could peer inside. He could see his bed, with the covers drawn up. He kicked the door open and stepped in. The stranger at the foot of the bed turned around.

"Jesus!" the stranger said, in Kipley's voice.

Vargas lowered the knife. "The hell are you doing?"

"Why aren't you in bed?"

"I got hungry and went down. Why are you creeping around the place? Why didn't you knock?"

Kipley drew himself up. "Come on," he said. "I need you. The Abadie family is cooked. There's about to be a play on their house."

"Who's coming for them?"

"A couple of the lads from town think the Abadies are lying about their son going missing. They think the parents killed him and are trying to cover it up. There's going to be hell."

"How do you know that?"

"I been pricking up my ears all day. Get dressed, come on."

Vargas steadied himself against the wall. "No."

"The hell do you mean, *no*?"

"No," he said again. "I didn't come here to be your second gun. You got another deputy for that." He had started down this path of resistance just to be difficult, but now, as he spoke, he found his indignation actually rising. The nerve of Kipley, slithering in here like this after dragging him all over the county with no decent meal, and no questions even about his well-being, and suggesting now that he take a couple of bullets breaking up a raid. "I'm too tired and I'm too old."

"I'm old, too, Anton—that's why you're needed."

"Maybe you should retire."

Kipley took a deep breath. "You know, I'm surprised I have to point out the similarity between this situation and another that cost you a great deal twenty years ago."

"That's low, Fred. That's low. I was being practical then, and I'm being practical now."

"Is that what you tell yourself when you keep your regrets company at night?"

"I don't got any regrets about that."

"The hell you don't. If you're so right with yourself, why are you here?"

"That's between me and him."

"And your guilty conscience."

Vargas stepped back for a moment to get right in his own head. He exhaled slowly. "All right," he said. "Give me your word that you'll take me to him, and I'll help you with this Abadie family business."

Kipley stood looking at him for a moment. He was thinking about it. Then the thinking was done. "No." He shook his head definitively. "But I *will* get word to him that you're here. That's the most I can do for you."

By the time they rode all the way out to the Abadies' place, the cabin was already surrounded. Vargas could tell that the raid was in its early stages: most everybody was outside and still mounted. He got his horse in among the men—maybe twenty in all, in various states of agitation—to see if he could catch the gist of what was going on. Somebody was usually in charge in a situation like this. Big pale Papa Abadie was standing out on the porch. He had the posture of somebody who had drawn the short straw to go outside and face the mayhem. That he had almost no English didn't help—he seemed not to understand that he was being asked, "Where is the boy? Where is he?" or to register the change in severity when the question shifted to "What did you do to him?"

Now the men were off their horses and roaming the house and grounds. Vargas followed a few of them inside. He found the Abadies in the back room, huddled all together on the mattress on the floor. Still, the men searched with fervor, as though the correct level of intimidation would cause the Abadies to confess the existence of a third, unseen room.

"Everybody all right?" Vargas asked the sad mass of Abadies.

Back in the foreroom, a crowbar had appeared and was being handed around to tear up the floorboards. There were already holes in the floor where it had been introduced. "Give it here," Vargas said, and the crowbar made its way into his hands. He carried it outside with him. Behind him streamed a gaggle of men, one of whom tried to snatch it from his grasp. Across the yard, he could see Kipley arguing with somebody who was holding a torch. The subject of debate seemed to be whether or not the torch should be applied to the house. "How do you reckon that'll help us find the boy?" Kipley was saying. Vargas went over to see whether the arrival of the crowbar might change the course of the argument.

"We've spent three days going up and down this valley," the man with the torch was saying. "Something's been done to that boy, or someone is lying about him being gone, and you're doing nothing about it. We want the marshal. Why haven't you called him out here?"

"And what is that boy to you?" Vargas shouted. "Who are you?"

That got the man's attention. "Who am I? Sir, who the hell are you?"

"I'm Anton Vargas—I come from these parts." There was a little too much silence at his back. He glanced over his shoulder to see what the pileup on his heels was up to—mostly, they were keeping their distance. Nobody had yet drawn a gun. Things looked all right for now. "But *you.*" He pointed at the torch wielder. "You're some cattle company shitheel, aren't you? Come in with your masters for the Stockmen's gathering. You never set foot in this town till last week—why the hell are any of us listening to you about what to do for our people? This is a good family. These are school-going kids. Their mother is heartbroken, sick with worry. You come to her door and threaten to burn her house down instead of asking what more you could be doing to bring the little fella home." He could feel Kipley rolling his eyes beside him. Well, that was fine. Kipley had never been cut out for this kind of crowd work. Let the burden fall to the one who is able, as the Lord God said. "Leave these good people alone and go on home. Go on home—you don't want to be waving that torch at me."

It had been Vargas's ritual to bathe after victories, whether they came to blood or not, so he asked for hot water to be brought up to his room. He filled the tub and eased himself into it. For a moment, he felt worse than he had in months. The water made his hands throb, as if he'd just come in from the cold. That was something he'd been told to expect: enhanced sensations, the specialist had told him, a more fragile tolerance of heat and cold. If only he had asked the specialist about dreams. Were they supposed to be relentless and bloated with detail? Sometimes, in these still moments, he couldn't help but think about the thing wandering around in his blood. The specialist had made it sound like a kind of seaweed, dislodged from its suspected place of origin in his stomach and catching now on every other organ in his body as his blood rushed back and forth: his lungs, his spleen, his guts, whatever other vile pink sacs his ribs were encasing. He had resolved to think about it as a kind of hostile cohabitant: they were occupying the same body, Anton Vargas from without, the cancer from within, and they were going to go along like this together, each doing the thing they were meant to do, until one of them gave up.

He opened his eyes to find Maura hovering in the doorway. "Towels?" she asked.

"Sorry—yes. Thank you."

She laid them on the chair. Then she sat down on the edge of the tub and leaned over where he was sitting. "Maura," he said. "Don't."

"I heard about you sticking up for the Abadies. We don't get a lot of men like you round here anymore."

"That's not true—there's men exactly like me every which where."

"You don't have to pretend to mind this so very much, Mister Vargas."

He had managed to get hold of her wrists, but that wasn't enough to dissuade her from leaning over him and putting her mouth against his. Her eyes were closed. Her forehead wrinkled in concentration.

"Maura," he tried, after a polite interval. "Stop. Your aunt. I knew your aunt."

This, at least, had the intended effect of puzzling her out of further attempts to kiss him. "My aunt?"

"Sadie and me—we were friends. And more than that, some of the time."

"Sadie?" She sat back on the edge of the tub and put her hands on her knees. "Sadie was my mother."

Vargas couldn't get her expression out of his mind on his march over to Kipley's place. To the solitary customer who had the gall to be standing in the newspaper office when he arrived, he said, "Get the hell out."

The man was a reedy, baffled-looking fellow. Kipley grabbed him by the arm. "Please disregard that," he said, forcing Vargas to stand there until ten pages of paperwork were signed and the customer was out the door. "Mister Vargas," he said. "How can I help you?"

"You told me Maura was Sadie's niece. Why?"

"That's what I was told."

"Horseshit. You knew it wasn't true." Kipley did him the courtesy of staying silent. "Who's her father?"

"How should I know?"

"Who is it?"

Kipley smiled oddly, mockingly. "Did you think it might be you?"

"She's the right age."

"A little too young, actually, which you'd work out if you weren't so damn doped up all the time."

"Who, then?"

Kipley stared at him. "Anton," he said. "Sadie led a very rich and adventurous life after you fucked off to parts unknown. Also, in case you failed to notice: Maura is *white*."

"People come out all kinds of ways. Half my kin are Puebloans, still my uncle had green eyes."

"Maura's not yours."

"Whose, then?"

A passerby chose this unfortunate moment to try to come in. Vargas threw his shoulder against the door. "Apologies," Kipley shouted through the glass. "We'll be back open shortly." He let the blind fall and stood with his back to Vargas, breathing loudly to steady himself. Vargas had the feeling that they were going to get ahold of each other, right there in the middle of the printing office. This was not his preferred outcome—he was still dizzy from his bath, and from the news Maura had inflicted on him. Besides, Kipley was limber, and well, and he had boxed once upon a time. Vargas did not want to give him the satisfaction of staving his face in.

Kipley finally composed himself. "This is a respectable place," he said. "We got a nice little town here. We got a school. We got the jubilee next week."

"I'll stop roughing up your nice little town as soon as you put me in the same room with Preacher."

"Why won't you leave him alone?" Kipley stood there, so obviously holding back tears that Vargas felt embarrassed. "Hasn't he earned his peace?"

A small, stout woman appeared at the bottom of the stairs in the very back of the room. Her arrival sent a ripple through Kipley. With some resignation, he stepped back to give Vargas a clear view of her, and gestured between the two of them.

"Anton," he said. "I don't believe you've met my mother."

Kipley's mother. Vargas stood there, astonished. She was short and plump as a grouse, standing there with her hand on the banister and her white hair up away from her face, which was, now that he was really studying her, unmistakably Indian. She gave an old-fashioned little curtsy and asked cheerfully, as if she hadn't overheard a word of their fight, "Anton, are you staying for lunch?"

He let himself be ushered upstairs, to a seat at the table in Kipley's apartment above the print house. He sat watching this tiny fabled woman as she moved around the stove. She talked incessantly. He only half-heard any of it. He couldn't believe he was in the presence of Kipley's mother—Kipley's mother! He had assumed she must be dead by now. That she was alive only in the handful of stories Kipley told about her—or, rather, in Vargas's poor recollection of those stories. Yet here Vargas was, sitting in her kitchen, while she nattered on about the weather, flitting back and forth in her slippered feet. This—*this!*—was the woman who had helped negotiate not one but two truces between the government and her nation. What tribe, exactly, Vargas was embarrassed to find he had forgotten. Bannock, maybe. It was on the tip of his tongue, this rogue detail he had known about her all his life. Right behind that missing word sat another, unfortunately available, one: *traitor,* which he had thought, without exception, every time Kipley had brought up his mother's upbringing, conversion, and eventual departure from her people. Vargas had never said it aloud, of course, not to Kipley, but he had thought it plenty, and that knowledge made him a little ill right now. It was all he could do to thank her for the meal and avoid Kipley's eye—because Kipley was glowering at him from across the table—and try to not look too conspicuously like he was imagining what it would have taken for his pleasant, soft-voiced host to kill her French trapper husband with her own hands and a length of trap wire one snowy afternoon when Jean-Claude Kipley had gone after Fred with a broken bottle for the hundredth and final time.

After she had brought out the rolls, she briefly disappeared downstairs for more butter. Vargas took the opportunity to lean across the table. "Don't be scowling at me like that, Fred."

Kipley laughed. "What are you going to do about it? Look at you—you're sick as a dog."

"I'm not sick."

"You been sick since you got here."

"Well, *you're* a goddamn liar."

"Say that again, Anton."

He repositioned his napkin inside his collar. "Mister High-and-Mighty. You said you would let Preacher know I'm here."

"And I will," Kipley said.

What he needed, unfortunately, was sleep. The chance to recuperate after this long, dreadful night-into-day, so that he could rally his strength for the Stockmen's Association banquet that evening. He was going to pile his two thin pillows one right on top of the other, and put both feet up on them, lie back on the bed, and surrender himself to oblivion and whatever the dream badger had in store.

But somebody was waiting in his room when he got there. For a brief, stomach-turning moment, he thought it might be Maura, looking for further engagement on the subject of her desirability.

But it was the Abadie matriarch, the stern handsome woman from the house. She was sitting in the chair under his window. The moment he stepped through the door, she got to her feet. She was holding a bolt of cloth to her chest.

Vargas removed his hat wearily. "Señora Abadie." Out came his mangled Spanish, strained to breaking point by his exhaustion. He struggled to put his words in order. "How did you succeed to be in my room?"

"You're Anton Vargas," she said.

"It is true."

"I wanted to thank you for interfering on our behalf this morning."

"It is nothing."

"My husband—you must understand. He's a big lout of a fellow, he talks loud and picks fights with the men in town. But he didn't hurt our son."

"No."

"Our son did vanish as we said, without explanation, without sending word."

"Six days before now."

"Yes." She stood quietly by. "Anyway, thank you."

"It was not any trouble for me. I'm only sorry you experienced fear." He let himself fall silent. Two or three more exchanges, and he would reach the limit of his ability to form a passable sentence. He needed to sit down, but she wasn't moving, and the gaunt insistence of her took up so much of the room.

"Is there any other thing I can make for you?" he finally asked.

She frowned. "Yes." She stepped toward him and held out the cloth she had been pressing to her chest. "You can save my son."

He held up his hands. "Money is not needed."

"Yes—you will save him. You will take this back to John Daisy."

He took the cloth from her. It was a velvet jewelry fold, soft and oddly weighted. He opened its top flap. Inside was a broken arrow about half a foot long, slightly mutilated from having been dipped in a substance that had since gone dry and black.

"I do not understand," he said.

"Please take this to Mister John Daisy. And tell him—my son, he's desperately sorry for the trouble. He didn't mean to take it. And if Mister Daisy is content with the return of this, he'll never see my son again."

Vargas wanted to be sure he understood. "Your boy took this from Mister John Daisy?"

She pressed his hands into the fabric of the envelope. "Please, just give this to Mister Daisy. Tell him there's no need to hunt for Jules Abadie anymore. He's gone away for good, and Mister Daisy will never have any trouble from him again."

"But what will I tell Deputy Kipley? He is with worry. He will not stop until he finds the boy."

She was looking at him as if he were some sort of idiot. "Tell him he must. If Mister Daisy agrees to stop searching, Mister Kipley must agree, too. I don't want this place to swallow my son."

"But what will happen to him?"

"Don't worry. El Hechicero will see him across the county—he's in good hands."

By the time Vargas had brushed down his good coat and gotten the pomade in his hair and stepped out in his evening best, such as it was, he was already an hour late to the Stockmen's Association banquet. He had the envelope with the arrow tucked into his coat, point side up. Maura whistled when she saw him at the top of the stairs.

"See?" she said. "You got another suit after all."

She seemed to have forgiven him. Or, at least, to have decided to rise above their shared previous embarrassment. He leaned over the counter toward her.

"You got tobacco and papers?"

"Sure do."

"Roll one for me, will you?"

He studied her while she worked. There was nothing of himself in her face, though he wished he had known his mother or his grandmother, so that he could be certain there was none of them in it, either.

Outside, he treated himself to a smoke, leaning against the hotel. He hadn't planned to indulge, but there was something about getting into his regalia that demanded it. A throwback to the times when he had felt most like himself. Or at least, most like the Anton Vargas everybody seemed to think he was. He stubbed out the end of the smoke, saddled up, and rode out to John Daisy's place. Torches were burning all along the drive, and the guests milled half in and half out of the house. A woman in a corset handed him a drink at the door. He had seen some ridiculous getups in his time, but the degree of duding up at the Stockmen's Association banquet far outstripped both Vargas's means and his tolerance. He drifted around the rooms, from one debate about cattle prices to another, trying to figure out what the hell he was doing there. A desiccated old rancher in crocodile-skin boots was assailing him with the horrors of a strange wasting disease that had recently begun taking root in the local wolf population when John Daisy finally found him.

"Mister Vargas." He held out his hand. "The deputy marshal failed to introduce us properly. Forgive me—I didn't realize, when I met you the other day, whose company I was in."

"Not at all," Vargas said. "Fred knows I'm particular about my anonymity."

"Well, that's understandable. You never know which of these young louts might get a notion. I suspect it's something you've had to deal with now and again. People thinking they might try you."

"They tend to keep those thoughts to themselves."

John Daisy motioned for him to come along, and Vargas followed him through an adjoining parlor and into the magnificent library. There, a whiskey from John Daisy's private stock was poured and handed to him. He wasn't sure whether to shoot or sip it, given the circumstances, and waited to see how John Daisy would proceed.

John Daisy, however, was here to talk. "You've been traveling the world with my friend Montana Jack and his beasts and savages."

"I help Jack out when I can."

"How *is* Jack?"

"Newly married," Vargas said. "I stood for him at the wedding."

"Well, Jack must miss you sorely—but his loss is our great luck. Can we expect you to linger?"

He told the truth: "I have no plans to return to New York."

"Do you intend to retire?"

"I'm of two minds."

"Well, if you're looking for a gesture of providence to consolidate your two minds, allow me to mention that I may soon need the aid of a man of your talents."

Now Vargas was supposed to say, *What talents do you mean, sir?* He wished he could tell people who spoke to him this way that he had heard it all before. Where were they getting it? Was there some etiquette pamphlet on the most inelegant way to invite a person into dubious work that had been passed down, rancher to rancher, for time out of mind?

"I think you may have the wrong idea about me," he said instead.

"Were you not a range detective out in Teewinot County?"

"Many, many years ago."

"That kind of work is sorely needed around here. We got cattle rustlers coming out of our ears, Mister Vargas. Or do you prefer Señor?"

"I prefer Anton."

"Is that short for Antonio?"

"No," he said, though he had felt sure all his life it must be.

"Well, Anton," John Daisy was saying. "How do you intend to pass the time? Surely you haven't come all this way just to help Deputy Kipley track down runaways."

Something about the way he said this irritated Vargas profoundly. Maybe it was the insult to Kipley, or maybe the suggestion that John Daisy had nothing to do with the particular runaway to whom he was referring. It set Vargas on edge, and being on edge made him want to lie, just to see the reaction it would elicit.

"I'm considering becoming deputized," he said. "So I can be of more use to Fred."

"Well! I'm sure Fred will appreciate the extra hands. He seems terminally unable to stay on top of things that go missing around here."

"We may have made some progress in that regard." He almost took the arrow out of his pocket. But something in him, something odd and small and quiet in the back of his mind, kept his hand at his side. In his other hand, he held the whiskey glass, still half full. He was aware that his stillness made him look a little insane. But the moment wore on, and still he stayed put.

John Daisy reached the end of his patience. "Have you located the boy?"

"No. But mention was made of a certain artifact that might be presented in exchange for his safe return."

"Presented to whom?"

"To you."

John Daisy looked at him oddly. "But I don't have Jules Abadie. How could I safely return him? I don't know where he is."

"The implication was that you might feel slighted enough by the theft of the artifact that his safety in this county would be impossible."

John Daisy nodded. "People shouldn't steal things whose worth they do not know."

"I imagine the artifact's worth was measured against all your other antiquities." Vargas gestured to the room. "You have so many."

John Daisy nodded. "Have you seen the artifact?"

"No," Vargas lied.

"It's an arrow of Miniconjou extraction. About that long."

Vargas studied the distance between John Daisy's hands and concluded that if the arrow were as long as the old man was indicating, it would, given its hiding place at that very moment, be sticking up through Vargas's clavicle and possibly into his ear.

"Twenty years ago, a prince of Austria came to these shores in a gesture of goodwill. It was his desire to see the great cities of our nation—Boston, Philadelphia, and so on—and to see the Great Plains as he passed through on his way to the port of San Francisco. A buffalo hunt was organized for him by my father. It was a great affair—hundreds of soldiers, hunters, dogs, Indian scouts. That's where I first met Montana Jack. Maybe he's mentioned it?"

"Actually, yes. Jack said the prince drank more champagne than any man he'd ever seen."

John Daisy laughed. "My God, that's right. How funny. I forgot. Well, on the second day of the hunt, the Miniconjou held an exhibition to demonstrate how *they* hunted buffalo. The old way. Spotted Horse shot a bull bison through the heart with an arrow he had made out of chokecherry. It was preserved in wax with the buffalo's blood still on it, and given to my friend the prince as a token of the Miniconjous' regard. When he died, the arrow was returned to me, along with a few other artifacts, for safekeeping." John Daisy sighed. "Now, to Jules Abadie, that is an ordinary arrow. As you say, no different than the others in my collection. Something for him to steal and sell. But to me, its significance is monumental. Not just because it is a keepsake of my dear friend." He jerked a thumb over his shoulder. "I presume you've seen the buffalo jump that was discovered when the foundations of this house were laid?"

"I have," Vargas said.

"Thousands of years old, Mister Vargas, and thousands of years in use. Beneath our very feet lie the bones and leavings of the ancients who preceded us. And it falls to us, the inheritors of their vast and remarkable history, to honor and remember them. To preserve the keepsakes they left behind. Jules is right in supposing that I take this responsibility seriously."

"Forgive me," Vargas managed to say through the ringing in his ears. "But haven't the inheritors of those ancients been sent to waste away in some barracks on the Tongue River?"

This did not succeed in provoking John Daisy. At all. It led him, instead, to lapse into a gentle smile that made Vargas angrier than all his previous little musings combined. What would happen, Vargas wondered, if he were to lay the old man out during a party under his own roof? Surely word of Vargas's presence in town would reach Preacher very quickly then. But he didn't want John Daisy's thugs, wherever they were lurking, to lay hold of him and haul him out of here before all the landed gentry of Sunrise and kick the shit out of him and then toss him into the pit with all the ancients' bones and leavings. You could alter the course of your life very quickly, giving in to your temper, even for just one moment. If he had learned nothing else in his lifetime, he had learned this.

Besides, John Daisy had more to say. "Mister Vargas, when you were abroad with my friend Jack, did your travels take you to London?"

"Sure."

"A remarkable city. There's a museum there that houses a most unique selection of Greek statuary . . ."

"I know it," Vargas said.

John Daisy paused in offensive surprise. "Really?"

"Yes." He had been bracing himself for more one-sided sermonizing, but was delighted now to be able to draw, from some dusty corner of his mind, the faint memory of an afternoon, ten years back or maybe more, when he had nervously accompanied a painter with whom he was smitten to that very place. Vargas could remember almost nothing of the painter, nor of his paintings, but he did have a vivid memory of the Greek sculptures, and in particular of feeling that they were surprisingly detailed in their attention to horse penises, and that something about this preoccupation made the whole thing feel obscene, because the horse penises were affixed to figures who were actually half-men. They were fighting each other, the half-men with the horse penises, and the faceless men with the human penises, but it seemed like what they really wanted was to be fucking—and while Vargas understood the complex connection between these two impulses, it had still embarrassed him a great deal to be standing there in his good suit and show boots amid all the penises while the translucent old English ladies fanned themselves and rain pounded the roof.

"I remember those statues," Vargas said. He felt compelled to add: "Though I don't pretend to be a sophisticated man."

John Daisy went on. "The lord who cut those stone people from the temple of Athena was called Thomas Bruce. He was no more Greek than I am. But he understood something very important: inheritance does not flow through blood, one generation to the next. The man who secured those sculptures understood that in his appreciation of them, in his embodiment of the ideals that moved their creators, he was *more* their inheritor than were the ragged Greeks and Mohammedans who happened at that time to occupy the land on which they had been built. Inheritance, Mister Vargas, is a matter of spirit."

When he got outside, still livid yet still somehow in possession of himself, the evening was cool and lively with the so-called inheritors of the ancients. Everywhere he looked, there they stood, huddling in groups of five or six, hatted, black-clad, and whispering, while the jittery torchlight burned in their spectacles. The goddamn Stockmen's Association. Some overserved guest leaned heavily against Vargas's shoulder in passing. Vargas accelerated him to the bottom of the steps, at which point the stranger got up, adjusted himself, and went off unsteadily down the sloping lawn, toward the distant lights of town. Vargas stood on the porch and watched him go.

He was furious with John Daisy, and furious with every soul in his line of sight, but above all, he was furious with himself. After so many years, and with so little of his own life left to safeguard, was it possible that he could muster no more potent response to John Daisy's inane blatherings than a smug little quip about the Cheyenne reservation on the Tongue River? It had dissolved against John Daisy with all the force of falling snow.

Vargas found some relief in pressing the tip of the hidden arrow against his ribs. Thank God for whatever instinct had led him to resist handing it over to Daisy.

He should return to the hotel and rest. It was cold—though at least it was that dry, sparse cold he loved. It wouldn't be damp again until spring, when the ground, wet from all the melted snow, started sending up little purls of moisture. The cold would be of a very different quality then. He would need a better coat.

Coat? he thought. *What for?*

The thought staggered him.

Every sinner on the torchlit lawn before him, even the white-haired men leaning on canes, had more time in his hourglass than did Vargas. Whether his plan came together, whether he found Preacher or not, he wouldn't be alive in spring to feel that dampness rising out of the ground. Of all the thoughts to paralyze him with fear, this one was unexpected. He didn't even like the spring. Didn't long for it. Found no comfort, as other people did, in the smell of last year's rotted leaves emerging. Why was he suddenly on the verge of tears at the thought of not seeing it again?

He took a lantern from its hook and went down the lawn to the buffalo jump. A strange thing, to have such a steep void so close to a party teeming with drunks. For good or ill, none of them seemed to be drawn toward it. Vargas was alone.

He knelt down at the edge of the pit and looked inside. A few feet below, he could faintly see roots and protrusions. He lowered the lantern, and its light bounced garishly across a stretch of teeth, a fragment of bone. With his free hand, he reached down and felt along the wall, his finger slipping occasionally into the socket of some stone-trapped beast. How long had they lain here? he wondered. How long had the earth taken to rise up, full of them, to this height?

He wished he could see to the bottom. How deep was the hole? Did anything living inhabit it? Vermin? Insects? Badgers?

As soon as he thought of the badger, he stood up. Then he got his horse and rode out to the Robles place.

It was farther than he remembered, and farther than the badger's dream had led him to believe. Vargas took almost an hour to get there, even riding, and he was exhausted by the time he arrived. Sometimes the pain left him wondering how the hours passed when he was free of it. It had a tendency to make him feel the full measure of every moment. He took a minute to catch his breath. The horse tolerated his leaning against it, accustomed as it was to serving this purpose.

The Robles place was one of the oldest homes in the valley, a dugout that John Robles had cut into the hill to give himself a dry place to lay his head. This had sufficed for John until Missus Robles joined him in Sunrise. She was a proper lady, a woman used to sunlight, used to music. Back home, in Oaxaca, she was said to have had a piano, a rumor she substantiated every few weeks when she came into town, sat wordlessly at the Lavinia's instrument, and played old love songs until John Robles came around to ask her what was for supper. That, everyone assumed, had been the inciting question the day she went home and blew his brains out in the middle of the night, right where he was sleeping on the cold dirt of the dugout. She had vanished by the time they found John, and the place had sat empty ever since, the haunt, ever afterward, of young people who liked to scare each other with the tale, and test whether they could provoke Robles's spirit out of the ground by calling his name.

Vargas did not want to be there. But then his dream belonged to the badger, and he recognized now that it was his obligation to abide by as many of its contours as he could remember. He had failed in this obligation so far, but he did not intend to fail again. He ducked through the doorframe and stood in the vacant darkness. Did it remember him, this horrible little place, which he loved just as he loved the rest? He wondered if John Robles's spirit, hanging upside down from the rafters or peering up at him from the floor, thought to itself, *Well shit, there's that boy who helped carry my stinking carcass out of here on a stretcher!* And would such a recognition be welcome? Preacher had made the coffin, but Vargas had, after all, been the one who draped a blanket over John Robles's face. Maybe John Robles's spirit would greet him as a friend.

In the badger dream, the hearth in the middle of the room had been unmistakable. But in real life, the whole floor was ash and dirt. He dragged his boot toe through it, searching for the place where it was thickest. Once he'd found it, he crouched down and began to move his fingertips through it gently. *What a lunatic I am,* he thought, finding nothing.

He was absorbed enough in thought that he failed to notice the light out on the road until it was almost at the door. It was a lantern. He crouched farther down to avoid being seen.

Someone was hurrying along outside, quietly by themselves in the dark.

He waited until the lantern had progressed up the road a ways, then stepped out and stood in the shadow of the Robles place and watched the light growing dimmer as the person carrying the lantern started up the hill.

Vargas didn't know the ground here so well. There were lots of the little houses and dugouts from the old days. Lots of holes and pits and mine tunnels.

He left his horse tethered and started after the lantern on foot. Its light was still visible in the distance, moving through the high brush where the road curved along the hillside. He had to run a little to catch up, and was lucky that the pain didn't hit him right away. When it came, it forced him to stop and watch the light continue hurrying away from him. There was nothing he could do until his body decided to move again. By the time this happened, the light had disappeared among the hills. He was determined not to run after it—no point to all this stealth and effort if he just gave himself away coughing and wheezing. Better to have faith that he would find it again eventually. Sure enough, from the top of the rise, he could see it in the next valley, flitting jerkily down the hill. Whoever was carrying it had gone off the path and was in the sagebrush now. Vargas cut across the hillside after them. Overhead, the clouds shifted and the moon came out, startling the whole valley with its brightness.

He emerged into a canyon pleated with unfamiliar features. It was from this vantage that he saw the lantern—so distant now that it was only a spectral little thing, like an orange star that had fallen out of the sky—reappear in what he realized must be the window of some kind of dwelling. As he stood there, the pain returned, so violently that he was forced to his knees. Doubled over like that, in the dark, in this unfamiliar terrain, he felt for the first time that he had done a stupid thing. He could feel something dimming the edges of his sight, and a whirling white streak seared his vision in two. The doctor in Cheyenne had told him that fainting spells would eventually come, and of course this was when it was going to happen. He was going to faint out here, alone and horseless. Probably get picked off by whatever lion called these cliffs home.

After a little while, he was able to stand up again. He stayed leaning against the ravine wall for support. The lantern was gone—had been put out. It was up to him now to try to remember where it had gone.

Then minutes later, he found it: the dugout Herman Remmick had built in the old days. Inside was a bed, and a table with the lantern on it. He could smell the smoke of its recent extinguishment.

"Hullo?" he said.

He knelt down and peered under the bed. A dusty little face was down there, looking back at him.

"Well," he said. "You must be Jules Abadie."

The boy said nothing. His eyes were huge and dark-colored. The tip of his nose was still round, like a toddler's, even though Vargas guessed the boy to be about eight or nine years old. He had the air of some rare animal that Vargas had cornered—no telling what he would do, startle or lash out. At least he wasn't very big.

"Looks cramped down there, friend. Care to come out?"

The boy did not. Vargas stood up. The bed was just a gaunt little cot with a straw mattress on it. Not that long ago, Vargas could have pulled it aside with one arm. He might still be able to, but he wasn't sure if he should take the chance. He sat down on the edge of the mattress. "You been sleeping on this? I've slept on rock softer 'n this."

The boy under the bed gave him nothing back. Vargas widened his stance, spacing his boots out carefully on the dirt floor. He wanted the boy to know that he was there, but still have room enough to get past his feet once he finally decided to emerge.

"Everyone's out looking for you," Vargas said. "Did you know that, Jules? Damn near got your house burned down with your nonsense. Why don't you come out and tell me where you're going?" He waited. "You going to see El Hechicero? Your mother told me."

After a while, he tried again: "You don't have to take off anyplace, you know. Your mother gave me the arrow you stole from Mister Daisy. I gave it back to him. You're safe to come home."

"You're lying," said a muffled voice under the bed.

"I'm not."

"You are. My mother said to get the hell out of here and never come back. She said John Daisy was gonna eat my heart because I stole from him."

"I don't know about that," Vargas said. "He's a weird old bird, it's true. But I don't know about him eating your hea—"

He was halfway through this sentence when the kid shot out from under the bed. Just a loud shadow, scrambling between Vargas's boots. It was so sudden that Vargas jumped. By the time he had recovered from the initial shock, the boy was already through the door. Vargas leapt out after him. All around him the shadows of the hillocks stood weird and twisted. He could hear more than see Jules Abadie, running out ahead of him in the dark. Noisy running, wildly indiscreet. Vargas started after him, but he had to stop because the sounds of his own breath and footfalls were drowning out the sound of the boy's escape.

"Jules?" he called out. Around him, the landscape lay silent. "Goddamn it."

"Why don't you fuck off?" the kid said, from somewhere out ahead. Vargas turned in the direction of his voice.

"I can't do that. I promised your mother I'd bring you home."

"Liar. I tried to go home. But it's too late. My mother told me to get out of here as fast as I can."

"And how do you think you're going to manage that? You don't got any food or water. Who's gonna help you?"

"Not you, I'll tell you that."

"Why don't you let me take you home. Plenty of grown men would tell you: there's no shame in being apprehended by Anton Vargas."

"Who?"

"Anton Vargas," he said again, figuring the kid hadn't heard him the first time.

"Are you the president or something?"

He stood there in silence. Feeling a little strange. A little stupid. As though he'd just stepped into a snare he'd forgotten having set. Everything about this situation enhanced his irritability. The soft throbbing in his temples. The kid's insolent, empty head, out there somewhere in the dark.

"Listen," Vargas said.

He heard the Abadie boy scramble up out of the bushes and take off. The sound wasn't far ahead—it gave Vargas the illusion that he might be able to catch up. He started running in the direction of the boy's footfalls. He hadn't gone more than twenty yards when something struck him with incredible force. Vargas flew forward. He was still airborne when the faraway crack of the rifle caught up to him, the sound following the bullet that had lodged just behind his right shoulder. It didn't hurt—it just startled him badly and left him facedown in the dirt. Somewhere far behind him, a man's voice was shouting, "Run, run, run!" in Spanish. Before long, he couldn't hear the boy's footfalls anymore.

Vargas found that he could not stand up. A dog was barking somewhere. Something about it brought him back to himself. Things couldn't be so bad—a dog was nearby, barking. What an ordinary thing.

Eventually, the dog reached him. It came tearing out of the bushes to his left, squat and mottled, ears like arrowheads, every tooth in its face bared crazily at him, but at least it didn't make contact. Vargas stayed where he was. He could hardly breathe. Whatever moisture had been in his throat had migrated out of his nose by way of snot. Through watering eyes, he could tell that somebody was walking along behind the dog.

"Son of a bitch," the unseen person said.

As soon as Vargas heard the voice, a calm spread through him. It was not what he had hoped for, not at all. He rolled over and tried a smile, though he knew it made him look utterly crazy.

"Hello, Preacher," he said.

Unlike Kipley, Preacher did not look the same. Vargas doubted that he would have recognized him if he hadn't heard his voice first. Preacher looked like someone who had, to put it simply, encountered dynamite. His left sleeve was empty below the elbow. His remaining eye, the one not obscured by an eyepatch, was the same glittering black that had first made Vargas avert his gaze back in Langsford Hole. Seeing it, Vargas realized he hadn't actually thought they would meet again. He felt fortunate that his own eyes were already watering.

"What's the matter with your eye?"

Twenty years, and it was all he could think of to say.

It was hard to read Preacher's expression in the dark, but Vargas could tell he was surprised. He hadn't known to expect him. He hadn't felt that Vargas was here after all.

"It's you," Preacher said. He wasn't smiling. That was all right. At least it would be over quickly. That was all Vargas wanted.

But Preacher lowered the gun. He pulled Vargas into a seated position. While he was yanking off his coat, the Abadie boy reappeared, out of breath, grinning wildly, as if he'd just won some sort of race.

"The hell are you smiling at?" Vargas asked through gritted teeth.

"You, you bastard."

Preacher squeezed the injured shoulder until Vargas cried out. "Why were you chasing this boy?"

"I'm taking him home to his mother."

"That's a *lie,*" the kid said. "My mother sent me out here so El Hechicero would get me across the badlands and away from all you people."

Preacher frowned. "Is that true?"

The kid nodded.

"Well, do you have a note for me?"

"I have a note for El Hechicero."

"You're a slow boy, son, but I'll give you latitude on account of the excitement you've just endured. Give me the note."

Finally, Jules Abadie saw the light. The man before him—disappointingly roughed up—was El Hechicero, the sorcerer in question. He fumbled around in his pockets for his mother's note, which Preacher stepped into the moonlight to read.

"Well, you're telling the truth," he said. "But we find ourselves in a bit of a predicament. Listen." He took the boy by the shoulders and spoke softly and steadily. "My horse is up on that ridge. Take him and ride into the east Warrens. Do you know Rabbit Creek?" The kid nodded. "Good. My house is about a mile down it. Go inside, get my medicine bag out from under the kitchen table, and bring it back here. Do you understand?"

"But—"

"There's no time. There and back before dawn. I'll take you to the river tomorrow night. That's an oath you have from me. All right? Good man."

When the boy had gone, Preacher braced Vargas up off the ground and led him into the dugout, where he dropped him unceremoniously onto the bed. Vargas's back was starting to hurt—just in time to have the wound pressed and prodded by Preacher, whom he could hear tearing off his sleeve. With impressive ease for a man working one-handed, Preacher packed the wound, tied the packing down, and thrust Vargas's rolled-up coat under his patient's injured shoulder.

Then Preacher crossed the room and sat on the ground with the ratty old cattle dog between his feet. Vargas lay on the bed, resting his boots on the bottom rail.

"How did you find me?" Preacher eventually said. "Did Kipley tell you?"

"No," said Vargas. "He wouldn't, the bastard."

"Then how?"

"Would you believe me if I told you I dreamt it?"

"No."

"Well, I did."

The stars in their scorching millions drifted across the window. Every now and again, one of them dropped as though it had been shot out of the sky.

A cough broke through him. He knew Preacher was listening carefully to it. Vargas hawked, spat, hawked again.

"It's not catching," he finally said. "In case you're worried."

"As far as I'm concerned, you're not even here."

"That's a relief." Vargas prodded the mattress with his bootheel. "I'm very relieved not to be here, freezing my balls off in this little shithole. Is this your house? Of course not—your house is down on Rabbit Creek. See, I'd've remembered that if I were here. But thankfully I'm not. So what is this place? Is it where patients from town come to wait for you? Goddamn it, I knew Fred was hiding you. 'I don't know where he is and even if I did, I wouldn't tell you.' Sanctimonious prick. No matter, since I'm not here. I wonder where I am. Maybe at the Gander, getting into some of that fine quail and stuffing. Bit of whiskey, bit of red wine. I probably don't even know I've gone missing!"

"You shouldn't be talking."

"Is that your medical opinion?"

"It's my personal preference."

Vargas stole a glance at Preacher. He hadn't budged. His good eye was closed, his intact hand worrying the dog's ears.

"I'm sick," Vargas said. "It's in my stomach. The doctor in Cheyenne says I got a few weeks at most. It's why I came here. To see you."

"This is supposed to move me, I'm sure."

"I'm not here to beg your forgiveness. My regrets are between me and whoever hears my prayers. They'll be with me when I take His hand. But I did want to give you a chance to take your revenge, if that's something you been thinking about. If that's something you been wanting to do."

Preacher finally looked at him. "My revenge?"

"I've gone around these last twenty years like I don't owe you a debt. If I'm going to die—and they keep telling me I am—I'd rather you kill me than the cancer."

There it was. He hadn't managed to say it as elegantly as he had planned, but for the moment, it was enough.

Preacher was frowning. "You'd rather *I* kill you?"

"That's right."

"Why the hell would I do that?"

"Because I wronged you. Enough for a few lifetimes, I think."

Preacher sat forward. "Did you think I would lay eyes on you and be so overcome with fury and raw feeling that I would just shoot you on sight?"

"Yes. But you fucked that up, didn't you? Look at me now. Shot and alive, the worst outcome of all."

"How completely like you, Anton. All this time while you were off hanging cattle rustlers and swirling around in circus arenas in Paris—oh, we heard about that, even in the Warrens we heard about that—did you think I was still twenty-seven? Still holed up in my infirmary back in Sunrise, furiously cleaning my gun and thinking of nothing but what I would do when you finally turned up?"

Why was he making it sound so preposterous? "I was thinking enough about it myself that I figured you must be thinking about it *some.*"

"And that I would 'take my revenge' by bloodying my hands, after all this time, sparing you from a slow and painful death. Do I have that right?"

"In detail, yes. But I can tell you've misunderstood the spirit of my gesture."

Preacher crossed his arms and his one eye glittered at Vargas with total amazement. "Anton, I wouldn't piss on you if you were on fire."

"You haven't changed a bit."

"Pardon?"

"You make believe that you are unimpeachable. But you have a way of misremembering things so that they align with only your most recent feelings."

"That's not true."

"It would serve you to remember that in the weeks, months, maybe even years after Greyrock, you did not object to *any* of the benefits that broke over our lives." He was pleased to find he had strength enough to raise his good hand and count off on his fingers. "You did not object to driving into Sunrise with the rotting corpses of the Salt Draw gang piled up in your dray. You did not object to your share of the reward for killing the Salt Draw gang. Nor did you object to how the incident was portrayed in the newspapers."

"I certainly did."

"Not until a good while afterward, when you'd soured on the whole thing. But in the first few years, you didn't turn down one free drink or one request to appear in public to relive it."

"That was all you and Sadie."

"It was not."

Preacher adjusted his eyepatch. "The fervor around the Greyrock shootout could only be kept alive by its most willing participants. And that was you, because you're a vainglorious bastard. And to a lesser extent it was Sadie, because she was a joiner."

"You can't lie to me, Preacher." He couldn't believe he was using his last breaths to pursue this argument. "A young man in town recently showed me some of the handbills from that time. You were all over them. A game part of our exhibitions. Until you found your high horse."

"I wanted to use our time on the stage to talk about matters of actual consequence. A single thwarted robbery did not merit that much attention."

"That's a very limited way of looking at it."

"*Especially* when the town's very existence relied on endless treaty violations with the Shoshone and the Cheyenne."

"Thank God they had you on their side. Look at all the good you did them."

"They were my patients, and my friends."

"Mine as well."

"*Actual* Indians, Anton. Not whatever Greeks and Italians Montana Jack had you dress up in war bonnets for his show."

He tried to laugh, but it just brought on another coughing fit. "You're so tiresome. You were always so *tiresome.* To everybody. Even me."

"Not Fred."

"Maybe these days. But back then—you realize everyone would just glaze over the moment you started talking about treaty violations?"

"That was their willful blindness. A deficiency of their character," Preacher said. "Not mine."

"And look at you now."

"Yes," said Preacher. "Look at me."

This was not going at all according to plan. Worse, it had gone sideways twice over. Preacher had shot him without killing him. And now here they were, squabbling over the usual details, instead of talking about all the things that had actually been on Vargas's mind for the past twenty years.

He had a sudden, dizzying thought. Maybe he had been mistaken about his significance in Preacher's life in more ways than one. Maybe there had been other loves for Preacher. Not just dalliances or infatuations, but loves. Maybe even marriage, maybe to some woman who was living with him, at this very moment, somewhere in the house on Rabbit Creek. Maybe there were children. What if Maura was *his*? Anything was possible. The man before him was not twenty-seven years old. He was neither weeping at the news of Vargas's cancer nor seething with rage. And in no part of their conversation did Vargas see evidence of the other thing. The love he had assumed, perhaps mistakenly, might still be there.

That had started with a fight, too, of course. Preacher had failed to see how important it was for Sunrise to wrest the county seat from Hemot City. He hadn't cared that the Greyrock Four were an instrumental part of gathering interest from the commissioners. Sure, Hemot City had gold mines and saloons and a new schoolteacher, the mayor and the council and the town money all seemed to say, but it did not have the Greyrock Four. Rather than give this the necessary attention, Preacher had made a spectacle of himself all over the county, jumping to his feet before this legislative body and that to rail against the expansion of the mines, the harassment of Indian traders, the guiding of city dudes to hunt elk and deer. "Earning," according to several regional newspapers, "the moniker by which he is known." The transgression that weighed on Preacher most heavily was the rebuilding and restaffing of Fort Searles. Why was the army back? Why were more and more of them arriving every day? Fort Searles, according to Preacher, should be left to rot in the sun as the United States had twice sworn before God and the sovereign nations of the plains that it would be.

To mark the town's fifth anniversary, the council threw a week-long party and called it a festival. They brought in a small circus from Montana, and for a week the streets of Sunrise swarmed with strange, exotic life, animal and human alike: fire-breathers and camels, stiltwalkers, zebras. The Greyrock shooting exhibition was to be a centerpiece of the entertainment. The stage at the Gander was transformed into a garish replica of the Greyrock station house and the surrounding woods, and Vargas personally signed the invitations for the county commissioners.

Vargas didn't usually wear makeup for these things, but just this once, he let one of the balcony girls line his eyes with something black and sticky so his expressions would be more legible from the back of the theater. He forgot that he was wearing the liner and he started rubbing his face in agitation when Preacher still hadn't shown up at fifteen, ten, five minutes to curtain. It had settled in every line on his face by midnight, when Preacher finally returned to the infirmary, where Vargas had been waiting for him since the abrupt and, as Kipley had put it to the booing audience, regrettable cancelation of proceedings.

"Where the hell were you?"

Preacher hung up his coat. "You look frightening."

"The performance, Preacher."

"Oh, the performance." Preacher pressed the heels of his hands into his eyes. "God, yes. The performance. To let down all those top hats from Cheyenne—I can just see them sitting there, dabbing their noses, wondering, *What about the performance?* I'm so awfully, awfully, *awfully* sorry, Anton. Can you ever forgive me?"

Vargas didn't know what to say when he got this viciously insincere.

"If you'd rather not be part of it anymore, just say so."

"I thought that was obvious."

"We're trying to do something, Fred and Sadie and me. We're trying to raise this town up. And the county seat—"

"Oh God, *yes,* the county seat."

"You don't have to help, if you don't want to. But at least don't revile what holds us all together."

"*Life* holds us together! What we do, what we talk about, what we feel. Not twelve hours of gunplay we somehow happened to survive four years ago. My God, Anton, isn't there anything more to you? Are you really going to continue through life, unthinking, unfeeling, yoked to the whims of the territorial legislature?"

He hadn't managed to work "unworthy" into this mix, but it was implied. Vargas had never felt so thoroughly eviscerated in his life.

"Few enough of us have your schooling, or your prospects," he said. His voice sounded oddly not his own. "We can't disavow the only worthy thing we ever did."

"*Worthy.* What was so worthy about it? What would have happened if we hadn't shown up at Greyrock when we did?"

"The Salt Draw gang would have kept stealing."

"Stealing flour and salt."

"They would have killed Sadie."

"Do you know how much killing and stealing washes back on us every day?" Preacher said. "What's a little more, in the grand scheme of things?"

"You're monstrous."

This, at least, gave Preacher some pause. He stood frowning at the ground. But then he came right back: "We're all monstrous.

We are the willing drudges of monstrosity. Nothing is more obvious to me, and yet nobody else in this town, in this whole damn country, seems to know it. Not even you. How? How can you stand it? To let them put you up on that stage so you can paint them a pretty picture of themselves? And to do it over and over again—my God."

"I don't tell them anything about themselves," Vargas said. "I tell them what happened to *me.*"

"You're a good man, Anton, but when I see you up there, mugging and twirling those guns for God and country, I can't stand you. It makes me wish we had died at Greyrock, all of us. Sadie, too."

He could tell that Preacher meant it, and it hurt him so deeply that he couldn't catch his breath. The only thing he could think to do was hit him. But Preacher would just take it without flinching, so what was the point?

Preacher was standing with his face in his hands. "I'm going into Fort Searles next week, before the new battalion arrives. And I'm going to disable their armory."

"Disable it? How?"

"I'm going to dynamite it straight to God."

Vargas realized that he meant this perhaps even more than he had meant the other thing. "You've lost your mind."

"Maybe."

"You'll go straight to the gallows."

"I'm all right with that."

"Well, *I'm* not," Vargas said. He felt like a child, standing there with his fists still clenched, so reduced by the gravity of this news and his own helplessness in the face of it. "I want you to live."

"Then help me," Preacher said. "We might still do some good. Help me next week."

He had drifted so close that Vargas could smell the soap he had used to clean his hands. "All right," Vargas said. "I will. Of course I will."

Preacher held out his hand—for Vargas to shake, perhaps—and that was how they ended up in an embrace. Preacher seemed to need steadying. His face was wedged against Vargas's shoulder. Vargas had merely intended to catch a little more of the breath coursing against his neck, so he would never really know which one of them dipped into the kiss first. He suspected it was himself, and the dimensions of this mistake made him dizzy. But by the time it occurred to him to explain himself, that he hadn't meant anything by it, that he had just gotten carried away, he realized it was still ongoing. He wished Preacher would open his eyes and reassure him that he realized it, too. Vargas's hat was on the floor, and Preacher's hands were cold against the small of his back. When Preacher tried for his coat, Vargas's elbows caught. That was it, he thought—in the instant it would take to free himself from the sleeves, Preacher would come to his senses and evaporate from his grasp. But this didn't happen. Preacher was still there. His jaw clicked a little. His neck was damp at the nape. Vargas kept revisiting the split edge of his lower lip. The air rivering over his nose and eyes meant that Preacher wasn't holding his breath to kiss him. Vargas had wanted to know that. He had wanted to know that Preacher's collar was worn out, that the taste of the licorice he was always chewing had infused his clothes, his hair. Preacher was after his buttons and his belt, but Vargas still couldn't manage to let go of him. To do so, he felt, would shatter everything.

The infirmary cot wasn't big enough for them. They were halfway on the floor, half-kneeling, half-standing, half-clothed. Vargas realized he didn't know the rules of this business, or what they were trying to accomplish other than to dig farther into each other. Maybe Preacher didn't know either, but he was trying to figure it out, gamely, one moment at a time. Later, Vargas tried to steady himself against the inevitability of an ending. He wanted to go back to that moment before the kiss and have it all over again, before the sounds Preacher was making dragged him into oblivion.

Sadie—that witch—had foreseen this moment. How had Vargas not?

This was life, then, for that single, astonishing week. They fucked, rode out to the lake, threw themselves off the cliffs into the freezing black water, fucked more, dozed in the sagebrush. Preacher never said another word about Fort Searles, and the closer the professed date of the attack came, the more convinced Vargas was that he had given it up. Here was a life he hadn't imagined for himself, with this fragile burning thing newly at its center. But five nights later, Preacher rolled over, drew his pack carefully out from under the bed, and said, "Here's the dynamite." He had planned everything, down to what they would wear. Just before dawn, in two days, they would enter Fort Searles under the pretext of seeing to an ailing soldier. Proceed straight to the armory. Take the dynamite out of their bags and let fly. It was the worst pillow talk Vargas had ever known.

They planned, debated, agreed, argued, planned again. On the eve of the siege, Vargas lay naked on the bed feeling, as he often did before a performance, nauseated and a little cloudy. Preacher was inexplicably asleep. Maybe that was what being certain got you: a full night's rest, no matter what.

It wasn't fear Vargas felt. Just a kind of low, swirling agitation with himself for having agreed to support Preacher in this terrible endeavor. Yes, he agreed on principle that what the army had done—was doing—to the Indians was awful. He'd seen it all, and was plenty disgusted by it. But did he let it gnaw away his life? No. He dreamt about it sometimes—burning tents and the smell of scorched flesh and the like, and all the precious tribal ledgers and painted hides thrown into the fire. But did this mean that he wanted to go now and get his head blown off trying to atone for something that wasn't his doing in the first place and couldn't be helped? No. Not at all. Exactly how much land or dignity or freedom would it restore if he ended up in jail or dead? Or if Preacher ended up in jail or dead? None. And it made him angry, Preacher throwing away not only his own life but Vargas's too, for the sake of a stand that would make absolutely no material difference at all. Whatever soldiers they killed would be buried. The fort would be rebuilt. Any Indians trading or hunting or fishing within a hundred miles of the fort would be rounded up, probably punished worse than they otherwise would have been as payback for the inconvenience to the army. All so that Preacher could know he had done *something.*

None of it made any goddamn sense to Vargas.

He was sweating. He got up and washed his face in the basin. It was still dark outside.

As far as he could figure, living was rife with horrors and injustices of every kind, but no man had the right to give in to despair because he could no longer stand the general course of things. It was selfish. It was ill thought out. And what about living for the things you wanted? If some desire for Vargas had been burning in Preacher for at least the last few years, didn't he want to stick around to see where it might lead, now that it had broken through to his real life?

But Preacher had always been this way. Letting his moral quandaries poison every goddamn thing. He couldn't take in a beautiful sunset or so much as sit in the grass without holding forth about the nature of civilization and how it didn't belong here, at least not as they had conceived it, not in wagon ruts and train tracks and church steeples, not in these shapes and shadows that they had drawn over whatever had stood here before. He couldn't go into town without finding quarrel with some stranger whose perceived misbehavior disturbed him. The part of Vargas that could settle on a beautiful thing just because it was beautiful, or inhabit a feeling of wonderment, apparently did not exist in Preacher. Everything had to be laced with this undertaste of guilt and ill feeling. It was exhausting. Vargas was embarrassed to have given in to it—and for what? His dumb gratitude at learning that Preacher did, after all, desire him? The overwhelming power of being naked together? That feeling attended first-time nakedness with anybody. He could get it for a few dollars at the Gander, up the street—and then return the following night and get it again from some other woman, all without the inconvenience of being strung up by the cavalry.

Preacher sat up when he heard him unlatch the door. "Where are you going?"

"Privy," Vargas said. It was, at that moment, still the truth.

After the privy, though, he went to the stable and stood among the horses and tried to calm himself down a little. He had slept in stables as a boy and found the small stirrings of life in them comforting. The mice in the hay. Spiders casting their silk in the corners. Here he was, looking up at the nest above where his horse was settled, wondering why on earth he was allowing the coming day to hold any power over him. There were plenty of unknowns in his life. Tomorrow did not have to be one of them. He could go back upstairs, make a futile attempt to talk Preacher out of his terrible plan, end up tangled in it anyway, and perhaps, by sundown, be standing on a gallows outside whatever was left of Fort Searles. Or he could saddle up right now and ride north to Hemot City. Down that course lay nothing but knowns: the twenty-five miles of road, the boardinghouse that would welcome him, the girl in whose bed he would spend the following night. Other knowns: the fact that Preacher would never forgive him. But also the knowledge that Preacher, robbed of an accomplice with whom to carry out his insane plan, would surely abandon it, and at least survive the day. Certainly that was worth more than all the rest.

He was in Hemot City by daybreak, and would be riding with Montana Jack's Light Horse Pioneers in Cincinnati, Ohio, before any word of the attack on Fort Searles reached him a year later.

Lying now in front of Preacher, with his stump and his absurd eyepatch, Vargas couldn't go into all of that. He had lost blood. He could feel the room beginning to crackle at the edges. So he just said, "It's not my fault you almost got yourself killed. I was trying to stop you. I thought if I didn't go through with it, maybe you wouldn't, either. Who the hell thought you'd be stupid enough to try it alone?"

"You might have, if you'd known me the way I thought you did."

They were silent for a while. Then Preacher said, "How sick are you?"

"Very."

"Can anything be done for you?"

"No."

"So," Preacher finally said. "If this plan of yours hadn't gone sideways, you'd be dead by now."

"That was the idea."

"But then you wouldn't have managed to tell me any of this."

"There was a letter."

Preacher sat forward again. "From you to me?"

"That's right."

"What did it say?"

"Does it matter? We've said everything we have to say to each other."

Preacher studied him. "Where would I have found this letter? Once I had shot you on sight, with my blood up like an adolescent's?"

"On my person."

"Is that where it is right now?"

He came over and knelt down beside Vargas. He checked the wound. Somewhere between the smell of Preacher's coat and the smell of his sweat sat a thin drift of something herbaceous and long gone. With his eyes closed, Vargas tried to isolate it. To dwell only on it. Preacher's hands opened his coat and went into the inner pocket. "Don't."

He made a half-hearted swipe for the envelope, but Preacher sidestepped him. Vargas watched him retreat to the other side of the room. There, Preacher sat back down on the floor and opened the letter.

And then what, Louise? What does the letter say? What happens next? Obviously, this is the end. You've got them to the dugout in the Warrens where Vargas was found. Have you decided yet whether Preacher will be killing him? If so, will he do it out of rage or mercy? The problem is you love these people and you don't want to kill Vargas, because once you kill him the book is finally over and you have to leave them behind. That's the *real* trouble. You've been thinking about them for so long that you don't know what's waiting out there for you once you move on from them. You're stalling, trying to find a way to stay with them for as long as you can. That's why you've suddenly decided you just *have* to go up and see Sunrise for yourself. Even though you've never felt the need to before, and you've written all of it just fine so far, and this Colin Yard character you're basically begging to show you around could not be less interested in your book or in anything else you're blathering about in your emails (which, by the way, you also keep writing pages and pages of so that you can delay finishing the book). But none of the stalling is going to make any difference. Eventually, you'll have to write the last line and put the thing aside. So what'll it be? Mercy killing? Revenge? Suicide? Obviously, Vargas has to die. That's in the history. Obviously, whoever shoots him can never be part of the official story. That's in the history books, too. What's left? What does the letter say, and how does Preacher react to it? Has Preacher, in fact, been holding this grudge as Vargas perceived him to be? If he has, then I guess it's possible that Preacher is the one who shoots him. But maybe some part of Preacher was relieved that Vargas abandoned him before the Fort Searles attack, because it meant not exposing Vargas to the possibility of death twenty years ago. Maybe that's what you need to stress in your next email. *Dear Mr. Yard—Colin, if I may. I've reached the limits of what I feel I can write, ethically and maybe even aesthetically. It's one thing, in my mind, to take artistic license with somebody's life, but I want to be careful doing so with somebody's death. These were, after all, real people. I have grown very close to the versions of them I think I know. However, other people are close to versions they think they know. People like you. I've seen that you often play Anton Vargas in the annual reenactment of the siege at Greyrock. I've read that you've occasionally played the much smaller role of Preacher, too. I would just love to hear your thoughts on both of these men. Do you think Preacher killed Vargas? Do you think Vargas ended his own life to avoid the horrors of his illness? I don't know. I just don't know.* The ending, Louise. What happens, I mean, how does it actually *work*? The whole thing is in Vargas's perspective, so you'll be tempted to make his death the very last moment in the book. But that would be a mistake. He has considered himself a dead man since he learned about his illness. He's not afraid to go. He's just a little sad. This is the biggest thing for you to wrap your mind around—you, who always ask, *Do they die at the end?* when someone recommends a movie. So if he's not afraid of death, what is he afraid of? It's not dishonor. It's not fading from memory. We've been through all of that in earlier drafts. I think it's just not getting a chance to see Preacher again. What he really wants, before he dies, is to put his wheels down on the track that should have been his life all along. So, if he's seen Preacher, and that goal is resolved for him, what is the feeling Vargas *has yet* to feel? Peace, relief, rest? That sounds right. He wants to come home to this love that he never really gave a chance. This love that really should have been his life. Are you going to give him that? I think you will. But how? I don't believe Preacher shoots him. And I struggle to imagine him taking his own life at the end, when Vargas finally feels that his outer self—the man called Anton Vargas—and his inner self are reconciled, and are both living the exact same life at the exact same time. Maybe for the first and only time.

So who, then? Who kills Anton Vargas?

Finish it, Louise. When's the last time anybody in your life actually saw you? When's the last time you sat down by yourself and had a cup of coffee without thinking only only only about these made-up people? Finish it and let them be.

AN INCIDENT
ON THE ROAD TO HEMOT CITY

September 2024

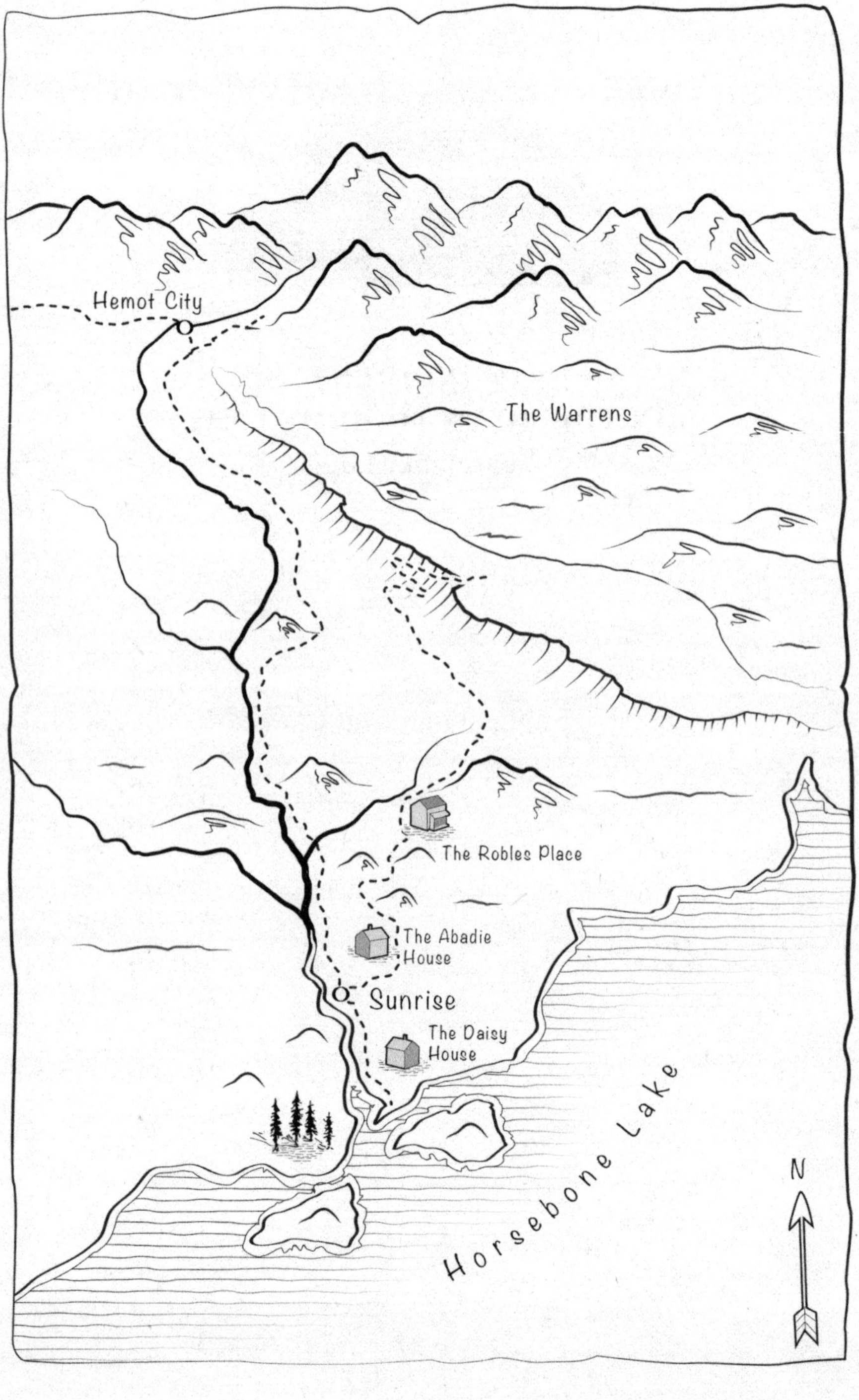

Hemot City
The Warrens
The Robles Place
The Abadie House
Sunrise
The Daisy House
Horsebone Lake
N

Day 6

If that's LT Hawley down there in the stable crawl space, then this, right here, the town Nina has been living in, must be Sunrise.

Nina is sure of it. Sure enough of it to rip the map out of the binder and stand with it in the square. She squints down the trail behind her. She squints up the trail ahead.

What are the odds that the Mint Green Bar is anything but the Lavinia? It's a bar. It's painted green. It sits right across from what was almost certainly a hotel. There's a garish mule deer head in it.

She rotates the map a little.

If this *is* Sunrise, then the lake where Ben's old Cessna fell—Horsebone Lake, according to the map—should be just south of where she is standing. And that's exactly where she finds it.

In that case, north of here, through town and past what appears to be a considerable obstacle course of woods, hills, and plains, sits Hemot City.

And Hemot City, she knows, is real. She's seen that name on a road map. It was one of the many words she had mispronounced on her and Ben's drive to South Dakota as she navigated through badlands where their signal was too sketchy to use the GPS feature. "*Hee*-mott," she had mused aloud, "like a gentleman moth."

Ben had laughed. "Not Heemot like Behemoth."

"No?"

"Hemot like *Hemm*-ott."

"Have you ever been there?"

He hadn't.

If Nina has learned one thing in this short and frightening life, it's to believe in symbols and signs. Her mother and Mrs. Tima are as adamant about the sanctity of this as the people teaching her about baroque painting have been. It would be incredibly stupid—hubris of the worst kind—to ignore the miraculous fact that this same Hemot City shows up in the manuscript she found in the crawl space under where she had been sleeping. Maybe Ben could ignore something like that. Maybe Ben could write it off as coincidence. But Nina knows better. If her mother and Mrs. Tima found out that she had done anything besides fall to her knees in gratitude and take up the message of this revelation immediately, they would disown her. And rightfully so.

If LT Hawley had done her research—and by the look of this binder, she had—and written Hemot City as it really was, big enough to have a train station way back in 1902, and if Hemot City is still relevant enough to appear on a contemporary map that Ben bought last year, then surely it's exactly the kind of place a person lost in the wilderness would be hoping to learn is just up the road. And only twenty-five miles away, according to LT Hawley.

Twenty-five miles is doable, even over rocky ground. Twenty-five miles is less than a marathon. Violet Devander runs marathons. She runs them with very little training. She puts them on her calendar three weeks in advance and just shows up at the starting line as if she's popped out to get the groceries. High-fiving spectators. Taking selfies across Staten Island, Brooklyn, Queens.

If Violet can run it, then Nina can walk it. She can walk it in a day, even with no carbs. Even with no training. Even with nothing but hope that she'll find people there.

Maybe you wouldn't need hope if you hadn't frontloaded so many Bulki bars, Neen. You're down to just three, and you have only yourself to blame for that. Couldn't hold out. Didn't have the common sense or the self-control. And now you've backed yourself into a corner: walk out or starve.

All day, every day, she feels as though someone has sunk hooks under her shoulder blades and is trying to pull her stomach out through her back. This feeling exists to the exclusion of all else. It erodes her thoughts. She knows it's affecting her. Keeping her still. Impairing her judgment. Would she go out there and try to walk the twenty-five miles to Hemot City if she were drunk? Or high? Of course not.

From the sound of things, the journey won't be easy. Her great fear, of course, is that she'll get turned around. She has no compass, and she doesn't know how to navigate by sunlight or moonlight or starlight or any other kind of light, terrestrial or otherwise. She could end up in the Warrens, fall down a mine tunnel, and die in slow agony.

You'll die in slow agony right here if you stay, though, Neen. That's for sure. You have several very good reasons to pack up and leave for Hemot City as soon as possible. Maybe even as soon as tomorrow morning.

Reason Number One: fall is coming.

The afternoons are still pleasant, but the days are getting shorter, the cold parts of the night colder. Yesterday, quite suddenly, Nina noticed that the glow had gone out of the leaves of the little bug-eyed grove on the hill just east of town. This diminishment came on the heels of two mornings in a row when she had emerged to find the lower peaks of the mountains white with fresh snow.

Reason Number Two: her period is also coming. Like the weather, this is beyond her control. She has two tampons in the bottom of her backpack. Once those are gone, she'll be out here in the wilderness, smelling of blood.

She knows the date of her *last* period, because she has a distinct memory of writing 08/10/2024 on the intake form at that urgent care center in Iowa, nine days before the crash. She'd had a dry cough for more than a week, and she wanted to make sure it wasn't a chest infection, rather than just fall allergies and shitty recirculated motel air, as Ben insisted.

When the nurse called her name, Ben followed them to the back. He sat in the chair beside Nina, holding her jacket while the nurse took her pulse, which was gloriously low, and her blood pressure, which was a little high. "All those tortilla chips," Ben said. The nurse ignored him while she typed up the results. Then she swiveled around to Nina.

"We just need a urine sample," she said.

"Oh, but I'm not—"

"Restroom's the first door on your right. Please read the directions carefully, all the way through. Just come back here when you're done."

In the restroom, Nina found a small cabinet with sample cups and labels and pens. Above it, the protocol for the clean catch was laid out in all caps. PLEASE READ CAREFULLY ALL THE WAY THROUGH. That insistence drew her into a detailed study of the instructions, just in case she had forgotten all the steps from the eighteen million previous clean catches she had done over her lifetime. Cleansing wipe. Another cleansing wipe. Hold yourself open. Pee a little, then stop—that was the hard part. Position the cup. Resume peeing.

At the bottom of all this, it said, "This is a safe facility. If you are a victim of domestic violence or are being held against your will, use the red marker to fill out the form on your sample and a provider will arrange to speak with you privately."

The red marker was just sitting in the cup among all the black caps. She wondered how often people failed to read the instructions properly and used the red marker by mistake, only to have to explain to the nurse that no, they hadn't meant to indicate that they were being domestically abused. What an absurd, terribly thought-out system. Who had come up with it?

She was describing it to her mother on the phone that evening, certain that they would enjoy a great chuckle about it together.

Instead, in a hopeful voice, her mother said, "So did you use it?"

Reason Number Three for leaving is the most important one: she is, eventually, going to starve out here.

Hunger lives like a goad at the center of her being. She has begun to imagine it as a living thing, wandering the streets of town, trying to intercept her as she goes about the daily rituals of keeping herself alive. It throws memories and cravings in her path in an attempt to make her eat more than her predetermined ration of Bulki bars. It knows, as she does, that the Bulki bars won't take the edge off her cravings. That whatever decision she makes, the Bulki bars will sit, sour and insufficient, at the bottom of her esophagus, while Nina herself goes on thinking about Mrs. Tima's *tulumbe.* And the chicken matzo soup she buys for the Devander girls at the deli on Columbus. And Violet Devander's summer risotto—bursting with roasted cherry tomatoes, and lightly sautéed sweet corn, and more butter in one bite than Nina would credibly believe Violet has eaten in her whole life. A sublime thing, that risotto. A true labor of love. The last time it was served, when the Devanders invited Ben over for a little getting-to-know you dinner ahead of this trip, Nina hadn't even gotten to enjoy it. The moment he'd shown up with that screw-top bottle of pinot grigio that had been hanging out for years in the back of his living room bar cart, Nina had known it was going to be a stressful night. She'd grabbed the bottle out of Ben's hand before either of the Devanders could get to it, and thumbed the dust off the cap while she introduced him to Dr. Michael and Violet.

"Man, you weren't kidding about his limp," Ben muttered as soon as they were alone in the den.

"Ssh!"

"He walks like he's eighty."

"Well, he isn't. He's a very nice man, and they treat me really well, so please lower your voice."

But he wouldn't let it go. As they wandered around, looking at the paintings in the study, he caught a glimpse of the master bedroom through a half-open door, and this set him off on an adjacent tangent. "How does he fuck her?"

"Ben."

"Do you ever hear them?"

She shook her head. She had never even imagined them doing it, though she had a tendency to imagine just about everybody doing it out of the sheer curiosity of observing one human body locked in such specific intimacy with another. There was something so whitely chaste about the Devanders that made this type of interrogation impossible. Her mind would just go blank. The camera would turn toward the window.

"I bet she's a squeak toy," Ben said. "I bet you'd have to cover her mouth."

He said these kinds of things only occasionally, not nearly as often as Melanie's boyfriend did, or even Gina's. Still, when he did say them, it tended to be because he was simultaneously amusing and turning himself on, and to her horror, she could see that this was the case now. She could see the idea electrifying him as he drifted from room to room, surveying the paintings and the bookshelves, and later in the way he plucked the figs from the charcuterie board before dinner. By the time they were all sitting down to the risotto, his eyes were moist at the corners, his pupils gigantic and black. Nina knew he wasn't *actually* drunk—he'd only had two glasses of wine—but he was swoony. It made her want to sink into the carpet, because she knew it was going to come out somehow, eventually.

"So," Violet said, cheerfully passing the salad platter down the table. "You two are high school sweethearts!"

"That's right." Ben smiled at Nina across the table. "We were lab partners in sophomore year. Dr. Ortan, chemistry class, last row of benches."

"Was it love at first sight?"

"For me it was," Ben said. "Finally convinced Nina to give me a chance in senior year."

It was a shame her mother wasn't here, Nina thought—she would have put it the exact same way.

"You have such a beautiful home," Ben was saying to Violet. "This kitchen. Just wow."

"Thank you!" Violet looked over her shoulder. "I designed most of it. There are still little things here and there that could use some tweaking. I'm not in love with these sconces. I thought I would be, but I think we need something different. Something more, I don't know. Robust. Something with a more masculine energy."

"I could get that done for you," Ben said.

He was purring. He didn't realize it. Nina stared down at her risotto so nobody would notice her expression. From the corner of her eye, she saw Dr. Michael sit forward a little.

"Are you an electrician, Ben?" he asked.

Ben, oblivious to the tone of the question, took another sip of wine. "I dabble."

"That's a pretty high-stakes thing to dabble in. What line of work are you actually committed to?"

"Oh," Ben said. "I'm a writer."

Nina jumped in: "He wrote a short story last year from the point of view of Ernest Hemingway about the time Hemingway lost a trunk full of manuscripts, and then found it decades later in Paris."

"Wow," Dr. Michael said.

"That really happened," Nina said.

"How did he feel when he found the trunk?"

"I believe he would have felt nothing," said Ben. "In the story, he's a completely different writer by the time he finds it, and he doesn't remember writing any of the stuff he finds. He feels alienated from it." He sighed. "That's what I'm worried is gonna happen to me if this story doesn't get published."

"Aw," Violet said. "Don't be so negative! I'm sure it will."

They made it through dinner, even though Nina could barely bring herself to eat anything at all, and she ended up pushing that cold, congealed risotto off her plate and into the trash. The trash! Then Ben went home to Alphabet City and Nina got the girls ready for bed. She didn't look at her phone again until after they were asleep, and by that point, Ben's expected *Come over* text was already more than an hour old. It had been followed by a *?????*. She turned the phone over. If he wanted to explore his desire to bend Violet Devander over the kitchen counter, he was going to have to use his imagination. Maybe Nina should do the opposite of coming over. Maybe she should let the good doctor indulge in the fantasies of which her mother suspected him and let him fuck her right out there in that same kitchen, beneath the not-masculine-enough sconces. How would that be?

She went out for a glass of water and found, to her horror, that Dr. Michael was *actually* in the kitchen. Standing there in his robe and slippers, taking his evening dose of Afrin. She hovered in the vast openness between the two marble-topped islands, certain that he could read her naked mortification over her own vengeful thoughts plainly on her face. He looked mad. Did he look mad? He looked like he knew *something*—but what was it?

"Can I make you some tea?" she finally asked.

"Only if you're having some."

Now she had to have tea. She hated this in herself, this impulse to hang around and make sure everything was okay. Especially when she so clearly knew it wasn't. She was stuck, drawn between the urge to pretend that nothing had happened at dinner, that they were all just imagining it, and the impulse to show the tired doctor that she knew, of course, that some line of decency had been breached by a person she had brought into the house. She wasn't an idiot. She was well brought up, courteous. Practically American. But to accomplish the latter, she would be inviting a discussion of Ben's behavior. And what would she even say? "Sorry, he was nervous and he got a little drunk"? Lie. "Sorry, he's a flirt." Truth. "Sorry, sometimes he doesn't know how bad things will sound coming out of his mouth."

While she was debating this, she realized she had put herself into exactly the kind of position with Dr. Michael that her mother had warned against. They were alone, clinking tea mugs, standing side by side in their sleepwear while the rest of the household slept.

"So," Dr. Michael said. "Cross-country road trip. Have you been out West before?"

"Only to Aspen, with you guys."

"That's right, that's right. I forgot." He rubbed his eyes. "Well, there's so much more than ski towns to see. Are you driving down south or up north?"

"Up north. To Montana. Ben says it's beautiful."

"He's been out there."

"The last two summers. He's been helping with trail work in some of the national parks."

"Is he thinking about a career in public works?"

"He likes being outside. But he's also trying to get his writing off the ground."

"Ah."

"I'm really sorry." It was the wrong thing to say, and the wrong moment to say it.

"For what?" Dr. Michael smiled at her. "I envy you. Before you know it, this part of your life will be over. When you look back on it from whatever great place you end up—and it will be great,

Nina—try to remember it fondly. Try to be kind to this young person you were. Take the good with the bad."

It was the kind of thing somebody might say right before they kissed you—and sure enough, here he was, coming toward her. She braced herself. It was actually happening. Just as her mother had predicted. She had come out here in her pajamas and initiated an overly intimate conversation with her boss, the father of two children she loved, the husband of the woman who was probably the only friend she had left, with plenty of foreknowledge that it could lead to something like this.

How was she going to explain it to Violet? How was she going to hide it from Ben?

Her elbow received the gentlest of squeezes as Dr. Michael passed her on his way back to bed, and that was it. That was all. She was alone in the kitchen and free to rummage around for the leftover risotto, which she heated up and ate with some bread and butter. She even went back for seconds.

Now, eons away from summer risotto, she's down to three Bulki bars and a little bit of trail mix that is essentially macadamia dust. Once they're gone, she'll have to face the prospect of eating the pickled eggs from LT Hawley's satchel and whatever has proliferated in them in the years since they were sealed. If, indeed, they were ever sealed. There are also some berries on the bushes around town—if she survives the eggs, she'll have to brave those next, but she's reluctant to even contemplate it because the ratio of risk to reward seems heavily balanced against her. And something as banal as food poisoning *does* seem a plausible way for her to die. Her mother has always been particular about food safety. Maybe she knows that this is how Nina dies. Maybe, all this time, she's been trying to warn Nina: don't eat berries of unknown provenance or pickled eggs you've found in a corpse's satchel.

Of course, there are many other ways to die. Exposure is an ongoing concern. What was the first, the most important thing Ben had mentioned when he'd told her how to survive in the wilderness? Shelter. She has often tried to remember the other basics, but her mind has, disastrously, blocked them out.

Maybe she would remember them if they hadn't come at the very end of such a terrible day.

Long before the incident on the road, Nina had felt that tingling in her scalp, the sense that she was very much alone, that the mood in the van was shifting and things could get out of hand. They had stopped at the Bradley cabin pullout in Nebraska. Ben had written whatever he had written on the panel, and they had driven on. She hadn't said a word to him about it. Maybe that had been her mistake. Maybe he was right: maybe sometimes she *did* provoke him on purpose. But she couldn't help it. She had fallen into thinking about the massacre. About how, exactly, Death had received his summons for it. Had he been there from the outset, lingering in the shadow of the watchful hoodoos until the army retreated? Or had he only arrived after the killing was done? Had he, at least, taken the children first? Or had he been obliged to wait while one or two tiny survivors lay, bawling and pinned under the body of the fallen Mrs. Bradley, until the night air turned to frost, and their cries grew quiet, and he could finally take them with him? The rules of his involvement were eternally elusive to Nina. Was he free to choose the moment of departure, or was there some other force, greater even than himself, that dictated how and when these things could happen?

Suddenly, everything around her had become tainted with grief. She didn't want to be out here, watching the utility poles flash by, looking up at the endless, flat-topped silhouette of yet another mine, moving the visor around to keep the last rays of the burning sun out of her eyes. She didn't want the other half of her lunch cheeseburger, which had congealed into a wad of fat and onion and damp bread in the cooler. She wanted to go home. Not to the Devanders, but to her mother.

And just as she was thinking this, Ben said, "I think we have to move out here."

She waved a hand to take in the darkening landscape. "What, here?"

"Well, not *right* here. Montana."

She shrugged. "I just don't get the appeal."

"Really?" Ben said. "There's such purity in empty space."

"Wow," Nina said. It just slipped out. She regretted it instantly.

"What?"

"Nothing."

"It's obviously *something.*"

She needed a word that wouldn't piss him off. "That's quite dark."

"What is?"

"Purity in emptied space?"

"I said *empty.*"

"Oh."

"You didn't hear me, Nina."

"I'm sorry."

"You need to actually listen."

"You're right, I'm sorry."

Whether he admitted it or not, "emptied" had been the right thing to call it. The accurate thing. But Nina knew better than to go any further with this. Ben was still in a good mood.

"Anyway," he was saying, "maybe we shouldn't go back. I think once we get to Montana, we should just stay there for good."

"Ha ha."

"I'm serious." He reached over and squeezed her knee. "Just leave it all behind and start fresh. Right?"

There was so much to say. She didn't even know where to start. "What about your mother?"

"She'll understand eventually. Hell, I've been telling her and telling her she needs to come out here and see the West for herself. Maybe this will finally make her."

"What about *my* mother?"

"What about her?"

She watched the white lines of the road breaking against the hood like tiny asteroids.

"Yeah." Ben was nodding to himself. "Aren't you done with New York? Aren't you done never seeing the sky and hauling groceries up and down subway stairs and sitting next to rude strangers from fucking . . . Zambeziland or wherever, and just catching everybody's bad energy all day long and then feeling like shit and then going to bed with all that noise outside, only to start the same goddamn day over again?"

"I only put in for two weeks of vacation."

"So what? Call up Dr. Bumleg and tell him you quit."

"I can't just leave the kids."

"Why not? Oh, I forgot. You love getting bitten and kicked by the big one. And you just can't get enough of cleaning up after a two-year-old who wears five-hundred-dollar cardigans but still shits her pants. Is that what you want? To be cleaning up baby shit for the rest of your life?"

"No." She rubbed her thighs. "But that's *why* I have to . . . you know . . . get my master's."

"Don't you just have to turn in your thesis?"

She could see that the plan was firming up in his mind and that any resistance to it would just agitate him further. Nina was getting agitated, too—she caught it before it got away from her and wrangled her pulse back down, a turtle in the mud. "We should crash with Zody for a while," Ben was saying. "He's got that big house in Eugene. He's always inviting me to come out and stay with him. Maybe I'll call him tomorrow."

"I've never met Zody."

"He's great."

"I doubt he'd be thrilled about you bringing a stranger to crash at his house."

"You're not a stranger. You're my high school sweetheart and the love of my life."

Way off in the distance, the red lights of an enormous power plant winked rhythmically on and off. She watched them until they fell behind the van, and then she watched the darkness.

"I have to finish my degree," she said.

"That's what Zoom is for." He was staring out onto the road, but obviously no longer paying attention to it. Nina was suddenly enraged with herself. Why had she kept protesting? Why hadn't she just joined him in the fantasy? They could be laughing together right now. He would have forgotten about it by morning. Instead, she had ensured that this plan of his was going to follow them around for the rest of the trip.

"We could open up a little burger shack." She didn't quite manage to make this sound as cheerful as she'd intended. "I've always thought that could be kind of romantic."

"Thanks for not saying anything when I said you were the love of my life."

"You're the love of my life, too."

"That's great. That's just perfect. I'm so glad to hear I'm the love of your life now that you've taken some time to think about it. *So* glad this is such an easy decision for you, since I'm the love of your life." He jerked the wheel to the right. The van shot across two lanes and skidded to a halt on the shoulder. Ben leaned over her and opened the door. "Get the fuck out. *Out.*"

She stood there on the gravel, watching his taillights grow smaller. The surprise of finding herself suddenly out of his reach had overridden, for now, the panic she should have been feeling. But then she started taking stock of her situation. She didn't know where the fuck she was. Nebraska? South Dakota? It was nighttime, and freezing. Her sweatshirt, wallet, and cheeseburger were out there in the void, moving away from her up a random county highway at seventy-five miles an hour. Her phone was in her pocket at least, but there was no one to call except Ben himself, and he wouldn't pick up. Who else could do anything for her, besides lay into her for being with him in the first place?

He would come back for her. She knew this. He always had before. She started walking along the shoulder after him, though she cursed herself for not having the strength to walk the other way.

By the time he returned for her, an hour later, she had covered about three miles on foot. During that interval, she had refused a ride from the only passing car that stopped to check on her. The driver was a man in his sixties, and if she knew nothing else, she knew that on American highways, Death drove an old car and held the door open reassuringly for you.

When she saw the next set of lights coming down the road, she thought it must be the stranger returning. But it was Ben. She recognized the van as it sped by where she was crouching in the bushes, and she ran out onto the asphalt to flag him down. Ben turned around, pulled up next to her, and rolled down the window with an air of resignation. As though he'd heard her panic and her prayers through space and time and just about managed to force himself to turn back. Nina wished she would just refuse to get in the van for once. Say *no thank you* to Ben, as she had to the stranger, and keep walking. Maybe next time.

"I got almost all the way to South Dakota," he said when she climbed in beside him. "But then I started thinking about you out here, all alone in your little green shoes."

Because she could think of nothing else to say, she said, "My little green shoes."

He looked over at her every now and again while he drove. "Do you even know what you'd need if you ever found yourself alone in the middle of nowhere?"

"Water," she mumbled.

Ben shook his head. "Shelter."

The rest of the list has been a blank. Food had probably ranked somewhere. But shelter had gotten top billing. Neither it nor water will be guaranteed on the walk to Hemot City.

Shelter has meant a roof over her head, but she has also learned that it means knowledge. Nina *knows* the weird little town of Sunrise. She has managed to persist in it. She knows the rhythms of its evening storms, the rustle of the wind when it rattles through the dead flower stack by the stable. She knows the sound of the beams in the Mint Green Bar, the smell of the wood warming up when sunlight hits it. She knows the fox who brings her pups through town on their way to whatever hidden place they call home. She knows the geese overhead. She knows the massive ravens who swagger around the ridgepoles of the houses.

She knows the unfriendlies, too. Not by name, but by inconvenience: the buzzfly, the madfly, the stingfly. The weird-faced monster wasp. The blue-assed gnat. The whirlybird suckermoth. The beady-eyed fuckoff bird. The oh-Jesus field rat. The relentless, smug-faced bushtit. All are her wretched companions in the town of Sunrise now.

And all will feast on your corpse if you wait too long and die here. They'll use your empty clothing for their nests.

Reason Number Four surprises her later that same afternoon. She's coming back into town from the sheltered little glade she uses as a lavatory. Right away, she knows something is off. The day is quiet and sunny. An early autumn chill lives in the shadows. Then something is in her presence. Or, rather, she is in the presence of something—she has arrived on the scene to find it already here, already waiting for her.

Nothing looks especially different. The trees on the hill are shimmering as the breeze stirs them faintly.

Then she hears it. Someone is calling out.

"Hello?" She can hear it up the road. "Hello? Anybody?"

She has been praying for this moment since she got here, for five whole notches on the stable door. Now that it's come, she's completely unprepared. She's aware only that she has no weapon to use if whoever is coming turns out to be an enemy.

An enemy. What is an enemy?

By your mother's definition: one who wishes you harm.

In a flash, she's in the hotel. Up the stairs, two at a time, then scrambling on her hands and knees all the way over to the big window that overlooks the street. Crouching there, she listens again for the voice.

You're a snake in a burrow. The earth is tight around you. It holds you in. You're going down, down, down, down.

She's finally calm enough to raise her head and look down. The breeze comes in, soft and lovely. The street below is empty. Across town, the river runs fast and bright, under the fence and away from here.

Then Ben comes around the corner of the schoolhouse just up the hill. He goes down the street, looking into the doorways, one by one.

Calling, "Hello? Anybody?"

He must be real. If she were hallucinating him, she would imagine him as he was the last time she'd seen him, not like this, with his sunburned bald spot, and the little scruffs of unshaven hair coming up the sides like a tonsure. His arms red, his nose a bright bulb down there in the street. His clothes dirty and shredded. Looking exactly as he would look after a plane crash in the wilderness.

She has been balancing prayers for his survival against the acceptance of his death. But now all she can think about are the last ten minutes of their doomed flight. Had he really pushed her out, as she has been telling herself, to save her life?

Hadn't she, in fact, jumped? Hadn't she just left him to his fate?

And if Nina has been asking herself this question, wouldn't Ben have been asking it, too? Wouldn't he have been thinking about it these past six days?

She watches him climb in through the window of the Mint Green Bar. What evidence of her presence has she left back there? Maybe none. Her backpack is mercifully on her shoulders. She's been careful about stuffing the wrappers of the Bulki bars she consumes back into it so that her bear won't get wind of them. LT Hawley's blanket is on the floor there, but to unknowing eyes, it will look like just another part of the chaos of the place.

If he's going around the buildings, one by one, he is eventually going to find her. He will come into the hotel and up the stairs, and stumble onto her crouching here by the window. Alive, to his amazement. Unhurt. Having hoarded all the Bulki bars. He will wonder if she searched for him as rigorously, as devotedly, as she should have. He will wonder if she'd prayed for him. Had she? And will she be able to convince him that she had?

She should take the opportunity of his being in the Mint Green Bar, where the windows are cloudy, to get out of here. Leave the hotel and run. Run anywhere.

She heads back toward the staircase, but it's already too late. The downstairs door is opening. She freezes. She is not hallucinating. It's real. She can hear all the different parts she has come to know of the door's musical progression: the loud creak when it first pulls away from the jamb, the thin squeal when the middle hinge rotates through rust. She hears two footfalls, and then the broken floorboard just after them. Then stillness. He's standing downstairs, just beneath the medallion where a chandelier once hung. He's looking around. What does he see? To his right, there's the empty room where the check-in desk is still half-standing. To his left, the room with the big tarped-up table. Has she left her sweatshirt there? No. She's wearing it. There's Munch, shrieking up at her.

She is staring straight ahead at the upstairs corridor, the open doors of the hotel's empty rooms. The back of the stairwell is directly in front of her. When Ben does finally come up, she will hear the three footfalls that bring him to the bottom of the staircase, and then the crack of the first step. There are twelve stairs in total, each more decrepit than the last, and one in the middle that he will have to jump over. Maybe there's still time to run. It's possible that as he comes up, the noise of the stairwell will mask the sound of her escape. But where would she go? Out the window and over the roof?

When he comes up, she will see the back of his head first, before he turns and sees her. Unless he comes up the stairs backward. Or sideways. Like some SWAT team on a cop show.

He's not moving. Why?

He doesn't like old places. Feels uneasy in them. As if he knows that they will sense his disbelief and test it by moving objects or making inexplicable sounds.

Maybe it would be better to try to prevent him coming up at all. Maybe she should scream. Let out some horrific animal noise that might dissuade him from further investigation. Maybe she should throw her voice into its lowest possible register and howl, "Get out." Or: "There's still time for you. There's still time."

Or something like that.

She could use her mother's voice again. He hadn't liked it on the plane six days ago, and he would like it even less now.

There has been a kind of violent glee to allowing herself to imagine, every now and again, what would happen if she used that particular voice on the Devander kids. If, just once, instead of saying, "Bo, it doesn't feel good when you hit me like that," she had said, "Put hands on me again, you little shit, and I'll raze you to the fucking ground." Just to see what would happen. Just to see if anything in the world could dissuade Bo once Bo got to hitting.

Maybe she should have tested this urge out on Bo first, instead of succumbing to it in the passenger seat of a Cessna flying through fog at fourteen thousand feet. Even if it *had* been necessary. Even if it had been a long time coming. Perhaps it would've given her a glimpse of just how badly it would go.

One of those huge, fat ravens is hopping along the roof. She can hear its mocking gurgle through the thin metal. Does Ben hear it, too? Will the noise bring him up here? He doesn't seem to have moved at all.

Does he see her, somehow, in some reflective surface she has failed to realize is giving her away? She doesn't want to be the first to cave to this horrifying silence. That's how she finds herself standing there for an hour, then two.

Finally, in the red light of the evening, she comes around the stairwell and looks down. There's nothing there. The downstairs landing is empty. She continues down the stairs, one at a time, until she's standing in the hotel foyer, alone. The front door of Sadie's isn't even open.

Here, then, is Reason Number Four: she might be going crazy, and not even realize it.

There's no sleep for Nina that night. She sits up in the dark of the Mint Green Bar and watches the windows for signs of movement. But phantom Ben, or whatever he was, does not come back.

Her mind is roiling with the list of things she has to bring on her journey to Hemot City. Her water bottle with fresh water from the creek. Her two remaining Bulki bars. Her dead lighter. Some of the dead flowers piled outside the stable, just in case she manages to start a fire somewhere, somehow. LT Hawley's blanket and jacket. The "Sunrise" binder. The pickled eggs.

Exactly how many of those things do you think you'll be using along the way?

It's not about using them. It's about not leaving them behind.

In that case, aren't you forgetting something?

Once she's had the thought, it lodges in her mind so decisively she feels the urge to reach up and touch her forehead. She can see its shadow spreading over the coming evening, all the little steps that will be required to accomplish it, all the terrors she will have to overcome.

You can't just march off to Hemot City and leave LT Hawley here. You have to bring LT Hawley with you.

Why would Nina do that? What possible difference is there between LT Hawley lying under the stable and all those other Sunrise people lying under the iron crosses down in the cemetery? None of their names have survived the wind and the rain. None of their people come to lay flowers at their grave markers anymore.

You know why. LT Hawley kept you alive. She gave you the answer to where you are.

Her presence has spread darkness over every inch of town, and every moment of Nina's time here. Nina is afraid of her—afraid of her sadness, her silence. Nina is afraid of her own ignorance, all the things she doesn't know about this person with whom she has been sharing this strange little place.

She does know *some* things. She knows that LT Hawley calls herself Louise—though to Nina, that seems too informal, too familiar. She knows that LT Hawley is the kind of person who writes herself notes at the end of an unfinished draft. Nina has done this herself plenty of times in the throes of frustration. But these knowns seem so paltry compared to the unknowns: Who LT Hawley is, where she lived, who her friends were. What she was doing here, and, most crucially, how she ended up under that stable floor. Nina knows more about the way LT Hawley puts a sentence together, more about made-up characters LT Hawley spent years writing about, than she does about how this woman lived and died.

And yet, of all the people who could have happened by to help Nina, the only one who actually did was lying here already, waiting, for who knows how long. Probably since Nina's childhood. When Nina's mother was applying for their visas, LT Hawley was lying under that stable. When Nina was learning English and struggling with math and asking the hairdresser down the street for an ill-advised pixie cut; when Nina was getting her period, and discovering lipstick, and counting her heartbeats relentlessly in the dark; when she was grieving her friend Andrea, and floating through her first blissful months with Ben; when she was translating the doctor's instructions for how her mother should treat the burn wound on her arm, and when Violet told her that she and Dr. Michael were finally expecting Belice because Violet wasn't afraid anymore—all that time, LT Hawley was waiting.

She was waiting, and you finally came. You can't just leave her behind.

Down in the crawl space, LT Hawley is in pieces. She is tangled impossibly in the clothes she used to wear, and Nina has to struggle to unwrap her. When she finally manages it, she takes the skull—or, at least, what's intact, the upper half. She's been afraid, all this time, of something gruesome, but it's just an ordinary old skull. Yellower than the skulls in the *vanitas* paintings have led her to believe. Oddly matted where bits of hair are still clinging to it. But nothing of LT Hawley's facial features remains to terrify her. No eyes. No skin. No tongue. LT Hawley is as barren and bleached as the face of Death.

Nina crouches in the creek and rinses the skull off and then lays it beside her on the blanket to dry.

Day 7

She sets off at first light to give herself the best chance of making it to Hemot City by nightfall. Her backpack is heavier than she intended, weighed down by the binder and the pickled eggs and the skull of LT Hawley.

At the top of the first rise on her way out, she stops to look back at the little ruined houses behind her. The river gleams between the buildings. Its movement makes the place seem alive. Inhabited. The hope that she will never see it again terrifies her. It feels like the kind of moment her mother would mark as ominous.

"She wanted never to come back" is how it would go in one of her mother's stories. "And she got *exactly* what she wanted." You'd have to wait for the punch line, but you could feel the hairs on the back of your neck standing up in anticipation. "Because, the very next day, they found her body in a ditch."

Down the next hill and then up again. She keeps the mountains to her right, as she did the day she encountered the bear. That feels like weeks ago—in reality, only three days have passed. In that short time, some of the vegetation has changed. The bug-eyed trees have dropped some of their leaves. Their nakedness makes them even stranger. A mean-looking bank of cloud sits over the mountains, obscuring their sawtooth peaks, making it impossible for Nina to see how much new snow has accumulated on them.

When she reaches the overlook where the creek comes out of the hillside, she pauses. The willows have gone from red to burgundy, and there are new trails through them, cutting this way and that. Perhaps made by her bear; perhaps made by some other huge thing she has yet to encounter. For a brief moment, she entertains the idea of making a true effort to find her phone down there. She'll need it when she reaches Hemot City. There'll be a place to charge. And imagine the look on her mother's face when Nina's name lights up her screen.

But the most she manages to force herself to do is glance around the ground as she speeds through the willows. It's hopeless anyway—half of what's beneath her feet is waterlogged, and the rest is spongy. Her phone is long drowned. When she gets home, she'll have Martin at the tech shop transfer its data into a new body—and while he does this, she'll regale him with the story of how it came to be lost in the first place. Martin's been working at the shop for six years, so he's heard it all—but she can guarantee he's never heard something like this.

She hasn't anticipated how difficult it will be to gauge her mileage on this walk. At home, on city streets, she can walk a mile in about fifteen minutes. Out here, she guesses it must take considerably longer. Maybe almost twice as long. Assuming that's true, two miles must already be behind her. Only twenty-three more to Hemot City. Maybe the journey will get easier before then. Maybe she'll find a proper road. Something paved. The important thing is, she is heading in the right direction. She is getting out of here. She is moving toward home. She's hungry, but her enthusiasm and sense of purpose are keeping her dizziness at bay. At this rate, she'll be halfway to Hemot City before she needs to eat again.

Within a few miles, she's descending into a huge, deep valley. The mountains look even bigger from the valley bottom. The trail has vanished, but she's pretty sure she is still following it. There's a kind of natural roll to the landscape, a place where the trail *would* lie. As long as she doesn't deviate from it, she'll be fine.

A herd of something large and dark-shouldered scatters over a nearby butte. She decides they must be elk—their grand white behinds, even at this distance, are unmistakable.

Emerging from another stretch of willows into an empty field, she finds a lone coyote mousing in the golden light of the afternoon. She stops for a moment to watch him. His back is turned to her. The head, with its arrowhead ears, tilts this way and that as he listens for movement underground. Then he jumps and the tall grass swallows him up.

The fulminating clouds that were sitting on the high peaks have magnified and come down off the mountains. The storm in them sends an occasional gust of wind her way. They are, luckily, miles east of her, and heading in the opposite direction, toward Sunrise. The rains think they will find her there, as they have almost every night since the crash—but they've got another thing coming. She's not in Sunrise anymore. No trace of her remains.

If she makes it out of this, she will put a pin in every map she ever owns to mark the place that kept her alive. She will tell every single person she meets about Vargas, and Kipley, and LT Hawley.

Within a few hours, it becomes clear that she won't be making it to Hemot City tonight. There's no way she's covered even fifteen miles. But that's all right. What matters is that Hemot City is *there.* It exists. It doesn't have to be a bustling metropolis for this to work out. She has only to walk into a situation marginally better than the one she left behind in Sunrise. Even if Hemot City consists of only one household, with one landline, with one car, she's saved.

It's like Violet always says: *You don't need a lot—you just need a little.* Pretty ironic, coming from Violet. But considered objectively, a heartening point.

When the sky takes on its evening colors, she makes camp. This is not giving up. This is Nina being reasonable. Using her energy appropriately. A bear in its den. A frog in its mudhole. What good would it do to wear herself out, to injure herself walking through the night? She finds a fallen tree to rest against, far enough back from the river she's been flanking for the last few miles so that the cold mist won't get to her. She makes a crude little lean-to out of a couple of branches, slings LT Hawley's blanket across them, and settles down to wait for nightfall.

Is it strange that she hasn't seen the contrail of a single airplane? Not one, this whole time? This means something, probably, but she doesn't know what. She has learned not to bother with things she can't interpret. If she doesn't know it now, she probably won't know it until she gets out of here. She hopes she'll be able to remember all the things she didn't know, so she can look them up.

For next time.

Her brain flashes reflexively through the thought, and she wonders: What next time? There won't ever be one. If she survives this, she will probably hole up in her mother's apartment in Carnation Towers and refuse all visitors. She'll be in therapy for the rest of her days. She'll probably never get on a plane again.

Of course, that's not very like the miraculous flight attendant her mother had told her about. She, with all her broken bones, had gotten on a plane within a couple of months of the crash. The difference was, the miraculous flight attendant had ended up in a coma because she had fallen thirty-three thousand feet onto rock, not two thousand feet into water. She didn't remember the explosion, didn't remember her own fear or the sound of the people around her screaming their last, so she had been able to get right back on a plane and fly again as if none of it had ever happened—because outside of other people's insistence that this had been the course of events that led to her lying in the hospital with practically every bone in her body broken, it effectively *hadn't* happened. Not to her. Neither her body nor her mind had any recollection of it.

Things are a little different for Nina. Nina can remember the abrupt, swinging dip of the plane and the change in Ben's expression. The sudden way he had let go of her hair, for once, without having to be begged.

There's something ceremonial about eating the penultimate Bulki bar. This is the moment she has feared for days that felt like weeks. Here it is. There it goes. If she had made the decision to stay in Sunrise, this would be a terrible moment. Instead, it's just another step on her way home. She stuffs the wrapper back into her bag, careful not to disturb the swaddled skull of LT Hawley.

She watches the sky. That massive storm is moving on, flashing and growling as it goes. It has completely erased the horizon. There's a thin, dark tendril unfurling in the underside of its main cloud. It looks odd. Out of place. As if it's drifting up from the ground.

It's probably nothing.

But still, she can't help but keep an eye on it. It doesn't disperse, though the other clouds around it lift, change, move on. In fact, it doesn't look like a cloud at all. Its movement is entirely vertical. Just a wavy black line, from ground to sky. Like smoke.

She tries to get control of her heart, but it won't be fooled. It knows: where there's smoke . . .

Nina stands and clambers up the nearest embankment. Puts a hand over her eyes and watches the smoke. The wind stirs it languorously. Sometimes it gets so thinned out that she worries it has disappeared. Night is falling, and soon she won't be able to see it anymore. But as the darkness comes, and the last traces of sunset go from purple to gray, she can still see not just the smoke but a veil of orange light. Faint, pulsing thinly against the bellies of the few remaining clouds.

It's fire. There's a fire.

She can't tell how far away it is. If she waits till morning to go to it, she will lose the light to follow it by. Or worse: if it's a campfire, the people around it will leave.

Only one problem, Neen. It's not in the direction of Hemot City.

No, but it's a good deal closer than ten miles. Even she, with her sputtering brain and her limited powers of navigation, can see that. Even with the light fading, she can make it over to that fire much faster than she can to Hemot City.

But you just set up camp.

So what?

You have a plan. Get to Hemot City, find the people there. It's a good plan. You've thought it out. You haven't thought this new thing out at all. You're tired. You're starving. It's dark. What if you're wrong? What if there *is* no fire?

But what if there is.

What if it's a wildfire, and you walk right into it?

But what if it's exactly what it seems like? What if *this* is the sign she's meant to follow?

Her progress is slow. Her sense of dread is overwhelming. She keeps checking her backpack, unable to shake the feeling that she's left something crucial behind. Over and over again, as she walks, she puts her hands in her pockets to feel for the penlight. Stops to make sure the very last Bulki bar is still there, in its pocket. Stops to check on LT Hawley. Hullo, Louise. We're on the move.

Her journey is not without mishaps. She stumbles a few times, badly enough to scrape her hands. But what matters is: she can still see the fire. Its glow, she's certain, is stronger now. It is dead center in her path, and she is moving toward it, one missed prairie dog hole at a time. Every now and again, the clouds draw up and shroud the sky, and the firelight spreads across their rumpled undersides like something magical. Like something she will tell Bo and Belice about.

Who's out there, sitting by that hearth? Backpackers, probably. College kids camping for fall break. Out on exactly the kind of trip she was supposed to be taking with Ben. Tents, s'mores, whiskey, weed. Maybe somebody has a harmonica. Maybe somebody has a guitar. She's going to give them a heart attack when she steps out of the brush. She has to come up with something to say as she approaches their camp. Like in *Winnie-the-Pooh,* the cartoon one, when the friends become separated from Tigger, forget he's still out there in the woods, and then lose their shit when he starts howling, "Hallooooooooo." The noise, according to Pooh, very like the scream of a Jagular.

That is crucial. Make sure they know you're not a Jagular.

Maybe go in shouting, *Don't worry, I am not a Jagular!*

Imagine this is how you meet your soulmate. The one person at the strangers' fire who stands up to greet you coming out of the dark, and actually knows what you mean when you say you're not a Jagular. Your soulmate for sure.

A shock wave of guilt is crouching at the end of this thought. It hits her so hard she has to stop for a moment.

Your soulmate, she thinks, is lying at the bottom of Horsebone Lake. All the little fish have picked his bones clean. You haven't even built a marker for him.

There won't be any marker, for him or for you, if you don't stop this insanity and turn around and get back on the road to Hemot City.

She's staring out ahead again when her leg drops down into a hole. She feels the impact in her jaw before she feels it in her knee—the thin thwack of her teeth as her body's forward momentum is interrupted. She's down over the knee before she can even register what has happened. And then she's lying there, howling into the damp earth under her hands. Somewhere behind her is her leg—the knee jammed, the hip a riot of pain.

You've broken it. You useless fucking idiot—why didn't you stay where you were? You were almost there. You had made camp.

She pushes back up and tries to pull the leg out of the hole. Her foot, which she can't feel, is somewhere underground, out of sight. Her knee, mercifully, can still bend. She squeezes it with both hands. She's crying, more from fear and shock than anything else. She can't even tell if it hurts. She grabs the leg under the knee and starts to pull. There's no pain yet, but there will be. At least she's getting the shoe to budge. She works her toes against the worn interior of her little green sneaker while strange bolts of feeling shoot around the thick mass of her leg. Then her foot is free of the sneaker, and she's finally able to sit back and pull the entire limb out of the hole. She lies there with the heavy length of it in both hands, howling: a wretched, howling little Jagular hugging itself in the dark.

It hurts to rotate her foot, to flex her toes. It hurts, but she can do it. The connection between her body and her brain is still there.

But the shoe is lost. She rolls onto her belly and peers down into the hole. How did her entire leg manage to fit in there? She can barely get her arm down to the elbow. Her fingers feel around hesitantly. They brush something that seems like rubber, but then never find it again.

She lies for a moment with her face pressed against the cool ground.

Is this how you die? Hobbling, half-shod, across these rocky wastes, all night long, toward nothing? Why didn't you stay where you were?

She straightens up to examine her surroundings. There's nothing between her and the glow of the fire but a short stretch of flat land and an eventual ridge whose silhouette is clearly outlined against the light. She's almost certain the glow is fainter than it was before. This means she's running out of time. Any minute now, that distant hearth will go out. The people lying around it will fall asleep. In their tents with their sticky faces, smiling through their dreams, they will drift off into the darkness, and she'll never find them. She'll walk right past them or fall short of reaching them, and they'll get up in the morning, pack their things, and leave.

Her injured leg is stiff. When she tries to bend it, the knee feels as though it's full of water. But it walks.

She limps on toward the faint light of the fire. Every once in a while, a bolt of pain crackles up her leg. The night is entering its coldest part, and now a thin rain has caught up to her. The distant moon, somewhere over her shoulder, sends its light in against the drizzle.

You're going to make it. Do you want to die here? No? Then there's no other choice.

Ahead of her is the ridge, and just beyond that the fire is burning. She climbs. The rain slants into her eyes.

From the top of the ridge, she looks down over a vast plateau of burrows. Just below her, in the middle of all that emptiness, is a sagging little shack. Beyond it there's just the endless dark, and in it the fire. It's there. It's consuming a lone cedar tree out in the middle of the badland.

There's no camp, Nina. There are no people.

Just the shack and the tree. This twisted lightning rod that must have caught a stray bolt whenever that first, massive storm came down off the mountain. The grass around it has already turned to ash.

You're dead. You left your path and spent the whole night walking toward a burning tree. You're lost.

The rain goes on soaking her hair. Her unshod foot, in what remains of an obliterated sock, is soaked. Rain lashes the burning tree, the ashen ground around it, and then while she continues to watch, it swallows up the smoke until the last of the fire is gone.

Eventually, she climbs down the ridge and heads into the shack.

At least there's shelter. She lies back against the wall, away from the dripping hole in the roof, and lays the last Bulki bar across her chest. She's going to have to give in and eat it. She knows that. She has depleted herself thoughtlessly, for nothing. She made a mistake. And now, she is going to have to pay for it by depleting herself even further. She breathes in, takes her time breathing out. She's a turtle in a bog. Around her, the mud is growing cold. She goes down, down, down.

Why? Why does this great, wondrous force her mother has always insisted is out there deal out such petty cruelties? Why is it waiting around every corner to turn a good thing into a bad one? To burden you with the exact antithesis of your most essential hopes? Doesn't it have anything better to do?

As a child, whenever she fought with her mother, she would pray for her own death. *God,* she would weep, holding the bathroom door closed against the onslaught of her mother's reproaches, *let me die. Let me die so she feels bad. Let me die so she feels something other than whatever this is.*

But then, in her sophomore year of high school, her friend Andrea had, actually, died. She had been struck by a car while cycling home from school, and taken off her ventilator two weeks later. Andrea's mother had organized a memorial somewhere in Gowanus. On the ride to Brooklyn, Nina had allowed herself a good cry so that she would not make a spectacle of herself at the service. To her surprise, however, she had emerged from the subway to find that the venue was not a church, as she expected, but some cavernous event space wedged between a lumber yard and a welding business. Nina, astonished, had gone in to what seemed, by all appearances, like a birthday party. A DJ was playing Andrea's favorite songs. A loop of photos from Andrea's pale gold childhood streamed over the distant wall. The buttercream whorled over the cupcakes was lilac, Andrea's favorite color. Nina was the only person there dressed in black.

Andrea's mother was dancing in a wild scrum of Andrea's other friends. Save for the occasional burst of tears, she seemed unaware that her daughter was gone. Or, rather, she seemed unaware that there was a material horror to her daughter's absence. Andrea hadn't simply wandered off to some faraway place from which return was prohibited. Her head had cracked open on the asphalt at the intersection of 29th and Lexington. Her soul, whatever that was, had gone out of her, leaving behind nothing but an empty carcass, and that empty carcass wasn't even here, at this party, in this room, but was instead lying alone in a lilac-upholstered coffin somewhere in Connecticut, forever underground.

Nina felt like she was trying to bring the sacred darkness of all this into the party with her but nobody else wanted to see it. They had cried during assembly, and spoken to the school counselors, and now they wanted to dance. They wanted cupcakes. They wanted to talk about Andrea in the present tense.

That night, for the first time in years, Nina crawled into bed beside her mother. She was still in high school. She hadn't kissed Ben yet or even registered his interest in kissing her.

She hadn't heard of Pieter Claesz, or unlearned her mother's fabrication about heartbeats for all the good it would do her. She was fifteen and afraid, and she wanted to ask her mother exactly how fast Andrea's heart must have been beating every day of her life for it to give out at such an early age. And *why* had this happened? Why had Death chosen Andrea over Mister Amadou down the hall, who had been dying of emphysema for the past six months, and who would say to anyone that he was not just ready, but eager to go, as if this confession were a plea that they might relay to Death on his behalf?

But Nina couldn't find a way to pose these questions. And she knew what the answer would be: it was Andrea's time.

"It was just her time"—is that what Nina's mother will tell herself when she finally realizes that Nina is dead? Will she find comfort in it? Or had she known all along that Nina would not be coming back from this particular trip? Is that why she had called so much? Is that what she had meant after the incident with the red marker, when she had whispered so that Ben wouldn't hear: *Nina, if you don't leave him, I'm afraid he's going to kill you*?

Nina has often imagined her mother in old age. White hair, a slower life. In this imagining, her mother has never undergone any physical or mental decline, only a softening. She wears looser, more elegant clothes. Speaks more measuredly. All the hard angles of her have been buffed out by tranquility and forgiveness. She has welcomed the dream of leaving her job at the call center, and she owns a little pastry shop of her own somewhere on Steinway

Street. She's made a few girlfriends from among her customers. They don't know who she was before she became this tender, white-haired woman. They love her for the person she is today. They accept her superstitions and her odd turns of phrase. They surround her.

But now, this imagined life will never happen. Now Nina's mother will become one of those hard people utterly broken by grief. This mistake of Nina's, this split-second decision to board the plane, undertaken in a moment of sleep-deprived vulnerability, will stretch into what's left of her mother's life in ways that no one could have predicted. In ways her mother had probably prayed against when they first came to America: *Don't let anyone bother us, don't let us accidentally break the rules, don't let us be scrutinized, don't let us be noticed, don't let something bad happen.* Into this cycle of entreaties, sent up into the ears of a God Nina knew her mother feared without completely believing in, *Don't let my child be lost and never found* hadn't featured explicitly. But it was the underpinning of all the rest of the things her mother *did* say out loud: *Let us be safe. Let us be healthy. Let us be.*

Her mother would be a lot of things in the wake of Nina's disappearance—a statistic, a hysteric, a thorn in the sides of law enforcement who'd seen it all before—but she would never just "be" again. Nina knows her mother. Her mother is not Andrea's mother. Whether this was the death predicted for Nina or not, her mother will sit for the rest of her life on the green velvet couch in their dark little living room until the upholstery sags around her, thinking about all the ways her life, and the life she had devised for Nina, had been leading to this moment. All along, she will think. All along. Despite all our dreams and plans, despite all the times I tried to warn her, this was going to happen all along. All along this had been waiting for them. A secret line painted across the path of their lives. There had never been a moment—while she was combing the knots out of Nina's baby hair, while they were laughing over dinner, while they endured those long years of Nina's high school strife—when this parting had not been in store. Now they had come to it, and it had rewritten everything that had preceded it. Recast their whole lives together in such a horrible light. Nina knows her mother will think this. Bowed over the kitchen table, she will think it and pull her own hair out one strand at a time. She will lose her job. She will lash out at her few hard-won friends. She will dwindle, in body and in mind, until she is as bent and bare as one of those driftwood sheds on the beach, a husk, half-breathing and half-remembered, like something out of the old stories.

Nina has to pinch her nose to stop the tears from coming.

Worst of all, her mother will never know the truth. She will never know that Nina had actually done it, had actually managed to leave Ben, or at least to leave him behind, in a moment of wild clarity, brief as it was, in those final seconds above Horsebone Lake. Her mother will never know about Sunrise, or LT Hawley, or this disastrous final walk. Her mother will assume that Ben had leveled up from throwing Nina into walls, or out of cars, and had finally put his hands around her throat somewhere between Nebraska and Montana, just as her mother had warned he would do, casting Nina into that abyss of eternal unknowns, along with the countless other daughters whose braces and glasses and school sweatshirts and Christmas pajamas and ceremonial braids and jingle dresses Nina had glimpsed on Missing posters from here to New York; last seen in May, last seen in March, last seen on her way to school, to work, to quinceañera rehearsal, to the convenience store, to worship, to pick up her children.

That's all right, Nina thinks. At least she'll be there, among them. And maybe someday, someone will find her the way she found LT Hawley. Maybe while her mother is still alive. By then, there'll be nothing left of Nina. Maybe a few scraps of clothing, a bone here and there. Maybe her skull. Hers and LT Hawley's, side by side. Just teeth and sockets keeping each other company in the great silence of the world.

Day 8

In the morning, Nina gathers up her things and starts back the way she came. It will take her hours to return to that first camp she made last night.

She climbs to the top of the ridge and heads right. At least the leg seems a little better. Her one remaining sneaker is throwing her off-kilter, but she doesn't dare remove it. If she can retrace her steps, she might be able to put herself back on track for Hemot City. She won't make it there by nightfall. She knows that. Even if everything else goes right, she's much slower now. But if she can keep her heartbeats steady and stay out of her own way, she might still be able to reclaim her plan. It would be better if she had the last Bulki bar, of course. There's nobody but herself to blame for that. If she had just done what she was supposed to do, she might be eating dinner in Hemot City a few hours from now, instead of staring down the barrel of her first zero-calorie day.

About an hour into her walk, somewhere in the distance, she hears a strange, echoing wail. It's followed almost immediately by another. She walks on along the ridge, scanning the surrounding landscape for its source. To her left is a hill covered in sage and tiny junipers. To her right is a scree slope, at the bottom of which lies some kind of drainage, where the water from several creeks has collected in a kind of half-submerged grassland.

She hears a huff behind her and turns around. A huge black dog is in the bushes just below her. For a moment, she thinks it must be following her, but its eyes are fixed straight ahead and it doesn't look up at where she's standing on the ridge. The size of it is startling—it must be closer than she thinks it is. Or bigger. Or closer. By the time she's crouching down to hide from it, she knows the answer: it's just huge.

She's never seen a wolf before. It's so tall that the tops of its ears are visible even after it has slipped in among the willows. It trots straight along, following the bottom of the ridge. Then it turns away from her and breaks into a run. Only now can Nina follow its intended trajectory to where the rest of the pack is already waiting.

They're trying to kill a bull elk down in that drainage. She watches the scene unfold. She has to blink every minute or so to keep focused on all the activity, which is extensive and simultaneous. Seven wolves are hard to keep track of, especially when they all look more or less the same: soggy, gray-white, and lean.

They swarm the elk, and he spears his massive antlers down at them. One by one they fall away, taunting him from this side and that, so close they must be making contact as they pass. He's soaked through, and he wheels on black caliper legs. That's when Nina's wolf bursts from the bushes and fastens onto the elk's hindquarters. The sheer force sends the elk to his knees. Water sprays around him. The huge crown of antlers roves heavily left and right, sweeping the field in front of him to keep the other wolves back. All the while, the bull is dragging Nina's wolf behind him. Every few steps, he stops to gather his strength, and that's when the wolf digs in its heels and starts jerking at the flesh of the elk's haunches like a dog playing tug-of-war. What a bizarre, incompatible sight they make: Nina's wolf, with its paws bracing playfully against the bull's backside, nibbling and tugging as if it's

Enid trying to get the stuffing out of a chew toy. And the bull, trailing a ribbon of blood, pulling with all his white-eyed, slack-tongued might to get himself out of the water, onto the bank, and out of the wolf's teeth. Any minute now, she thinks, the others will descend and finish him. But they don't. They just go on standing around. Shaking themselves off. Water from their bodies glints in the sun. One pale wolf sits down to scratch an ear. They seem to think that Nina's wolf has it handled—and for all intents and purposes, it does. And then, quite suddenly, it doesn't. The bull bucks it off and breaks for dry ground. There is such desperate triumph in his pumping legs, the water spraying all around, that Nina almost resents him—stupid, useless thing, thinking he has a chance. Even if he gets away now, what's left for him but to die of his wounds? Does he really believe that he'll be dragging that stripe of blood and colon to brighter days?

But he's running, and suddenly the wolves seem to realize he means business. They're swarming him on both flanks. One of the smaller members of the pack races around the front, leaps for the bull's face, and seizes him by the snout. With the weight of it on him, pulling his head down, the bull stumbles. Laden with water. Laden with wolves.

What's awful is the not-knowing. If he stopped fighting right now, he would know. He would be less tired, at least, when the end comes. But as long as there's that other possibility, even the slightest chance of it, he'll have to keep trying. Even if it exhausts him.

Now he's up again. Even from the ridge, Nina can tell it's his last attempt. He won't be able to make another. With Nina's wolf hanging from his throat, he rises out of the water and picks his way onto a sandbar. Nina's wolf, dwarfed by the sudden immensity of the elk, hanging there like Grandma's old stole, gives its head a mighty shake. This makes no difference. There is nothing left for the bull to keep back. He runs. The pack tighten around him, and together they disappear behind a hill.

Nina doesn't see him fall, but some time later, a wolf reappears in the field with one of the elk's legs in its jaws. It comes through with the same triumphant waddle that powers Enid after she's found a particularly good stick. The wolf pursuing this victor does so with the same jealous zeal of any other play-yard dog. They grab two ends of the leg and drag each other across the grass. While they're doing this, Nina's wolf appears with another, larger, more indistinguishable piece and settles down to enjoy it. This does not go uncontested, even though the rest of the pack have a huge swath of entrails at their disposal.

Nina's knees have gone numb, but she doesn't dare move. The wolves seem too playful, too distractible. Maybe if she'd gotten out of there while they were making the kill, instead of crouching here in the bushes with her mouth open—but no, now it's too late. Now it's her fate to stay and watch while the pack scatters the elk all over the killing field. His big tinsel insides, shockingly reflective even at this distance, have brought ravens out of the sky. They saunter and squabble, gorging themselves.

When does Nina realize what she has to do? It's not so much an idea as a feeling of inevitability. Maybe, she thinks, this is how the ravens feel, knowing their turn has come.

To leave her overlook on the ridge, she will have to stand up and be in full view of the wolves. What will they do when they see her? She doesn't know anything about wolves. She knows that they howl at the moon. She knows that they dress up as grandmothers in stories, and that their neon outlines appear on horrible shirts in the worst tourist traps she's ever seen. Until this moment, she thought—falsely, it seems—that they were confined to national parks. And say she makes it all the way down from the ridge without having them surround her and rip her to shreds—what then? She has nothing to cut into the carcass with. She'll just be standing there, gingerly trying to yank something edible out of the elk, while the wolves and the ravens swarm her.

The shit from the intestines is another problem. Imagine surviving this long only to die while competing with wolves for a kill—not a victim of the wolves themselves but of wolf-killed elk contaminated by its own shit.

Get a grip. That is *not* how you die. If anything, the wolves eat you. A wild way to go, but quite classic.

Who, in her life, would have ever imagined that she would find herself here, contemplating this predicament?

Not Dr. Michael and Violet.

Certainly not Ben.

And not her poor mother.

But her mother would be proud. She knows this now, in a way she hasn't really known it before. If she knew about this wild demise, her mother would say: *Do you know how my daughter died? When she was starving, she fought wolves for food to eat. She ran across an open field, straight into their midst, waving her arms and screaming, even though she was so tired. She was so tired she could barely stand, and she had been crying all night long, alone, and she had a skull in her backpack, and she was wearing a corpse's coat, and she knew that her death was waiting to meet her out here, but she did it anyway. See how the wolves recognize despair when they see it? See how they know not to fuck with it?*

Nina's in the carcass now. Both of her feet are in the elk's gore. She's not afraid of it. Her heart hammers out wildly, freely, expansively. The organs are sticky and still surprisingly warm. Everything between the ribs is mangled all to hell—not that she could tell spleen from kidney if this were a perfect dissection, but she had wrongly imagined there would be some sense of order to the cavity, when really the elk is broken in half and strewn all over the place. Nina is the third arrival to it, and between the wolves and the ravens, it's down to the scraps. It smells awful. But still the meat is red. The ribs sit there like a huge red crown in the field.

She is waving her arms at a raven that's flapping its wings back in her face, and her heart is thundering away, bright flashes of blood zooming through her at a fantastic rate. She must be pulsing with light. She's so dizzy she can hardly see. And yet it's all right, it doesn't hurt, it doesn't frighten her anymore to let these heartbeats clamor out of her so recklessly. She wants to kiss her past self on the mouth. Wants to grab her own frightened little face with these sticky hands and breathe this new life into her.

With a fistful of innards under her arm, she scrambles back up toward the ridge. One of the smaller wolves follows her a little way. Learning, she thinks. Learning what she is, what to do about her.

"Get away!" she shouts. "Fuck off! Go!"

The wolf, chastened and a little disgusted, turns back. She scrambles the rest of the way up the ridge, sliding here and there where the scree lets her down. Her heart is hot with her own blood. Her mouth is covered in the elk's. A raven is riding a column of wind over the slope. She follows. It's there waiting for her when she gets over the top.

If this were one of her mother's stories, now would be the moment the shepherd arrives. Small and stricken. Just standing there staring at her, up to her elbows in elk gore, while the wolves below look on in bewilderment.

But this is not her mother's story, it's hers.

So it's not a shepherd. It's a truck.

The truck is just sitting on the ridge, as if it's been there all along. As if she simply missed it earlier.

She's not sure whether it's real, or whether the sudden overloading of her system with adrenaline and raw elk is leading her to imagine it. This can happen, she knows. She's not even sure that going up to the truck and touching it will convince her of its substance.

But she doesn't get to do that. Because just then, the driver turns around from where he has been pissing into the bushes on the other end of the truck.

Everything about him is surprising. She hasn't seen another person this close up in so long that the only thing she can think is: Is this how men hurry to zip up their pants? Is this what people wear? Buttoned shirts and jeans? Is this how humans move?

He seems to be wondering more or less the same thing about her. He stands there with his mouth open. It's hard for her to read his expression, because there's something the matter with his face. It looks burned somehow, glossy and gouged all over with deep scars. These scars extend all the way up to his forehead and beyond, into the faintest hairline.

"Jesus," he says. "Who are you?"

She won't tell him. She's not sure why, but she won't. It seems like such a personal question, *Who are you?*

"Miss? Are you okay? Is that your blood?"

He's still standing exactly where he froze when he first saw her. He doesn't know what to do next, and that's all right. Nina doesn't, either.

"Do you need help?" he says. "You do. You need help. I'm gonna call for help."

He takes out his cellphone and presses it between his shoulder and his ear. While he's waiting, he opens the passenger-side door and starts spreading a blanket on the seat.

"No signal," he says, waving his phone apologetically.

"I know."

Nina's voice surprises her almost as much as it surprises the stranger. He waits for her to speak again, but she climbs silently into the truck and sits there, watching him pace around outside, scratching his head, scratching his arms, hanging up and trying again.

The truck is old. It smells of leather and dust. Nina's feet rest on a pile of junk that clutters the floor of the passenger side. She lowers the sun visor and opens the vanity mirror. What she sees there is unrecognizable. She returns the visor to its original position and watches the man outside. He's standing with his back to her, still trying to make the call. The back of his head is very nearly bald. Only a few wisps of gray hair cling to his skin, like bits of morning cloud.

He gives up on the phone call. She can tell he's trying very hard to figure out how to approach the truck without frightening her. He comes around her side, then thinks better of it and keeps going. He opens the driver's door and leans in over the wheel.

He says, "I'm gonna give you something to eat, okay?"

From a cooler in the back seat, he produces a sandwich. He holds the bigger half out to Nina, and when her brown-tinged fingers move to take it, he draws it back, wraps up the bottom in cellophane, makes sure that's the part she's holding on to as she shoves it into her mouth. Nina doesn't know how to ask for privacy in this moment—she doesn't want somebody watching her eat bread for the first time since she fell out of the sky. He seems to sense this and steps back to give her room. She can see his hip framed by the open door.

After a while, he sticks his head in again.

"How you doing in here?"

She nods.

"I want to give you more," he says. "But I don't know what the rules are about this."

"Okay."

"I'm pretty sure that if you're starving, too much food all at once could make you very sick." He's got both arms leaning against the roof of the car, and she can hear his fingers up there, drumming nervously. "Where are you from?"

"Queens."

"Queens?" He repeats it a few times, as though he can't quite understand, as if she has traveled here by wormhole. "You mean New York?"

She tries to explain: "There was a plane crash."

"Where?"

"The lake."

"There's a plane down in Horsebone?"

"A small one."

"Are you alone?"

The question should terrify her, but it doesn't. She nods.

"I'm going to drive you into town. There's a hospital. I don't have any signal out here, but I'll call them as soon as I'm in range to tell them we're coming. Okay?"

"Okay."

"Don't be afraid."

He climbs in beside her, and they set off down the road. Everything feels alien, especially the thrum of the car. She holds her backpack on her knees. Will they search it at the hospital? Almost certainly. They're going to have a lot of questions, and they'll have even more once they find the skull of LT Hawley. But that can't be helped. She's not going to ask this man—if, indeed, he is here, if he's real and not some chemical delusion she's experiencing as her body unwittingly shuts down back there somewhere amid the wolves—to pull over so she can leave LT Hawley behind now.

She doesn't want to examine the stranger too closely, but she can tell he's stupefied. Worried, even. And how could he not be? Because she's studying his face, she sees it change the moment before he slams on the brakes.

"Jesus," he says.

She looks ahead through the windshield to where he's pointing, and there, standing in the road, is Ben. She can tell it's him from the way he's waving a piece of torn fabric back and forth. And this time, he's real. He must be, because the stranger sees him, too.

"What the *fuck* is happening here?" the stranger mutters. "Who the hell is this now?" He slows down and looks at Nina. "Is he with you? Are you two running some kind of con?"

"No," she says. "No no no."

"Because I got a gun in this truck, young lady, and I'm not in the mood to get robbed by a couple of little punks today. Do you understand?"

"No."

"Jesus Christ."

"What are you going to do?" Nina asks.

"I guess I'm gonna pick him up."

"Please don't," she says. "Please take me to the hospital."

"I can't just leave him here."

"But you don't know anything about him. He could be anybody. Please."

"I'm sorry, I can't."

She unbuckles her seatbelt and climbs, against the stranger's protestations, into the back seat. From here, she thinks, she can jump out when he slows down. She can take off back the way they came, or into the woods.

The stranger slows down and pulls up alongside Ben. He looks entirely and yet not at all like himself. He's at least twenty pounds lighter. A massive black bruise has formed a mask over his face. He is sunburned almost beyond recognition, so sunburned his nose appears nearly blue. His lips are chapped. Fresh tears are carving pathways through the dust that reddens his face.

"Do you need help?" the stranger says.

"Oh my God," says Ben. "Thank God."

"Bit of a weird day," the stranger says, jerking his thumb toward Nina. "We're heading to the hospital. Hop on in."

This is when Ben squints into the back and sees her. Or whoever she's become now.

"Nina? Oh my God, Nina!" One of his hands shoots across the seatback toward her, and she jerks away from it so hard that her head slams into the headrest behind her.

The stranger turns to look at her, too. "So you *do* know him?"

She stays very still and says nothing.

"Is that your name? Nina?"

"Nina! Babe, it's me."

"You'd better give her some space," the stranger says. "I think she's in shock."

They set off down the road again, Ben with his elbow kinked back over the seat, occasionally holding out his hand to her. She stays where she is, huddled in the corner amid the blankets and packages and random detritus that crowds the stranger's truck. She's sitting on something very uncomfortable—a pile of leaves and thistles—but to get it out from under her, she would have to move, and she can't bring herself to do that.

"Honey, are you all right?" Ben is staring at her. "I can't believe you're alive."

"Is this your girlfriend?" the stranger asks.

"My fiancée, actually. We just got engaged two days ago." He shakes his head. "No, not two days ago. Two days before whatever the fuck happened to us."

"She said there was a plane crash?"

"She spoke?" He angles around to get a better look at her. "Nina, can you talk? Do you know who I am? Do you recognize me?" But his car sickness doesn't let him stay sitting like this for long. "What else did she say?"

"Not much. I gave her half a sandwich. You want the other half?"

"That's okay—she might need more." Ben sits in silence for a while, glancing back at her. Every so often, a sort of half-hearted smile makes it into the mix of expressions playing out across his face. "How far is the hospital?"

"Another twenty-five miles, give or take."

"That's not so bad."

"What the hell happened to you two?"

"We were flying to Moraine from Hollis, and we had a bird strike."

That's not all, she wants to say. A bird hit us, yes, but before that you hit me. You hit me and for the first time I hit you back. Then the bird hit us.

"Jesus. How did you survive?"

"I put the Cessna down in the lake, but we got separated." He glances back again and smiles, and for a moment, he's the Ben she knows. "I thought she was dead." He leans toward her. "You hear that, Neen? I thought you were dead. But it looks like you did all right, huh?"

"How long were you out here?"

"What day is it?"

"September seventh."

Ben whistles. "Eight days."

"Eight days! Eight *days*! That's got to be one of the wildest things I ever heard." The stranger shakes his head. "And separately! You each thought the other was dead?"

"That's right." Ben twists toward her again. "Isn't that right? You thought I was dead?" He searches her face. "I thought *you* were dead for sure. When you jumped out of the plane—at that altitude? Jesus. I thought you were smashed to pieces."

"How did *you* survive?" the driver asks him.

Yes, Nina thinks. How.

"Well, the plane hit the water and I swam out. Spent a couple of nights on the far side of the lake before I swam to a bigger beach and started walking. It was cold down there, man. Freezing at night. But I rigged myself a little rod, stripped down some bark, found plenty of worms. I tell you, though, I don't think I'll ever eat another fish again as long as I live."

They drive on. After a while, Ben says, "We're in the Whitetooth Mountains, right?"

"That's right. Kipley County."

"You live here?"

"I live in Salt Draw. That's where the hospital is."

Ben reaches a hand across the center console. "I'm Ben Robbins. That there's Nina Terzić."

"Colin Yard," the stranger says. "Coll."

The one-lane road curves around a small hill, and a log cabin springs up on Nina's right. Small, weather-beaten. The roof is low and painted red. Glass wind chimes cast brilliant pinks and greens all over the porch.

"What's this?"

"Hemot," the stranger says. "Let's see if Doris is home. She might have some Gatorade for you or something."

He pulls into the driveway, turns off the engine. Up on the porch, he knocks and peers through the transom. Nina, in the back seat, prays to Doris. Doris, please be home.

Ben is watching her with a worried smile. "You're gonna be okay," he says.

The stranger comes back down the steps. "No luck. We can stop for a minute here to rest and grab some water—Doris always leaves the door open in case. Or we can press on."

Ben thinks about it. "Let's press on. Just in case—I'm worried about why she's not talking."

"All right."

"Thanks so much, man. I'm so sorry, my mind's totally fried—your name again?"

"Colin," the stranger says, pulling back onto the road. "Coll."

"Thanks, Coll."

It takes a long time for the realization to start boring through to Nina. When it happens, it doesn't come on all at once. She is slow to it. She floats among the disparate pieces—that name, the letter in the book's final pages, the half-grinning skull now hidden in her backpack. Her worn-out brain tries and tries and tries to pull these knowns together into the shelter of a single thought.

She still doesn't have it.

But then she looks down at her legs, at her own scrawny, blood-caked, sunburned thighs resting on all these parched thistles held together with string. And she has it.

"Who are the flowers for?" she asks.

Ben whips around at this first sound out of her. "Neen! Oh my God!"

"There she is!" the stranger says. "I told you."

"Who are the flowers for?"

"Speak up, Neen, I can't hear you."

But the stranger can. "What flowers?"

"These flowers." She pats the seat. "These ones."

"They're wildflowers," the stranger says.

"They look like the ones I've been seeing up in Sunrise."

"Yeah, they grow all around here."

"Who were you bringing them to?"

"I'm sorry?"

"Who were you bringing them to?"

He frowns, puzzled. "No one."

"But they're bundled," she says. "Look."

The stranger shakes his head.

"They're just like the ones outside the stable," she says.

Ben is frowning at her. "Babe, you're not making any sense."

"Were you bringing them to her?" Nina asks.

"Who?"

"I think you need some water, Neen."

"Her. Under the stable. Her."

"Miss," the stranger says, "I don't know what you're talking about. But I agree with your guy here: you need to calm down and have some water."

She *is* calm, though. There's an absolute stillness in her. She can barely feel her own pulse. Ben is trying to get her to take the water bottle from his hand. When she doesn't, he tries to press it closer to her mouth.

"I don't want it," she says, pushing it away. "I don't want it."

"Nina, you have to drink something, okay? You have to *listen.*"

The stranger is watching her in the rearview. "Where'd that blood come from?" he says. "That blood all over you?"

"Elk," she says.

"Jesus, Neen, I didn't even see it."

"Not that elk the wolves took down in the drainage?" the stranger asks. She nods. He drums the wheel, rubs one eye. "Wolves in these parts got a terrible pathogen. It's called canine wasting disease—you see it in other animals too, but round here it's the wolves that have it. Jumps from canid to human like that. Very few people survive it. Very few. Certainly no one I've seen covered in blood like that. I'd be afraid you're looking at a horrible death."

"What?" Ben turns to face him. "What do you mean?"

"But aren't we on our way to the hospital right now?" Nina says.

He looks away from her in the rearview mirror.

"It's a terrible thing to survive this ordeal you been through, and suddenly be facing what you're facing."

"What am I facing?" she says.

He gestures to his own reflection. Meaning, maybe, his scars. Meaning, maybe, himself.

Something strange is happening to Nina. An odd, swoony feeling is descending on her. Pressing down on her from above. She should be growing more agitated. But she's not. There's an absolute stillness, as if someone's turned off some mechanical sound that has been whirring inside her all her life. Now that the sound is gone, in the silence that has replaced it, she feels only relief. As if a straining fridge in the other room has cut out, and now she can finally hear how quiet the house is supposed to be. She sees the bars of light slicing through the window. The wind gently ruffling the front of her sweatshirt and the flowers around her bare, blood-blackened thighs.

And then, to her surprise, she sees nothing.

From somewhere near the front seat, Ben screams, "Oh my God! Nina? Neen! Pull over!"

Her body is devoid of all sensation. She can't feel her head, her arms, anything. She's not even sure if she's still sitting up. There's only the distant sound of things, remote as if in nearby water. She hears the screech of the brakes, and then seconds later the rear door beside her opening. It must be Ben—he's there beside her, his footsteps uneven, heavy. He's trying to get her out of the truck, staggering under her weight. He's saying, "Nina! Nina! Call 911!

Neen!" First from right by her ear, and then, after a thump that she realizes must be her own body hitting the ground, from right above her.

Somewhere much farther away, she hears the stranger's voice: "Did she faint?"

"I don't know. I can't find her pulse."

"Move over."

She has a pulse. She can feel it crouching in her, way, way at the bottom of this warm, dazzling blackness she has slipped into. Secret, solitary, hers alone.

"I can't find it," the stranger says.

There's the sound of Ben pushing him away, and then the sound of Ben beginning CPR on her. Two deep breaths, which she can hear blowing around in the hollows of her sinuses. And then the chest compressions: "One, two, three, four, five, six . . ."

Poor Ben. It's such a long, long way to thirty.

The stranger's footsteps pace slowly somewhere overhead. She can hear him going back and forth, pausing at each end of his loop. He's thinking. She can tell. He's thinking about whether to just jump back in his truck and leave them both here. What to do about this second body that's about to complicate his life. A mountain of dead flowers later, another dead woman on his doorstep. Wait till he realizes that the skull of the first is in the second's bag, right there in his truck.

Ben is counting again, but his pumps are becoming interspersed with sobs. Not long now, she thinks. He'll start to panic and lose the rhythm.

There it is.

She can hear him sitting back on his heels and starting to wail. As he does this, the darkness inside her sends up a single, solitary beat. It's warm, enormous, echoing. *Ba-boom.* She can feel the blood shooting out of her heart in all directions. She never realized how warm it is, the strange and lovely sensation its flight through the body produces, a kind of gathering of all the faraway parts of her. Then her heart goes quiet, and everything goes still again.

Just in time, too, because Ben is back, with a clearer, more determined tone. He says, "Stay with me, Neen!" And counts loudly. He's shouting numbers into her face. She can't see, but she's certain spittle is involved.

The stranger is still there. "Son," he says. "Son."

The nearby truck engine idles on. For a moment, it's the only thing she can hear. Then Ben draws a deep, ragged breath of despair and resignation from somewhere just below her chin, and she can tell he's slumped down on her chest. She still can't feel his weight. He's whispering her name: "Nina, Nina, Nina."

"I'm so sorry, son," the stranger says. "I really don't know what to say."

Sobs are shaking poor Ben, who has sat up again, away from her. "Call. Nine. One. One."

"There's no signal out here. Won't be for another five or so miles."

"Well, let's get her in the truck—let's—let's go, let's get going. Come on, don't just *stand* there."

There's a long, drawn-out scrape, and she realizes from the angle of it that Ben has grabbed her by the arm and is pulling her body back toward the truck. Another heartbeat pulses deliciously through her and settles back down to wait.

"Son, look at her." The stranger's footsteps come around her head, and then she can hear him crouching down beside her. He's probably feeling around for her pulse again. "Nothing," he says. "She's gone."

Ben sobs and sobs. The stranger is patting his shoulder. The sound of them moves up and away from her. Boots on gravel. The stranger has pulled Ben to his feet and is walking him, slowly, staggeringly away from where her unfeeling body lies.

"Take a minute," the stranger says.

"I can't breathe."

"Just relax. Put your head between your knees."

Inside the darkness all around Nina, a small, gray smudge is beginning to appear. Faintly, faintly at first, then returning the contours of the world to her. Her eyes are open. Maybe they have been this whole time. The sky above her is white, filled with blinding clouds. Black trees tilt into the frame overhead. Another heartbeat booms in her ears. Then another. Fainter as they grow faster.

She manages to sit up. The world is still in gray scale, still thin and shimmering at the edges. Trying to fill itself back in. She looks over her shoulder. The men are standing just down the road, behind the pickup, with their backs to her.

Nina rolls to her feet, pushes up, and runs.

"What the *fuck*!"

The stranger's voice is there behind her, but it's too late, she's in the truck, she's at the wheel, she's shoving the hand brake down with all her strength, and the truck rolls forward, heavy, immense. For a brief moment, in the rearview, she sees the stranger catch the edge of the truck bed, with Ben just beginning to break into a run at his heels. But then Nina slams down the gas. The truck gurgles violently, crashes through a pothole, bounces on the other side, and then the two of them are just dust-washed blurs back there in the mirror, standing side by side in the road. One of them—at this distance, she can't even tell which one—is grabbing at his face in frustration.

Her gray hands are shaking on the gray wheel. The light is coming in from all directions, white, blazing, caught in the faint cracks of the windshield, the water in the potholes, the stream far, far below the road as she speeds along the ridge. The clouds overhead blind her. Past the next bend, the road drops fast, and canyon walls rush up like outspread wings to envelop the vehicle. Grayish hills ahead, pleated where the water came and went and came again. Brownish now, growing slowly brighter, maybe faintly yellow, maybe gold. The whole world is coming into color, and with it another heartbeat. *Boom.* She's hurtling along. The track is trying to wrench the wheel out of her hands. The ride has jostled LT Hawley out of Nina's backpack. There she is, on the seat, bouncing madly around, grinning away. Stands of yellow aspen lean out over the canyon to watch them pass.

In the distance, at last, Nina can see the highway stretching out in either direction. She's almost made it. She's almost to the junction. There's a little fenced-in obelisk down there, across the road beyond the cottonwoods. Another car, red and brilliant, is just leaving, pulling away from the turnout where it sits. Nina honks as she crashes through the potholes toward the car, but that other driver doesn't hear her, doesn't stop, leaves her behind. She slows as she glides in under the trees. Before her tires finally grip the asphalt, before she turns the wheel to follow the red car wherever it's going, wherever she's going, wherever she's bringing LT Hawley, she looks up. The cottonwoods are immense. She's never seen them like this. Their orange crowns are swollen with light, full of wind. They are casting themselves up into the wild blue yonder.

Acknowledgments

The love story in this book was born more than a decade ago. The rest was written in a time of monsters. I am grateful to the family, friends, book lovers, and fellow writers who continue to make this world bearable, and beautiful, and worth fighting for. I am lucky to live in your midst.

Like all books, *Sunrise* was supported by a small army of early readers, without whom it would have fallen apart many times over. I am thankful to Dan Sheehan and Parini Shroff for their relentless optimism and availability; to Rachel Sobel, who always asks the best questions; and to Matt Daly, who has continued to teach me so much about my sweet Wyoming home. Thanks are due, as well, to the brilliant Marie-Helene Bertino, without whose musings, texts, and voice notes this book would not be what it is. And to the Teton County Library, and its irrepressible crew, and that chair by the fireplace that served as my home away from home.

It is my great fortune to still be sailing along with the encouragement and belief of Seth Fishman, Rebecca Gardner, Will Roberts, and Caspian Dennis at my back.

I'm also indebted to Sara Birmingham and Azraf Khan for championing this book through its many drafts; to Bonnie Thompson and Cara DuBois, who always challenge me to look at my prose with fresh eyes; and to Maria Braeckel and Peter Dyer, who have once again assumed the thankless task of turning me into a temporary extrovert.

Finally, just about every good thing in my life can be traced back to Dan, who manages to care so well for so many of us, and who lives each day with courage and integrity. We love you, Fini.

About the Author

TÉA OBREHT is the internationally bestselling author of *The Tiger's Wife, Inland,* and *The Morningside.* Her novels have won the Orange Prize for Fiction and the Southwest Book Award, and have been finalists for the National Book Award and the Dylan Thomas Prize, among other honors. Her work has appeared in *The Best American Short Stories, The New Yorker, The Atlantic, Harper's Magazine,* and *Zoetrope: All-Story,* among many other publications. Originally from the former Yugoslavia, Obreht now resides in Wyoming.

teaobreht.com
Instagram: @teaobreht